TRIPLE PURSUIT

TRIPLE PURSUIT

A Father Dowling Mystery

Ralph McInerny

St. Martin's Minotaur
New York

R

www.minotaurbooks.com

Library of Congress Cataloging-in-Publication Data

McInerny, Ralph M.
    Triple pursuit / Ralph McInerny—1st ed.
        p. cm.
    ISBN 0-312-26948-X
    1. Dowling, Father (Fictitious character)—Fiction. 2. Catholic Church—Clergy—Fiction. 3. Illinois—Fiction. I. Title.

PS3563.A31166 T7 2001
813'.54—dc21

                                                                00-045854

First Edition: April 2001

10   9   8   7   6   5   4   3   2   1

For Connie

Better long wed than soon hung . . .

TRIPLE PURSUIT

❧ Prologue ❧

A young woman in a yellow raincoat, its hood pulled halfway over her head, stood near the back of the group waiting impatiently for the light to change. Standing on tiptoe, she tried to see across the street, her smile flickering as she searched for him. At last the light turned green.

Cars began to move at varying speeds, lurched forward, slowed, darted into other lanes to get out from behind trucks that blocked the view of motorists anxious to get home. The timing of the lights did not take into account all these factors, to say nothing of wet weather conditions. The intersection of Dirksen and Lincoln at five-thirty of an autumn afternoon, with the rain falling and the street lamps on, store windows and headlights aglow, would please an observing eye. But cars and pedestrians flowing through the intersection of Dirksen and Lincoln were intent on being elsewhere, not on the aesthetic enjoyment of their surroundings. A distracted glance at most, or a look up at the large clock that stands in front of the First Fox River Bank.

The clock related the activity at the intersection to the slow revolution of the Earth around the sun whose system forms part of the Milky Way which, like all the other scattered galaxies, is governed by a single set of laws and by its originating cause. Can any part of this vast cosmic order be random or accidental?

The young woman in the yellow coat, her smiling face uplifted as if to catch the falling rain, moved toward the opposite curb, searching for someone who would be waiting there. She was the last to cross before

3

the light changed. Gears shifted, impatient horns were heard, cars and trucks moved north and south, gathering momentum. On the sidewalk, the young woman was jostled by impatient people who eddied around her, muttering. And then she saw him.

Her smile broadened and she began to run. Now he saw her and he in turn ran toward her. For a moment they were blocked from one another's view, but then once more each saw the other, and they seemed to swim through the sea of people into one another's arms. Suddenly a cry went up. The young woman staggered toward the street, arms wheeling as she tried to regain her balance, and then as if by the force of a push fell into the path of the onrushing traffic. Horns sounded, brakes squealed, but tires found no immediate traction. Cries of piercing anguish went up from the horrified observers who milled helplessly about as vehicle after vehicle thumped over the fallen body on the wet pavement.

Because a death was involved, the event was singled out and subjected to scrutiny. The police arrived and those who had been in the vicinity were questioned. Did the young woman fall? Did she jump? Was she pushed? Eyewitnesses agreed and disagreed. The investigation fell to the Detective Division of the Fox River Police Department, Captain Phil Keegan presiding. Reasons, causes, culprits must be found. The detective's universe is as logical as the larger one. Events have causes. Sometimes the causes are actually found.

Keegan drove his underlings, sparred with the press, grumbled about the case with his old friend Father Dowling, and doubted they would ever find the one responsible for the death of the girl in the yellow coat who had ended like a crushed fallen leaf on the wet pavement of Dirksen Boulevard. Keegan took the problem home, finished his weak whiskey-and-water nightcap, and got into bed on his side although his wife was dead and either side might now be his. He pulled the covers over him and had the eerie sense that Marge was there, that if he stretched out his leg their feet would touch. . . . The memory of his wife was evoked by death, by sad inexplicable happenings, by the sense that all our hopes and plans sooner or later will be crushed in the traffic of time.

❧ Part One ❧

1

The reaction to the young woman's death was pronounced at the St. Hilary Senior Center. Apparently being jostled about in a crowd was one of the recurrent fears of the elderly. They were aware of talk about the burden old people represented and of the increasingly positive chatter about euthanasia.

"What have you learned?" Father Dowling asked his old friend Phil Keegan, who had stopped by the rectory just in time for the evening meal.

"Well, her name is Linda Hopkins." Phil took the cigar from his mouth and scowled at it. "Roger, the coroner's report is no help in determining whether or not it was an accident."

"Aren't there witnesses?"

There were witnesses, but their testimony conflicted and not all of them would be willing to swear to what they thought they had seen. Perhaps no investigation would have even begun if the local paper had not seized upon the event. Soon accounts of the young woman began to appear, interviews with the women with whom she had worked on the cleaning crew at the Hacienda Motel.

She was from a small town in Wisconsin, a hundred miles north on the Fox River, and had come to Chicago to escape the limitations of life in her native Appleseed. She had done this against the express wishes of her parents, and her father took his daughter's death as confirmation of the wisdom of his prohibition. It was when Anton Hopkins refused to accept responsibility for his daughter's burial that Cy Horvath asked Father Dowling to accompany him on a visit to the parents.

Appleseed, Wisconsin, might have been Fox River, Illinois. Apparently Linda had been somewhat overwhelmed by Chicago itself, and migrated west to Fox River where, in a replica of the town she had fled, she took a job she never would have taken at home. On the drive north through falling snow, Cy told Father Dowling what he had learned from interviews with members of the cleaning crew at the Hacienda Motel.

"I think they wondered what she was doing on that crew. Not that they didn't like her. From Ruby Otter, the head of the crew, on down, they have nothing but good to say of her."

"Do they think it was an accident?"

"They think it was murder."

"Do they have a murderer?"

"A guy she was going with."

"Have you talked with him?"

"We can't find him."

"Maybe they're right."

The body of Linda Hopkins was taken to the local morgue while Father Dowling and Cy went immediately to the Hopkins home, a frame house whose driveway was cleared of snow. A face appeared at a window when Cy drove in and, when Father Dowling got out of the car, a man emerged from the house and stood looking at the priest who came toward him.

"I'm Father Dowling from Fox River, Illinois." He extended his hand and, after a moment's hesitation, Anton Hopkins took it. His eyes now went to Cy. "This is Lieutenant Horvath."

He asked them in, still reluctant, and they found Mildred Hopkins seated at the kitchen table, eyes red from weeping and wide with confused grief. "Did you bring her?"

"Yes."

"Thank God."

It seemed the resolution of an argument the bereaved parents had been having, but Anton too seemed relieved that the decision had been taken from his hands.

"She should have stayed home," he said, but there was little conviction in his voice. Perhaps he thought he had lost Linda the day she boarded the bus for Chicago, defying his wishes, going off on what he had been certain would be a fateful trip. Whatever consolation he had derived from knowing that the worst had happened deserted him now. He sank into a chair across from his wife. She in turn rose to welcome these unexpected visitors. Soon they were all seated at the table, coffee before them, and Cy was telling them what he knew of the death of Linda. Father Dowling was grateful Cy neglected to say that witnesses of their daughter's death thought she had been pushed into traffic on Dirksen Boulevard. However it had happened, their daughter was gone and this official notification had the finality they must have longed for. Rumor had become fact and their grief was unalloyed. Father Dowling noticed the parish calendar on the wall and suggested that they call their pastor.

Mildred looked at Anton who said nothing. She nodded to Father Dowling.

Father Kommers was in his seventies and his gruff unsentimental familiarity calmed the desolate parents. He called the funeral director who had provided the parish calendar and arrangements were made to transfer the body from the morgue. While Cy talked to Mildred about her daughter, Anton withdrew to the living room with the two priests.

Half an hour later, Father Dowling walked down the driveway with Kommers.

"You in the Chicago archdiocese?"

"That's right."

"So she didn't end up in Chicago after all."

"We're to the west of the city."

"Young people don't stay here now if they can get away."

"What kind of girl was Linda?"

Father Kommers thought about it. "A good girl, as far as I know. It's a good family." He rubbed his chin with the heel of his hand. "They lost a son in Desert Storm."

"Any other children?"

He shook his head. "Was she in your parish?"

"Not registered. Apparently she went to Mass there." He was relying on Marie Murkin's word for this.

"Good. Good. Did you tell the parents?"

"Yes."

"Good."

Had that been their fear, that she would go off to the big city and shuffle off all they had tried to give her? Cy was pensive on the drive back, but then he always seemed pensive. The visit to the Hopkinses might have induced thoughts of the futility of life, the sadness of parenthood. At least Anton Hopkins had stopped thinking that his daughter had followed the path of the Prodigal Son. Up to a point. Linda would never walk up that shoveled driveway again.

"Is there any hope of finding the boyfriend, Cy?"

"We'll find him."

2

Colleen Gallagher's Aunt Ruth had taught her a little prayer when Colleen was a girl, long before there was any reason to think that she would still be single at the unsettling age of thirty-two. She had added the prayer to her little repertoire of devotions, orisons murmured hurriedly as she dressed in the morning, but it scarcely engaged her mind until she reached thirty. It was just a little jingle like "Now I lay me down to sleep," to the tune of which she drifted off into maidenly dreams. Eventually something like desperation crept into her saying of Aunt Ruth's prayer. *Good Saint Anne, get me a man as quick as you can.* On Sundays, after communion, she knelt with hands clenched in prayer, eyes tightly closed, and sent up her petition to Saint Anne. She wasn't quite clear who Saint Anne was, but Aunt Ruth had told her the prayer was surefire.

What a joke the petition had seemed all those years ago, with the future stretching ahead in all its green promise. Colleen had no one she cared to ask to the senior dance when she graduated from Holy Angels Academy, but neither did Jane, who was the most beautiful girl in the class. It was a source of amazement to Colleen that she and Jane were such good friends. The reason, it turned out, was her brother Tim, who was a student at Georgetown and not at hand to be asked to take Jane to the dance. But Jane's fastidious patience had paid off; she too went off to Georgetown and it was there, rather than in Fox River, they fell in love. Colleen was a bridesmaid at the wedding and at the reception, her full lips moist with champagne, Jane said, "I owe it all to Saint Anne."

Colleen had told her about Aunt Ruth's advice and Jane had wanted to know the prayer.

"I said it every day until it worked," Jane confided, all radiant on her wedding day.

After that, Colleen repeated the prayer so often she would sometimes find herself murmuring it without realizing what she was doing. But her petition went unanswered and she felt almost betrayed by her patron. It seemed unfair that she had told Jane the prayer with much girlish giggling and now Jane was a wife and mother while Colleen rose each day to hurry downtown to the offices of Mallard and Bill where she worked hard as a paralegal as if to drive away the thought that she was doomed to do this into spinsterly old age. And then Mario Liberati joined the firm.

He seemed to be all those wonderful Italian singers rolled into one, with dark wavy hair, olive complexion, romantic eyes, and a smile which lit up the office.

"You're a marvel, do you know that?" he said to Colleen about her legal research.

"It's my job."

"You make mine easier to do."

Mario's forte was the courtroom. In Britain the barrister is distinguished from the lawyer, and Mario would have been a barrister there; increasingly he was the preferred man to argue a case in court. Judges were as susceptible to his persuasion as were juries and he won cases Mallard and Bill had been prepared to lose.

"I think you're the one who's considered the marvel here."

Their first lunches together were in his office, food sent for so they could continue working, but after one signal triumph he had asked her to dinner. They would go directly from the office, but she noticed he too had come to work dressed for the evening ahead. Colleen had taken a lot of kidding about her ankle-length skirt and spangly blouse but she laughed it off and all day long murmured her prayer to Saint Anne like a mantra. When they left together, Aggie, a spanking new lawyer, watched them go with envious desolation. But the dinner was a battle, not the war, and Colleen knew that the bright and breathtakingly endowed Aggie was her most dangerous rival with Mario.

Colleen had been prepared to lie about her age, assuming Mario was younger than she. She found it difficult to tell how old he was, since he had reached a peak of manly perfection that would no doubt endure until retirement. He could have been any age. It turned out he was older than she, thirty-five. This surprised her because at the time he had been with Mallard and Bill for only three years.

"I was a late bloomer," he said, displaying his perfect teeth. After college, he had spent several years in a broker's office before entering law school at Northwestern.

"You would have been wasted in anything but the law."

"Some people expected me to go into criminal law."

"Oh, no." It was much more fitting that he should represent the victims of others' negligence or malice and bring them to justice.

After that, at the office Aggie brought out the heavy artillery. Her skirts became shorter; she had a way of crossing her legs that seemed designed to expose her thighs, a trick doubtless learned from watching women on television. She was shamelessly predatory. Aggie had thick brown hair, a perfect nose, and lips that in repose might have been those of Michelangelo's *David*. Colleen too stepped up her campaign. Thus it was that she stopped by St. Hilary's rectory and asked to see a priest.

"You mean Father Dowling," the housekeeper said. "There's only one."

"My parents were in this parish. Is Father Dowling a Franciscan?"

Mrs. Murkin scowled. "Certainly not. What is your business?"

"I want to have a Mass said for a special intention."

This softened Mrs. Murkin and she forgave the allusion to Franciscans. Friars had the parish before Father Dowling came, and for Marie Murkin the change had been one from cheery incompetence to the serenity of a well-run parish. Of course Marie took some credit for that, her genius as a rectory housekeeper having been unleashed by the going of the Franciscans.

"What was your parents' name?" Marie asked when Colleen gave her name.

"Gallagher is my family name."

Marie Murkin stepped back in surprise. "I assumed that was your married name."

"I'm not married."

"I don't believe it."

Colleen smiled, feeling at ease with the housekeeper. "Now you know my special intention."

"You couldn't have a more powerful advocate than Father Dowling."

"And Saint Anne?"

"Saint Anne, of course."

3

Marie took the young woman to Father Dowling in his study and did not stay to eavesdrop, having learned the purpose of the visit beforehand. Gallagher, Gallagher . . . Marie prided herself on her prodigious memory for parochial affairs. After all, she had served here longer than any pastor, but she hoped Father Dowling would never be reassigned. And there was little danger of that.

When Marie first heard the story of Father Dowling's fall from grace as a prestigious member of the archdiocesan marriage tribunal, she could not believe it. Of course she had noticed the pastor never drank, and that was odd in a priest, not that they weren't usually abstemious. She would give even the friars that. But it seemed almost a religious duty to take a stand against the puritanism that had eventually driven the country into a hedonist culture and given religion a bad name. A sip in time saves nine, was Marie Murkin's philosophy. In her apartment, reached by the back stairway, she kept a bottle of sherry, making it do for a month. She liked to take her ease before the television of an evening, with a wee glass on the table beside her and her knitting in her lap. As often as not, she nodded off in her chair before finishing the sherry and then grumpily got ready for bed. She felt she was striking a blow for decency and civilization when she turned off the television.

"What was that all about?" she asked Father Dowling when his visitor had gone.

"She wanted a Mass said."

"Did she tell you what for?"

"A special intention."

Marie looked knowing. "A very special intention."

"Don't tell me you wormed it out of her?"

"It is the kind of thing one woman tells another."

"That sounds like an advertising slogan."

"She is understandably anxious to marry."

"Anyone in particular?"

"That is not a question one woman would ask another."

Marie swept grandly from the room. She did not often leave the study with the sense that she'd had the last word, but such was the case on this occasion. It irked her all the more that she could not remember the Gallagher family. She decided to go over to the parish school and see if the photographs of graduating classes would jog her memory. On the way along the path from the rectory to the school, she tried to guess what class it would have been, moving backward from Colleen Gallagher. The girl couldn't be thirty, and if her father had graduated at thirteen . . .

Coming toward her along the path was a couple, two of the seniors who frequented the parish Senior Center into which the school had been turned when the decline of young families in the parish made a school less and less feasible. If St. Hilary's had been an inner-city parish, the doors of the school could have been opened to any child who cared to come, offering an alternative to the jungle the public schools had become. But there were not enough children, Catholic or non-Catholic, in the part of Fox River where St. Hilary's was located. The couple consisted of pretty little Maud Gorman and a man who must be yet another in the string of beaux Maud attracted despite the fact that she was seventy-five if she was a day. How an old woman could have preserved a kind of girlish beauty, and coquetry as well, into her eighth decade was one of those mysteries that eluded Marie. Maud was a mother and grandmother, had led an exemplary life, and still did as a widow, except for the flirting that more than once had sown dissension in the ranks of the old men who came to the Center. Maud had a way of reminding them of better days and they responded as much from memory as from passion.

"Running around like chickens with their heads cut off," Marie had humphed to Edna Hospers, who directed the Center. "They're on their last legs and don't know it."

"It's harmless," Edna said.

"There are still sins of thought in old age."

There was a perilous moment when Marie feared that Edna would defer to her greater authority on that question. But it passed.

"Their minds are weaker than their bodies." Immediately Edna regretted the remark. She always took the seniors' part against Marie's criticisms. "It gives them something to do."

"That's what you said when you talked Father into buying that pool table."

"Good afternoon, Mrs. Murkin," Maud said now in her lilting little-girl voice. "Isn't it a beautiful day?"

Maud sounded as if she herself had brought about this lovely November day. The leaves were turning gloriously, and there was the slightest nip in the air despite the sun.

"There is nothing like an Illinois autumn," Marie pronounced.

"I think it is even more beautiful in Wisconsin. I was raised in Ellsworth." Maud said this more to her companion than to Marie. The man seemed to resent Marie's interruption. "You know Austin, I suppose," Maud said. "You know everyone."

"Austin Rooney," the man said, abruptly putting out his hand.

"From this parish?"

"For three generations there were Rooneys in St. Hilary's. I went to school here."

"Just the man I want," Marie cried. "Tell me, were there ever Gallaghers in the school?"

"Why do you ask?"

"A young woman named Gallagher told me her father went here. . . ."

"Colleen?"

"You know her?"

"She is my niece. My sister married a Gallagher. Jack. He was in my class here at St. Hilary's."

Maud followed this with a dimming of her sunny smile. She felt put to one side, an outsider, and she preferred being the center of attention. "I never met anyone named Gallagher," she said, as if to change the subject.

"He should come here," Marie said. Austin Rooney frowned, but Marie went on. "I'll tell Colleen to suggest that to him."

"Don't," Austin said.

Marie professed to be astonished. "Why, is he dead?"

"No, my sister is dead."

"God rest her soul."

Maud made a little fluttering sign of the cross. "Amen."

And that was that. Maud put her arm through Austin's and off they went in the direction of the little grotto. Marie, her mission having been unexpectedly accomplished en route, went on to the school anyway. It was important to her authority that she show the flag there from time to time.

4

"I ran into Maud Gorman and her new conquest on the way over."

"Which one? She has half the men at her feet."

Edna Hospers said it with something of the reluctance with which any woman attributes such power to another. In earlier years she had known women like that, effortlessly drawing men mothlike to the flame. She had not expected to have a recurrence of the phenomenon in the Senior Center, but with someone as old as Maud it could almost be enjoyed.

"Men are fools," Marie burst out, and then fell silent. Edna said nothing. Their own men had not been the most fortunate of creatures. Marie's had simply disappeared, and Edna's was serving a lengthy term in Joliet.

"Celibacy would be better for most of them."

"Not a good prospect for the human race, Marie."

"Don't worry about the human race."

Somehow this had turned into one of those conversations. Father Dowling had assured Edna she had complete authority in the parish center and he would make that clear to Marie. Edna did not blame the pastor for not succeeding. Marie sometimes acted as if she were the pastor and Father Dowling her assistant. She was notoriously nosy, and bossy besides.

"What brings you here?" Edna asked.

"A young woman named Gallagher told me her father had gone to school here, and for the life of me I can't remember."

"Why should you?"

"Edna, I pride myself on my memory of such things."

"But that must have been long before your time."

This was said without ulterior motive but it mollified Marie. "I suppose you're right. Austin Rooney says this Gallagher is a relative of his and they were in the same class."

Marie really did treasure such little tidbits of parish lore, though why, Edna failed to understand. Sufficient for the day were the evils thereof. Of course Edna knew Austin, a distinguished-looking newcomer who had been unable to resist the blandishments of Maud Gorman. How would the other smitten old men take being supplanted by the newcomer? How would, for example, Desmond O'Toole?

Although Desmond had been a barber, he took pride in saying that he had been associated with the *Fox River Tribune*. "The literary page," he had explained to Edna importantly. He was a thin rail of a man whose complexion had been marked by some childhood disease. He had a way of seeming to call to order any group he joined in order to make some pronouncement or another. Old people on the shelf needed a sense of importance, and enhanced memories of what they had done usually figured in this.

"What does that mean?"

Desmond made a fluttering gesture with one of his long-fingered hands. "Arranging for book reviews. Interviews."

"That's what you did?"

"That's what kept me alive, spiritually. Cutting hair was drudgery."

"The *Tribune* doesn't have a literary page," Austin Rooney had remarked on his first day, when Desmond had mentioned his past eminence.

"Did you work there? I don't seem to recall you."

"No, but I've read the paper all my life. There are only a few book reviews on Sundays, and most of those are short."

"I did many of them myself," Desmond confessed.

"They seemed to have been plagiarized from the dust jackets."

This had been the beginning of Austin's campaign with Maud, since up until then she had been ever at Desmond's side.

"Some people read books, others read reviews."

"I taught literature," Austin said.

"What high school?"

But Austin had been on the faculty of the local campus of the University of Illinois. Here was eminence indeed. It was the last time Desmond mentioned his literary past. But enmity toward Austin had entered into his soul. To compound his fault, Austin was a magnet to more than Maud, and his apparent indifference to female attention increased it. From his second day at the center, he always had a book under his arm. It might have been a warning to Desmond. Maud, of course, wanted to know what this fascinating man was reading, and soon Austin was giving an impromptu little lecture on the author he was reading—"Of course I mean rereading"—James Joyce.

"A fallen-away Catholic," Desmond said in solemn tones.

"Whatever the faults of his practice, his mind and imagination remained Catholic."

"I don't see how that is possible. Either you're a Catholic or you're not."

But Austin was telling Maud of Nora Joyce, the author's wife, and she leaned toward him as if from fear of missing a word. Desmond's day with Maud was clearly over. He came to Edna.

"I want your advice."

"Of course." Edna dreaded that Desmond had come to seek her aid in winning back Maud.

"I think I should go to Father Dowling about this, but since you are the director of the center I felt I should talk to you first."

"What is it?"

Desmond had taken a seat in her office and was arranging his bony limbs as he searched for a way to say what he had come to say. "It doesn't seem right to have a man in the center who advances heretical opinions."

"You mean Austin Rooney?"

"You've noticed it too?"

"Austin was a professor. . . ."

"Exactly."

"What has he said that disturbs you?"

"I am not worried about his disturbing me. But there are those who may not recognize how dangerous his opinions are until it is too late. His comments on James Joyce could not be made by a sincere Catholic. And he actually claimed that Willa Cather was one of the most important Catholic writers in American literature!"

"Isn't she a good writer?"

"Excellent. But she wasn't a Catholic. She was Episcopalian!"

"You should tell Austin."

"I did. He already knew. He says that does not affect his judgment of her as a Catholic writer."

Desmond's shock doubtless owed more to losing Maud than to what Austin Rooney had said. It did not seem to Edna that such remarks were harmful to her wards in the Senior Center, but she could think of no way to get rid of this lanky Torquemada.

"Maybe you should talk to Father Dowling."

"I will!" And Desmond sprang from the chair. "I'll do it right now. I will tell him that we discussed it."

2

1

Colleen Gallagher's relations with Mario Liberati ascended to a new plateau after their dinner together, but then seemed to be stuck there. When she dressed in the morning to go to work, she realized she was dressing for him. She would not of course go so far as the miniskirts Aggie affected, even though she was certain she had far better legs. Such display seemed out of place in the offices of a firm as prestigious as Mallard and Bill. But whenever Aggie crossed her legs in the studied way she had, every senior partner paid attention. All Aggie's alleged independence seemed canceled by this shameless appeal to her feminine charms. Her theory was that she would make it in a man's world with her talents and her mind, but her popularity with the partners owed far more to the ritual exposure of her shapely thighs. Colleen wavered; she actually tried on some short skirts, but she could not bring herself to buy one. She had assumed that Mario was as susceptible to Aggie's allurements as the other men in the office. How wrong she was.

"If she were my sister, I'd tell her to go home and get dressed." There was real distaste in his tone.

"Oh, lots of women wear short skirts."

"Not any woman I respect."

Colleen wondered if Saint Anne had been protecting her unbeknownst to herself. But Mario was not through.

"Why can't she just act like a lawyer?"

"Do you want her to wear slacks?"

"Why not?"

Colleen was half ashamed to take such pleasure in this revelation of Mario's distaste for Aggie. "I don't like touchy-feely women, not in the office," he said, and that was the end of it. But Colleen heard more in the rest room.

One of the secretaries swore that Aggie had made a play for Mario, putting a hand on his arm, moving close and lifting her face to his, ostensibly to hear his reply to a legal question she had posed.

"He actually shook her off and went around behind his desk. So what did she do?"

"What?" chorused half a dozen voices.

"She half sat on the side of his desk, crossed her legs, of course, and began examining her knee."

"No!"

"He left the office. He left her sitting there. It was a full minute before she strutted off to her own office."

This was sweet indeed for Colleen. Still, a rival dispersed is not a victory won. Her relationship to Mario settled into that of co-workers. Colleen was no longer at the disposal of the other lawyers; it came to be understood that as a paralegal, she was permanently assigned to Mr. Liberati. Simply on a professional basis, he was a joy to work with. He had an unerring sense of what was relevant and irrelevant in a case, and nothing stimulated him so much as an opponent with a battery of lawyers and limitless supplies of money to sustain those lawyers. Given the prestige of Mallard and Bill, he was not often cast in the role of underdog, but his suit against a major pharmaceutical firm for selling a supposedly surefire way to quit smoking, was David against Goliath.

"The judgments against the tobacco companies gave these people a license to steal." Mario's client was suing because he had not quit smoking after using the product longer than the minimal period during which his desire for tobacco was supposed to have faded away.

"Does he still smoke?" The client, Harrison, a burly little man, bald, both his arms and legs bowed as he stood, had never asked to smoke during the depositions.

"No, he quit."

"But . . ."

"There's no relation. It was months afterward. He went on retreat and made a novena to Saint Anthony of Padua. He hasn't smoked since."

"Saint Anthony!"

"Haven't you heard of him?"

"Of course." Colleen was about to tell him that her special devotion was to Saint Anne; and then she did—why not?

"I was stationed at Santa Ana when I was in the Marines."

"Santa Ana," she repeated. "What a coincidence."

The pharmaceutical company settled out of court. Mario was more than ever the rising star in the firmament of Mallard and Bill. He and Colleen had their private celebration in the same restaurant where they had dined before, but not until after an office party in which Mallard himself announced that young Liberati was to become a junior partner in the firm.

"I met your brother," Aggie said to Colleen one morning. "You didn't tell me there was a lawyer in the family."

Aggie had met Tim at a legal seminar. Her eyes widened as she spoke of him and Colleen forgave her. Let this lithe Venus with the petulant lips talk of married men. It seemed an ultimate concession of defeat.

"Is everyone in your family blond?"

Her raven-haired mother had marveled at her four blond children, as in a way had her father until his sister, who had married Austin

Rooney, reminded him of the golden-haired Gallaghers among their relations.

"Ireland is alive with blonds," her aunt told Colleen, she of the prayer to Saint Anne. "It all goes back to the Danes."

Aggie tapped her plush lower lip with a philosophical air. "Of course Italians go wild for blonds." And Agatha Rossner shook her brunette locks as if they explained her failure with Mario.

Their private dinner was only intermittently private. Mario had informed Luigi of his good fortune and Luigi and his family surrounded their table and serenaded them with Neapolitan songs. Is this what the wedding would be like? Mario's own parents had returned to Sicily and a property where they would receive the news of their son's triumph, looking out at the azure Mediterranean.

"If you saw the place, you'd understand why they went back."

"I'm sure it must be beautiful."

He hunched toward her over the table. "So Timothy Gallagher is your brother. I should have known."

"Did Aggie tell you?"

He nodded, but there was a frown on his face. "Tell your brother to buckle on his chastity belt around her."

"He is a married man with children."

"It would take more than that to deter Aggie."

She did not pursue it. Her brother was married to Jane, a most beautiful woman, now a wife and mother. What more could a man want? But of course Tim was a man.

"I'll warn him," she finally said.

Mario laughed. "I'm only half serious."

But would he become fully serious about other things? The night seemed ideal for a declaration and any number of times she was certain it was on the tip of his tongue. But then the restaurant was not the place for it. He took her to her door and lingered there and some dark instinct told Colleen she should ask him in. What that might lead to was hazy in her mind but wasn't this the time to cast aside all barriers and let him know how much she loved him? It was remembering his remarks about Aggie that deterred her. Suddenly he took her in his arms and hugged her as he had so many others at the office celebration.

"You've made my big day perfect."

A chaste kiss on her cheek and then he was gone. Before she went to bed, Colleen scolded Saint Anne and then, repentant, repeated the prayer. *Good Saint Anne, get me a man as quick as you can.*

"Now that I've got him, make him mine," she added.

2

"Did you see the young man with Colleen Gallagher at Mass this morning?" Marie Murkin said to the pastor one Sunday.

"I leave it to you to survey the congregation during Mass, Marie."

"Pooh. I ran into them in the vestibule."

He remembered Colleen and her request that he say a Mass for her special intention.

"I told her that you never miss."

"Good Lord, I hope you didn't say that."

"With the young fellow right there beside her? Don't be foolish."

Marie Murkin's faith was a mixture of rigorous orthodoxy and half-superstitious beliefs. The former sat in judgment on the latter, but in moments of emergency, Marie resorted to almost magical rites. A dash of Lourdes water at a reprobate would bring him to his knees in repentance. A novena was not a sustained petition but a guarantee of the outcome. How much such advice Marie dispensed in the parish Father Dowling was not sure, but it had never got out of hand. Marie was a good woman and he did not like to think what his life at St. Hilary's would be like without the housekeeper.

"You'll be marrying them before long," Marie predicted.

"We'll see."

It was that day that Edna Hospers sent Desmond O'Toole to the rectory with his complaints about the heterodoxy of Austin Rooney.

"You know the author James Joyce, Father."

"Of course."

"They won't even let the man be buried in Ireland. There was a petition but the Church and everyone else opposed it."

"I didn't know that."

"It's all in Edna O'Brien's little book."

"I don't know the book, I'm afraid."

"I reviewed it for the *Tribune*. I was involved in the literary page, you know."

"I think you've mentioned that before."

"And now comes Austin Rooney with the most outlandish statements to these good old people. It is shocking that women and men in the twilight of their lives should be subjected to such opinions as his. The professor of literature!"

This last was said with disdain, and then a litany of complaints. Joyce was a difficulty, but surely the remarks about Willa Cather were understandable. A woman who had written *Death Comes for the Archbishop* and *Shadows on the Rock* had a claim to be called a Catholic writer, with the emphasis on "writer."

"The woman lived and died a devout Episcopalian."

There was woolly-headed ecumenism abroad, no doubt, but there was also a narrow sectarianism. Not that Father Dowling felt that Desmond O'Toole was motivated by a passion for orthodoxy. Edna had forewarned him of Desmond's coming and made it clear that his heresy hunting was part of his campaign to win back Maud Gorman from Austin Rooney. It seemed an ignoble indignation.

"Tell me about your literary work."

"I would have severed my connection with the paper if any book by James Joyce was reviewed in the *Tribune*."

"Well, I suppose his reputation is secure."

"I don't know how much of Joyce you've read, Father."

"I was going to ask you the same question."

"Oh, I read it all. As a professional duty. The poetry is a thing apart, lyrically beautiful, but things already start to go wrong in *Dubliners*."

Father Dowling rose to stop the oral book review he was certain threatened. He told Desmond that he would have a word with Austin Rooney. Of course he did not say what about.

"You are a good pastor who looks after his sheep," Desmond said unctuously, and left.

"He's just jealous of Austin," Marie said when he was gone.

"Oh, you heard. I didn't realize he was speaking so loudly."

Marie ignored this. "Austin, by the way, is Colleen Gallagher's uncle. Her mother was his sister."

"Was?"

"She's gone to God."

The following day Father Dowling stopped by Edna's office and they talked generally about the Center. Under Edna's direction it had flourished. She knew how to strike a balance between too much fuss and too little, leaving alone those who just wanted to be there, providing games, excursions, and shopping trips on the parish shuttle bus for those so inclined.

"I've talked with Desmond O'Toole."

Edna's eyes drifted heavenward. "About the dance?"

"Dance? He came to me about Austin Rooney's literary opinions."

"Well, the dance has just come up. Austin and Maud got the idea when he did a few waltz steps with her in the gym and others applauded the performance. Austin invited the others to dance, but they held back, and that's when he suggested that the center have a dance some evening, with a band and everything. The enthusiasm carried them all right up to my office. What do you think?"

"Why not?"

"For one thing, it would take their minds off that girl who was pushed into the street during the rush hour a few days ago. Some find a morbid fascination in her death."

"Her name was Linda Hopkins. I've talked with Phil Keegan about it."

Edna observed a moment of silence.

"A band would cost money."

"I have one restriction, Edna. No rock band. It must be a band that plays music."

"Oh, there's no danger of rock with this group. They want golden oldies. Desmond O'Toole is a lonely voice in opposition."

"How can he oppose a dance?"

"I didn't encourage him to tell me why."

Desmond was downstairs, a dour Savanarola surveying the inane recreation going on in the converted gymnasium.

"I haven't had a chance to speak with Austin yet, Desmond. Is he here?"

"He is doubtless off on the primrose path of dalliance with some unsuspecting lady."

"The mark of the literary page is still on you."

"Perhaps you will support my idea of an excursion to visit the cathedral."

"That's quite a distance."

"But such an objective."

"Work it out, Desmond. But be sure to schedule it to avoid peak traffic times."

"It will only be possible if we take the interstates."

"Keep me posted."

Austin Rooney was seated on a bench, looking pensively over the parish grounds. Father Dowling sat beside him, intending to have a word about something or other with Austin, to redeem his promise to Desmond.

"Why so somber, Austin?"

"Life is a mystery and a maze, Father Dowling."

"How so?"

"Take the actuarial tables. They assure us that it is the female that outlives the male, yet look at the people who come to the Center. It is almost fifty-fifty. I was thinking of my own case. I did not retire at sixty-five, as I could have, but decided to teach until I was seventy. Seventy came and I still was not willing to step down. My wife and I could postpone the delights of retirement. But of course she died before that time came."

"Retirement may be oversold, Austin."

The former professor chuckled. "Young people now begin to talk of retirement before they've done any work. Do priests retire?"

"We're given much the same leeway as professors."

"My niece is going out with an Italian."

"They have souls too."

Austin Rooney laughed aloud. Father Dowling asked him to come on to the rectory. In the study Rooney explored the books on the pastor's shelves before taking a chair. He accepted a cup of tea and they chatted about James Joyce.

"He was an odious person, Father, no doubt of that. But it is not for his person that he is acclaimed."

That was all. Austin did not parade the knowledge he no doubt had.

"Don't misunderstand my remark about my niece and her Italian. I was thinking that Italians have a stronger sense of family than the Irish. If she marries him, we will lose her."

"Isn't that the definition of marriage?"

It was pleasant to hear Austin Rooney's educated laughter. Among the mysteries of life he probably had not been pondering on that bench, was that he should be attracted to someone as silly as Maud Gorman.

3

Thirty years before, having financed his college education by joining NROTC, George Hessian was commissioned and spent two sickly years in uniform before he was given a medical discharge for the diabetes that had escaped the attention of the physicians who had given him the pro forma physicals paving the way into college and then into the Navy. He had his first attack in San Diego and was assumed to be drunk when he was discovered on the floor beside his bed in the junior officers' quarters. The hangover remedy he was given restored him and he himself passed off the episode as due to the uneasy excitement he felt as he waited for the ship to which he had been assigned to come into port. The second attack was on shipboard where he was attended by a physician who recognized the symptoms because of the experience he had had with a diabetic younger sister. George spent his first voyage helping out in sick bay, was put ashore in Hawaii, and flown back to the mainland. Until his ultimate discharge he spent hours in the base library where he conceived the ambition of becoming a writer.

It is the nature of such an ambition to be alluringly vague. His mind was flooded with images of himself in the flush of fame, a fame of which he quickly tired—imagination can exhaust whole lifetimes in a matter of days—and he began to see himself as a Salinger sort of recluse, fleeing from his excited readers and intrepid reporters. When he returned to Fox River, he took a job in a bank where he worked for decades, moving slowly up the lower rungs of the financial ladder. The work was boring but welcome, since he saw it as his incognito. Who, when they sat beside his desk arranging a loan, suspected that they were dealing with a writer who would become a legend?

He wrote nothing. At first it was a matter of postponing the great effort, then his daily work proved more distracting than he would have believed. Finally, he dreaded the thought of sitting at his typewriter and trying to make words he actually wrote conform to the inflated image of himself he had devised. After retirement he took a job as gate guard at the retirement home where his mother now lived. It was in the solitude of the guard shack that a great project had come to him. He would write the history of St. Hilary parish.

"I'm not sure there would be a great demand for such a history," Father Dowling said.

"It is a matter of setting down the record."

"I suppose publishing it would be expensive."

"My proposal is to write and publish it, Father."

"Ah. You're retired?"

"More or less."

There seemed no need to mention his job as a guard at the retirement home where his mother now resided. Father Dowling's kindness seemed the result of an effort. George had the sense that he was being condescended to, however unconsciously. He smiled, sustained by his carefully cultivated self-image. In the end the pastor saw little reason to refuse him. George would have recourse to the parish records, he would need a letter that would gain him entry to the archdiocesan archives, he would interview graduates of the school.

"Of course the school will be a central theme."

"You know that it has become a Senior Center?"

"All the better. As a school, it has a beginning, a middle, and an end."

"Have you written such a thing before?"

"History is a new departure, Father Dowling. But a writer's craft can be applied to many subjects."

If he rather easily received carte blanche from the pastor, Marie Murkin, to whom Father Dowling referred him—"She is a walking archive, George, the animate history of the parish"—was a tougher nut to crack.

"Why on earth would you want to do such a thing?"

He looked at her. "It's not easy to talk about."

"Why not?" She had insisted that he take a cup of tea. They were seated at the kitchen table in the rectory.

"I suppose I could talk with you."

"Of course you can."

"Equally, of course, I could not do this without your help."

Marie Murkin liked this acknowledgment of her importance in such a matter. He added, "In all justice you would have a claim to be co-author."

"Co-author!" She threw up her hands, but could not master the smile that came. "I will leave the authoring to you."

So he was given access to the records of the parish, most of them stored in the attic, and Edna Hospers let him use what had once been the school nurse's office, just down the hall from the principal's office where Edna was installed. He brought his laptop computer with him to rectory and nurse's office and established a routine that, in a short time, made him all but invisible to those he moved among.

"You grew up in the parish?" Edna asked.

"I attended the school."

The school records, nine large file cabinets, were transferred to the nurse's office by a protesting school janitor and the parish mainte-nance man. They stood around until he tipped them each five dollars. He closed the door after them. The first thing he did was ascertain which of the cabinets contained the records of his own years in St. Hilary's parish school. Then he settled down to work.

4

As Father Dowling had told Colleen, weddings were a rarity at St. Hilary's given the changed character of the parish. There were young families, happy possessors of the large houses that were sold for a song by those anxious to flee the parish after it had been hemmed in by the a triangle of new highways meant to facilitate the daily flow to and from Chicago. Old parishioners were just that: old, their families grown and gone. This had prompted turning the parish school into a meeting place for seniors, and under Edna Hospers the idea had expanded and flourished.

"The next pastor may want to turn it back into a school," Father Dowling said.

"This is a pretty healthy bunch, Father."

"I was thinking of the growing number of children in the parish."

"Oh, sure. As soon as my kids are grown, there'll be a parish school again."

But Edna was not unhappy. The local public school was spared the usual problems because of its insulation by the new highways and teaching positions there were eagerly sought. Edna's children were being well taken care of, educationally, and she was as effective a mother as she was as director of the parish Center.

Father Dowling found that he was looking forward to giving marriage instructions to the young couple. His years on the archdiocesan marriage tribunal made him a firm supporter of the new requirement that those about to marry should be made aware of the permanency and obligations of the state they were about to enter.

His thoughts turned to the bereaved Hopkinses in their empty nest to the north. There was still no news of the missing boyfriend whose absence had taken on new significance, from what Linda's fellow workers at the Hacienda Motel had told Cy Horvath.

"They all hated his guts. I don't think they thought he was worthy of her."

"What did he do?"

"Drove a cab."

"Wouldn't that make him easy to trace?"

The chauffeur's license appeared to have been taken out in a name devised for the occasion, Harry Paquette. But the photograph on the license had been sent out in a routine fashion to other police departments, along with a fax copy of the application form. Cy remained keen, but Phil Keegan considered the investigation, such as it was, a waste of time. If it had not been a slow time in the Detective Division, Phil would have put an official stop to it.

"We don't even know that a crime has been committed."

"How about the witnesses?"

"To what? Someone might have bumped into her, she might have been pushed. She might have just lost her balance."

But one witness was certain that she could identify the man she had seen push Linda Hopkins into the path of traffic on Dirksen Boulevard. She was less sure that the photograph on the chauffeur's license application was that of the man, though other witnesses thought it was.

"I will never forget that face as long as I live," Mabel Wilson repeated nonetheless.

"We'll see," Phil said. His tone was the skeptical one of a cop who had known the certainty of witnesses to evaporate when they realized they could be called to testify in a trial. "If there is a trial, which I doubt, Roger. The prosecutor is not eager to pursue a case he is sure to lose."

But Cy Horvath had met the parents and he had talked with other members of the cleaning crew at the Hacienda Motel. Cy's face communicated neither optimism or despair. But so long as he could, he meant to go on trying to unravel how it was that Linda Hopkins had met her death.

1

Life had smiled on Tim Gallagher and he knew it. That he should have found such a wife as Jane was an unmitigated blessing. He tried to remember when he had thought of her as just Colleen's friend, someone thrown in his way without the need to search for her and, having found her, win her. But it had not been until he ran into her on the Georgetown campus that she ceased to be just one of Colleen's friends. In Fox River, he had never taken her out or, to tell the truth, even thought of it. At Georgetown he thought of it, and the envy of which he was the object when he was seen about campus with Jane was not lost on him. The film of familiarity lifted and he saw Jane as a very attractive young woman. She was fun to be with; they were immediately at ease with one another, perhaps because they already knew so much about one another. Within a semester, there was an understanding. They would marry as soon as Tim was through law school.

In the event, they married after he got his B.A. He had been offered a full ride in law school and there seemed no reason to postpone their marriage. It was a glorious wedding and although Tim had become used to being regarded by other men as fantastically lucky to have won someone like Jane, the wedding gave that realization a boost. Law school went easily by. Jane worked in the admissions office until the first baby came. With children, she became a mother, an amazing transformation. A great offer from Anderson Consulting was topped by a Loop firm, and the outstanding legal career that all his professors had predicted for him began. They lived in Barrington, not far from Fox River where they had grown up—not far in distance, that is. In another sense they inhabited a different universe. Their parish was St. Anne's, something that delighted Jane.

"What's special about that?"

"Oh, nothing. But I have to tell Colleen."

There were Jane, the three kids, wonderful kids, the house, the constantly rising line of his career—what more could he ask?

And yet there were times when the very fact that he had all he could ask for made him want more. What the "more" might consist of, he could not have said. But with forty looming, the future seemed more confining than alluring. They had special plans for the kids' education; his financial plan conceivably could have made retirement at fifty-five feasible. They had a condo on Long Boat Key that they rented out when they weren't using it. With Jane on his arm he still felt king of any hill you could mention. She seemed more beautiful than ever now, with a mature beauty, a silver thread or two in her dark hair that did not age her but added something mysterious to her beauty. They said family prayers together at night and he listened to his children thank God for Mommy and Daddy and all their grandparents and uncles and aunts and cousins. There was much to be thankful for. So why was he discontent? He could not forget that sleek and sexy young lawyer from Mallard and Bill who had come up to him as if they were involved in a conspiracy.

"I know your sister."

Her name tag told him she was from Mallard and Bill. "Colleen?"

"That's right, but you cheated. You peeked at my name card." She tilted it toward him in what seemed an almost suggestive manner. Did she have a blouse under that suit coat? As for the skirt, with legs like those, who could blame her? "I signed up for the morning seminar on investments."

"Are you in trusts?"

"More or less. You are, I know."

"How do you know?"

"I told you I know Colleen."

Other men noticed her interest but their reaction was different from the one he got when he was with Jane. This girl—"They call me Aggie," she corrected when he called her Agatha—was both all business and gave the promise of adventure. He took a seat on the opposite side of the table from her and down at one end, when they went into the seminar. But it was like an admission that she had gotten to him.

Lunch was one of those lunches, everybody chattering about the morning seminars, and then back they went till four.

"I'm dying for a drink," Aggie said at his elbow.

"I forgot my flask."

She actually punched him in the ribs. "There's a bar downstairs, or we could go up the street."

Just like that. Well, she was a business girl and they were colleagues of a sort. They had their drink up the street, in a bar crowded with people, many of them looking like singles.

"Do you come here often?"

She laughed a trilling laugh. Apparently he had made a joke. She made him feel that he had been far away on a long voyage. He never stopped for a drink in the Loop. He hurried to catch the train that would take him back to Barrington and allow him to go on working on the way. They had the drink and parted in the street.

"I am so glad we've met at last."

And then she waved and went in a leggy walk up the street. Tim found himself staring after her.

2

One of the attractions of his parish of which Father Dowling was ashamed to boast, was that in a sense, so very little went on there. His tasks were the essential tasks of the priest—to offer Mass, dispense the sacraments, visit the sick, and bury the dead. There were very few weddings, so the arrival of Colleen Gallagher and Mario Liberati at the rectory to make arrangements for their wedding was an event. He became aware that they were in the house when he heard voices in the front parlor, among them Marie Murkin's. She seemed to be subjecting them to a preliminary inquiry before turning them over to the pastor.

"I'm back," he said, looking into the parlor.

"Where've you been?"

"I assumed you thought I wasn't in."

Marie was not flustered. "Father Dowling, you remember Colleen. This is her fiancé, Mario Liberati."

"Aha." He shook Liberati's hand. "You make a very nice couple."

"Father, we want to make arrangements for our wedding."

"Somehow I guessed that."

The parlor was a better place than his study for this. As they got seated, Marie asked if anyone would like tea or coffee. Nobody did. Reluctantly Marie withdrew. As a precaution, Father Dowling shut the door.

Mario, of course, was a cradle Catholic. Did he practice his faith?

"I intend to from now on." He looked at Colleen.

Father Dowling explained the new requirement that they meet several times before the actual wedding date. Some parishes had marriage preparation courses going nonstop throughout the year, but at St. Hilary's they could be more informal.

"On the first occasion I will speak to both of you, like this. Then with each of you alone. The fourth meeting will again be with both of you."

The requirement had been initiated because of the fear that young people had only a hazy understanding of marriage as a sacrament. The world is too much with us, and it is fatally easy to pick up one's notion of marriage from the culture around, not a good thing to do with half the marriages in the country ending in divorce. Divorce had become common among Catholics as well, and applications for annulment were at an all-time high. The idea that marriage was a promise for life, through thick and thin, had weakened. Hence the requirement.

"Sounds like a good idea," Mario said.

Colleen looked blissfully at her intended. Once upon a time a pastor simply knew the people who came to be married—he had seen them grow up, knew their parents, knew their outlook on life—and such meetings were unnecessary. Of these two, he had met Colleen only once, scarcely enough to know her.

"So we're agreed?"

"Whatever it takes," Mario said.

"So let's fix some dates. When would you like to be married?"

"Would June be possible?"

"Of course. You can have any Saturday in June you want. We don't have a great many weddings at St. Hilary's."

"It's such a lovely church," Colleen said, looking first at Mario and then at Father Dowling.

"It's a very serviceable parish plant. Of course we've put the school to a different use."

"What use?"

So he told them about the school and of the Senior Center. "Your uncle is often here. Austin Rooney."

"He is? Dad should come too."

"Of course he's welcome."

"He moved out of the parish after Mother died."

"That makes no difference."

It was only after the couple had gone, having arranged to return the following week, that Father Dowling remembered Marie's report of

Austin's reaction when she suggested that his brother-in-law come to the Center.

Austin was a rare bird among the old people, few of whom had led the kind of active life he had.

"Active life? Father Dowling, you must realize that a professor's life is no more active than a . . ."

"Than a priest's?"

"That isn't what I was thinking."

Active or not, Austin was happy enough, when prompted, to talk of his days as professor of literature. It was amazing the things Austin knew and loved—and those he did not. Bloy and Maritain and Claudel were only names to him.

"I taught American literature, Father."

So they talked of Scott Fitzgerald and John O'Hara and Hemingway.

"Hemingway was a kind of Catholic, you know."

"How many kinds are there?"

They often sat together in Father Dowling's study but if the pastor thought he was preserving the man from the attractions of Maud Gorman, he was wasting his time. The professor emeritus was as smitten as half a dozen others had been before him, and there are some things beyond the reach of reason. Besides, such infatuations among the elderly had always proved to be short-lived, however intense.

"The little vixen actually came to the door when the two of you were speaking," Marie said when Austin had gone.

"What did you tell her?"

"That you preferred to hear confessions in the church when a lady is involved."

"You must never turn a penitent away, Marie."

"Oh, it was I who brought up confession, not she. She scampered away at the mention of it."

Marie was incorrigible, and like many women she was particularly hard on her own sex. Edna Hospers told Father Dowling that Austin was a good influence on Maud.

"She's never without a book now."

"Does she read it?"

"That may come."

"How are plans for the dance progressing?"

"Everything is all set. And we won't have to pay for a band. Desmond O'Toole has put together a trio. He himself is a marvel on the piano. And he sings."

"Desmond?"

"He is now enthusiastic about the dance. He sings like a bird. He plays by ear and he knows the lyrics of any song you can name."

"But that will keep him off the dance floor."

"It's just as well. Then he can't be turned down if he asks Maud for a dance. Anyway, I think his ardor has cooled."

Father Dowling could see that Edna was relieved. It would be difficult to have to tell people twice her age to grow up. Then he told her about the wedding and that the bride-to-be's father might be coming to the center. "He is Austin's brother-in-law."

"The one he hates."

"Did he say that?"

"Oh, he's too smooth for that. But Desmond told me all about it."

"Maybe Desmond is trying to start trouble."

Edna thought about it. "He really does sing like a bird."

3

Some days later a tall, silver-haired man without an ounce of fat on him stood in Edna's doorway, wearing an apologetic smile on his handsome face.

"Mrs. Hospers?"

"Yes."

He crossed the room to her and took her hand in both of his. "My daughter told me what you are doing here and I had to see for myself."

"Your daughter?"

"Colleen. I am Jack Gallagher." He said this as if throwing off a disguise. "And there is to be a dance?"

There were posters everywhere about the school, as he must have seen on his way in. She managed to free her hand. Jack Gallagher was decidedly a charmer and age had not dimmed his conspiratorial good humor.

"You must come."

"Wild horses couldn't keep me away. In the phrase. The very anti-quated phrase." He stepped back and looked around the room. "This was Sister Ellen Joseph's room."

"You attended this school?" Edna asked.

"For eight years. Eight of the most . . ." He stopped and gave her an apologetic smile. "The most eight years of my life. The nuns were saints, all but a few."

"Are you still in the parish?"

"Is that required?"

"Not at all. I just wondered."

"No, I am now filed away in a condominium, awaiting the grim reaper."

"You're retired."

He gave her a look. "Flattery will get you everywhere. Yes, my voice has been stilled."

"What did you do?"

"Why should you remember? I was on the radio. *Jack in the Box* was my show but my most popular program was at night. Two hours of soothing music and murmured philosophy. I came on at nine. I had a devoted audience. Of course that was long ago. I did not make the transition to television. The accent is on youth. On radio, a voice might be of any age, but who wants to see their grandfather on television?"

"So you have grandchildren?"

"Three. Not that they would have listened to me. It is just a phrase.

When my fans died away my voice was stilled. For some years I did audio for commercials, making far more money than I had in my ascendancy."

Edna had the sense that he could have gone on and on, and the truth was she almost wished he would. First Austin and now this man. The Center was coming up in the world.

All the old people knew who Jack Gallagher was, or at least what he had been. He was surrounded by what could only be described as fans when Edna went downstairs. Austin was nowhere in sight, but a bright-eyed Maud regarded the newcomer from afar.

"Did you know him?" Edna asked Maud.

"Know him! Only his voice, of course, but it hasn't changed a bit. Did you ever hear him?"

"I don't think so."

Maud closed her eyes and brought her hands together. "His program was heavenly. The sweetest, saddest music, and he would talk, say things, sometimes recite poetry—it was so restful. I am sure everyone in this room listened to that program religiously."

"*Jack in the Box*."

"That was during the day. The evening program was called *Love's Old Sweet Song*."

Desmond O'Toole was in the first rank of the admiring circle, and Jack Gallagher remembered Desmond from their time as boys in the school. Within hours it had been arranged for Jack to alternate with Desmond on the night of the dance. It seemed Jack had a beautiful tenor voice. For Jack to show up just a week before the dance was a bonus Desmond would not have believed.

"I wasn't sure he was still alive until he walked in here," he said to Edna.

"You haven't kept in touch?"

"It isn't that. How incredible that a man who enjoyed that kind of popularity could sink into total oblivion. Wait until you hear him."

"I was coming in order to hear you, Desmond."

"Of course, my voice is bass."

"Don't run yourself down."

She had told a joke. What next?

1

"Your father is all excited about St. Hilary's school," Jane said. The kids were in bed, Tim and Jane were having hot chocolate in the den, catching up on one another's day. She sat on a couch, her legs drawn up beside her, wearing a shawl, the fire making her face a pattern of shadows. How beautiful she is, Tim told himself, as if he were surprised.

"He already graduated from there."

"Ha ha. The place has been turned into a center for seniors."

"He wouldn't admit that he is one."

"You're wrong. There's going to be a dance and he will be emcee or something and he really is excited."

"It's time he came out of his shell."

When his father had left the station, he had been given boxes of tapes, music, mainly recordings of his own programs, and Tim had the awful feeling that his father spent all day listening to himself in that lonely condo. For all his popularity, Jack Gallagher had retired with not a lot more than Social Security. But the sale of the house, and a little help from Tim, had enabled him to move into a very comfortable apartment in Western Sun Community. The idea was that he would be near things, able to walk or take public transportation, and not have to bother with driving. He was a terrible driver. But he had become almost a recluse. It was a major event when they got him to the house, despite

49

the fact that they picked him up and returned him. Of course his father had never really been at ease with Tim since the great accusation.

One summer his father got Tim a job at the station, on the television side. It was then that Tim first realized that his father was obsolescent, a man who did radio and not television. On that station, there was no room for such specialization now. For a time it had even been thought that radio itself was obsolete. No one then could have imagined the plague of talk shows that lay ahead. When Tim heard gossip about his father's pursuit of the girl who did the weather, he broke out into a little sweat of embarrassment. It was one thing to learn that his father's status at the station was sinking, it was another to hear him mocked—and about such a subject. That night at home, he confronted his father with the accusation. His father almost sprang from his chair, took Tim by the arm and steered him out of the house.

"Do you want your mother to hear such nonsense?"

"They're all talking about it at the station."

"And you believed them?" His father was capable of theatrical tones at home but this was as unmodulated as he could make his voice. The words penetrated Tim and made him feel the deeper shame of doubting his father. Then he was in his father's arms, his back being patted, friends again.

"Actually, Tim, she's in pursuit of me."

Thus in a joke had it been passed over. Why did he remember that now? Because it conveyed more surely than any other consideration how a child reacts to anything that threatens the home. Husbands and wives might have formed their union voluntarily, but the child is born into it as his only world. When Tim heard his father spoken of in that way, in pursuit of a weather girl, it was like his first travel by plane when he realized there was literally nothing but miles of air beneath the floor on which his feet rested.

As that summer wore on, Anita, who did the weather, seemed to be flirting with everyone. She even stopped at Tim's table in the commissary, gave him a look of appraisal and chucked him under the chin.

"Be careful, Anita. That's Jack Gallagher's son."

Her eyes widened and she stepped back. "Then I better be careful."

By then Tim had learned that many meaningless things were said at the station. But what an odd memory to have when Jane mentioned his father and St. Hilary's school.

"He went there as a kid, Jane."

"And now he's back. He's seeing friends he hadn't seen in years. Your uncle Austin hangs out there too. And there's going to be a dance."

Much of Jane's enthusiasm was relief that his father had any news at all to tell, let alone all this. He realized how the old man's loneliness had weighed upon them. Maybe the fact that Colleen was getting married at last had snapped him out of it.

Jane was a little disappointed when Colleen suggested they have dinner in a restaurant in order to meet Mario.

"She's thinking of you having to prepare the meal."

"I know, but still."

"Maybe she thinks the reality of domestic life would scare him off."

"Tim, he's Italian. Colleen is going to have to learn how to cook *modo Italiano*."

"You make him sound like an immigrant. He is the shining light at Mallard and Bill. They've already made him a partner so he can't be lured away. All the youngsters there are jealous and angry." Of course he was thinking of Aggie and she was probably not a good example. She had called Mario "the cardinal," making an unintelligible reference to Cesare Borgia.

Mario Liberati probably would have been created a cardinal if he had gone into the priesthood. Tim liked him immediately.

"I never go to court, so it's not surprising we haven't met before. Colleen has given me an underling's view of things."

" 'An underling's'? Most of us get credit for the work she does. I know I do."

Every effort to get him to talk of the firm was similarly deflected.

Tim liked that. Mallard and Bill would have liked him less if they thought he discussed the firm with outsiders, even with a prospective brother-in-law. He was not a lot more forthcoming about his family.

"I was raised in Milwaukee, but got my first job here in Chicago after graduation."

"Isn't Mallard and Bill your first job?"

"This was before law school. I was a financial adviser for several years."

This opened up a vast area of conversation, at least for Tim and Mario. Colleen must have known about it already but Jane was simply bored with money. They had enough, more than enough, and that gave her the right to ignore it. Except, of course, for a careful keeping of the household accounts, but this was an exercise in mathematics rather than economics. Jane tuned back in when Mario's family came up.

"My parents married late and I am one of two children, almost an only child. Not many Italians can say either. They've retired to Sicily."

"We'll see them on our honeymoon," Colleen said.

"Of course Americans think of Sicily as Italians think of Chicago. It's one of the most beautiful places on earth, all of it, but on the southern coast, it is breathtaking. There's the sense that you're in touch with the roots of civilization. Syracuse was a Greek city. Plato visited there."

"You sound like you want to move there yourself."

"No, but I'm gratified they are in such a place."

Colleen said, "Tim met Aggie at a conference, Mario."

"Who's Aggie?" Jane asked.

"A femme fatale," Colleen confided, leaning toward Jane. "Skirts up to here, neckline down to here, all slinky and predatory. She tried to steal Mario away from me."

"Definitely not my type."

"What did you think of her, Tim?" Jane asked.

"As little as possible," he lied.

"I don't want any femme fatale stealing you away from me."

                              * * *

Later she and Tim talked about Mario and agreed that he was a good
match for Colleen, who had been her old self again.

"I suppose she must have wondered who she'd meet in an office,
and what other chances were there?"

"He was worth waiting for."

"What a gallant guy you are," Jane said, lifting her face to be kissed.

2

Desmond O'Toole regarded the arrival of Jack Gallagher at the Center as providential. Maud might be awed by the fact that Austin had
been a professor of literature, but she would remember Jack from his
radio days. Just about everyone did. They crowded around Jack, who
responded in a way that made the women want to get closer and just
touch him, but didn't make the men resentful; they were as
impressed as the women by the presence among them of someone
who had been an undoubted local celebrity. And his voice! On radio
it had been seductively gentle but it was even more so in person. He
might have been inviting the ladies to get closer so they could hear
his every word.

"You sing a little too, if I remember, Jack," Desmond said, estab-
lishing himself as Jack's right-hand man.

Jack put on a shamefaced look. "I used to sing along with the
records sometimes."

"Oh, I remember," Maud said. She had finally gotten right next to
Jack.

"The reason I mention it, Jack," Desmond said, "I was going to do
a few vocals at the dance, and if you would spell me . . ."

The squeals from the women brought back memories of the Sinatra
phenomenon. Jack raised his hands, as if in self-defense.

"All right. But I'll count on your being hard of hearing."

"What?" said Desmond, cupping his ear. It got a big laugh.

"You'll have to dance too," Maud cried.

"Of course he'll dance," Desmond assured her. It no longer hurt so much that Maud's interest in him was fading. He would be sending Jack in as the second team and routing Rooney from the field.

Rooney was nowhere in sight during this triumph, which dimmed it only a little. Austin had made a point of saying to Desmond how much he looked forward to the dance, speaking with Maud on his arm, so he could scarcely back out. The night of the dance Austin Rooney would be replaced by Jack Gallagher.

Austin Rooney was with his niece Colleen, who had a strange story to tell.

"There isn't anyone else I can tell, Uncle Austin. I can't tell Father, and of course Jane must never know."

"What on earth is wrong?"

And then she told him the story of Aggie, the office vamp, who, having lost out to Colleen with her now fiancé, had decided to get revenge by seducing Tim.

" 'Seducing'?" Austin said with a little laugh. "That is an activity that usually goes in the opposite direction."

"You don't know Aggie."

"I don't think I want to."

"She has to be stopped."

"Have you talked with her?"

"I wouldn't give her the satisfaction. That's what she's after, to avenge herself on me."

Austin had lived his life in the hothouse of faculty life and was not disposed to dismiss his niece's fears. He supposed an office could be like a campus, a place where petty quarrels sometimes blew into major storms. Male professors often acted as if they had droit du seigneur with their female students, and women faculty, wed and unwed, often entered the competition on the excuse that they were protecting students. When Austin had begun teaching, the profession was high-minded, moral and responsible. The notion that female students were legitimate prey would have shocked and horrified both male and female faculty. But now seminars were sponsored by national organizations decrying the alleged McCarthyism of monitoring the misbehavior of faculty with students. What a professor did behind the closed door of his office was nobody's business. No matter that the student was vulnerable, flattered by an attention which was at first equivocal and then unmistakable. And they were dependent on the professor for their grade. Something akin to the Hollywood director's couch was now operating in too many faculty offices. On this analogy, however limping, Austin was disposed to take Colleen's concern seriously.

"Surely you don't doubt your brother."

"He won't know what hit him. Already they're meeting regularly for drinks. People have noticed."

"Colleen, I am trying to think what I can possibly do."

"In part, you've already done it. I had to talk to someone."

"Sweetheart, you can always talk to me."

What he could not tell her was that his receptivity to her fears was strengthened by memories of her father's misbehavior. Jack had been a notorious womanizer during his golden years. When Austin had learned of this, he had gone to his brother-in-law, told him what he had heard, and asked for a denial. Jack's brows had lifted in humorous disbelief.

"Do you have your stole with you?"

"Is it true?"

" 'It'?"

"Are you running around with other women?"

"That is an interesting figure of speech, since the point is to get them stopped and horizontal."

Austin hit him in the mouth, with his open hand, then drove his fist into his stomach. Jack staggered backward across the room into a rack of records which continued to cascade down on him when he was prostrate on the floor. Austin left Jack's office and the two men had not exchanged a civil word since. Was Jack's son now to go the same route as his father?

Austin had gotten out of the studio before anyone came running in response to the crashing records. Jack must have told some lie about what had happened, since the charge of assault Austin half feared his brother-in-law would bring against him did not materialize. But the rumors about Jack's behavior continued.

This precedent did not make the thought of speaking to Tim attractive, but he resolved to do something.

"Where have they been having drinks together?"

Colleen gave him the name of a bar near Water Tower Place, the Willard.

"And that's all it has been so far, a tête-à-tête in a bar?"

"I hope so."

One afternoon at four-thirty, Austin took up his station in the bar, off in a corner, sipping a martini. The Loop was being swept by November winds and he had felt carried along by them when he walked from his car to the bar. What he had really wanted was a cup of coffee, but this was not the kind of bar that expected such an order, certainly not at this time of day. It was ready for an invasion of tense and ambitious professional people wanting the supposed relaxation of a couple of quick drinks before they headed home. In the event, he ordered a second martini, finding a species of warmth in the icy drink. The place eventually became so crowded he began to fear his nephew could be there and he wouldn't know it. So with his drink in hand he waded into the crowd. From its center he caught a glimpse of Tim and a young woman who lived up to Colleen's description.

What to do now? He had imagined a less hectic setting in which he could pretend to happen upon Tim and by his presence set the stage for any further talking to that might be needed. In this noise, it was doubtful anything he said could even be heard. He was reassessing his plan when Tim turned and their eyes met. It was all there on his nephew's face; no need to wonder if this were an innocent rendezvous. Whatever it was, Tim was ashamed of himself. People crowded between them and Austin lost sight of Tim and the young woman, but he had the sense that, in a way quite unplanned, he had fulfilled his mission.

The following day, Colleen phoned to tell him that the ineffable Aggie had let it be known in the ladies' room that she was involved with Colleen's brother.

"She told you that?"

"Oh, no. Not directly. Of course, she counted on the story being told to me."

"Is she *capable* of shame?"

Colleen laughed. "She is proud of what she is doing."

"Your brother isn't."

"Have you talked to him?"

"Our eyes met in that bar when he was with her."

"You went there?"

"With a grandiose and impractical plan. Fortunately, it proved unnecessary. When our eyes met, it was plain as could be what he was up to and how he felt about my seeing him."

"How long ago was that?"

"This is Friday? It was Wednesday night."

"But Aggie claims the big event took place at her apartment Thursday."

This was bad. When he had hung up, he called Tim at his office and was told that he was away for several days. And then he called Jane.

"Tim's out of town, Austin. Is there anything I can do?"

"It's nothing important. Just tell him I called. Have you heard about the dance we oldsters are having at St. Hilary's tomorrow night?"

He entertained her with the story of it, leaving out the fact that her father-in-law was now regarded as the main attraction of the evening. If he could have thought of anything else to make his call seem less abrupt, he would have been delighted, but only that idiotic dance came to mind as diverting small talk.

3

It was when Mario was going on and on about what a wonderful couple Jane and Tim were that Colleen burst into tears.

"Colleen, what is it?"

He put his arm around her and tugged her to him. She could not remember when she'd had such masculine reassurance and protection, and she sobbed helplessly. After that, she had to give him some indication of what worried her.

"It's Aggie," she said.

"Aggie!"

"You know what she's like?"

"What in God's name does she have to do with your brother's family?"

"Not the family. Tim."

He quickly understood, having been the object of Aggie's pursuit himself. This enabled Colleen to tell the story in an almost coded manner.

"He can't be that dumb. Would he jeopardize his family for that . . ." The word he used both shocked and delighted Colleen.

"My uncle saw them together and said that Tim looked guilty as sin. But after that, Aggie was letting everyone know in utter confidence that she had a thing going with my brother."

"How did your uncle know?"

"I told him. It was an awful thing to have to do, but the thought of her ruining Tim's marriage was worse."

"Someone has to talk to Aggie."

"What's the point? She has no conscience."

Mario began to talk of what he would do to Aggie at the office, make life hell for her, drive her from the firm, but his voice soon lost conviction. Any campaign against her would surely bring a suit, the kind he himself could win in a walk.

"It's not what she's doing in the office, Mario." She moved more closely against him. "At least not anymore."

"Why can't she settle for Fremont?"

Albert Fremont was a lawyer who had been hired at the same time as Aggie and clearly would have loved to be the object of her attention, but what kind of challenge was that for Aggie the man-eater? If only Albert would drop his heroine-worshiping expression and make himself interesting to Aggie, the trouble with Tim might dissolve. But placing one's hopes in Fremont seemed the definition of despair. A week ago, Fremont had come to Colleen as to a sister with the story of his lack of luck with Aggie:

"You're too available."

"She doesn't know I exist."

"Just ignore her and see what happens."

Fortunately, Fremont was a better lawyer than he was a lover, and it soon became obvious to Colleen that Aggie was picking his brains for her own work. But any chance that Albert Fremont might be the answer came apart when he and Aggie were working on a case together and she turned in their work as her own. When the work proved to be full of flaws, she said that Fremont was the author of most of it.

Fremont exploded. "Aggie, that was preliminary stuff. Why the hell did you turn it in?"

Aggie looked at Fremont. She could hardly tell him that she had wanted to steal his work and the credit she was sure it would bring.

"You sounded as if we were through."

" 'We'? This is finished work!" He waved it in her face and then took it in to a senior partner.

"Did you tell him what happened?" Colleen asked.

Fremont lifted his chin. "Certainly not. I apologized for the earlier work and replaced it with the finished product."

"But Aggie . . ."

Fremont's expression seemed to indicate that he was cured. Aggie's perfidy had drained love or desire or lust, whatever it had been, from his heart, and from then on he seemed immune to her.

"She's lucky you are a gentleman," Colleen told him.

4

Western Sun Community was a graded development through which the elderly could move from antepenultimate through penultimate to the ultimate stage where total care was provided those whose sun was definitively setting. George Hessian's mother had taken up residence in a condo at first, but had since been moved to a building where she had a room, nurses in attendance, but could still be relatively independent.

"I hate it here."

"I know, but it is best that you be looked after."

She looked at him as at a traitor. There were those, George's friend Rawley among them, who embarrassed George by congratulating him on his filial piety, but in truth he shared his mother's estimate. How could he not feel like Judas when he kissed her good-bye and left her with the television she loathed and the four walls whose blankness seemed reflections of her mind? It was better when he visited during mealtimes and could sit at the corner of the table where two other elderly women who had been pushed up in their wheelchairs watched resentfully as he told his mother of his day. Leaving her in company cushioned the blow because his mother knew how envious her table companions were of her dutiful son. When he visited between meals he would push her about in her wheelchair for whatever diversion that might afford.

"If only there were something to do."

"You have spent a lifetime doing things."

There was a covered walkway connecting the building with the common room where those who lived in condos went, and sometimes he took her there. This was a failure. She was dressed in tennis shoes and a running outfit, an ironic commentary on her immobility, and her presence made the more mobile residents uneasy. She represented what awaited them, they could only hope, in some misty future. But it was there that he heard that the great Jack Gallagher had moved into one of the condos.

"Who is Jack Gallagher?" he asked his mother.

" 'Who is Jack Gallagher?' He was on the radio. Where is he?"

He was holding court on a couch surrounded by adoring fans. His mother insisted that he push her over. Jack Gallagher fell silent when they arrived before him and George felt compelled to say that his mother had been a great fan of his.

"My dear lady, how wonderful." Jack Gallagher rose and took her hand. "Where on earth did you get that chair? I want one."

Laughter all around. George was filled with gratitude at this gracious gesture and his mother was delighted. For days afterward, she cherished the memory but seemed to have no desire to repeat the experience, thank God.

"So Jack Gallagher is living here now," George said to Rawley now.

"The man himself."

"My mother was a fan of his."

"Everyone was, if you can believe them."

Sitting in the guard shack, talking to Rawley as their shifts changed, George thought how their status had changed since Rawley was in the financial office of the university and George was a representative of the bank. Their contacts were regular enough to transcend mere business, and soon they were friends. Rawley was a widower.

"I never married. Responsibility for my mother devolved on me."

They attended the Chicago Symphony together, Rawley finding that he liked Mahler despite himself.

"But I prefer the baroque."

"Is that what brought you to Western Sun?"

"I get paid for reading. I sit here and cars go in and cars go out but they require only minimum attention. I give 'em a wave."

"I am writing now in my off-hours."

"Ah."

"The history of St. Hilary's parish."

Rawley was an agnostic, so religion was a subject they avoided. If Rawley had not liked music they would have avoided speaking of that. Music, like religion, cannot be explained to the disinterested.

"You really believe all that stuff?"

"Catholicism? Of course."

"I never even had a faith to lose."

But they went to the exhibit of Vatican art and Rawley managed to avoid negative comments.

When Jack Gallagher showed up at the St. Hilary Senior Center he was mobbed as he had been at Western Sun. The man could not be too much younger than George's mother but he seemed hale and hearty. And then George learned that Austin Rooney was the brother-in-law of the newcomer.

"This place will be too tame for him," Austin said.

"Western Sun is tamer."

1

The former gymnasium that had been transformed into a recreation room for the seniors was now transformed into a ballroom. The lighting was subdued, the tables ringing the dance floor had candles or floral arrangements in their centers and four to six senior citizens breathing heavily between dances. The rest were on the dance floor, moving to the slow rhythms of the songs that had fueled the imaginations of their youth. The improvised bandstand, with Desmond at the piano, old Oliver Deutsch at drums, and Pinkie Kunert on bass, provided accompaniment for the crooning Jack Gallagher. The onetime radio host was an expert mimic, able to sing in the manner of Sinatra, Vic Damone, Dick Haymes, and even Crosby, so that the dancers concentrated on him rather than their unsure feet. Desmond proved to be a virtuoso of the keyboard, stitching the numbers together with riffs and changes of tempo so that one song smoothly followed another until it seemed that another decade was being reenacted in the makeshift ballroom.

A punch had been provided, mild enough but sufficient to bring nostalgic tears to the shuffling couples on the floor. Maud had to be taken from the floor for an interval, overcome by a number that had been the favorite of her late husband's. Except for that sentimental interlude, she was in the arms of Austin Rooney, an expert dancer whose lead made up for Maud's hesitation. On the dance floor, at least, she followed rather than led.

Father Dowling had come over to smile a brief benediction on the dance, puffing on an unlit pipe, with Marie Murkin half frowning, half smiling on one side of him, and Edna Hospers on the other.

"This could become a tradition," Edna said enthusiastically.

She was still surprised at how little all this was costing the center. It was as if the only contribution the parish had made was the locale. The piano had been brought down from the first floor where it had once provided march music for students when they filed in from recess and returned, but the other instruments were provided by the musicians who played them. The punch was also donated by the dance committee, plus the candles and other items of festive color. Maud was wearing a corsage provided by Austin Rooney. Her loyalty was divided between her partner and the crooning Jack Gallagher, who directed his tremulous lyrics at her as she passed beneath his microphone. Austin's efforts to keep as far from the bandstand and singer as possible were not always successful, and if Maud looked up with glistening cow-eyes at Gallagher, Austin stared into space at some distant star where the likes of Jack Gallagher were absent.

And then Desmond took over, playing and singing at once, his style his own but the words the words of Jacob. Jack Gallagher stepped onto the dance floor and tapped Austin imperiously on the shoulder, but his regard was for Maud alone. The transfer was made smoothly, in the approved manner, but for a moment Austin looked bereft of a purpose in life. He drifted toward Father Dowling.

"A great success, Austin."

"It brings back the past."

Desmond was now giving a particularly maudlin rendition of "Sentimental Journey." A sigh had gone up when he began the lyrics, and many couples swayed in place to listen. He went on to "Let it Snow, Let it Snow, Let it Snow," perhaps in deference to the light snow that had fallen earlier in the day. Now they were singing along with

Desmond, and Jack Gallagher was crooning the lyrics into the receptive ear of Maud, who had closed her eyes as if she might just drift heavenward on the memories evoked. Austin Rooney stepped forward and tapped Jack's shoulder. In response, Jack swung Maud in an elaborate pirouette and they disappeared among the other dancers. Austin's face was dark with anger and embarrassment.

"I thought when someone did that, the partner had to be given up," Father Dowling said to Edna.

"He should have! That isn't right."

Marie said she wondered why one man, let alone two, could be interested in Maud Gorman.

"Two?" said Edna. "Several others had to concede defeat to Austin."

"Jack Gallagher hasn't," Marie said, and it was difficult to tell from her tone if she had taken sides.

Meanwhile, at the microphone, Desmond was intoning "Dream," but his eyes were following Jack and Maud. He had seen the rebuff of Austin's attempt to break in—it had happened just in front of the bandstand—and he looked prepared to sing on forever if Maud could be kept from the arms of Austin Rooney.

Austin had circled the floor, and suddenly stepped forward and tapped Jack's shoulder again, more forcibly this time. Jack merely shrugged and once more swept Maud out of harm's way. This time Austin waded into the dancers, gripped Jack by the arm, and said in a voice audible through the soothing strains of Desmond's singing, "When someone taps your shoulder it means he wants to break in."

The dancers turned to look and then began to dance more slowly, fascinated by what was happening.

"And when there is no response, he should give up."

Maud had stepped out of Jack's arms and stood in her pretty rose gown looking back and forth between the two men. Austin was unable to keep his anger from showing, but Jack, head tilted back, looked at Austin with amusement. That was when Austin hit him.

Jack reeled backward, moving through the dancers like a bowling ball through tenpins, and crashed to the floor at the feet of Desmond O'Toole. Desmond raised his hand, the music stopped, and then he was kneeling beside Jack.

"Give him air. Give him air."

But Jack was already rising. He started toward Austin, but Desmond, after a moment's hesitation, stopped him.

"Is he all right?" Father Dowling asked Edna.

"What can one punch do? So long as they don't have a real fight."

Father Dowling strode to Desmond, told him to play something rousing. "Do you know 'MacNamara's Band'?"

"MacNamara's Band" was played, and Jack, restored, divided his attention serially among half a dozen delighted women. Off to the side, Austin and Maud were in earnest conversation.

"I think it's safe for me to leave," Father Dowling said to Edna.

"Thanks for coming by, Father."

Marie was not ready to return to the rectory. She seemed to fear— or was it hope?—that the violence was not yet finished.

2

She was right, but its continuation took place long after Marie had gone back to her apartment in the back of the rectory. The two adversaries met in the parking lot after the dance had been completed, with the mandatory playing of "Goodnight Irene."

"I think I owe you something, Austin," Jack said, tapping his brother-in-law on the shoulder as he walked to his car. When Austin turned, Jack swung a haymaker. A mistake. Austin had ample opportunity to step out of its way and drive his fist into the stomach of the beau of the ball. Gallagher doubled over like an Olympic diver after he has left the board, and Austin, for good measure, gave him a push that sent him stumbling backward. When he sat, it was in a puddle of melted snow.

Maud Gorman looked on enigmatically; Austin helped her into the passenger seat of his car and slammed the door possessively when she was seated. Maud had come with Austin and she always went home with the man who brought her. But as they drove off, her wide-eyed gaze was directed back toward Jack Gallagher, sitting ignominiously in a puddle in the parking lot of St. Hilary's Senior Center.

❧ Part Two ❧

6

1

"Maybe I should assign half a dozen officers to your next dance to keep the peace." Phil Keegan was enjoying himself immensely with the story of the quarrel between two old men over an ancient woman.

"How did you hear of it?" Marie asked. She herself had heard of the fight in the parking lot the following morning from Edna.

"Because Jack Gallagher came downtown to swear out a complaint against Professor Austin Rooney. He insisted on the 'Professor' part. He nearly fell into the hands of Skinner in the prosecutor's office."

"Is that a name?" Marie asked, shifting her weight as she stood in the doorway of the pastor's study. Keegan was at his ease in his favorite chair and Father Dowling, behind the desk, his pipe going satisfactorily, waited while Phil answered Marie.

"Flavius Skinner, assistant to the prosecutor, a lean and hungry man who proceeds on the assumption that all citizens are potential criminals."

Since little more than Gallagher's self-esteem had been injured in the attack he described, the usual thing was to soothe the accuser and promise to say a few harsh words to his attacker.

"Everybody came in to hear him tell it," Phil said, smiling at the memory. "That's how Skinner heard about it, so he came down the hall on the run. Gallagher liked having an audience, I'll tell you that, and if he thought we found it hilarious that he was talking about a tiff between rivals for the hand of a woman in her mid-seventies, he gave no sign of it. Before you know it, Skinner has whisked him off to his office, seeing what prosecutable possibilities there might be in the story."

Phil took a sheaf of papers from his inside pocket and handed them to Father Dowling.

"There it is."

It was Skinner's account of the interview with Jack Gallagher in his office.

"Does he pass these around?"

"My secretary knows his secretary."

"Can I see it?" Marie said.

"I wonder if Phil wouldn't like some tea, Marie."

"Tea! I will take some coffee, if any's made." Marie turned to go, and he added, "I couldn't let you read official stuff, Marie. It's not for the laity."

She gave him a look.

The account Jack Gallagher gave of the evening of the dance was not without its contacts with reality, but by and large it seemed to have come from his imagination. Austin's attempts to break in on him when he was dancing with Maud were lost in an account of the rude assault made on him, the manhandling, the blow that had sent him careening through the dancers to land on the floor by the bandstand. Jack described it as a "sucker punch." His enemy had later stalked him through the parking lot where he sprang on him from the dark. Only the element of surprise had enabled this attack to take place, Jack assured Skinner. "Then the blackguard sped away in his automobile."

" 'Blackguard'?"

"He talks that way, Roger."

"He's quite an entertainer."

"I hate to see a man who climbed so high bring dishonor on himself in his old age."

"Wasn't he a local radio announcer?"

"Roger, he was a radio legend. My wife loved that program."

"So what will Skinner do?"

"He asked me to look into the particulars of the case." Phil laughed. "It's a slow time and if anyone can handle those old people with respect it is Cy Horvath."

"Phil, what of that girl who was pushed into ongoing traffic on Dirksen Boulevard?"

Phil frowned. "I don't think we'll ever learn what happened there. Of course Cy won't let it go."

"Good for him."

"I appreciate the sentiment, Roger, but now he can distract himself checking out Gallagher's complaint."

"Do you think charges could actually be brought against Austin Rooney? I don't approve of people hitting one another, particularly men of an age when a little can do a lot of damage, but there was certainly provocation. The lady in question was Austin's date of the evening and Gallagher tried to commandeer her. But it doesn't seem to have the makings of a criminal case, Phil."

"You have to know Skinner."

2

The night of the dance, George Hessian and Rawley were at McGinty's Irish Pub drinking Guinness and trying to convince one another that the activities they were engaged in after retirement were more satisfying than they were.

"I am reading systematically through the novels of Trollope," Rawley said, his lips creamy with stout.

"I've never read him."

Rawley looked at him in disbelief and for forty-five minutes extolled the merits of the English novelist. George had often been impressed by the former financial officer's knowledge of literature.

"You must have thought of writing yourself."

"It is not my gift."

"You should try."

Rawley looked at him. "I did try. That is how I know it is not my gift."

It was more difficult to convey to Rawley the satisfactions George derived from writing the history of the parish of St. Hilary. His youthful dreams of authorship might seem mocked by the project that now engaged him, but in the privacy of his own heart he could admit to himself that however modest a parish history might be it did not detract his efforts from anything more impressive. Immersing himself in the school records brought him back to his beginnings. Long thoughts were induced by comparing the grade-school records of those whose subsequent careers he knew. Dallying over the details of such records did not advance his task, but then he was still in the preparatory phase of his great effort. He wanted to recover the spirit of lost times and these old records were a catalyst to remembering his own years in the parish school. Recently he had been tracking Austin Rooney and Jack Gallagher through their eight years at St. Hilary's school. Each report card had a mark for deportment which was glossed by a line or two from the teacher. Austin from his earliest years had been recognized as docile, inquisitive, bright. His IQ score as well as his grades were higher than Jack's, about whom teachers tended to write with more unction and enthusiasm. It was difficult to know the basis for this higher estimate of Jack Gallagher. It helped to think back from the man Jack had become and imagine that those long-ago nuns had foreseen something of the shallow fame that would be his.

In sixth grade Austin and Jack were thought to have possible vocations to the priesthood. They were both altar boys, Austin the president of the John Berchmans Society, of which all altar boys automatically became members. The rivalry between Austin and Jack seemed present from the beginning, though they excelled at different things. Jack had been the athlete of the two, something that seemed ironic when George learned that Austin had knocked Jack to the ground twice in the course of the much-heralded dance.

"Did you see it?" George had asked Edna Hospers.

"I saw Jack Gallagher on the floor."

She seemed to be suppressing her partisan feelings for Austin in the dispute.

"What was it all about?"

"Maud Gorman."

George learned that as schoolboys Austin and Jack had once fought on the playground during recess, but then it was Austin who had been vanquished. Nonetheless both boys had been summoned to the principal's office, equal in the offenses they had committed.

"Didn't you fight him when you were students here?" George asked Austin.

Austin took a step backward. "How would you know about that?"

"What was that fight about?"

A rueful smile. "He intercepted a note I had written to someone."

"A girl?"

"I was not in the habit of writing notes to boys."

It was that afternoon, in the nurse's office on the second floor of the school, that George Hessian had an inspiration. His history would become a memoir tracing the lives of Austin Rooney and Jack Gallagher from boyhood to old age. They had married sisters, they were both widowers now, and the fight over Maud Gorman seemed to bring them full circle. Memoir or novel? George's mouth was open, he stared at the wall without seeing it; he was suffused with the ambition he had first known in the Navy. He had found his material. He *would* become a writer, a real writer. As he thought, he unconsciously brushed the notes he had been taking on St. Hilary's school to the edge of the desk. But the idea for the history had been providential, paving the way to this moment of inspiration. He smiled.

3

Tuttle and Tuttle consisted of Tuttle, the second occurrence of the name commemorating the father whose faith had sustained him through law school but had long since gone to that great appeals court in the sky. Clients were not plentiful and Tuttle was making do with part-time secretarial help: a battle-ax of a woman sent over from Tempting Temporaries, Hazel, who cleaned up Tuttle's correspondence, real and imaginary, in a couple of hours. Since he had her for the day, he asked if she wouldn't do something about putting order into his files.

"I could burn them. Those drawers are full of junk. Old newspapers, letters still in their envelopes. *Bills.*" The last was said with a none-too-subtle emphasis.

"Well, just clean up generally."

She dropped the phone book on his desk. "If you want a maid, they're in the Yellow Pages."

For all her severity, Hazel had a way of looking him over appraisingly. "I don't see any pictures of the wife and kids."

"Whose?"

"You're not married?"

"I took a vow."

"That's what you do when you marry."

"Are you married?"

"That's pretty personal, isn't it?"

"To the spouses."

Her laughter did not sound joyous, but she took to sitting in his office, which had the effect of cutting into his nap time.

"Do you have any clients at all?"

"I am on retainer to most of them. I don't get a lot of walk-in business."

"I'm not surprised. Hidden away on the eighth floor of this dump with an elevator that has a will of its own."

"My new premises are being readied."

"Where, at Resurrection Cemetery?"

There was no doubt of it, she liked him. Tuttle was frightened. He had the sense that if Hazel decided she wanted to move right in he would not know how to stop her. Thank God he had only hired her for the day. The next time he availed himself of the services of TT he would specify anyone but Hazel Barnes. Peanuts Pianone, his bosom companion, looked in the door, saw Hazel at her ease in Tuttle's office and beat a hasty retreat. Tuttle shouted after him, but Hazel closed the door of his office.

"I thought you didn't get much walk-in business."

"That's a friend of mine."

"As opposed to a client?"

Tuttle felt imprisoned in his own office. Hazel's expression had softened. "This place is a god-awful mess."

"I've always had trouble with help."

There was a knock on his inner door and Hazel was on her feet, unnecessarily smoothing her skirt. She pulled open the door and slipped past the caller with her face averted. The man looked after her, then at Tuttle.

"You're Tuttle?"

"To whom am I speaking?"

"Matthew Skinner, prosecutor. Captain Keegan mentioned your name."

"In what connection?"

But Skinner had come to the desk and now thrust out his hand. "I think we can be of mutual benefit to one another."

It was a sentiment that had seemed to emanate from Hazel but minutes before. He could hear her banging around in the outer office. Was she going to clean up those files after all? That might turn out to be an equivocal favor.

Meanwhile Tuttle asked Skinner to be seated. Of course he had heard of Skinner, though apparently Skinner had not heard of him. Skinner was regarded by many as a comic figure, eager to put the full authority of the prosecutor's office behind the most trivial of cases. But Tuttle had an open mind. He certainly wanted to know what mutual benefit Skinner had in mind.

"You doubtless remember Jack Gallagher."

Tuttle thought about it but no recognition came. "Go on."

"He is, of course, the legendary personality of radio Chicago. He has been attacked on several occasions by his brother-in-law, most recently last Saturday night, twice, at a dance held at the Senior Center at St. Hilary's."

"Father Dowling's parish."

"You know him?"

"Professionally."

"That may be helpful. Gallagher says the priest was a witness to one of the assaults. This took place on the dance floor itself, in full view of all those at the event."

"What is to be done?"

"That is why I have come to you. I had thought there were sufficient grounds for prosecution, but I have been overruled." Skinner paused as if he would like to go on about his travails in the prosecutor's office. But he overcame the impulse to self-commiseration. "As a criminal case, I fear it is a dead issue. But it grieves me that such things can be done with impunity. I do, however, think there is a sure-fire civil case. Are you interested?"

"Is Jack Gallagher interested?"

"How could he not be? He was publicly humiliated by this man. He is seething with a desire for . . . I was going to say 'revenge.' Let us say, for justice. A skilled lawyer could win a suit for considerable damages."

"You say the assailant is his brother-in-law?"

"A man named Austin Rooney. A man of means. He is a retired professor of literature at the local campus of the University of Illinois."

"Ah."

"Captain Keegan described you as a bulldog of a lawyer."

"You must remember that Captain Keegan and I are old . . ." Tuttle stopped. ". . . acquaintances. I have known Keegan throughout my career as a lawyer. I'm surprised that you needed a third-party recommendation of my skills."

"This is only my second year in the prosecutor's office."

Tuttle smiled at such infancy in the profession. "Even so."

"As soon as Captain Keegan mentioned your name, I hurried to you."

"Wise," Tuttle said. "Very wise."

He drew toward himself an appointment book and shielded its blank pages from Skinner's view. "I could take on the case. If there is a case."

"Do you doubt it?"

"It's what Jack Gallagher thinks that matters."

"I could take you to him immediately."

Tuttle did not fancy the idea of an intermediary. "Why don't I just drop in on the man? I will, of course, mention your name." Tuttle picked up a ballpoint pen. "Just give me the particulars."

"Of the assaults?"

"Maybe not. His address will do for now."

Skinner read it out of a pocket diary he had plucked from his pocket. Tuttle's ballpoint seemed to be dry. He fished several more from his desk and found one that would write. He jotted down the address and phone number of Jack Gallagher with apparent indifference. But his pulse was racing. With an ally in the prosecutor's office, his path would be smoothed. He could pick Skinner's brain for the most effective approach.

"And your own address?"

Skinner handed him a card. Tuttle read it with care and envy. It had been some time since a supply of business cards had been a high-priority item.

"I'll keep in touch."

"How I wish I myself had been given the go-ahead on this."

"If things work out as you suggest, perhaps a reference fee . . ."

Skinner made a horrified noise. "No, no. I couldn't take it. It would be unethical."

Tuttle nodded affirmatively. "It is well to be sure of the professional ethics of a colleague."

"But you mustn't suggest that I am a colleague in this. Even coming here . . ." Skinner's voice drifted away.

"Mum's the word," Tuttle said. "And Arrid too. Have no fear. No mention shall be made of your visit. Except, of course, to Jack Gallagher."

"Couldn't you portray it as something that had occurred to you as a lawyer?"

His more fastidious colleagues frowned on such solicitation of clients, but Tuttle was not adverse to the metaphorical ambulance chase. He thought of Amos Cadbury, the custodian of legal proprieties in the community. What a reception Skinner would have gotten if he had gone to Cadbury with this scheme! Tuttle himself understood the junior prosecutor's zeal. He had hesitated to ascribe revenge as a motive to Jack Gallagher, but doubtless Skinner dreamt of being vindicated by a Tuttle triumph. Tuttle hoped he was right.

4

The collapse of the prosecutor's interest in taking Austin to court was not bitter to Jack Gallagher. He had been publicly humiliated. But a suit would tell the world of the absurd rivalry for the attention of a seventy-five-year-old woman. Maud had retained her girlish ways, no doubt of that, and in his arms she had proved a marvelous dancing partner. His one regret was that his return from obscurity, if only at a parish dance, had been marred by Austin's unsportsmanlike behavior. This was the man who had once had the nerve to scold him about his behavior. Now he was panting like a teenager over the likes of Maud. When his daughter Colleen called and said she was dropping by that afternoon, his reaction was mixed.

"I'll take you to dinner," she said.

"What's the occasion?"

"I'll tell you then."

He had little doubt that she had heard of the contretemps at the St. Hilary dance and wished she would just come out with it. It would help if he had some inkling of her reaction. With apprehension he readied himself for dinner with his daughter. It was never clear to him how much his children knew of his checkered life as a celebrity. Could anyone who had not been in the same position appreciate how someone as famous as Jack had been then would be the target of amorous advances? It was never a question of going in search of occasions for dalliance. It would have taken an anchorite to be indifferent to the swooning females who had pursued him in those golden years. Perhaps not all of them knew what precisely it was they wanted, or expected, but he had been able to take his pick of potentially yielding female fans. This presented no danger. These were one-night stands— well, one-afternoon stands—and never threatened his marriage or his professional life. It was simply one of the perks of the position, and he had felt he would have been a fool to scorn the opportunities. If Austin were a rational man Jack could have explained that to him when he burst into the office and began to rail righteously about the folly of Jack Gallagher's ways.

Colleen's reason for wishing to see him came as a complete surprise.

"Tim?" He was shocked. For a moment Jack sensed what Austin's reaction had been on that memorable occasion.

"Oh, I don't blame him. This woman is unbelievable. You've met Mario."

Earlier Colleen had brought the young man by to introduce him, and Jack had been affable if unbelieving that Colleen would at last get married. For years he had assumed that she was contemplating a religious vocation. Why else would an attractive young woman put off the joys of matrimony? This was not an ironical phrase. Jack, despite his weaknesses, considered that his marriage and family life had been exemplary. He had convinced himself that Julia did not know of his dalliances, but in her last illness she had looked at him ruefully.

"For God's sake, behave, Jack."

He did not pursue it, but he had the sudden certainty that all his flaws and foibles had been known to her all along. Confessors had always been understanding, once he could assure them there had been no long-term relationship involved, just a moment of weakness. He had shopped around the city for a new confessor each time he fell, not wanting the priest to recognize his murmuring voice. Of course he had disguised his voice, certain that anyone with a radio would know who he was. One priest asked him if he'd had this trouble in the past.

"The flesh is my great weakness, Father."

"Do you mean this is a habit?"

"I have confessed this sin before."

"With the same woman?"

"Oh, no, Father."

"Are they prostitutes?"

Jack became indignant. "Father, I have come here to confess a serious sin, not to provide you with an autobiography."

"Then they are prostitutes."

"They are not."

Silence from the other side of the grille, then a sigh, and he was given his penance. He made special note of the priest's name when he left the confessional. He wanted his confessors to be as serial as his falls from grace, but there was always the off-chance of running into the same priest. He was particularly resolved not to tell his troubles to Monsignor Keefe again.

"You're sure you're not exaggerating Tim's danger?" Jack asked Colleen now.

"Uncle Austin agreed to look into it and—"

"Austin!" The other diners looked at him as they once had for other reasons.

"I went to him with this."

It was painful to listen to Colleen tell him how she had confided in Austin Rooney, and that the ass had actually gone downtown and spied on Tim in a bar. If Austin could have gotten near Tim, he might have assaulted him.

"Colleen, this is a family matter."

"Austin is my uncle."

"By marriage, dear. By marriage. I wish you had come to me in the first place. A father knows how to deal with these matters, efficiently and kindly. Your uncle has a hair-trigger temper and not the least understanding of the human heart."

"The human heart has little to do with Aggie."

"Aggie . . ."

"The woman. Agatha Rossner. She is a lawyer at Mallard and Bill."

"Mallard and Bill?"

"The firm I work for. Had you forgotten?"

Actually he had. It occurred to him how little interest he had in his children's lives. The fact that Tim was now accused of engaging in the same peccadilloes as his father pained Jack. He felt a shame for his son that he had never felt for himself. How could he do this to Jane and the children? But of course he had managed to push thoughts of his own obligations from his mind when one of the yielding devotees had put in her appearance.

"I am not surprised that Austin failed."

"He thought just finding Tim together with the woman was enough."

"Well, we must come up with a more effective plan."

In the course of listening to Colleen, Jack's interest had been piqued by her description of the woman. Vague memories of past encounters teased his mind. She sounded like a type he knew well. The plan formed naturally.

"I want you to introduce me to this woman."

"To Aggie!"

"To Aggie. It must appear quite casual, I will come by the offices of Bullard and Mill—"

"Mallard and Bill."

"Just so. You can introduce me around. My name may be known to some. It doesn't matter. And you can include this Aggie among them. I will take it from there."

"But what will you do?"

"I shall find an occasion to speak to her as a daughter."

"It won't work."

"Trust me."

7

1

Father Dowling had grown fond of his conversations with Austin Rooney, who had such resources of literary information and general culture, but his notion of the man had been inevitably altered when he saw him throw a punch at Jack Gallagher, sending him crashing to the floor. And then to hear that he had been at it again in the parking lot! A hot temper is not like freckles, a gift of nature, but something acquired by losing one's temper frequently. The image of a street brawler did not go well with that of the knowledgeable retired academic. To his credit, Austin was thoroughly ashamed of himself when at last he showed up at the rectory. Marie brought him to the study as if she felt her life was in peril from this testy pugilist.

"He is the only man I ever struck in my adult life, Father. And I have floored him three times overall."

"Good Lord."

"You have to know the man to understand. First, I've known him since we were kids. Second, he is my brother-in-law. Third, he was an inveterate womanizer during the years of his fame. Women fell over him, he said. That was meant to be an excuse. I suppose they did, I'll grant him that. He is an attractive if wily rascal. But he was married to my sister Julia and I made up my mind to do something about it. His reaction was too much for me. I hit him and he went down under a pile of records."

"And that brought an end to his misbehavior?"

"No."

"I never tried that remedy on anyone but I don't think I would have had much confidence in its curative effect."

"There was the satisfaction of hitting him."

"Fleeting, I am sure."

"My fear was that Julia would hear of it. It was never clear that she was aware of Jack's reputation, and I didn't want to be the cause of burdening her with the knowledge."

Was it possible for one spouse to so completely deceive the other?

"I suppose I am telling you this for its extenuating effect. The other night, when he was dazzling poor Maud Gorman, I was reminded of what Jack had always been and . . . Well, you know what I did."

"I was there."

"The incident in the parking lot was different. There he attacked me. He came up behind me and tried to surprise me with a punch. It was easy to dodge. Then I dropped him in a puddle of water."

Father Dowling did not want to give the impression that he approved of such behavior. The extenuating factor was the age of the men and of the woman over whom they were seemingly quarreling. It was difficult not to be amused at that, but he sensed that Austin would not appreciate being made to seem doubly foolish.

"I will tell you something in confidence, Father. Now his son seems to be up to the same tricks."

And Austin told the story of Tim Gallagher and the young lawyer whom he had seen together in a Loop bar, having been asked to look into the matter by his niece Colleen.

"It runs in the family, Father."

"The human family. We're all affected by Original Sin."

"Jack Gallagher doesn't have an original bone in his body. His fame rested on the accomplishments of others, the musicians and singers he played. His accompaniment was a sort of *Reader's Digest* uplift philosophy and a knack of imitating the voices of singers. As an imitator, he was good. You heard him the other night."

Hearing about the son and of Colleen going to her uncle with the story, hoping he could bring the young man to his senses, saddened Father Dowling. The doctrine of Original Sin did not lessen the tragedy of the actual sins it disposes us to. What if Colleen had come to him with that story? What would he have done? It seemed further evidence of Original Sin that he was glad he had not had to face that challenge.

"I am told that the prosecutor has dismissed all thought of bringing charges against you."

"The prosecutor!"

"Jack Gallagher went to the police with the story of what had happened."

A dark cloud came over Austin's face, and Father Dowling was sure that if Jack Gallagher were there he would have been knocked down one more time.

"It was simply a zealous junior prosecutor who wanted to pursue it. But he was vetoed and that's an end of it."

"Thank God."

"Indeed. Quite apart from your own discomfort, it would not have been the kind of notice the Senior Center needs."

"I am truly sorry this happened, Father Dowling."

At Matthew Skinner's insistence Cy Horvath had come out to St. Hilary's and spent some time speaking to the old people and to Edna Hospers, and then he came by the rectory.

"A tempest in a teapot, Father Dowling."

"Still, a pretty good tempest for a teapot."

"Gallagher attacked Rooney in the parking lot—any number of people say so. It sounds like he got what he deserved. The prosecutor would have been an idiot not to stop Skinner."

And Cy gave Father Dowling a thumbnail sketch of the avid prosecutor.

"So now you can go back to serious business. How are you coming on the Linda Hopkins investigation?"

"The coroner is waffling."

"How so?"

"He's not prepared to say with any certainty that there was foul play. The girl may simply have tripped and fallen into the path of traffic."

"But weren't there witnesses who said that she was pushed?"

"They're having second thoughts too. It doesn't help that we have no suspect."

"No luck finding Harry Paquette?"

Cy never indicated by his expression what he was thinking so his next remark was a bit of a surprise. "These things take time." But Cy had the look of a man who would not let go. Perhaps he was remembering the girl's parents in Appleseed. And he had interviewed the women Linda had worked with at the Hacienda Motel.

"A woman named Ruby Otter was her boss. She liked Linda and she hated Paquette. She's sure Harry killed her because she wouldn't live with him."

"Do you think he did it?"

"One witness is positive she can identify the man she saw push the girl into traffic."

"Because of the picture on Paquette's application for a chauffeur's license?"

"She's not sure there's a match."

But if that witness did not think the application photo was that of the man she saw push Linda, finding Harry Paquette seemed less urgent. "Any other possibilities?"

"I'm on the Jack Gallagher thing now." And Cy permitted himself the slightest alteration of expression. There was little doubt which matter he thought should take priority.

2

Jack Gallagher was an enigma even to himself. In the days of his celebrity he had often thought of himself as a spectator to his own career, attending to the mellifluous voice that enthralled listeners as if it were that of some stranger, not his own. This separation of self from self had made his intermittent affairs possible. He loved his wife, he loved his family, but the Don Juan who took advantage of women so eager to be taken advantage of did not seem quite himself. Oh, he took responsibility, of course, confessing his falls, but the role he seemed to be playing made demands that could not be ignored and he had not ignored them. When he retired, the station had made a great thing of it, and his last weeks on the air had been the most triumphant of all. The banquet at the Palmer House had been grand and it was pleasant to hear all the speeches. His children were there to hear their father praised, but he felt sorrow that Julia had not lived to see this send-off. Her words to him as she lay ill had had their effect on him, but the obscurity into which retirement plunged him also had removed those tantalizing occasions of sin. He did not regret their going. He no longer felt a divided man, but simply the Jack Gallagher he thought he had always basically been.

From time to time the thought came to him that he could have had his way with the ladies even independently of his celebrity, but he had never put this to the test. He had retired as a womanizer as well as the toast of late-night radio—or so he had thought until Colleen mentioned Aggie.

His daughter's very horror of the woman whom once would have been called a homewrecker made her a fascinating creature in

Jack's imagination. When he had suggested that Colleen introduce him to Aggie he had known a moment's fear that his daughter would suspect his motives. But what were his motives? He was seventy-one years old, and if his mirror gave back to him an image of a vigorous man who still had his looks—silver hair is one of age's gifts—he knew otherwise. Or thought he did. The recent popularity of pharmaceutical aids to cancel the effects of waning desire filled him with distaste. But there was a question whether he was up to the task of lover, illicit or otherwise. Austin Rooney might amuse himself with the improbable Maud Gorman, but there was little threat that this would advance beyond what amounted to a schoolyard romance. It was with such confused thoughts and troubling questions that Jack betook himself to the Loop one afternoon and called at Mallard and Bill.

Colleen was expecting him, of course, and he was pleased with the way she paraded him around, introducing him to Messrs. Mallard and Bill as well as to a bevy of lesser partners. And then they had come to Aggie.

The young lawyer was in conference with a fellow named Fremont and had been facing away when he entered the office with Colleen.

"I want you to meet my father," Colleen trilled, and the two lawyers looked up.

Aggie was everything he had been led to expect—lithe, mannishly dressed, but in such a way that her essential femininity was enhanced. The expression in her eyes when she looked at him was one Jack Gallagher recognized. She extended her hand and Jack pressed it with apparent indifference, looking about the room they were in.

"Where are all the law books?"

"They're in the library." Aggie meant the firm's law library. "Hasn't Colleen shown it to you?"

"Why don't you?" Colleen said.

Jack realized why his daughter made this suggestion, but the ostensible purpose of his visit had faded from his mind as soon as he set eyes on Aggie.

"Let's go," she said cheerily, putting her arm through Jack's and taking him down the hall to the library. She closed the door after them.

"And here are all the books."

" 'Here's the church, and here's the steeple,' " Jack said.

She looked puzzled.

"Surely you know that."

"Tell me."

So he interlaced his fingers, repeated the words, and then turned his hands over to reveal his wriggling fingers. " 'And here's all the people.' "

Her laughter was throaty, as if he had just confided something intimate and personal. She stepped back from him, wearing a quizzical little smile.

"Now I know where Tim gets his good looks."

"He took them all," Jack said. Increasingly he felt on familiar ground with this voluptuous wench.

"Oh, I wouldn't say that. I think it's the silver hair."

"Yeats's poem to Lady Anne Gregory."

"You say the most mystifying things."

" 'Only God could love you for yourself alone and not your yellow hair.' "

"Or silver."

"You were going to show me the books."

"I have. Surely you don't want to read them."

From that point, it was Aggie who escorted him on the tour of the offices. It was then four o'clock. Jack frowned at his watch.

Aggie said, "Are you taking Colleen home?"

"We go in different directions."

"I have an idea."

Why didn't they leave now and go somewhere for a drink? Jack felt that his celebrity days had returned. When they left the office and were saying good-bye to everyone, Jack gave Colleen a small conspiratorial smile.

1

There were housekeepers who complained that a rectory was a boring place where nothing much happened, but Marie Murkin was not among them. She sat now in her kitchen having a cup of tea with Stella Morris, who had worked at a string of rectories, never yet finding one to her sufficient liking to remain. When possibility called elsewhere she was ever ready to respond, but within months her disappointment began again.

"I feel that life is passing me by, Marie."

"Then get married, for heaven's sake."

"Don't talk to me about marriage. I may be dissatisfied at Sacred Heart but I haven't lost my mind."

"You never thought of it?"

"Thinking doesn't get you married."

"Or much else."

"How long have you been here, Marie?"

"I was already here when Father Dowling was given the parish."

"That doesn't answer my question."

"It's all the answer you'll be getting. Next you'll be asking me my age."

"I wish I had your stamina and contentment."

Marie wished that Father Dowling could hear this unsolicited testimonial. The truth was, she had little sympathy for Stella's wander-lust. What had it got her after all? She might have been a woman changing husbands again and again in hopes of finally getting the one she wanted. Life was what you made it, Marie thought, and she was content with her lot, having brought the parish near the mark she had set for it.

"Of course, here you are in a place where excitement never stops."

" 'Excitement'!"

"I know all about it, Marie. Aged men fighting for the favors of an equally ancient woman. Everyone is talking about it."

"They should find a more useful way to occupy their time."

"Marie, I have come here for the real dirt and you have to tell me."

" 'Dirt'! What a thing to say. It is all perfectly innocent and silly. The problem is the woman, the flirtiest little seventy-year-old you ever saw in your life. She acts as if she were sixteen, and of course these old goats are enthralled by it. In that particular area of life, men are the greatest fools."

"Women aren't much better."

"I am talking about the men. Neither one of the men in question would have given a nod to Maud when they were in their prime. Of course, both were married then, but so was Maud. Honestly, it makes one wonder if it is wise to pray for a long life when you see what it does to so many."

"I'm told that one of them is Jack Gallagher." Stella had a way of slurping when she took her tea and she had just lowered her cup and not quite swallowed.

"Are you drooling?"

"Marie, I used to hurry with the dishes, get my kitchen spick-and-span and then go off to my room to listen to that man." Stella closed her eyes and swayed. She began to hum.

"I know all about it," Marie said impatiently. She herself had been a Gallagher devotee for years, a secret pleasure she had kept from the friars and from Father Dowling when he came. What would a pastor say if he knew his housekeeper was swooning over the songs of her girlhood while the soft and intimate voice of Jack Gallagher spoke in her ear or sang along with those immortals that once had been? Marie had been reminded of these things the night of the dance, but she had wondered if she had felt as foolish as the old women who oohed and aahed over Jack Gallagher. Desmond O'Toole had been, in his way, better, using his own voice at least, and if his interpretations were echoes of familiar ones, they were not mimicry as Gallagher's were.

"If I had known he was to be here I would have bought a ticket to the dance myself."

"Stella, it was a very successful affair. We actually made money on it."

"Did you charge extra for the fight?"

This was unworthy of Stella. Marie preferred her going gaga over Jack Gallagher than constantly alluding to the way the evening had ended. Thank God there had been no word of it in the newspapers, as there surely would have been if the prosecutor had decided to act on the matter. Jack Gallagher's stock had plummeted in Marie's estimate when it became clear that he had taken the matter to the police. But Cy Horvath had come and satisfied himself that there was nothing serious enough to merit attention. Nor had Jack Gallagher put in an appearance at the parish center since that memorable night. And Austin Rooney, though a frequent presence, seemed to have distanced himself from Maud, putting Desmond back in the running.

"Are you thinking of leaving Sacred Heart, Stella?"

"Why do you ask?"

"I'm just asking."

Stella had sat forward. "Are you thinking of retiring?"

"Retiring! At my age? Don't be ridiculous."

After that, the visit was not what it had been and Marie was not at all sorry when Stella sighed and said it was time to get back to the salt mines. The suggestion of retirement took Marie upstairs to her little apartment where she tried to surprise her reflection in the mirror, walking past it and throwing a quick glance, as if she might catch herself not looking. How old did Stella imagine she was? But the truth was that Marie Murkin was the age of many of the regulars at the parish center. Nonetheless, in her own mind she was fifty-five and she meant to remain that age forever. Her joints ached and her limbs were not as agile as they had been but she prided herself on keeping these signs of age hidden from the pastor and all others. Retirement! She intended to die with her boots on. The only way she would leave St. Hilary's was in a box.

It was in this testy frame of mind that she came downstairs and found the ineffable Tuttle at the door.

"Is the boss home, Mrs. Murkin?"

"How may I help you?"

"I meant the other boss."

"Father Dowling is making a day of recollection."

"A day of recollection. How I envy the man. Most of us could use a day of forgetfulness."

"Speak for yourself, Mr. Tuttle."

Once, the little lawyer had had the gall to entertain an amorous interest in Mrs. Murkin, which suggested he would have lost his shirt guessing ages in a carnival. For all that and for all her starchy manner, Tuttle's lapse into romance had softened the housekeeper toward him. It gave credence to her view that her remaining single had been a matter of refusing a series of offers. Not that she could forget the absent Mr. Murkin, gone God-knows-where so many years ago, without so much as a note of farewell. Sometimes Marie imagined that he had been shanghaied and had been serving all these years as a slave on some communist vessel. He had been in the Navy when Marie met him. Or had he fallen into the Fox River the worse for drink and been swept away by the tide, eaten by fish, his bones scattered along the riverbed from here to Aurora? These macabre thoughts were preferable to the apparent truth that he had simply tired of her and, there being no children, decided to be absent without leave indefinitely.

"Actually, I was hoping to make these preliminary inquiries with you first."

She had opened the inside door before Tuttle said this, and now she felt like closing it on him.

"What preliminary inquiries?"

"Could we sit in the parlor?"

"If you take off that hat."

Tuttle wore an Irish tweed hat in all seasons, pulled low over his face, as if he feared recognition. But the hat was what everyone recognized. He swept it from his head, and his hair seemed to rise into free air, then settled softly on his round head. He had pulled out a chair from the conference table, but waited for the housekeeper to be seated first.

"It's about the assault on Jack Gallagher."

" 'Assault'? What nonsense."

"I gather you weren't a witness."

"I saw the whole thing."

Tuttle pulled out what looked like a schoolboy's spiral notebook and licked the tip of his ballpoint, leaving a little dab of purple on the tip of his tongue. "If you keep that up, you'll look like a chow dog."

"Speaking of which . . ."

"Speaking of what?"

"Chow. You wouldn't have a cup of tea for a weary man, would you?"

"I just threw it out."

But she took pity on him. She rose and told him to follow her. They could carry on this conversation in the kitchen as well as in the parlor. There she put the kettle on and Tuttle pulled up to the table as if he expected a meal. She put a plate of cookies on the table and he sat staring at them as if he had just been released from obedience school.

"Have some, for heaven's sake."

"I thought I'd wait for the tea."

"Now, what is this nonsense about an investigation?"

"Mrs. Murkin, I am not even sure that I will take the case."

"Case? What case?"

Tuttle rubbed his chin. "There you put me on the spot. There is professional confidentiality involved."

"Keep up that kind of double-talk and I'll take the kettle off the fire."

"Let me just say a word or two and whatever surmises you make are your affair. The victim of assault was Jack Gallagher?"

Marie just looked at him.

"Jack Gallagher took the matter to the police," Tuttle said. "The prosecutor considered the matter and decided not to proceed."

"I already knew that."

"And you considered it to be a thing of the past?"

"Of course."

"As it is, taken as a criminal case. Civil law is another thing. The matter can be pursued in the form of a suit."

"Has Jack Gallagher hired you?"

Tuttle shut his eyes and bisected his pursed lips with a fat little finger.

"You're not denying it."

"I told you your surmises were your own."

Marie was stricken. She had indeed considered the matter to be over and done with, as well it should be. No one could possibly gain anything from publicity about such a ridiculous episode. It made matters worse that Gallagher had selected a lawyer as inept as Tuttle, for whom publicity, good or bad, was food and drink. Tuttle loitered about the courthouse to pick up just such tidbits as this and it would have been like him to suggest a suit to Jack Gallagher.

"I will go further," Tuttle said. "When the prosecutor came to me—"

"Came to you?"

"While the case had not risen to the level of their concern, there were those in the prosecutor's office who thought that such an attack on an elderly person, even if by another elderly person, should not go unpunished."

"Mr. Tuttle, everyone you talk to will tell you that Gallagher provoked Austin Rooney. He was repeatedly rude on the dance floor, cutting in on Rooney and then, dance after dance, refusing Rooney the right to reclaim the silly woman he had brought to the dance."

"That does not sound like reason enough to strike a man."

"And later in the parking lot, he sneaked up on Austin and threw a punch at him. And missed. Austin didn't, and down went Gallagher again. If anyone is guilty of anything, it is Jack Gallagher."

The kettle was singing and Tuttle was drawn by its music. Marie made him his cup of tea, and it and the cookies soon disappeared. She did not offer him a second cup. She wanted to warn Edna Hospers what was afoot.

At the front door, hat in hand, Tuttle thanked her profusely. "For your candor, but even more for your hospitality." He had a look in his eye that suggested there was another suit he would like to pursue. She pushed him out the door.

"Your heart is in your belly."

"You're a poet, Mrs. Murkin. A poet."

And he hurried away in the direction of the school. Marie ran to the phone to warn Edna.

2

Colleen had told her fiancé that she had confided their fears about her brother Tim and Aggie to her uncle Austin, so she thought it was only right that she tell him that now her father had taken the matter in hand.

"What did your uncle do?" Mario asked.

She described for Mario the scene in the crowded bar when Tim had looked at her uncle with guilt and shame on his face. "He couldn't do more at the time, but he was sure that their meeting of the eyes would do it."

"But it didn't?"

"Not if Aggie can be believed."

"Ah, that's the question. So now your father has talked to her?"

"Yes."

Mario looked thoughtful; perhaps he was recalling her father's age. That seemed to reassure him. "I wouldn't rely on shame in her. Your father is a well-preserved and good-looking man."

"Once, he was a celebrity."

"My sister in Milwaukee remembers our mother swooning over his program. Was he ever on television?"

"He preferred radio. It wasn't always easy to repeat on television the success one had on radio. When am I going to meet your sister?"

He had told her things about this married sister, but there always seemed to be a point where reticence took over. Colleen began to sense that his brother-in-law, whose name was Kane, was the explanation for this.

"What does he do?"

Mario had hesitated a moment. "He has an insurance agency."

Now he told her more, perhaps prompted by the fact that he was learning things about her family that seemed to give him an unfair advantage.

"Every city has the type. Jimmy Kane has been indicted any number of times but never convicted of anything."

"What was he accused of?"

"Colleen, he is little better than a gangster. The irony is that my sister, by marrying a non-Italian, thought she was entering the American mainstream. It's more like mainline."

"Drugs?"

"Of course he would never use them himself."

Meaning that he dealt in them, or was thought to deal in them. "I wish they would get sufficient evidence and put him away. At least, I would wish that except for what it would do to Lucy. She lives her life under a Sword of Damocles. Sooner or later, it will drop."

A trip to Milwaukee no longer had its former attraction for Colleen, though she did long to meet Mario's sister. "Does she ever come to Chicago?"

"I could ask her."

"Oh, would you?"

"That might be the best way. If you never met Jimmy Kane, I wouldn't be sorry. He is the reason I would never practice law in Milwaukee."

One morning Lucy drove down from Milwaukee and they had lunch in the Loop. Lucy was pretty, with olive skin like Mario's, her hair worn long, but her wide eyes had the look of a deer caught in headlights. She held Colleen's hands and looked at her and then the frightened look went and she smiled a lovely smile. "So you are going to be Mario's wife."

There were no children nor, Colleen gathered, would there be. The great irony, as Mario called it, was that his macho brother-in-law was impotent. "He blames Lucy, of course, knowing it is false and she tolerates it."

It is not easy for a woman on the brink of marriage to preserve the exaggerated hopes and dreams of the years ahead when all around her marriages are not what they should be. Tim's weakness had come to Colleen as an earthquake. How completely irrational it was for him to find Aggie anything other than repulsive compared with Jane and the kids. Would he risk all that for some fleeting excitement with a woman like Aggie? The incredible answer seemed to be yes. Poor Jane. But if that marriage could be jeopardized, it seemed that any could. And now the story of poor Lucy and her unsavory husband who, if justice was done, would apparently spend the rest of his life in prison. It was not easy in these circumstances for Colleen to retain the conviction that she and Mario were different and their marriage would be perfect.

"Like my parents'," she promised him.

"And like my own. We will visit them on our honeymoon."

It was while they were lunching with Lucy that Mr. Mallard dropped by their table and was introduced to Lucy.

"Just 'Lucy'?" he asked affably.

"Lucy Kane," she added. "We live in Milwaukee."

Colleen could see that Mario would have preferred that she not mention Milwaukee along with her married name, but what else could Lucy have done?

At the office Aggie, the cause of so much anguish to Colleen and the frequent topic of conversations with Mario, became subdued. Her skirts were as short as before and she still leaned toward men as if to give them a chance to verify the effects of her décolletage, but less frequently now. Colleen thought that the young lawyer had decided to make a serious play for Albert Fremont. They had quarreled once, but still they must work together, and they seemed almost as friendly now as before. And then one night Colleen heard Aggie suggest to Fremont that the two of them have a drink somewhere and she could have cheered. She called her father to thank him.

He was embarrassed by her gratitude but took it in good grace. And then he begged off when she suggested dinner that very night.

"My dear, I am with my lawyer."

"Your lawyer!"

"It's a long story, but of course I cannot tell it now."

3

Tuttle's days were now filled with trepidation as well as the excitement attendant upon having been handed the case of the half-century by Skinner the assistant prosecutor. The trepidation was caused by Hazel, late of Tempting Temporaries but now, as she put it, freelance, who had come to the office and in effect hired herself as general factotum.

"General what?"

"I will make your life orderly and efficient."

"Hazel, in the present state of my practice . . ."

She held up a hand. "You are going to clean up with the Gallagher suit."

This vote of confidence was welcome, but Hazel's presence was not. He could not afford her. He did not want her even if he could afford her. Years ago he'd had a regular secretary but a time had come when cutting back was imperative and he had let her go. Ever since, the office had been a bachelor haven. It was here that he and Peanuts Pianone, an officer in the Fox River Police thanks to the influence of his powerful and equivocal family, whiled away hours, feeding, communing in silence, dozing off. Hazel had gotten a glimpse of Peanuts, but he had gotten a glimpse of her as well, and he did a 180 in the hall and headed back to the elevator.

"Who's he?"

"Peanuts. Pianone."

"He related to the crooks?"

"He is my closest friend."

Hazel looked at him but said nothing. Clearly her plans for his future did not include Peanuts. But then, what of those golden hours spent with Peanuts eating Chinese in his office, exchanging information in their scarcely articulate way, feet on the desk, hat on his head, litter all over the place from the sent-in meal? Such idyllic scenes would certainly be irrevocably over if Hazel continued to camp herself in the outer office, a place Tuttle no longer recognized. It was neat and orderly; she knew where everything was. She fired up the computer and had proved to be a whiz with it.

"Was this brought over on the *Mayflower* or what?" She was drumming her fingers, waiting for the computer to perform an operation.

"That is practically new." Tuttle did not like to think what he had paid for it in an imprudent moment. He was to learn that computers have no resale value.

"A computer is obsolete before you get it out of the box."

"When we need a new one we'll talk about it."

A fatal remark. It sealed their bargain. "We"? Good God. But she had put together and made sense out of his inquiries into the Gallagher case, handing him a manila folder filled with a fat sheaf of very important looking papers, the gist of which was that Austin Rooney had punched out Jack Gallagher twice at the St. Hilary senior dance. Armed with these, he set out on phase two, acquiring Jack Gallagher as a client.

Always in favor of face-to-face contact, preferring a rebuff from one he could see to a long-distance kiss-off, Tuttle drove to the condo in Western Sun Community where Jack Gallagher was living his twilight years. It was an elegant little community, with a guard at the gate, shoveled drives, Christmas decorations already atwinkle in the late afternoon dusk.

"Mr. Gallagher," Tuttle called to the suspicious-looking fellow in the guard shack.

"What about him?"

"I'm going to call on him."

"Is he expecting you?" Tuttle was wishing that he had brought Peanuts along to handle this Keystone Kop.

"Do you know who I am?"

The fellow stepped from the shack, crouched, and looked in at Tuttle. There was a look of indecision in the guard's eye. Tuttle reached out and patted his arm.

"I'll tell Jack you're doing a helluva job, Rawley." Tuttle had finally made out the nameplate which hung askew from the uniform blouse. He eased up on the brake and his car moved forward. Rawley stepped back. He was in. In the rearview mirror, he saw Rawley go back into his guard shack. Did he have a phone in there? If he called Gallagher, the point of just dropping by was lost.

He found the number of Gallagher's condo and parked. He walked up the shoveled walk to the door and hit the buzzer. A woman who had been exercising her dog came up the walk.

"Who are you looking for?"

"This is Jack Gallagher's apartment, isn't it?"

"Yes, but I doubt he's in. This time of day he is always at the club."

"The club?"

She pointed into the gloaming and Tuttle saw a low building with windows all aglow.

"I'll check over there."

"If you give me a moment to put Richelieu inside, I'll come with you." Richelieu was the dog. The woman was of indeterminate age, but given his recent experience with Hazel, Tuttle was wary. But she was his entrée to the club. He waited while she went inside. She was back in a minute, an expectant smile on her face. "He hates being alone."

"Jack?"

She laughed. "I meant Richelieu, but you're right. That's true of Jack too."

She got in on the passenger side and seemed to be waiting for Tuttle to close the door. He was already behind the wheel. He reached across her and struggled to reach the door handle but it eluded his grasp. The lady against whom he was pressing began to laugh.

"A gentleman waits for the lady to get in and then closes the door after her."

"I'm no gentleman."

Giggling, she gave him a little push and he sat upright. The car complained before starting, but then they were on their way to the club and, with luck, Jack Gallagher.

Music emanated from the club, there was now the promise of snow in the air, and the lamps lining the development's streets glowed softly. The woman waited for him to open her door when he had parked. Tuttle went around and opened.

"At your service, Mrs. Richelieu."

"Call me Isabel."

She took his arm and they entered the club. There was a huge fireplace in which gas logs were burning merrily. There was a bar, tables and booths, maybe twenty-five people steeling themselves for the night ahead.

"There he is," Isabel said.

Jack and a young woman were seated near the fire, a small table and not much else between them; she followed what he was saying with fascination. Isabel hung on Tuttle's arm as they advanced toward the couple by the fire. Neither Jack nor the woman looked up until Isabel spoke.

"Jack, I've brought someone who wants to see you." To Tuttle she said, "Take off that hat."

He had some of the business cards Hazel had ordered in the hat. He handed one to Jack Gallagher. "Skinner at the prosecutor's office suggested I speak to you."

"Skinner?" Gallagher was annoyed at the interruption, and given the looks of the girl, Tuttle didn't blame him.

"No need to interfere now, Mr. Gallagher, but the sooner we get together, the better. I share Skinner's view about Austin Rooney."

This caught Gallagher's attention. He studied the card. "You're a lawyer?"

"Can we meet sometime tomorrow?"

"Are you free in the morning?"

Tuttle closed his eyes in thought. "What time?"

"Be here at eleven and we can talk. By 'here' I mean my apartment."

"Eleven o'clock."

"Aren't you going to introduce me, Jack?" Isabel said in lilting tones.

Tuttle got out of there, but not before he heard Gallagher growl, "Aggie, Isabel. Isabel, Aggie."

He stopped at the guard shack on the way out and gave Rawley a buck. "So you'll remember me tomorrow morning."

"I don't work mornings."

Tuttle felt like asking for the dollar back.

1

Even weeks afterward, the fate of the young woman who had been pushed into oncoming rush-hour traffic from a crowded sidewalk continued to be a source of conversation in the St. Hilary rectory.

"Even if it was an accidental bump, the person who did it should have come forward," Marie said.

"Maybe it wasn't accidental," Father Dowling said.

"That's why he didn't identify himself."

" 'He'?"

"Whoever." But Marie was certain it had been a man. The witnesses who had become unsure from being sure had spoken of a man, so doubtless Marie was right. But it had struck a philosophical node in the housekeeper's brain. "Just think of it, walking along, going where you're going, and then suddenly, the Particular Judgment."

Marie's expression was pensive and sad. How fragile life was. A person wasn't even safe on a public street. Death was everywhere.

"People keeling over from heart attacks."

"Some die in their beds after prolonged illnesses."

"I don't want to talk about it."

"You brought it up."

Marie went back to her kitchen, doubtless to meditate on the Four Last Things. Edna had told Father Dowling that the old people at the

Center were obsessed with the accident too. The skirmishes at the dance had taken momentary precedence, but now they had returned to it.

"Many of them sense resentment of their age on the part of younger people. All this talk of euthanasia and grumbling about what those still working could expect from Social Security causes apprehension among the elderly."

Father Dowling pondered all this, wondering if he could address it in a homily in a way that would reassure the regulars at the Senior Center. Cy Horvath was the only one who still hoped the bulletin they had sent out would serve to locate the missing fiancé.

"Not a chance," Phil Keegan said. "Cy hates loose ends; it's what makes him such a great detective. But that guy is gone with the wind."

Father Dowling asked Cy out to the rectory in order to hear the lieutenant's thoughts on the matter. Their trip to Linda's parents in Wisconsin was a spur Phil Keegan did not have.

"If he is found, those witnesses will get their memories back," Cy said. "They probably think he is lurking around and are afraid he'll shove them into traffic too, if they sound too sure about what he looks like."

Cy had pieced together an account of the relationship between Linda and Harry. She had moved to Fox River a year before the accident, and it was here that she had met Harry Paquette, who was driving the cab she hailed one rainy day—for her, a luxury. He had driven her to her door before she realized he hadn't turned on the meter. On the way, she had babbled on about herself as one will to strangers. When he parked, he turned and looked over the seat back, and asked if she'd like to go somewhere for something to eat. It was all so improbable, she had thought it romantic.

Her work in a local motel on the housekeeping crew put her on the margins of a more interesting life than she led. Harry was the first guy she had gone out with since coming to Fox River, and he became a staple of her conversation with the other girls at the motel. Harry too had come to Fox River, not long before Linda herself. Two uprooted people had found one another, and she, at least, regarded it as the fruition of her reason for leaving the small town in Wisconsin for the excitement and promise of a larger city. Chicago was too large, but Fox River had not been as intimidating.

The fact that Harry had given Minneapolis as his place of birth was either another lie, one he had used again on his application at the license bureau, or maybe an opening into his true identity.

"Maybe he went back there," Father Dowling suggested.

"We'll see."

Harry had lived in an obsolete motel that had been turned into a kind of rooming house for men like himself. Special weekly rates. What kind of future had Linda imagined with him?

"From things she told the girls at the motel, he apparently wanted her to move in with him, but she was holding out for marriage. He told her they were engaged—wasn't that something? But she wanted a wedding. She wanted it to be legal."

There were times when Father Dowling felt an infinite sadness at the lives people led, at the things that moved them, at the ineradicable sense of right and wrong that survived the most demanding tests. Linda Hopkins's upbringing in Appleseed continued to have its effect. Had the girl been tempted by Harry's offer that she become his live-in girlfriend? Not enough to accept it, apparently, but living with him as his wife had certainly attracted her.

It was odd that a tragedy undergone by a stranger could eclipse the events in his own parish. Or perhaps Linda Hopkins's death put things into perspective. For some days Father Dowling had been concerned with this quarrel among two old men for the attentions of an elderly lady, a concern that had been magnified when he learned that someone in the prosecutor's office threatened to turn it into a cause célèbre. The industrious Skinner had been overridden by his superiors and had become the object of mockery by Phil Keegan. But not by Cy Horvath.

"If it weren't for Skinner, I would have been told to forget about Linda Hopkins," Cy said. Beyond that he did not go. It certainly wasn't a blanket endorsement. But Skinner had confided to reporters about the Hopkins death and that had kept the matter before the public. Did Skinner hunger and thirst after justice, or was he, as Phil said, trying to secure his foothold in the prosecutor's office? Father Dowling knew nothing of Skinner, but his admiration for Cy Horvath was unbounded, an attitude he had first learned from Phil Keegan, whose protégé Cy was. There was something dogged and matter-of-fact in the huge Hungarian's unwillingness to write off Linda Hopkins's death.

"I saw her body in the morgue," Cy said in explanation.

No one of Harry Paquette's name was known in Minneapolis—he certainly had never driven a cab there—but Cy had been in contact with a similarly dogged detective in the Twin Cities and this produced the first movement in the investigation.

"It's the handwriting," Cy explained. "Not a strong basis, but Nelson is sure that the man who signed the chauffeur's-license application here is a man who has a record there."

"What name do they know him under?"

"Lloyd Danielson. Of course they have prints. Nelson has sent out an APB on Danielson."

These routine inquiries were exchanged by the thousands between the police departments of the nation, and Cy was not sanguine—only hopeful. Father Dowling thought of the WANTED posters in post offices, of the pathetic pictures of lost kids on milk cartons and at stations on the tollway. The APB on Danielson was like a ticket in the lottery—but it was less far-fetched than hoping that some department would turn up the man under the name of Harry Paquette.

"Has Tuttle been out here?" Cy asked Father Dowling.

"I think Marie said he dropped by the other day."

"Skinner wants him to persuade Jack Gallagher to bring a civil case against Austin Rooney."

"Good Lord." His estimate of Skinner had risen slightly, but now it plummeted.

"Would Jack be such a fool?" Father Dowling asked Austin later that day.

"Not if he thought it wasn't foolish."

"He hasn't been back to the Center since the night of the dance."

Austin's own infatuation with Maud Gorman, if that's what it was, had cooled, and Desmond O'Toole was back in the ascendancy.

"Do you know Cicero's *De senectute,* Father?" Austin asked.

"Only the title."

"I found rereading it salutary."

That was all, but reading a Stoic meditation on old age had apparently helped. Austin winced now at any reminder that he had actually floored Jack Gallagher because Jack wouldn't let him cut in on Maud at the dance.

"I used to think age brought wisdom."

"Wisdom is a gift."

"Of the Holy Ghost." And Austin rattled off the Seven Gifts of the Holy Ghost, memorized long ago when he had prepared for confirmation, right here in St. Hilary's school.

" 'Fear of the Lord' is the one I never lost."

The remark seemed to refer to the possibility that he would be sued by Jack Gallagher for assault and battery and public humiliation.

2

Jack Gallagher sat in midmorning in the living room of his apartment, drapes pulled, breakfast done, dressed and ready for another day. The phone was off the hook. His mood was one of depression. The supposed fling with Aggie had turned out very differently than he had thought it would. Bringing her to the clubhouse here where he lived had been done in a spirit of bravura, to give the other residents something to think about.

When he had awoken this morning she was long gone, having left a note on the kitchen table: *Mmmmmm. Aggie.* It unnerved him that he had not heard her get up and go. He felt no triumph in his conquest, perhaps because he had been the conquered one. It had become clear that he had become a project of hers, a target of opportunity, and the delusion that youth had returned made him susceptible. What he felt now did not qualify as remorse; it was more like embarrassment and shame. The girl was younger than Colleen. Colleen!

He could not forget the little smile they had exchanged the afternoon he had left the offices of Mallard and Bill with Aggie on his arm. Colleen had assumed that Jack was going to read Aggie the riot act about Tim. Aggie had mentioned Tim, not Jack, and then only glancingly. The topic of their meetings became Jack Gallagher and his stellar career. It seemed to him now that he had been wooed and won. That he was a trophy of sorts was made clear when Aggie called.

"Thanks," she breathed, without feeling any need to identify herself.

"Aggie?"

"Who else?"

"I didn't hear you go."

"Oh, I'm good at that."

"What time was it?"

"When will I see you again?"

"I'm still half asleep."

"Have a rough night?" She laughed throatily.

"Don't you remember?"

"Mmmmm."

"So that's how to read your note."

"Call me later." She hung up.

Call her? In the shower he had stood in water as hot as he could tolerate, wanting to wash away all memory of her. A metaphor of confession. How long had it been since he had knelt in the confessional and whispered his sins through the grille? That act always made him feel like a boy again, bringing back his adolescent confessions when he had knelt in agony, willing to listen to any scolding or gentle advice, if only the priest would give him absolution and he could get out of there, out of the church, and be just good old Jack Gallagher again. And so it had been whenever he had confessed a serious sin.

He had the living-room blinds pulled so he could not see the pictures of Julia, his wife, of Colleen, of Tim and Jane and their kids. Maybe, if Aggie had noticed those photographs and made any comment on them at all, he would have had the sense to give her a drink and then send her on her way. He would have taken her home in order to get rid of her. But she had been in control from the moment he had let them into the apartment. Five minutes after the door shut behind them they were in bed, their clothes scattered about the room. He almost felt that he had been raped.

The doorbell rang and he jumped to his feet. For a crazy moment he thought she was back. He put his eye to the viewer and recognized the little fellow who had come to his table with Isabel. Tuttle the lawyer. He opened the door.

"Mr. Gallagher."

"Mr. Tuttle."

He came into the room still wearing his hat. His unbuttoned overcoat had lost its shape and the green sports jacket looked as if he had slept in it. Scuffed shoes, of course. But he promised diversion, and at the moment Jack Gallagher needed diversion from his conscience.

Tuttle plunked down in a chair, still wearing his overcoat. He did take off the hat. "As I mentioned last night, Skinner in the prosecutor's office referred me to you."

"What can I do for you?"

"Do you remember Skinner?"

"I don't think so. Would you like some coffee?"

"Only if it's made."

"I just made this for breakfast."

Tuttle followed him into the kitchen, talking as they went. Skinner was the eager young prosecutor who had hoped to bring a criminal suit against Austin Rooney for striking and humiliating Jack Gallagher before dozens of witnesses at the St. Hilary senior dance. The prosecutor's office had decided against proceeding, but Skinner continued to think that something should be done.

"That's why he came to me."

Tuttle had accepted his mug of coffee and then waited for Jack to precede him back to the living room. Before sitting down, Jack opened the drapes.

"So what's the proposition?"

"A civil suit, demanding a considerable sum of money."

"Rooney has no money."

"There you're wrong. He taught until a year or two ago. During those years he amassed a retirement benefit close to two million dollars."

"Austin?"

"This is common with professors. They pay a certain percentage of their salary over the course of their career; their institution matches, even doubles it. Month after month, year after year. It goes into a national plan. The total amount of money sounds like the national debt. In recent years the book value of those benefits has skyrocketed. Austin Rooney has money."

It turned out that Tuttle had already engaged in preliminary investigations. "To see if it was worth our while, to see what kind of witnesses could be called. You do realize that Father Dowling saw the whole thing."

"You'd call him?"

"In a shot. He would be reluctant, but he would tell the truth. And the truth is devastating. Other witnesses would serve to add color to what the priest had said."

Tuttle no longer looked like an impecunious buffoon. And wasn't he just the sort of lawyer you would want for such a suit—shifty and hungry?

"How much do you mean by 'a considerable sum'?"

"Two million dollars."

"A million a punch."

"We won't get that, of course. But we should get at least a million."

" 'We'?"

Tuttle looked at him. His lips were moving but no sound emerged. Then he said, "I'll ask twenty-five percent. That is below standard, but like Skinner I don't think this sort of thing should go unpunished. Furthermore, I will work on spec. All you need do now is give me one dollar and I am your lawyer and we are under way."

Jack Gallagher gave Tuttle a dollar. The prospect of punishing Austin Rooney seemed a way of compensating for the fool Jack had made of himself with Aggie.

"Who was that beautiful young woman you were with last night?" Tuttle asked when he rose to go. There was a man-to-man smile on his face that Jack did not like.

"A friend of my daughter's."

"Lovely girl."

And then he was gone. The sound of his car not starting went on for a while but then the battered Toyota wended its way through unplowed snow, back to the entrance of the development.

3

Colleen was in Mario's office working with him when Aggie looked in.

"Hi. I had a date with your dad."

And then she was gone.

Colleen looked at Mario, who had resented the interruption. "She means they went for a drink when Dad was here."

Mario wasn't interested. They were going through the research she had done for him, a process she always liked, because he was difficult to please and her work always pleased him—after he had gone over it with a fine-toothed comb. But Colleen had been upset by Aggie's pop-in remark and disappearance. A few minutes later, she excused herself and went to the ladies'. Aggie was there with a few other girls, talking. She fell silent when Colleen came in, and then the other women left. Colleen heard their laughter as the door closed.

She was certain Aggie had been telling them some story about her father. She was trembling with anger as she thought of it. But she rinsed her face and leaned toward herself in the mirror. With calm came a thought that altered her mood: Her father had talked like a father to Aggie about Tim and this was Aggie's way of getting revenge. She must have suspected that it was Colleen who had enlisted first her uncle, and then her father, to stop Aggie's pursuit of her brother. Of course Aggie would strike back. But she was doing more harm to herself than to Jack Gallagher.

Tim laughed when Colleen spoke to him about it, and told her to relax, the old man was way past that sort of thing. Had he forgotten the story of Susannah and the elders? But in this case, it was Susannah who was leading an old man astray. If she could be believed. That of course was the problem with Aggie's bitchy boasting: There was no way to know whether what she said was true. Aggie's tailored suits must have affected her hormones. Imagine a woman boasting of her conquests! And of course, in talking with Tim, Colleen knew things he didn't know she knew. Unless he suspected that she had sent Uncle Austin to that bar. She thought she saw a reflective look in his eye, wondering if he, too, had been the subject of such washroom gossip.

What a paragon Mario seemed, compared to Tim and her father.

He had at once recognized and repudiated Aggie's seductive manner. The comparison both pleased and disconcerted her. Tim's disbelief was contagious, and she scolded herself for being taken in by Aggie's tale of supposed conquests.

"Women like that are usually frigid. They have to up the ante to get anywhere near what normal women feel. She would probably call a cop if anyone laid a glove on her."

There was a disturbing authority in Tim's voice. Had he been lured into such a reaction? She almost hoped it was so. Sinning in the heart was one thing, not likely to threaten his home and family. The more she thought of it, she simply could not imagine Tim and Aggie . . . well, doing anything like what Aggie claimed. And as for her father . . . ! Now she felt ashamed of herself for being taken in by the sleek young lawyer with the body of a goddess.

"Of course you're right, Tim. But you can imagine what it's like, having that kind of whispering going on in the office."

He gave her a hug and that was that. Colleen left with the sense of a great weight having been lifted from her shoulders.

4

Tuttle tucked the dollar bill into his shirt pocket and headed for the gate, thinking that he had earned back the dollar he had given that guard the other night. But as he approached the entrance, he slowed, then stopped. He had a client and he could go ahead and file the suit he had already drawn up, which waited, typed and authoritative, on his desk. Typed by Hazel, of course. With the imperious Hazel there, his office no longer felt like a haven. Normally he would have returned there to bask in his victory, maybe call Peanuts and have him come over with a pizza and a six-pack so they could celebrate. Now that was out of the question. Peanuts had not been in his office since Hazel had installed herself there.

Tuttle put the car in gear, and again headed for the gate. He would go downtown and see Peanuts there. Hazel was not going to come between him and the one true friend he had in Fox River.

Peanuts might be almost mute, and seemingly retarded, but he was a loyal friend, so long as that loyalty did not conflict with the loyalty he owed to the Pianone clan. Once, it had been thought that the Pianones had gotten Peanuts into the force in order to have a mole within the enemy's camp, but with the passage of time Peanuts's dim ineptitude allayed that fear. There had been an intermediate theory, that Peanuts was just playing dumb and that, sly as a fox, he was the eyes and ears of the Pianones in the police department. But that suspicion too had withered away, and the remaining task was to give Peanuts assignments where he could do no harm. His great resentment was the young black detective, Agnes Lamb, who outshone him in every aspect of police work and brought out all Peanuts's primitive racism and male chauvinism. It occurred to Tuttle that Hazel provided a new and powerful bond between himself and Peanuts, Hazel matching Peanuts's Agnes.

Tuttle found Peanuts in the press room where the coffee and the company were better than in the division run by Captain Phil Keegan. Peanuts sat with his coffee before him, staring straight ahead. He could sit like that for hours, saying nothing, doing nothing, apparently oblivious to his surroundings. He might as well have been a Buddhist. Tuttle poured a cup of coffee and sat across from Peanuts and received a nod of acknowledgment. The little lawyer had learned the knack of mindless contemplation from his friend. Well, not mindless. Tuttle's thoughts were always going a mile a minute. The whining voice of Mendel of the *Tribune* engaged his attention and he turned.

Mendel was a hirsute, resentful reporter who often talked of the book he was writing that would blow the lid off Fox River. Most of his stories were edited to blandness on the advice of the paper's legal department, and knowing this would happen he composed outrageous screeds which he read aloud to his disinterested brethren in the press. Tuttle got up, caught Mendel's eye, and moved his head, indicating he wanted to talk with the reporter.

"What the hell do you want, Tuttle?"

"I've admired the stories you did on the tragedy of Linda Hopkins."

"You should have read them before they were rewritten."

"Your reward will be great in heaven."

"I'm an atheist."

"Well, wherever you end up. My one criticism is that your laudable concentration on that matter blinded you to another."

"Yeah?"

"The police treated it as a comic matter."

"What the hell are you talking about?"

Tuttle went to the heart of the matter, steeling himself for Mendel's derisive laughter. His account of the events at St. Hilary's was in the legalese of the brief he would file that afternoon. Mendel did not laugh, but beyond that showed only minimal interest.

"That's been dropped, Tuttle. Skinner tried to stir the conscience of the prosecutor, with predictable results."

"The criminal case is indeed a dead letter."

"What else is there?"

"This will have to be kept under wraps until . . ." He pulled back his sleeve and consulted his ancient Timex. "Until two o'clock this afternoon."

"What happens at two?"

"You'll hold the story until then?" He had Mendel's interest now. The reporter looked over his shoulder at a group of his colleagues playing bridge.

"What story?"

"A civil suit is going to be filed on behalf of Jack Gallagher against Austin Rooney."

"That's your story?"

"Think about it. A onetime entertainment legend is assaulted in his twilight years by a resentful academic."

Mendel liked it. Tuttle promised him a copy of the complaint he would file. They parted as allies, however mistrustful of one another.

Tuttle returned to Peanuts with the sense that he had begun his campaign. Always at such moments, he thought of the prim and proper Amos Cadbury, dean of the Fox River bar, a byword for rectitude and professional ethics. Cadbury would be furious that such a suit should be filed since it would bring his good friend Father Dowling's parish into the news in an unflattering way. Just a bonus of the good turn that was taking place in Tuttle's life.

"Peanuts, could you do a stakeout?"

The squat detective came alert, probably because he thought Tuttle was referring to outdoor grills and food. Food was the dominant appetite in Peanuts's makeup.

"Can you get an unmarked vehicle?"

"They all have dents in them."

"Here's what I want you to do."

He and Peanuts would spell one another on a mission that had occurred to Tuttle when he left Gallagher's residential development, the Western Sun. He had already done the fundamental work on the case; he had interviewed Marie Murkin, Edna Hospers, and half a dozen of the old people at the Center. Their sympathies were divided between Austin Rooney and Jack Gallagher, but their accounts of what had happened were devastating to Rooney. Desmond O'Toole was a great plus. He hated Austin Rooney.

"Because of what he did to Jack?" Tuttle had asked O'Toole.

"That, of course. And the woman in the case."

"Maud Gorman?"

"Maud Gorman. Austin lured her away from me with his pompous professorial baloney."

In ordinary circumstances, a rejected lover might be of only equivocal help, but the case was between Austin Rooney and Jack Gallagher. O'Toole gave a vivid account of both assaults, the one on the dance floor and that in the parking lot.

"You witnessed them both?"

O'Toole nodded. "Jack asked me to come with him when he went after Rooney outside. He was too much of a gentleman to avenge himself inside the school."

"But he got roughed-up again?"

"A lucky punch."

"He went out there to settle matters?"

"Yes. Rooney has the luck of an Irishman."

Since all the principals were of Irish descent this was an odd remark, but what Tuttle wanted was the statement that Jack Gallagher had gone into the parking lot to settle matters. A jury could be made to understand that he had gone out to offer the hand of peace and friendship and had been assaulted again for his pains.

With all this material already gathered, Tuttle's concern could be for his client. His opponent, whoever it might be, would doubtless look into Jack Gallagher's life to find there a basis for describing him as a hot-tempered prima donna, forever getting into scrapes. Tuttle wanted to make sure that no such account could be offered, at least one that would come as a surprise to him. Hence the stakeout.

"I'll be out this afternoon, Peanuts. We'll get something to eat before I take over." He paused. "You've seen my new secretary?"

Peanuts scowled.

"You're right. Peanuts, you have Agnes, I have Hazel."

The mention of Agnes Lamb brought fire into Peanuts's narrow eyes. He drove off with the idea that somehow the favor he was doing for Tuttle would strike a blow at the hated Agnes.

5

When Isabel Ritchie moved into her condo at Western Sun Community a year after her husband passed away, she had no idea of the excitement that lay ahead of her. Jack Gallagher lived in the apartment next to hers! Jack's program had been a bone of contention between Isabel and her husband Ozzie. The sound of the theme song of the program would bring a howl from Ozzie, and no matter how low Isabel turned the volume, the syrupy music and even syrupier voice of the host—Ozzie's description—drove him wild. Only the purchase of a Walkman had gotten them through the crisis. From then on, seated across from Ozzie in the den, headphones on, Isabel listened to Jack Gallagher with impunity, although it gave her the sense that she was being unfaithful to her husband. But how could she be unfaithful with a voice? A voice that entered her ears and then curled through her with an intimacy of which she was half ashamed.

She had seen photographs of Jack Gallagher and was not surprised to find that he had the looks of a matinee idol, but it was the voice that had won her and many thousands like her. The songs he favored went back to the time before Isabel had met Ozzie, and gave her the illusion of being a girl again, still awaiting her destiny. In that recapturing of youth, Jack Gallagher had become her ethereal lover. She learned to bless the person who had invented the Walkman. She could sit a few feet from her husband and be transported into a world that excluded him entirely.

After Ozzie went and she moved to her condo—not yet realizing who lived next door—she continued to use her Walkman, but there was no longer the voice of Jack Gallagher to invade her inner ear and inner being. And then one day she saw him coming up the walk. For a mad moment, she thought that he had found her, the woman to whom he had been making radio love for all those years. She ran to the door and opened it, to find him putting the key into the door next to hers. He looked at her over his shoulder and gave her a beautiful smile.

"You're Jack Gallagher!"

He turned, the smile grew brighter, and he extended his hand. Isabel all but swooned, as she had once swooned over Sinatra and as later generations of girls had swooned over Elvis and the Beatles. She managed to tell him her name.

"So we're neighbors."

Neighbor to Jack Gallagher. He let himself into his apartment and as he closed the door, gave her another smile. Isabel stared at the closed door. When she had buried Ozzie she had told herself her life was over. Now she felt that it was about to begin.

The truth was that she made a pest of herself with Jack—she always called him Jack in her own mind—and could see that his patience was tried. Not that he ever acted other than in the most gentlemanly way. When the little man in the tweed hat had asked about Jack, Isabel had taken him to the clubhouse and marched him up to Jack's table, where he had been seated with a very well-endowed young woman. Isabel had withdrawn discreetly after the little man had left.

Later, in the bar, a hand was laid on her shoulder and she turned to look into the face of Jack Gallagher, only inches from her own. Her heart stopped beating. She was sure that all eyes in the bar were on them, and she gloried in it.

"Forgive me for not introducing my niece, Isabel. But that lawyer interfered . . ."

"Oh, think nothing of it. What a lovely girl."

"Just so you understand." He signaled to the bartender to give Isabel another drink, touched her shoulder once more, and then was gone. The new drink was put before her though she had hardly touched the one she had ordered. She pushed that aside in favor of Jack's propitiatory gift. How incredibly intimate her name had sounded coming from his lips.

* * *

That night she hardly slept. Thoughts raced through her mind. Jack was a widower, she was a widow, they had been thrown together by fate. She could close her eyes and hear him say "Isabel" as if she had her Walkman clamped to her ears. She slept fitfully but when dawn broke she felt refreshed and renewed. It was her practice to put in half an hour on the treadmill in the exercise room of the clubhouse, and she got into her gym clothes and Michael Jordan sneakers and had a glass of orange juice. When she opened the door, Jack's niece was coming out of the next apartment.

"Good morning!" Isabel cried, and they set off together down the walk. "You're too young to know what your uncle meant to women my age."

"My uncle?"

"Jack."

The girl finally smiled. "Our family is so close I don't even think of him as an uncle."

"Of course not."

The girl looked at her curiously, then opened the door of the cutest little car and stepped in. Isabel would have expected her to roar off in such a machine, but she crept away from the curb at ten miles an hour and accelerated only when she was halfway to the gate. The treadmill was demanding exercise, but Isabel felt that she was walking on a cloud. Now she had met one of the family.

1

The news that Jack Gallagher had filed a civil suit against Austin Rooney was brought to Father Dowling by a shocked Marie Murkin.

"Just when it had all died down."

"Surely there can't be a case."

"You'll never guess who his lawyer is: Tuttle!"

Father Dowling did not laugh. Jack Gallagher was not in good hands but that did not ensure that there would not be unwelcome publicity. Quite the contrary. Sometimes it seemed that only the local press took Tuttle seriously.

"He was here quizzing me and I never guessed what he was about. He's such a nosy little man, I thought that's all it was. And he talked with Edna too, and some of the old people. How were we to know he was gathering evidence? I'm surprised he didn't talk to you. But then he would have, if you'd been in."

Marie keened on and Father Dowling felt no disposition to calm her. This was indeed a dark moment. Some moments later, an ashen-faced Austin Rooney was at the door.

"Father Dowling, I had no idea that even Jack Gallagher would stoop this low."

"He must be getting very bad advice."

Austin had come for reassurance as well as to make an apology, but Father Dowling did not know what to tell him. For better or worse, Austin and St. Hilary's parish were in the same boat. That was Amos Cadbury's view when he telephoned.

"I would like to talk with Austin Rooney, Father."

"He is with me now."

"Would he still be there in half an hour's time if I came?"

"I'm sure he would."

"Good. I will be coming as the attorney for the parish, Father. I would not like it thought that I was soliciting a client."

"No one would think that, Amos."

This was good news indeed. If there was a legal way to handle this crisis, Fox River's premier lawyer would know. His question had suggested that he would arrange for someone to defend Austin Rooney, perhaps from his own firm. But Amos had even more than that in mind.

"Is anyone representing you, Mr. Rooney?" Amos asked when he arrived. Tall, dignified, his white hair accented by the dark suit, as it had been by the black overcoat and hat Marie had taken from him, Amos Cadbury was an imposing and reassuring figure when he took a seat in the study and put this question to Austin.

"I just heard of this on the radio. I came immediately to see Father Dowling."

"That was wise." Amos looked expectantly at Austin Rooney.

"Could you suggest someone, Amos?" Father Dowling said.

"If I were asked."

Father Dowling too now looked expectantly at Austin. Austin said, "I would be grateful for any help you can give me."

Amos stretched out his arm, causing a starched cuff to appear, and shook Austin's hand. "Very well, since you ask, I shall act as your attorney."

"You yourself, Amos?"

Amos nodded. "It is these nuisance suits that are . . . well, the greatest nuisance. It is imperative that they be taken with the utmost seriousness." He paused. "Tuttle filed the suit on behalf of Jack Gallagher."

"Who is Tuttle?" Austin asked.

"You will learn the answer to that question soon enough," said Amos. "Now then, I took the liberty of obtaining a copy of the complaint. It is a very vivid statement. And I have to say this—surprisingly effective, to have come from Tuttle's office. They are asking damages of two million dollars."

Austin Rooney laughed. But immediately sobriety returned. The sum was symbolic. The suit was meant to impoverish him.

"My own fee will be a mere token," Amos said. "I am on a retainer from St. Hilary's parish and I shall treat this suit as effectively aimed at the parish as well as you."

Amos's retainer was *a façon de parler*, a hundred dollars annually, which would not cover a fraction of an hour of his working day. Austin was understandably relieved. A retired professor could not contemplate the expenses of such a lawyer as Amos Cadbury without blanching.

The defense strategy had been worked out in large part by Amos as he was driven to the rectory. Young Joseph Castlemar would do the legwork. He would be at the parish the next day and everyone with information about the set-to between the two men must be interviewed and depositions taken. It was Cadbury's hope that such a mass of exculpating evidence could be gathered that he could convince the judge to throw out the suit. But the mention of a judge made him thoughtful.

"Bertha Farner has been assigned the case."

He looked at Father Dowling. The name meant nothing.

"I take it she is a judge."

"She is a judge. Having raised her family, she went to law school, after which she clerked for old Francis Reiner. When Reiner retired, she was named to take his place. All her legal experience is from the other side of the bench. She is known somewhat irreverently as Big

Hearted Bertha, when she is not known simply as Big Bertha. Of course, those who use the latter name have no knowledge of the Krupp cannon also so named. Judge Farner is a sizeable woman, doubtless glandular, as I am told she eats like a bird. I could have wished for another judge, but be that as it may."

"She does not sound lean and hungry."

"No, she is rather plump and compassionate. Mr. Rooney, I would like to begin with you, and now, if that is agreeable."

"Of course."

Lawyer and client adjourned to the front parlor and immediately Marie looked in.

"What did he say?"

"He is in consultation with his client in the parlor."

"His client! Oh, *Deo gratias.*"

As he had shared Marie's apprehension, so now Father Dowling shared her relief. "Marie, you might see if Amos would like tea brought to the parlor."

Amos was an unstinting admirer of Marie Murkin's tea. She bobbed her head and was off. In a moment she was back. "And I have some of the oatmeal cookies he loves."

"With raisins?"

"Of course."

"Marie, if Amos should want me, I will be at the school. I think Edna should be told what portends on the morrow."

"What does?"

"One of the young lawyers in Amos's firm will be here to do what Tuttle apparently already did."

Edna sat at her desk with a blank look on her face. Obviously she had heard the bad news. Father Dowling was glad to be able to give her the good news.

"Amos Cadbury himself? I almost feel sorry for Tuttle."

"We must not be overly optimistic. There are other factors." He told Edna of Judge Farner.

"Oh, I like her." Edna too was in favor of the underdog and had followed accounts of Judge Farner's compassionate decisions in the local media. It did not occur to her that as the plaintiff, Jack Gallagher would be considered the underdog in this matter.

"One of the lawyers from Amos's firm will be here tomorrow to talk with those who witnessed the events."

"So he'll talk to you too, Father?"

This thought had occurred to Father Dowling as well, and he felt decidedly ambiguous about it. Amos was right to see that the parish was implicated in this suit, if only because the events had taken place on the premises. But it did not behoove Roger Dowling as a priest to take sides in the matter. Jack Gallagher had, after all, been knocked down twice. But how could he avoid being deposed? He had witnessed Austin knocking Jack Gallagher down on the dance floor. After he told Edna to alert those who would need to be deposed by young Castlemar, he walked slowly back to the rectory. If only Austin Rooney had controlled his temper.

It had been decided that Austin would go to Amos's office in the morning to repeat his account of what had happened so it could be taken down for the record. After Austin had left, Amos waxed eloquent about Marie's tea. "And the oatmeal cookies, Marie. If I were a decade younger I would make love to you."

A confused and giggling Marie retreated to the kitchen. Amos once more took a chair in the study.

"They were quarreling about a woman," he said wonderingly.

"Maud Gorman."

Amos looked surprised. "Maud Gorman!"

"Do you know her?"

"Yes, I know her." Amos paused. "During a period of prosperity, the Gormans belonged to the country club. Maud was one of the prettiest women I have ever known. Even in middle age . . ." His voice drifted off. Father Dowling wondered what would have happened if Amos had come to the senior dance and attempted to cut in on Jack Gallagher.

"It no longer seems completely farcical, Father."

"She has cut quite a swath here."

"I often wondered what had become of her." Amos had half a dozen years on both Austin Rooney and Jack Gallagher, but there was something in his voice that suggested that what had been regarded as comical in those two had stirred in Amos's breast as well.

"If you like, Father, I will depose you myself."

"Is that necessary?"

"You were there, were you not?"

"Yes."

"Then it is imperative. You may be sure that Tuttle will be calling on you. I gather he missed you on his first foray. We must be prepared for whatever nefarious use he attempts to make of your testimony."

That night Phil Keegan came by, his brow clouded. "It almost always happens, yet I am always surprised."

He was speaking of the death of Linda Hopkins. Apparently there had been a copycat attempt at a local stop of the El. Someone had brushed past a woman standing on the platform, deliberately, and for a terrifying moment she had teetered on the edge of the platform, the tracks below, a train pulling in. But someone had grabbed her coat and pulled her back. By then the culprit had fled. Once safe, the woman had fainted, 911 was called and paramedics had restored her to a measure of calm. She had shuddered at the thought of taking a train so officers had driven her to her door.

"Now I suppose there'll be more."

The world had become irrational in its violence. Drive-by shootings took the lives of people unknown to those who fired at them. Violence on the expressways at least had some semblance of motive, perhaps a car cutting into a lane and nearly shearing off the fender of the vehicle it passed. Of course, no one could justify a motorist who had been given such a scare chasing the reckless car down the expressway; on occasion, efforts had been made by the victim to force the offender off the freeway. Judge Farner had handled such a case and her sympathies had whipsawed between the two offenders. But then she came up with a Solomonic decision. The two drivers must take turns driving one another to work for a month. At last report, they had become fast friends.

2

Tim Gallagher called his father and said without explanation that he would stop by his condo on the way home from work. Jack had been pleasantly surprised by the media reaction to the suit he was bringing against Austin Rooney, although he had not liked the reference to the "battling brothers-in-law." That aside, the stories had dwelt on Jack's formidable career as the former king of Chicago nighttime radio. Testimonials were sought from old fans, and they were fulsome enough even for Jack. Of course Tim would have heard of the suit. Jack looked forward to discussing it with his lawyer son. The references to Tuttle had been equivocal, but there seemed to be the suggestion that just such a street fighter as Tuttle was needed in a case like this. The assumption that he had his pick of attorneys caused a moment of regret. Maybe he should have shopped around before taking Tuttle on. Perhaps it was not too late. . . .

When the doorbell rang, Jack pulled open the door. "Don't tell me you resent the fact that I took another lawyer."

But Tim brushed past him and flung himself into a chair. "What the hell is going on with you and Aggie?"

In a flash Jack remembered the occasion years ago when his son had confronted him on just such a matter. For all that, the question came as a surprise—his head had been full of his coming revenge on Austin Rooney. But now he remembered that Colleen had enlisted his help because of her fears that Tim was misbehaving with Aggie.

"Just the question I was going to put to you, Tim," Jack said, delighted by his own cool aplomb.

"What is that supposed to mean?"

Jack sat and adjusted the crease of his trousers. He assumed a sad expression as he looked at his son. "Colleen came to me with her fears. This young woman had apparently been bruiting about the office that she was having an affair with you."

All Tim's accusatorial superiority dissolved. Guilt was written all over his face.

"First she went to your uncle Austin."

"Oh my God."

"Then she came to me, as she should have in the first place. Tell me about it, Tim. Man-to-man."

Tim looked at his father abjectly, destroyed by the suggestion that they were peas in a pod. After a minute he said, "Can I have a drink?"

"What will you have?" It was tempting to say that he would be happy to have a drink with his son, although he could not promise to be as good company as the young lady. But he was in the catbird seat so why should he crow?

"Whiskey and water."

Jack poured the same for himself, very light on the water. This was Jameson, and it was sacrilegious to dilute it.

"Now, what is this about Aggie?"

Tim, robbed of his righteousness, was laudably confused. Jack had the tactical advantage of having been enlisted to save his son's marriage and family. While Tim searched for a way to put it, Jack added, "Of course she chose to divert suspicion to me."

Tim looked at him desolately. No need to dilate on the significance of that, of course. His son had suspected that in his heyday Jack had strayed from the beaten path, but now must think it ludicrous to imagine that a man his father's age was still susceptible to sins of the flesh. Jack himself had been surprised to learn that it was not ludicrous at all. Nonetheless, he was glad to be rid of Aggie. Her disconcerting phone call the morning after had given him some moments of unease. But it was foolish to think that such a delectable damsel would dally with him when there were more youthful pickings to be had.

"I've never known anyone like her," Tim said.

"And you would have been better off remaining ignorant that there are women like that. Women are different from you and me, Tim. I shouldn't have to point this out to a married man. Or perhaps I should. A woman who is wife and mother is one thing, liberated from the purpose of corralling a man. But the professional woman is a new phenomenon. She wants to be conquered so she turns to conquest as being second-best. It means nothing, finally. If she really wanted to settle down, nothing would be easier. But she prefers to compete in a man's world. Her psyche is altered in ways we have yet to understand."

He was enthralled with the sound of his own voice, of its message of world-weary wisdom. He himself had succumbed to the unaccustomed directness of Aggie, the New Female. He sympathized with Tim, a far less experienced man.

"Have you resolved to put all this behind you, son?"

"Oh, God, yes. It was the stupidest thing I ever did in my life. She was so obvious, but somehow that didn't seem to matter."

Jack nodded sagely. After a moment's silence, he said, "Do you know what I thought brought you here tonight?"

"What?"

"I have filed a suit, through my lawyer, against your uncle Austin."

"Good God."

"I am assured that I have a very good chance of enriching myself at his expense."

"But, Dad, the publicity . . ."

"I have never been a foe of publicity, Tim. In itself, it is neutral, it can be turned to good or evil. Austin has always been a sanctimonious ass. It may be good for his soul to be exposed as a fool."

"Are you sure that is how it will come out?"

"Tim, it is safe as real estate. If you could see the spontaneous expressions of support I have received!"

"But a suit goes before a judge. Do you know who will hear the case?"

"Judge Farner."

"You live a charmed life."

"Hadn't you heard of the suit?"

Tim had not heard. Publicity is an odd thing, touching some, leaving others untouched. Fame was like that. For a select few he had once been a god, but even then there had been countless millions who had never heard of Jack Gallagher. Concentrate on those affected and ignore the rest, that was the trick. Tim wanted to hear of the suit, if only as a diversion from his woes; Jack cast himself in the role of initiator of the action, seeing intuitively that there was redress to be had for what Austin had done to him.

"How did you end up with Tuttle?"

"Do you know him?"

"He is a laughingstock. I am surprised he hasn't been disbarred. Amos Cadbury has done everything possible to drive him from the bar."

"Amos Cadbury. I believe he is representing Austin."

"You're doomed!"

"Tuttle is a diamond in the rough, no doubt, but shouldn't I have a man like that in a case like this?"

"Only if you want to lose."

"Whom would you suggest?"

"I don't know many trial lawyers who would be willing to go up against Amos Cadbury."

"Isn't Mario Liberati a trial lawyer?"

Tim was struck by this remark, Jack saw it. Everyone sang the praises of Mario's courtroom pyrotechnics. "You couldn't afford Mallard and Bill."

"Tuttle is doing it on spec."

"That is not unusual. The problem is that Mallard and Bill would not want to get involved in such a suit. Dad, think of it. It's incestuous already. You are taking your brother-in-law to court. And you want your future son-in-law to represent you?"

"It's worth a try."

"I wouldn't count on it."

"I'll put it to Colleen."

"I suppose it can't hurt. What will you tell her about me?"

"That nothing happened. On the proviso that nothing ever will."

"I give you my word of honor."

"That is more than enough for me. I'll fix it with Colleen, don't worry."

Tim embraced him and Jack felt a fleeting impulse to tell his son that they were alike sinners. "Get along home to Jane."

When he opened the door to let Tim out, there was Aggie.

"Am I interrupting?" she asked, unperturbed.

"Right on the button," Jack said, consulting his Rolex. And then, to Tim, "Aggie has agreed to give me her legal advice on my suit."

Tim seemed to accept that. The sight of Aggie obviously made him want to flee. Aggie and Jack stood in the doorway, waving him on his way to wife and family.

"What was that all about?" Aggie asked, when the door was closed.

"Have you heard about my suit?"

"Birthday?"

"Be calm. I thought we would go over to the clubhouse."

"Only if you insist."

"I do. How often does the Old Man of the Sea have an opportunity to be seen with a naiad like you?"

"I know you will explain that to me."

Jack draped a camel-hair coat over his shoulders, marveling at his own calm reaction to her surprising appearance on his doorstep, and at such a moment. A lesser man would have collapsed at her appearance, but he had brought it off nicely, if he did say so himself. Everything he had gained with Tim would have gone out the window if he had expressed the surprise he felt at seeing Aggie in his doorway. The suggestion of the clubhouse had been an inspiration. He had to get this fascinating young female out of his apartment, bringing as she did memories of his dalliance with her the other night. But perhaps he might ask her back for a nightcap. After all, the sun of life was setting and opportunities for carnal folly were not apt to be many.

When they left, deciding to hoof it through the light, early-December snow, Jack noticed the drapes of the next condo flutter and then fall still. Dear Isabel, the snoop. Well, let her play Leporello to his Don Giovanni. Another allusion he would have had to explain to the voluptuous but unsophisticated Aggie.

3

Tuttle, who was serving in tandem with Peanuts at this juncture of the stakeout, witnessed these comings and goings. Not that he recognized Tim as he did Aggie, but both their visages were registered on the hard drive of his memory.

"Know him?" he asked Peanuts.

"Nope."

"Know her?" he asked sometime later.

"Nope."

Tuttle had recognized the girl who had been with Jack Gallagher in the clubhouse when he had first introduced himself to his eventual client, in company with the adhesive Isabel. This gave him an idea, bolstered by the fact that he too had noticed that fluttering drape. He could enlist Isabel's help to keep current on Jack Gallagher's activities.

And then Jack emerged with the young woman on his arm and they traipsed off through the gently falling snow toward the clubhouse. Soon they were lost to sight.

"I'll be right back," he said to Peanuts.

"Where you going?" But there was disinterest in Peanuts's voice. Indeed, he yawned as he asked the question. They had consumed a bottle of Chianti done up in plastic webbing with their pizza and Peanuts had the air of one about to slumber. Tuttle shut the door gently on his somnolent colleague and strode through a snowy world to Isabel's door, where he pressed the bell once and then again.

"Jack doesn't answer his door," he said, when she peered out at him over the security chain.

"I didn't see you knock."

"Perhaps you've heard that he is my client."

"Are you a lawyer?" Her voice rose with the question. He had earned distinction in her eyes.

"I thought you might have heard it on the news."

She undid the chain and opened her door. "Tell me about it."

It was sweet to give her an account of the suit he had filed on Jack Gallagher's behalf. Isabel was a good audience, in contrast with, say, Hazel, who listened to his braggadocio with a look of scornful skepticism. Still, Tuttle detected in Hazel's manner the growing conviction that she had boarded a ship that would not sink. Isabel was more forthright in her admiration.

"Someone actually assaulted him?"

"You can read all about it in the papers."

"But I would rather hear it from you."

"I'd be delighted. By the way, I was surprised not to find Jack home."

"You just missed him. He and his niece went over to the clubhouse. I was thinking of going over there myself."

"Niece?"

"Yes, he explained all about it. I think he was feeling badly about the way he received us when we went up to his table that night."

"I don't blame him at all. No man likes to be interrupted when he is having a drink with a girl like that, even if she is his niece."

"Her name is Aggie."

Tuttle resisted her suggestion that he accompany Isabel to the club. "Maybe you're right," she said reluctantly. "Once was an accident. Twice might seem suspicious."

"I envy you your sensitivity."

"Oh, Mr. Tuttle."

Peanuts was asleep when he got back to the car. The permanent occupant of the bottom rung of the Fox River Detective Division had crawled into the backseat and was now violating the winter quiet with sonorous snoring. This afforded Tuttle a welcome opportunity for thinking.

The news that Amos Cadbury was representing Austin Rooney had shaken Tuttle. He had no illusions about his own courtroom presence, but to go up against Amos Cadbury was to invite unwelcome comparisons from a jury. They were as unalike as comic and tragic masks. Tuttle had the unsettling feeling that Jack Gallagher would be advised to entrust his suit to a more prepossessing lawyer than himself. The young man who had stopped by had had a legal look about him. Perhaps the treachery was already under way. Tuttle was no stranger to rejection. Time and again when he had seemed to grasp the nettle success, or whatever it was, the prize had been snatched from his grasp. Jack Gallagher had listened avidly when Tuttle explained to him what a litigious opportunity Austin Rooney had presented him. The idea was new to Gallagher and he had found it easy to identify the project with Tuttle, the one who had explained it to him. But at the urging of others he could be persuaded to exchange attorneys. It would be explained to him what a formidable adversary Amos Cadbury was. It would be explained to him that, on the other hand, Tuttle was . . . No need to complete the thought. Tuttle was not without self-knowledge. Keeping an eye on his client could thus serve a double purpose: the original one, and as a hedge against being dumped by Gallagher.

He jotted down the tag number of the car the young woman had come in, as he had that of the young man. Maybe she was Gallagher's niece, and maybe not. Isabel had not shown an ounce of doubt about it. But then her eyes were clouded by the brilliance of her next-door neighbor. In the backseat, Peanuts turned over, with much snorting and blowing, and then slid down onto the floor. A moment of silence, and then the rhythmic inhalations and exhalations began again. Peanuts was a barrel of laughs on a stakeout, all right. It would have been nice to just voice his thoughts, consider all the angles out loud. Tuttle smiled at what must have been Amos Cadbury's reaction when he found out who had filed the suit on behalf of Jack Gallagher. But then his earlier suspicions began again.

The young man who had come earlier indeed had the look of a lawyer. Don't ask Tuttle what exactly that was, but he could recognize another lawyer at a distance of a hundred yards. Whether they saw their ilk in him, he did not know. The trouble with sitting in a parked car, looking out through steamed windows at a snowy world, was that there was no protection against wild surmise. It got into Tuttle's head that the man had been an emissary from Amos Cadbury, sent to brief Jack Gallagher on the less-than-illustrious career of Tuttle. Tuttle told himself he had been frank with Gallagher. He didn't claim to be Perry Mason but they had one helluva complaint and he was sure he could win. Not that he thought it would be necessary to go to trial. He hadn't mentioned this to Gallagher, since the old ham seemed to relish the thought of publicity. Publicity was a grand thing, of course, and Tuttle craved it as much as anybody, but a settlement would be better all around. Tuttle would settle for a couple hundred thousand, if pushed. His slice of that would be a pretty good paycheck. This had come up when Hazel's eyes widened at the amount of damages being sought.

"You're nuts," she said. "Not a nickel less than a million."

"Do you know how much two hundred thousand is?"

"Do you know what the Cubs are paying that no-good Folwell with an ERA of six-point-three who has lost more games than he's won?"

"There is no chewing-gum empire involved here."

"They made that bum a millionaire! Four-point-five for three years! And you want to settle for two hundred thousand miserable dollars."

"It is just a contingency plan."

"Well, you better think again."

Who was working for whom here? It was getting more difficult to tell. Somehow Hazel's imposing presence brought in business too, a few wills, a divorce case.

"I don't handle divorces."

"You what?"

"I don't handle divorces. My father was against them."

"Your father."

"He's the Tuttle in Tuttle and Tuttle."

"Which one?"

"Reading from right to left."

"You don't have to approve of divorce to help someone with it legally, do you?"

"I would feel I was betraying my father. He put me through law school." That simple phrase covered the six and a half years it had taken Tuttle to get through law school, plus another seven while he tried to pass the bar exam. Finally he had hired someone to take it for him. Between Tuttle and the memory of his father there was a link that approached the religious. Sometimes he thought his penchant for Chinese food disposed him to ancestor-worship.

"Was your father divorced?"

"No!" The thought shocked Tuttle. Hazel might have been suggesting he was illegitimate, or adopted. He didn't remember his mother, but according to his father she had been a saint. Well, his parents were together now, strumming on those harps or whatever you do up there, and while it was his father he thought of as smiling down on his lawyer son, he supposed his mother was proud of him as well.

4

"That was your son," Aggie said.

"That's right. Timothy."

"I've met him."

"I know."

She squinted at him as they walked into the swirling snow. She had pulled the hood of her long coat over her head but snowflakes sparkled here and there, got caught in her eyelashes and were batted away. Jack found her even more attractive than he remembered her. "How do you know that?"

"Don't all lawyers know one another?"

"That's it. We met at a seminar. His name made me think of Colleen so I spoke to him and he was her brother!"

Inside the clubhouse they stamped their feet, took off their coats, and then were drawn toward the open fire.

"It's a night for eggnog," Jack said.

"I couldn't drink it."

"Why not?"

"Calories." And she ran a long-fingered hand down her side, through the indentation above her hip, over the gorgeous thigh, and then down her leg to her shoe which she removed.

"To avoid calories you'd have to drink water."

"Scotch and water."

There were no waitresses here, so he went for their drinks. When he returned, she was staring into the fire, a leg drawn up under her, the shoe lying on its side. Jack Gallagher became wary. Thoughtful women were trouble and she looked almost melancholy staring into the fire.

She took her drink and sipped it. "There's more about your son."

"I know."

"What do you know?"

"Colleen told me what you told the girls in the ladies' room."

"Colleen! I never said anything to her. It was . . . well, impulsive."

"My son has a wife and family."

"Oh, God." She pouted. Was he going to preach to her?

"Maybe that was the attraction."

"What's that supposed to mean?"

"Think about it. And, of course, to zing it to Colleen."

Her smile engaged only one side of her mouth. "Have I been under investigation?"

"Colleen was worried about her brother. It is difficult for women to believe the folly of men."

"Is it?"

"She talked to her uncle about it, and he went to the bar where you and Tim had formed the habit of having a drink. Tim saw his uncle there and looked like a boy caught with his hand in the cookie jar."

Aggie's smile had turned pensive. "So that's what happened."

"Your last drink together?"

"Then I met you." She got her leg out from under her and pressed her knee to his. Ah, the flesh is a traitor. After the drink, they hurried through the snow, arm in arm, back to his apartment.

Snow fell gently for hours and lay like a disguise on buildings that had not existed three years before. Once this had been farmland. Before that it had been a prairie full of wildlife and Native Americans, its rivers awaiting the first probes of Europeans. But for centuries these coordinates of space had known the wisdom and folly of the human animal. He and Aggie were not setting any precedent.

At three in the morning, Aggie slipped from Jack Gallagher's condo and hurried, head down, to her car. It came to life and she drove off, past a car behind whose steamed windows a hatted figure slumped not quite out of sight.

5

A secret of Cy Horvath's success as a detective was his ability to replicate the nutty thought processes of the guilty. The incident at the El station had been labeled a copycat deed by Phil Keegan, and that was the accepted wisdom. But Cy had a hunch that Harry was back and was attempting to create just the impression that Phil had formed. Cy drove over to the Hacienda Motel to have another talk with Ruby.

"I read about that," Ruby said. "It brought it all back."

"I wonder if Harry is back."

The whites of her eyes glistened. "Do you think so?"

"It's possible."

"What's wrong with a guy like that?"

"It's been wrong for a long time, whatever it is."

He told her to go on working, and he sat in a chair while she made the bed, took the plastic bags from the baskets, carried an armful of towels from the bathroom. Next would come the vacuuming, but she put that off. All the while she had been telling him again what she had told him before, about the honey-blond girl from rural Wisconsin, the only white girl on the crew. Large blue eyes and an oval face and teeth like an ad.

"She didn't know she was beautiful. But the guests did."

"Did she ever go out with a guest?"

"Not from want of being asked. She thought they were kidding. She was so innocent." Ruby stared down some corridor of memory toward the image of her own prelapsarian self.

"Anyone in particular?"

"Sometimes they're here for days. For meetings. There was one man especially . . ."

"When would that have been?"

"Two, three months ago. They was lawyers, I think. It was when Harry was trying to get her to move in with him. She had actually thought he had an extra room that would be hers." Ruby rolled her eyes. "That girl. You wanted to protect her, you know. Like a daughter. One of my girls has sort of blond hair."

"So what happened?"

"With her, nothing. But, once, they went up the road to a restaurant, after Linda was through for the day. Then he came back several times, but she was always working then, and I told him she couldn't be goofing around while we were cleaning."

"So you'd recognize him?"

"Oh, sure." Ruby looked at him. "But nothing happened. She was shocked when she found out what he was after, and told him he ought to be ashamed of himself. Can you imagine? She found out he was a Catholic like herself and she reminded him of what they both believed. That was the last of him."

Lawrence, the assistant manager, had the look of a man trying to seem busier than he was. Of course there were records of past events held in the motel; why did Horvath ask?

Cy showed him his badge. "Just routine."

Two and a half months before, there had been a legal conference at Hacienda. Cy went down the list of registered guests for those days and came upon the name of Tim Gallagher. It caught his eye because of the fuss Jack Gallagher was raising.

Cy went out to his car.

The former motel in which Harry had lived was still operating as a rooming house. There were pickups and semi cabs parked in the lot. In the manager's office a middle-aged man sat sneering at the television.

"Did you ever see such crap?"

"I don't get much chance to watch daytime television."

"Well, that's what it is." He gestured at the inanities on the screen, then pushed the MUTE button on his remote control. "What can I do for you?"

For the first time he looked at Cy. "Not you again."

"I wondered if Harry had come back."

The man shook his head. "They almost never do. A month or two in this dump is all they can take."

"How long have you been here?"

"I told you before."

"Remind me."

To the manager's disgust, Cy went through all the questions he had asked him weeks before.

"If you wrote this down it would be easier to remember."

"I remember. So far, your story is the same as before."

" 'Story.' "

"You remember that the reason I came was that a girl Harry had been going with was pushed into the path of a car and killed."

"And you thought Harry did it."

"He disappeared, didn't he?"

"You bet he did. He owed me for two weeks' rent. But I'll keep his things until he pays up."

"His things?"

"What was in his room. I packed them up so I could put someone else in there."

"You have them in storage?"

The manager had jammed what Harry had left behind into a cardboard box and a large shopping bag.

"You want me to go through those here or take them downtown?"

"I told you why I kept them."

"I'll give you a receipt."

The manager hesitated, as if searching for a way he might benefit from this.

"I'll forget you didn't tell me about this stuff before," Cy said.

"Take it. I don't think even Goodwill would want it."

"You looked it over?"

"It's all there."

The sound of the television began as Cy closed the door of the manager's office. His name was crudely lettered on the door with a magic marker: *P. J. Sherman. Mgr.*

Cy turned the box and the bag over to the lab, where Lapin looked up at him with pink, nearsighted eyes. "What am I looking for?"

"I don't know."

"I can't get at it right away."

"When you can."

He went past the press room where Tuttle was sleeping, slumped over a table, his tweed hat fallen to the floor. Cy went in, picked up the hat, and put it on the lawyer's head, waking him up.

"Horvath, how are you?"

"You ought to sleep nights."

"Thanks for the suggestion."

"How's your big suit going?"

Tuttle looked sly. "It will all come out at the trial."

Cy pulled up a chair. "What do you think of Jack Gallagher?"

"What's to think? He's got a just complaint and I'm representing him."

"You're up against Amos Cadbury."

"Not even Cadbury will get Austin Rooney off on this."

"They're brothers-in-law."

"I know that."

"How many kids does Jack have?"

"Two. A boy and a girl. Of course they're a man and a woman now."

"What do they do?"

"Both involved in law. The son lives over in Barrington."

"Timothy Gallagher?"

"That's the one."

Cy thought of it as the Gallagher tangent. Any investigation, however halfhearted, turns up unusual things. He had no reason to suppose that Gallagher was the lawyer who had tried to put a move on Linda Hopkins. He could easily find out; if he had a picture of the man, he could show Ruby. Maybe he would do that, while he waited for the lab to see if the junk he had brought from Harry's motel could tell him anything he didn't already know.

6

Father Dowling was surprised at Amos Cadbury's appetite for irrelevant minutiae when he came to depose the pastor on the events at the now famous dance. He had also decided to depose Maud Gorman; Edna had promised him the use of her office for the occasion. Father Dowling had never before been anxious for a visit of Amos's to be at an end, but he was wary of everything he said, lest he seem to have prejudged the issue. Legally, it was still to be decided, and morally it was difficult to think of either man as the injured party. But what he dreaded was being asked to testify in the case.

"They will come begging for a settlement long before we get to court," Amos said.

"Wouldn't that be best?"

"When they do, I will know they're beaten. I will refuse. Eventually they will withdraw the suit."

"You are sure of that?"

"No. But it is the goal I am pursuing."

"I will make that an object of my prayers."

Amos Cadbury was a pious man, a man who often thanked God for the many good things that had come his way in a long and successful life, but for a fleeting moment the idea that special Divine intervention might be needed for the practice of his profession brought a twitch of impatience to his luxurious silver eyebrows.

"Of course you're right, Father. And I will do the same."

And so Father Dowling relived the night of the dance. Amos wanted all the particulars as to why a dance had been held in the first place—who had suggested it, how everything had been arranged. Nothing seemed too trivial for the little tape recorder he had placed on the pastor's desk.

"And will it be a regular thing now?"

"After what happened the once, how can you ask?"

"A dance is a wonderful thing, Father. A real dance, I mean, with music you can bear and dancing that is graceful and dignified."

"Do you dance, Amos?" The priest's mind was suddenly flooded with a vision of the stately attorney sweeping around the floor, his partner held lightly but masterfully as he guided her among the other dancers with precision and grace.

"I danced. But I should like to dance again."

"Perhaps we will have another, then. After a time."

"You mustn't let two foolish old men spoil a grand idea."

And so they came to the night of the dance. Now Amos's curiosity about the music, the songs that were sung, seemed to go well beyond the limits of professional curiosity. That Jack Gallagher had been able to mimic the great singers of yore enthralled him. "Was Dennis Day in his repertoire?"

"He was. He sang 'Danny Boy' as Day would do it."

Amos wanted to know if Gallagher had sung "Dream" and "Smoke Gets in Your Eyes." He had.

"And 'Goodnight Irene'?"

"Desmond O'Toole sang that, a version that went on at least five minutes."

Amos sighed. His eyes were moist. "My dear wife's name was Irene. Whenever I hear that song . . ."

But in a moment he regained control of himself, and the re-creation of the night of the dance went on. Father Dowling was surprised by how much he was able to recall. When Jack stepped down from the microphone and Desmond took over, he had tapped Austin on the shoulder and then Maud was in his arms.

"That woman can dance," Amos said fervently.

"They danced well together. And during the next dance, Austin tried to reclaim his partner, with disastrous results."

"All of it, Father. I want to hear it all."

So Father Dowling told of the repeated attempts on Austin's part to break in on Jack Gallagher and Maud.

"How many times, would you say? This is important."

"A half-dozen?"

"More? Less?"

"More."

"Unbelievable rudeness! A dance is a rite and ceremony, Father, there are rules that must be kept." The lawyer's animosity against the man who had brought this ridiculous suit was now strong and unwavering. But the climactic moment when Austin Rooney threw the punch that felled Jack Gallagher excited Amos more. "Good man, good man," he said.

Father Dowling was relieved when the deposition was done, and Amos got ready to go over to the school to interview Maud Gorman. Since the dance, he had doubtless tried to forget that night, but now it was almost more vividly present to him than it had been at the time.

"I wish you had witnessed the set-to in the parking lot, Father."

"Maud can help you there."

"Good grief." He looked at his watch, fishing it from a pocket of his vest. "I mustn't keep the woman waiting any longer."

"How was it?" Marie asked.

"Like making a general confession."

"Confession? Nothing that happened was your fault."

"I meant it as an analogy, Marie."

"Even so. Cy Horvath is here if you can see him."

"Has he been waiting long?"

"He's been in the kitchen. I gave him a little snack."

The lieutenant came into the study and sat when Father Dowling asked him to.

"We got a message from Kansas City. Harry Paquette has been seen there."

"Didn't they arrest him?"

"They got a positive report when they showed his picture around. We got a picture from Minneapolis. They'll find him."

"And then?"

"We'll find out why he left Fox River in such a hurry."

That night Phil Keegan stopped by the rectory and, forgetting his previous indifference, was triumphant, praising Cy's tenacity to the skies.

"I suppose it will be difficult to prove he actually pushed her into the path of that car."

"It won't be difficult for Cy. He has kept in touch with the witnesses, keeping their memories fresh. He is sure that when he produces the man, they will identify him."

It was odd how one's attitude changed. When the search for a culprit seemed unlikely to succeed, it was easy to think of him as a monster, but once the trail grew warm he seemed a hunted wretch. The man might have a record as long as your arm, as Phil put it, but it was hard not to fear for him as the tenacious search closed in on him. Lines from Francis Thompson's "Hound of Heaven" came to Father Dowling. Guilty as Harry Paquette might be, the priest hoped to see him if and when they caught him. A criminal must be punished, of course, but he was also a sinner and as such, a candidate, like all of us, for Divine mercy. Phil sometimes grew impatient with this "lost sheep" business, but in his heart he understood. His interest and Roger Dowling's might differ, but they were compatible.

The pastor of St. Hilary's sat up late this night, Dante open before him, but his thoughts often elsewhere. The events he had spent over an hour recounting to Amos Cadbury seemed comic compared with the matter Cy was pursuing. Two old men vying for the same old woman at a dance, on the one hand; a man pushing a woman to her death because she refused advances she seemed once to have accepted, on the other. But were they so different? What Austin had done to Jack Gallagher easily could have had more serious consequences. Jack might easily have been injured when he fell; a man his age might have had a heart attack as a result of such rough treatment. Of course the still-unknown Harry had meant to kill his erstwhile love; certainly, to injure her seriously. Still, the anger behind both deeds was in many ways the same. In any case, Harry's presence in Kansas City seemed to exonerate him from what had happened at the El station in Fox River. That seemed to make it what Phil had called it, the work of a copycat. Surely Harry was not to blame because some poor devil had tried to do a similar thing.

7

George Hessian heard that Joseph Castlemar from Amos Cadbury's office would be taking depositions from those in the school who had witnessed Austin Rooney striking Jack Gallagher. This was welcome news, strengthening the symmetry of the book he was now in the process of outlining. Part one would evoke St. Hilary's school of yesteryear, establish the ethos of the place, introduce the class, but largely as background for the two protagonists of the book, Austin and Jack. Their rivalry, the resort to blows, would provide the base for the following parts. George was certain that there was something deeply significant in the fact that each man had married the other's sister. Dark thoughts of secondhand incest blew through George's mind, but he let them blow on. Let the reader think such thoughts if he chose; George would merely chronicle. Their careers seemed parallel rather than a continuation of their rivalry, but Tuttle had found that wasn't true.

"You interviewed at the station?"

The tweed hat bobbed in assent. Tuttle was lying prone on the examination table of the former school nurse's office George used. The hat once more fell over his face.

"Do you have notes of those interviews?"

"It's all in my head."

"That's equivocal."

Silence from beneath the tweed hat. But Tuttle told George of the remembered visit of Austin Rooney to the station. When Jack Gallagher went down he took a fortune's worth of records with him.

"I'm surprised he didn't sue him then."

"I wasn't advising him then."

It was tempting to tell Tuttle what Rawley had reported on the way the little lawyer was haunting Western Sun Community. "I think he or his partner are out here all night," Rawley had said.

"What are they looking for?"

"They're keeping an eye on Gallagher."

"But Gallagher is his client."

"Lawyers are nuts."

Rawley worked various shifts, not really caring whether he put in his eight hours in daylight or darkness, but he preferred the graveyard shift, from midnight to eight in the morning. "I can read then without being interrupted."

Tuttle had been satisfied with George's assurance that he could be of no help to him on what had happened between Austin and Jack. That provided an excuse to get the story from Tuttle, who became a compendium of all the accounts he had gathered from his interviews. What George learned was better than he had expected. The fact that Austin had attacked Jack in his office at the station, provided continuity with their playground scuffles and the events at the St. Hilary

Senior Center dance. All these resorts to blows had involved women. Somewhere in these attacks a theme lurked, and George Hessian was intent on finding it. Had Maud been the bone of contention early and late? She had been a student when Austin and Jack were in St. Hilary's school. None of the comments on their deportment had linked Maud to the two boys, but it seemed to George that a little poetic license could at least suggest that she had been the object of their rivalry from the beginning.

"A little old lady?" Rawley asked. He puffed between sentences, causing his mustache to flutter. "You mean the one in the condo next to Jack's?"

"Who's that?"

"A widow named Ritchie."

"Mrs. Oswald Ritchie?"

"That's right."

"You remember Ozzie."

"Do I?"

Rawley refused to find George's enthusiasm contagious. He wanted to talk books, at least the book he was reading at the time— that was *Indian Summer* by William Dean Howells.

"It could have been written by James."

"Is Jack interested in the widow?"

"What do you mean by 'interested'?"

"Oswald Ritchie was in the same department at the university as Austin Rooney."

"How do you know that?"

"I cleared his loan at the bank. When he bought his house."

"What a memory for trivia you have."

But links suggested themselves to George Hessian, whose imagination was now in full flow. Maybe Maud had a rival. After a shift change in the guard shack, he called on Isabel Ritchie.

"I knew your husband from the bank."

"It broke my heart to sell that house," she said, when he had given her more details. Isabel was no Maud Gorman, but she was cute enough, for an old lady. George's lack of experience in matters of the heart made anything seem equally possible or impossible in such matters.

"And now you live next door to Jack Gallagher."

Her eyes brightened and she sighed. "Such a man, such a voice."

"He was a favorite of my mother's."

"He was everyone's favorite."

"I wheeled her over to meet him at the clubhouse."

"Wheeled her?"

"She's moved on to assisted living."

Isabel did not want to know any more. Life at Western Sun was calibrated to degrees of dependency and Isabel was still in the part where she was as independent as she would have been if she had kept her house.

"I suppose you remember Austin Rooney."

"We weren't close to the Rooneys."

"He is Jack's brother-in-law."

This lent Austin significance in Isabel's eyes. "What a small world."

"A marble in space. Do you and Jack go to the clubhouse often?"

"We're often there together."

No need to pry further for the nonce. Had she been dissembling in claiming not to have been close to the Rooneys? George would pursue the spoor further with Austin. But discreetly.

11

1

The phone call from his brother-in-law Jimmy Kane in Milwaukee came to Mario Liberati at his office at Mallard and Bill, and Mario was furious.

"Mario, I'm in real trouble this time. I need the best defense lawyer I can get. That means you. Lucy has kept me up to speed on your career."

"Jimmy, I'm a member of the firm. I don't decide the cases we take. I'll ask about lawyers in Milwaukee."

"I want you."

Mario closed his eyes in frustration. He had managed to keep the anger from his voice, but he was fearful he would unleash it at Jimmy if this conversation went on. All his reasons for not wanting to practice law in Milwaukee came back to him. In Chicago he had started with a blank slate; no one knew his sister was married to a man thought to be behind the drug trade in the city to the north.

"Mario, Lucy wants to talk to you."

"Mario?" My God, it was Lucy. "Can't you help him? It really does look bad. I tell myself he deserves whatever happens, but as his wife I can't stick to that."

"I told him I will look into who in Milwaukee would be best."

"Mario, we know the lawyers here. The only ones who will take the case would make Jimmy look guilty before the trial begins. They're always in court with guilty people."

"Isn't Jimmy guilty?"

"Doesn't he deserve the best defense?"

"Lucy, I'll call you tonight from home. Let me think."

He hung up. Think? There was nothing to think about. All he had to do was to appear in a Milwaukee court with Jimmy Kane as his client and everything he had managed to build up since law school would go down the drain. Of course he would respond to Lucy's plea, but he would not, he could not, be Jimmy Kane's lawyer. For a member of the firm of Mallard and Bill . . . He did not have to complete the thought. He was sitting at his desk doing nothing at all, staring blankly before him, when Colleen came in as scheduled.

"What's wrong?"

"Shut the door."

She did so and then came around the desk to him. He seemed to be trembling. "Mario, tell me."

He found he did not want to tell her there, did not want to foul his nest further with talk about Jimmy Kane.

"Let's get some coffee."

They went into the room set aside for breaks, and though it was crowded it was better than his office. A dozen conversations were in progress, no one would imagine what he had to tell Colleen. At a corner table, Aggie sat with Albert Fremont and made a point of ignoring Mario. But then Fremont seemed pretty intent on what he was telling her. Mario held his coffee in both hands and told Colleen about the call from Milwaukee. She understood immediately why he was upset. As the conversation went on, he did as he would do in his office when they talked, making cryptic notes, now on a paper napkin he had pulled from the container on the Formica table.

"How can I tell them that helping him would jeopardize my career?"

"It isn't as if you are in private practice and can just take on clients."

"I said that. My sister got on the line."

"Oh, Mario."

Was this some sort of retribution for what he had been feeling about the troubles in Colleen's family—her uncle, her father, her brother? All that seemed like nothing compared to the threat posed by Jimmy Kane. Not even Jimmy's best friends would think him innocent. Least of all his best friends.

"I don't mind telling him to go to hell. It's my sister. Of course he made her get on the line."

"Just tell them you can't do it."

"Of course I can't do it."

Thank God for Colleen. What would he have done if he had no one to talk to about this? He crumpled the napkin and sent it in an arc to a wastebasket.

"Three points." There was applause from those who had noticed. Colleen smiled. He took her hand in his.

"They can't make you do it."

"Of course not."

Before the call came, if he had thought about it, he would have realized how well his career had gone since coming to Mallard and Bill. And here he had met Colleen. Some of her attraction was due to the contrast with the predatory Aggie. But of course that had just been the beginning. They worked so well together, but that too was only a part of it. They might have been waiting into their thirties for one another.

He had been driven by the need to free himself of his Milwaukee connections. The memory of the day Lucy had married Jimmy Kane was a painful one. Throughout the Mass, afterward at the reception, recognizing many of the questionable characters who had shown up and who were impossible to ignore at the reception, he kept telling himself he should have done everything he could to dissuade Lucy from marrying Jimmy Kane. But what good would he have done if he had tried? She was in love, hard as that was to accept. She had fallen for one of the most disreputable men in the city. The one time they had talked about it, it was clear she knew all about him.

"He is going to change, Mario. He promised. It was a condition of my acceptance."

"And if he doesn't?"

"He will. He *promised*."

Ever since, he had been waiting for the kind of phone call that had come today. Sooner or later people like Jimmy Kane were brought low. Then they whined and cried and sought help wherever they could find it. He could imagine Jimmy promising him that if he only got out of this, he would be a changed man. Well, he wouldn't get out of it. Jimmy was shrewd enough to know that this time it was different. And he wanted Mario Liberati in court with him so they could all go down together.

The following day, Mario was wanted in Mallard's office. Bill was there as well, two symbols of rectitude sitting in shirtsleeves, one behind the desk, the other in a chair in the corner.

"Something disturbing has arisen, Mario," Mallard said.

"Yes, sir."

"Do you know a man named Jimmy Kane in Milwaukee?"

"He is my brother-in-law."

Two pairs of eyebrows raised. "I have looked over your original application and find no mention of that. You remember the section that asked if there were any compromising facts in your background that could affect the reputation of the firm?"

"He lives in Milwaukee."

"That is no excuse. You appreciate that it is a serious matter if one of us is connected with a known racketeer?"

"I am not connected with him. My sister is. I have never had anything to do with him."

"He is currently under indictment in Milwaukee."

Mario said nothing.

"Did you know this?"

"He called me."

"Here?"

"Yes."

"Did he call you as a brother-in-law or as a lawyer?"

"Both. He asked me to defend him. Of course I said no."

"Of course."

The two partners allowed a long silence to develop.

"What do you want me to do?"

Bill spoke. "This is a sad day, Mr. Liberati." Mr. Bill was always formal.

"What do you think you ought to do? You will appreciate that for us the reputation of the firm is paramount. We have never—never— represented anyone like this Jimmy Kane. Everyone deserves legal representation, true. But not from Mallard and Bill," Mallard said.

"Do you want me to resign?"

"You have been one of the best hires we have made in years. You have fulfilled every expectation we had of you."

Bill said, "We will make it as financially attractive for you as we can, Mr. Liberati."

He was being asked to resign; he had known that the moment he walked in. Somehow they had heard of Jimmy Kane and his connection with the star of the firm, and painful as it might be to them, they could not permit him to continue with the firm. It would not do that one of them had such connections.

"We can hope that none of this will reflect on Mallard and Bill despite your departure. But I needn't tell you what the situation demands."

"How did you find out about this?"

"That scarcely matters, does it?"

"Did he call you?"

"Good God, no." The idea that someone accused of what Jimmy Kane was accused of would have the temerity to call either of the senior partners of Mallard and Bill shook the two men.

"Your severance package will serve to cushion the blow somewhat, Mr. Liberati," said Mallard.

"I cannot tell you how this grieves me, Mario," added Bill.

"I understand."

"We were certain you would."

When he emerged from the office, in a daze, Aggie was in the hall, just dipping toward a water fountain. She stared at him.

"What's wrong?"

"Not a thing."

"Mario, if there is anything I can do—"

Why did he think that she had already done all she could do?

Colleen was waiting for him in his office. "What did they want?"

"Does everyone know?"

"You know this place. Aggie has been spreading the word."

"Aggie! How did she know?"

"Mario, everyone knows. Is it bad?"

"I am being let go. I am to get together with the accountants to discuss a historic severance settlement."

She flew into his arms and, embracing her, unable to hold back, he wept. That quickly the life he had built was destroyed. He had proposed to Colleen in the full confidence that his future was secure. How could he hold her to their engagement now, when he did not know what he would do next?

"It was about Jimmy Kane being your brother-in-law."

"Of course."

"I'll talk to Tim."

"Why?"

"You know how he admires you as a lawyer. Everyone does."

"His firm will probably have the same objection. Now I'll know better than to try to conceal the fact that my sister married that bastard."

"Don't be silly. How many firms are as staid as this one? Have they bothered Tim about Dad and Uncle Austin?"

"They're not drug dealers."

She pressed herself more closely against him, as if she wanted to draw all his pain into herself.

"Colleen, about the engagement . . ."

"Don't you say another word. Not one."

"If I love you I should free you."

"I am going to leave here too."

He stepped back. "That's crazy."

"Is it? I am very employable. I do not need Mallard and Bill and neither do you."

They had dinner together, they went to her place and talked until midnight. Outside, snow was falling steadily, huge moist flakes. While he drove home, all the strength and reassurance he had drawn from Colleen seeped away. For the rest of the night, before at last he fell asleep, he thought back to where he had begun, a kid in Milwaukee, prospects dim. Mallard and Bill presided over his dreams, two implacable judges in their expensive snow-white shirts, pointing like angels his way out of the Garden of Eden.

2

Tuttle was seldom surprised that following someone around for a few days turned up odd things. Jack Gallagher's niece was not his niece but a lawyer who worked in the same firm as did his daughter; Mallard and Bill, a starchy outfit that made Amos Cadbury look like a free spirit. Tuttle was impressed against his will that a man Jack's age was still at it. He had gotten some sense of his client's character from the program manager at Jack's old station.

"So you're representing Jack." Hove was short, fat, bald and a master of sarcasm. "I always hated that pompous son of a bitch."

"I have to know everything I can about my client."

"You've come to the right fella."

Hove was a font of carping criticism of the onetime star of the station. Jack was a notorious womanizer and the women acted as if he was doing them a favor. He received them in his office as if he were a prize bull and they had come to be serviced. Listeners loved him. It was not a restful thought to think of one of Amos Cadbury's acolytes interviewing Hove. Tuttle asked Hove if anyone else had talked with him about the case.

"I wish they would. Do you know that I am one of the few people still here that worked with Jack? His photograph is on the wall in the reception area, but no one who works here now remembers him. One day he was king, the next . . . What does he do with himself nowadays?"

No need to mention the bogus niece. "He is enjoying his retirement."

"Retirement. If what he did is work, I'm a brain surgeon. Judy made the musical selections, Jack just improvised when he was on the air. He had nothing to do with preparation, he was above all that."

"Judy?"

"She's the other survivor of those days. Do you know that one day his brother-in-law came here and punched him out because he had heard of how Jack was playing around? His son worked here one summer and of course he heard the buzz about his old man."

Tuttle was almost sorry he had come. Hove would make Cadbury's case for him, if Amos condescended to check out his opponent. It was difficult to imagine Amos in this smoke-filled office, listening to the sarcastic twang of Hove.

"Is Judy here now?"

"You want to talk to her?"

"Yes."

Hove picked up the phone and dialed. "Judy? Jack's lawyer is here. The one who is representing him out in Fox River. He was knocked down twice and now wants to win the fight in court."

The upshot was that Judy would talk to Tuttle. Her office was next door to Hove's.

"I wish you had come to me first. Hove always hated Jack."

"So he told me."

"He was jealous."

Judy weighed maybe a hundred pounds, skin and bone and buck teeth that didn't look too bad when she smiled, which was a lot, as if someone had told her.

"Jack Gallagher was a giant of Chicago radio. A giant. The irony is that he would have flourished in the present era too. Radio is all talk now and Jack was nothing if not a talker."

"You were his assistant?"

"I was. He was wonderful to work for."

Is everybody made up of as many different people as those who knew him? Maybe nobody really knows anybody. Judy got out old promo material for Jack Gallagher's radio show, offered to give him tapes of typical shows.

"I called him to offer my sympathy when I heard what had happened to him, but he just laughed it off."

"Do you see him much?"

"See him? The last time I saw him was when he walked out of here on his last day. He was too proud ever to come back."

"Why did he leave?"

The smile faded. "Radio stopped being what it was. His ratings dropped; advertisers wanted something else, they didn't know what. There was not the slightest gratitude for what he had done for them and for the station. He read the handwriting on the wall and left with his head high. Of course he was given a big phony send-off at the Palmer House."

"What about him and women?"

"That's slander. Several times he called me to his office to help him get rid of some overwrought fan. One was actually pulling off her blouse when I got there, tugging him toward the couch. Of course women like that would talk to get back at him."

"So there was nothing to it?"

"Nothing like what you hear."

"Hove said his son heard about his dad when he worked here one summer."

"The poor boy. Why do children think so little of their parents?"

Tuttle thought of his own father. He could not imagine himself and his father in such a situation.

"It's a mystery."

He left with an armful of promo material and his pockets filled with cassettes, tapes of the Jack Gallagher show. If he had a machine, he might play them.

Driving back to Fox River, Tuttle felt that he did not know his client at all. The guy was likeable, no doubt about that. Tuttle liked him, despite the lie about the niece. If Cadbury sent one of his minions to the station, Judy and Hove would cancel one another out. Tuttle's next step was to look into Austin Rooney's background. Or it would have been.

When he awoke the following day and listened to his police radio while shaving he nearly sliced off his nose. He stopped and listened. A woman's body had been found in the West End development where Jack had his condo. Strangled and left in a snowbank. Her name was Agatha Rossner and she was a young lawyer in a prestigious Chicago firm.

❧ Part Three ❧

1

Phil Keegan couldn't sleep late if he wanted to, not anymore. Once he could lie in bed for twenty-four hours, out like a light, but after his wife died and his kids moved away and there was only himself, he woke without fail at five-thirty. Thanks to his bladder, of course, but even without that biological alarm clock he was sure he would have been wide awake and eager to get going on another day. Staying busy was a necessity; that and visits to Roger Dowling when he could think about what his life might have been like if he hadn't flunked out of Quigley because he couldn't get the hang of Latin. He would have been annoyed if anyone suggested that police work was therapy for him, what kept him from going bonkers. But there was truth in this.

That morning the call from the department came first, and he listened to the radio on his way to where the body had been found, but all he could find were talk shows, dozens of voices violating the morning air with dogmatic comments on one thing after another. He turned it off.

Dr. Pippen was already at the scene when Keegan got there, looking as if she had yet to go to bed, but fresh as a daisy and more beautiful, the adornment of the coroner's office. The paramedics had called her as soon as they had checked out the body; the woman was clearly dead and beyond their jurisdiction. The crime scene was already

169

tainted by all the people who had been tramping around in the snow that had fallen during the night.

"What do you make of it?" Keegan asked her.

"Strangled with her own scarf."

The medical examiner's wagon arrived and all hell was raised about the fresh footprints around the scene. The place was finally staked off, and the photographers went to work. Pippen huddled in her fur, her auburn hair hanging in a ponytail down her back, as if she were the animal whose skin she wore. Cy Horvath got there twenty minutes after Phil did and they had a conference.

"She live here?"

"The identification in her purse gives a Chicago address."

"So what the hell was she doing here?"

That question would have to wait. How anyone could sleep through the commotion out there on the street was hard to understand. But as Phil looked around, all he could see were drawn drapes, no sign of light, as if this was just another morning.

Pippen checked out the body again after the medical examiner's crew had finished. She indicated that the body could go. Agatha Rossner was zipped into a rubber bag and taken away.

"Anyone bring coffee?" Pippen asked.

"Want to go get some?" Cy replied, and Phil frowned. Pippen was Cy's Achilles' heel. He was mesmerized by the beautiful young doctor, liked to hang around her, innocent as could be but not very damned smart. Pippen seemed to think of Cy as her big brother.

"Send someone," Phil said.

"No reason for me to stick around," Pippen said.

"How'd you find out about this?"

"My buzzer."

"You wear it to bed?"

"I was still up."

"At five?"

"My medical-school class had a reunion. It went on and on."

"So you've got your car."

"I've got my car. See you later. Much later."

Cy watched her walk off, scrunching through the snow toward her car that she had left by the guard gate. He turned to Phil.

"I am going to check out the woman."

"Which one?"

Cy held up a purse. "I kept this. I'll turn it in to evidence later. I want to check out her place. The keys are here."

"Without a warrant?"

"She lives in Chicago."

Phil nodded. Getting a warrant in Chicago would consume most of the day. Besides, the Chicago police would want to get in on this and they might never see the inside of the apartment.

"I'll come with you."

She had lived in a remodeled house near Old Town, on the edge between the fashionable and the bohemian. Large windows looked out of her second-floor apartment onto a street where dogs were walked, couples strolled, and the curbs were lined with parked cars, bumper to bumper. The girl herself had rented car space some blocks away. A little plastic tag with the address was on her key ring: Kopcinski's Parking. Her car was not there, and Phil sent a message to have the Western Sun development searched to see if the car was out there. Otherwise it was a Chicago matter. The two Fox River detectives were careful not to leave signs of their passage as they went through the apartment. Not much furniture, not many books (and those were of the jumbo glitzy paperback type—hundreds of thousands of words of improbabilities to soothe the civilized breast), a very elaborate sound system with speakers in all the rooms. Cy checked the CDs. She seemed to have liked everything.

"Lots of old stuff."

"Classics."

"No, 'popular music of yesterday.' " Cy was reading from the blurb. "Jack Gallagher stuff."

The remark was prelude to a number of surprising things. The number scrawled on the pad near the phone proved to be Jack Gallagher's. Not that they rang the number while they were in the apartment. In the bedroom, where a large mattress lay on the floor without benefit of bedstead, there was a framed photograph of Jack Gallagher, signed. *All the best, Jack.* Cy frowned at the picture.

"That's an old frame."

"So?"

"I mean it's a picture that's been in that frame for a long time."

"Why would this woman even know of Jack Gallagher?"

"She likes old music?"

"But this is an old photograph."

When they left it was with thoughts of Jack Gallagher on their minds, and they just looked at one another when they got Jack's address from downtown. The body of the girl had been found twenty-five yards from Gallagher's condo.

When Phil rattled the knocker on Jack Gallagher's door, the door of the next apartment opened, and a lady in a kimono leaned out with her finger to her lips. "Shhh. He never gets up until noon."

"A lot of commotion here this morning."

"What do you mean?" The glassy look suggested contacts. Cy showed her his identification. Her mouth rounded and she stepped back. "It's that car that's been parked out there for days, isn't it?"

"What car is that, Mrs. . . ."

"Ritchie. Isabel Ritchie. That's with one *l*."

"One's enough," Cy said. "What car has been parked out there for days?"

"I don't know one car from another. But there were two men, sometimes only one, and they just sat there, for hours, day and night."

"Did you complain about it?"

"I mentioned it to the gate guard and he said he'd look into it."

"But the car remained?"

Wrapping her kimono more tightly around her, she stepped outside in her big floppy slippers. "It may be out there still." She stopped. "What are all those people doing?"

"That's why we're here, ma'am."

The theory was that retired people took out their hearing aids when they went to bed and could have slept through a bombing of the city. Whatever the explanation, the body had been taken away, patrol cars and meat wagon were gone, nothing was left to commemorate the finding of the dead girl's body but a yellow plastic ribbon marking off an irregular rectangle at the side of the road, a rectangle in which the freshly fallen snow had been trampled thoroughly by dozens of feet.

"Who reported the body?"

Phil looked at Cy. "Good question."

They decided to postpone visiting Jack Gallagher for a while. They had the 911 tape relayed to them several times. Cy looked at Phil. "If I had to guess, I would say that is Tuttle trying to disguise his voice."

Then they headed back to Jack Gallagher's door.

2

Jack Gallagher was in a mood when he opened his door at the crack of dawn, going on eleven o'clock, to find Cy Horvath and Phil Keegan on his step. Cy opened his wallet and Jack squinted, pretending he could read it.

"What can I do for you?"

"This may take time, Mr. Gallagher."

" 'Mr. Gallagher'! Come on in, there's fresh coffee."

The apartment was a little steamy and the fragrance of showering drifted from the inner reaches. Taking in the place, comparing it to his own modest digs, and to the place in Chicago from which they had recently come, Phil decided it was basically a motel suite, one room made to look like many—living area, another area divided between the kitchen on one side and the dining table on the other, and beyond the inner sanctum, bedroom and bath. The living room was cluttered with photographs, most of them including Jack, if not exclusively of him.

"We found the body of a young lady in a snowbank beside the street outside."

Jack had gone into the little kitchen area to fetch the coffee. There were mugs set out on the little ledge that separated it from the living room. He had no reaction at all.

"Did you hear me, Mr. Gallagher?"

"Not unless you call me Jack."

"A dead girl was found in the snow just outside your apartment. All hell broke loose around here in the early hours."

"You're kidding."

"You heard nothing?"

He shook his head slowly back and forth. "One of the selling points of these places is the acoustics. They're built with a common wall but the claim is that all the walls, not only the common one, assure absolute quiet and privacy. It's true."

"The girl's name was Agatha Rossner. Does that mean anything to you?"

"Of course. She worked with my daughter Colleen at Mallard and Bill in the Loop. That's a legal firm."

"Why would her body have been found here?"

"I suppose people can die anywhere."

"She was strangled, Jack."

He stared across the room as if contemplating the fragility and folly of life. He shook his head. "She was younger than Colleen."

"You yourself were acquainted with her?"

"Oh, yes. We had become pals. Several times she came by here and I took her over to the clubhouse for drinks."

"She just stop by or what?"

"By invitation. I had met her when I was given a grand tour of Mallard and Bill some time ago. She ended up being my tour guide. We had a drink and it was pleasant but a little hectic so I asked her out here to see our clubhouse."

"When did you last see her?"

"Last night." He had hesitated. "Last night was one of the times she came by for a drink."

"At the clubhouse?"

"We came back here afterward."

"When did she leave?"

"I don't know." Jack looked from Cy to Phil and the macho look faded from his face. "I was asleep."

"Was that the first time she stayed?"

He shook his head.

"So it was an affair?"

"Of sorts. Driven by curiosity on both sides. Of course, we liked one another."

"Never quarreled or anything?"

"When there is a great disparity of age there is little to quarrel about, or to agree about, frankly." His shoulders slumped. "It was a damned foolish thing to get involved in."

Cy took him through every stage of his relationship with Agatha Rossner, the tour of the firm, the drink downstairs afterward, the mutual kidding that had proved to be a prelude to her coming by the condo, the visit to the clubhouse where he had displayed her as a kind of trophy, but Jack claimed to have been surprised when it went beyond drinks and talk. "I have always been the aggressor in such matters. Being seduced was a novelty. Before I realized she was serious, we were in bed." He looked agonizingly at Cy. "I hope to God none of this has to be made public."

The telephone rang and it was Jack's son Tim. After Jack hung up, he smiled ruefully. "He advised me to say nothing. That comes a little late. Since I have been forthcoming I hope you will do what you can to keep me out of this."

"Keep him out of it," Phil said as they walked to the car.

Cy got behind the wheel and paused before starting the engine. "He never once asked about the girl."

3

When Marie Murkin heard the news that a young woman's body had been found beside the road in a West End retirement development, she had no reason to think of it as anything different from the dozens of dreadful happenings with which the radio listener becomes acquainted over his toast and coffee. Murder, mayhem, rape, and bombings, are digested along with the morning meal and scarcely rise to the level of consciousness. Marie's antennae were sensitive enough but even she had become dulled over the years by the din of disaster with which her day began. But her head snapped up from her Wheaties when she heard "Western Sun Community." She sat with cocked head, chewing methodically, then shrugged it off. Later she would claim that she knew from the beginning that Jack Gallagher lived there and that all this had to do with him.

"Imagine his gall, suing Austin Rooney," she said later, when Phil Keegan stopped by.

Father Dowling and Phil turned to Marie when she made this remark. Phil Keegan had begun telling his old friend about the investigation that now occupied his detective division.

"That is a non sequitur, Marie."

"You bet it is. Almost Divine retribution."

The story Phil had come to tell was not exactly a logical sequence in itself. Things seemed to stick together and not stick together at the same time. The young woman, a Chicago attorney, had been found on the street not far from Jack Gallagher's condo. She had worked with a Loop firm in which Jack's daughter Colleen was a paralegal. Perhaps she was a friend of the daughter's?

"Pretty much the opposite."

"Have you talked with Colleen Gallagher?"

Phil made a face. "Not yet. She didn't come to work today."

Only when Marie was out of earshot did Phil let Father Dowling know the direction in which suspicion was tending to gather.

"Jack Gallagher!"

"Roger, the guy is a cool fish, no doubt about it. He owned up to things which turn out to be incriminating as can be. He was carrying on with that young woman. Cy hears that she was a woman who went after whatever she wanted, and she decided that Jack Gallagher was it. He paraded her around like the cock of the walk, and there is no doubt that it had been going on at least a week, hot and heavy. She stayed over at least twice, including last night. He claims he doesn't know when she left. But as far as we can tell, he was the last one to see her alive."

"But why would he do her physical harm?"

"Is there an alternative?"

The alternative seemed to be someone lurking around, waiting for her to appear. But why would anyone think that would be before full daylight?

"Somehow Jack Gallagher seems a feeble adversary for Austin Rooney. If he is embroiled in this, his suit against Austin will seem weaker than it did."

"He'll probably drop it."

Amos Cadbury stopped by at ten, on his way to his office. He was a good friend of Nathaniel Bill of Mallard and Bill, and learned that the young woman, Agatha, had been notorious in the firm. Not that Bill had heard this until after his young associate was dead. Amos tried hard for a delicate way to put it.

"She boasted of her conquests, Father. A staple of talk in the ladies' room was Agatha's daily bulletin of her activities. Apparently she was making a run of the Gallagher family."

"How so?"

"First it was the son, Timothy." Amos shook his head. "However flamboyant the father, Timothy Gallagher is the picture of rectitude. It would be dreadful if her claims to have had an affair with him should be publicized."

"But is it true?"

"Truth and publicity are strangers, Father. It wouldn't matter whether it was true if it became the subject of idle chatter."

"The only Gallagher I know is the daughter, Colleen."

"She is a paralegal at Mallard and Bill."

"And she plans to marry a man who was just recently made a partner in an unprecedentedly brief period."

Amos traced the line of his jaw with a manicured hand. "What is the young man's name?"

"Mario. Mario Liberati."

"Oh my."

"What?"

"One of Nathaniel's confidences was that they are letting Liberati go. Apparently he concealed from the firm his connections with underworld figures in Milwaukee. That is his native city. They will give the young man what Nathaniel referred to as a golden parachute, but he has been let go."

"What kind of connections with the underworld?"

"His sister is married to a man who has just been indicted on a drug count. By all reports, he is the head of the Milwaukee drug racket."

"Poor Colleen."

The two old friends sat in silence. Father Dowling longed for a return of the almost innocent shenanigans in which Jack Gallagher and Austin Rooney had been engaged. Folly is one thing, but murder quite another. The last time he and Amos had spoken, Father Dowling had told the attorney of the senior dance and all the events of that adventurous evening. Then, he had been anxious about bad publicity coming to the parish; now those events had sunk to the level of a playground quarrel.

"Do you think Gallagher will drop his suit against Rooney?"

"Why should he?"

"Phil Keegan is proceeding on the assumption that Jack Gallagher strangled that girl."

Amos thought about it. "Even so, he might find it difficult simply to walk away from that capricious undertaking."

"Surely you won't hinder him."

"I was thinking of Judge Bertha Farner. Whatever sympathies she might have felt for Jack Gallagher as the object of Rooney's assault, will be reversed when she learns the kind of Lothario he is."

"But surely that is irrelevant."

"Trial-procedure relevance is one thing, Father. But what a judge finds relevant in the privacy of her own mind is quite another thing. She is likely to want him to pay a price for bringing the suit before her when his own hands were tainted. Whether or not he is accused of the death of that young woman, I suspect Judge Farner will insist that the civil suit go forward."

"To what end?"

"If he loses, he will have to pay court costs."

"That's fairly vindictive, isn't it?"

"To Judge Farner, it might seem to be simple justice."

"Did you find Maud Gorman helpful when you deposed her?"

Amos immediately brightened. "That woman could be a female Dorian Gray. Somewhere there must be an image of her that is showing the ravages of time, but in person I found her the same delightful woman I knew at the country club years ago."

"Men find her attractive."

"Men." Amos shook her head. "It is demeaning that such a woman should be dragged into this ludicrous dispute."

"There are those who think she encourages attention."

"Nonsense. There are those who fail to understand the manners of such a lady. It is her femininity that is misunderstood. I doubt that any woman has been more willing to accept the gender God gave her than Maud." He paused. "She told me that 'Smoke Gets in Your Eyes' was sung that night. I am surprised it hasn't been embargoed in the current puritanical climate vis-à-vis tobacco."

It occurred to Father Dowling that, styles apart—as well, of course, as the object in view—there was some similarity between Maud Gorman and the predatory young woman Amos had described who now lay in the morgue.

4

In the Senior Center, Maud Gorman was being treated with awe and wariness. Her presence was acknowledged, but no one seemed willing to engage her in the ordinary sort of conversation that characterized the Center—no one but Austin Rooney, that is, and he was grateful to be able to speak with Maud without kibitzers.

"To think I actually danced with him," Maud said, shivering.

"This should put a stop to his effort to impoverish me."

"Would it have been so bad?"

"It would have been devastating if he had won. I think Amos Cadbury underestimates the resources of a lawyer like Tuttle."

"That a man should treat his brother-in-law like that."

"Are you referring to Jack or to me?"

"Oh, Austin." Maud laid a delicate hand on his sleeve. "Perhaps I shouldn't say it, but I was proud of you. Both times that you hit him.

You must realize that a lady is helpless if her partner refuses to acknowledge someone who wishes to cut in."

"I got his attention finally."

"Indeed you did." And she looked up at Austin as at a hero.

Austin had spoken to Maud obliquely of the mess Jack was apparently embroiled in. The old rake. Well, it would serve him right if his philandering brought his name into disrepute. Not that Maud could imagine him actually strangling the young woman. She could not imagine anyone strangling anyone else, for that matter.

"Would the two of you like to come to my office for tea?" Edna Hospers asked, appearing at their side.

"What a lovely idea!" Maud cried, turning as a flower turns to meet the sun. "I seem to be something of a pariah here this morning, heaven knows why."

"Celebrity comes in all forms," said Edna.

The office of the director had all the attractions of a legendary place to Maud. She had been there only once before, the other day, when she had spoken with Amos Cadbury. Of course, she had known the office as the principal's when she was a child.

"How I remember this place," Austin said.

"That's right," Edna said, busying herself with putting the water on. "You went to school here."

"This was the principal's office."

"No wonder I feel apprehensive," Maud said, making a little face. "Called to the principal's office."

Mrs. Hospers was warmer to Austin. Maud noticed that without concern; other women often were a little resentful of her. Perhaps that is why she felt more comfortable with men. The other day, when Amos Cadbury had asked her what had happened at the dance, Maud's mind had been flooded with memories of a better time, when Paul had been doing well and for several years they had belonged to the country club. Paul had golfed and played tennis and taken advantage of their membership but Maud had been content to sit in the shade at a table not far from the pool and read her magazine. Just being there had a significance she found it difficult to describe.

It was not that she had married down in marrying Paul—their backgrounds were similar—but their imaginations were poles apart. Maud had freely indulged the familiar fantasy that she was adopted and had fallen from a great social height. It was so much easier to accept her parents when she considered them as really strangers, good people who had undertaken to raise this daughter who had come from elsewhere. A few at the club, preeminently Amos Cadbury, had accepted her for her real and secret self. Paul hated to dance but Amos was a sure and graceful dancer and Maud had always been able to count on him as a partner at the weekend dances. Not that even he was allowed to monopolize her time. She was swept from partner to partner and sometimes the other couples watched as she was whirled around in the center of the floor. It was not unusual for there to be applause when the number ended. When Amos was her partner on such occasions, Maud allowed herself to entertain slightly subversive thoughts.

If her parents were not really her own, Paul could seem an almost imaginary husband. He was ensconced in the bar during dances and scarcely noticed how feted and petted she was. That she could think a man as proper and upstanding as Amos might dance her right out to his car and drive away with her into the unknown, was no doubt due to the exhilaration dancing gave her—or anything else that put her in the spotlight of attention. She could sense the resentment of the women, but that was a small penalty to pay for such attention. Such a feeling had come over her at the senior dance when she was in Jack Gallagher's arms.

It had thrilled her when he had ignored Austin's attempts to reclaim her. Of course he meant to keep her, he meant to take her away from the Center, from St. Hilary's, from Fox River, and . . . Her thoughts always grew fuzzy as her imagined self disappeared over the horizon with a man other than Paul. For the moment Austin Rooney was Paul, and Jack Gallagher was doing what she had always dreamed of Amos Cadbury doing. Secret thoughts, secret dreams. And now, when she heard of the life Jack Gallagher was leading, keeping a young woman in his apartment overnight . . . Well, it took her breath away. Now she could enjoy the thought that she had been rescued from a fate worse than death.

That side of her marriage had been forgettable. Paul did not have a romantic bone in his body. Of course there were children, but that was something that had occurred without Maud's mind being engaged. That she had grandchildren now was another of those incredible things you could not doubt, but which scarcely seemed real. With her granddaughters Maud felt almost like a contemporary and everyone raved at how well they got on.

"I don't know how much you two know of what has happened," Edna said.

"Only what I read in the papers."

"Pretend we know nothing, Edna," Maud cried. "Tell us everything."

"As far as one can tell, all this happened after the dance."

That was the sentence that burned itself into Maud's memory. Of course. That had been the reason Jack had decided to make a fool of himself with that young woman; it was a way of avenging himself. On Austin? Don't be foolish. It was not the blows he had received, the physical blows, but the fact that he had lost his chosen partner irrevocably and publicly. How could she not sympathize with his wounded pride? Austin and Edna went on about that poor young woman, as if she were the explanation. Maud sat with a little smile, inhabiting the world where she was queen, the still point around which the cosmos whirled.

"That must be a brutal way to die," Edna said.

"I wonder who killed her," Maud asked.

Edna Hospers and Austin just stared at her.

13

1

Colleen Gallagher did not go into work. She was up and dressed and ready to leave when she heard the news on the radio and stopped. My God. She was assailed by a flurry of dreadful thoughts. Last night she had been with Mario, commiserating over the injustice that had been done him by Mallard and Bill, and again Colleen had suggested he contact her brother Tim. He shook off the suggestion.

"I never thought I would be rethinking my life, but that's what I have to do."

"What do you mean?"

"Of course I am now back at square one. Only it is not as it was when I got out of law school. There were all those interviews and then the offer from Mallard and Bill. When I decided on that, the whole future seemed to fall into place."

Colleen was frightened. In the immediate aftermath of Mario's summons to the office of the founding partners, she had been prepared to release Mario from his commitment to her. But it was he who had brought it up and he had been so relieved when she simply dismissed the suggestion. But time had passed since then; time when not all his thoughts had been known to her. It went without saying that their marriage-preparation sessions with Father Dowling would have to be postponed. She was fearful now that Mario regarded the prospect of marriage in another light. And of course now he knew of her family.

Her family. That is when the dark thoughts began. Aggie's body had been found near her father's condo and of course that meant suspicion would turn on him. Aggie had been as bad as she claimed. Imagine, pursuing a man her father's age, a man who had always been vulnerable to flattery. He was only human to have succumbed to what Colleen was sure had been a deliberate and relentless campaign on Aggie's part. She remembered when her father had left Mallard and Bill with Aggie on his arm, and had thrown her a little smile that only she could have understood.

"It's all my fault," she said aloud. "I threw them together. I invited him to the office specifically so he could meet Aggie and talk sense into her about Tim."

She had reached the nadir of her fear and dread: Tim. Tim, who had once accused his own father because he had heard of his philandering at the station. It was all too easy to see whatever had happened at Western Sun Community as the sequel of that long-ago suspicion. Only this time the target was not Jack Gallagher.

The phone rang and she snatched it up, certain it was Mario, but it was Tim on the line.

"Have you heard?"

"Just now."

"I've canceled all my appointments in order to be with Dad. I couldn't talk to him when I called the condo because the police were with him so I am going out there."

"I'll come with you."

"No." A silence on the line. "I want to have a serious talk with him. I'll call you from there."

"As soon as you can."

"I have an errand to do first, but I'll call as soon as I can."

"Tim, what is going to happen?"

"Who knows? God, what a mess. Mario and I may be in the same spot before this is over."

He left her with that dismal thought when he hung up. She called Mario then, but he did not answer the phone. Normally at this time of day, he would be walking in the door at Mallard and Bill. But there would be no rush this morning. He could be still asleep or in the shower. Five minutes later he called her.

"Mario! I just telephoned your place."

"I'm on my cell phone. Are you going to work?"

"No."

"I didn't think so. I'd call in and leave a message, though. Can I come over now?"

"Of course."

"Good. That's where I'm headed."

Her earlier doubts fled and she was waiting expectantly when he rang the bell. She pulled open the door and then she was in his arms. Oh, thank God for him. Thank you, thank you, Saint Anne. She had not prayed that prayer in weeks, but it had been answered and was not rescinded.

"Colleen, what you have to do is avoid reporters."

"Reporters!"

"Think about it. They're bound to want to talk to you. You have to get out of here. Quick, pack some things and I'll take you to a motel."

"A motel?"

"There's one in Fox River where we have had conferences. The Hacienda Motel. That way you'll be near your dad and no one will be able to find you."

She realized how much she had wanted someone to tell her what to do. She ran into the bedroom, got a small suitcase out of the closet, and began to pack.

"I'm going to steal a cup of your coffee," Mario called.

"Of course. Go ahead."

She packed only casual things; what she was wearing would be nice enough for—She stopped the thought. For what? Did she think she and Mario would be enjoying candlelit dinners at a time like this? She was going into hiding to avoid the press. This thought spurred her on, and in several minutes she emerged with her suitcase. Mario grinned.

"Did you have that packed and ready to go?"

"Ha."

He took the suitcase. Colleen slung her computer bag over her shoulder, picked up her purse, and followed Mario down the back stairs to the garage and then outside where his car was waiting. Colleen began to believe that she really was being pursued by vultures of the press who would dig up every humiliating thing they could to add spice to their stories about Aggie's death.

"Of course they'll talk to the girls in the office." She had pulled the door shut but Mario cursed his frosted windshield and then got out to scrape it clear. When he slipped behind the wheel, she mentioned the girls at the office again.

"If I know Mallard and Bill, they will have forbidden everybody to speak to the press."

"Isn't this ironic, after the fuss about your brother-in-law?"

"I am trying to think of that as liberation. Do you know what suddenly occurred to me last night? A lifetime at Mallard and Bill would have been stultifying. We'll come up with something far more exciting and interesting."

She huddled against him as he maneuvered toward the side street and then found the expressway that would take them west to Fox River. Alone, she had been so full of dread and apprehension—and she still was, but it was different now that she had the reassuring presence of Mario. He had never seemed more confident and sure, and he could believe that the tragedy at Mallard and Bill was no longer the devastating rejection it had seemed at first. Of course, it would be necessary for him to get past it and face the suddenly redefined future.

When he turned off the expressway, which had been cleared of snow by highway crews, they came onto roads that required more driving skill. Colleen remembered the Hacienda Motel. She had not attended the conferences the firm had held here, but she had been in on the preparations. Only lawyers had been involved, of course. It was when Mario pulled into the parking lot and stopped that Colleen was suddenly overwhelmed by what had happened.

"Poor Aggie," she cried, and then she began to sob helplessly, finally finding an object for her grief and anxiety.

"She was heading for a fall." But he took her in his arms and comforted her. Aggie was now beyond any human appraisal of her life.

"May she rest in peace," Colleen murmured.

"Amen."

Inside, he took a seat as she registered and then rose to go with her to her room. When the door of the unit was shut behind them, he said, "This place is as nice as I remember it."

A sudden thought gripped Colleen. "Did Aggie attend that conference?"

"Not that one. Not everyone did. Albert Fremont was here." That thought reminded Mario of the eminence from which he had fallen, and a shadow passed across his face.

"Tim called," Colleen said.

"Has he talked with your father?"

"He was on his way to the condo."

"Colleen, if it comes to that, and your father needs an attorney . . ."

"Oh, Mario." And once more she was in his arms.

It was a dangerous moment. She had seldom felt so vulnerable, and here they were in a motel room alone, unbeknownst to anyone. But Mario was stronger than she was and he released her. He picked up a packet of matches with the motel number on it.

"You just stay put. I'll keep in touch." At the door he paused. "Better not call anyone, Colleen." He hesitated again. "Or if you do, don't mention where you are. That would defeat the purpose."

"Bless you."

This almost surprised him. "You too."

And then he was gone.

2

When Peanuts had been woken at his vigil by the arrival of his cohorts, having slept through the arrival of the paramedics, his first thought had been to get the hell out of there. His second had been to let Tuttle know that something was up; maybe he thought this had been the purpose of the stakeout. But Tuttle had had to get the news of what had happened from police radio. Tuttle was not really surprised that his almost autistic friend really hadn't had the faintest idea that the body of a young woman had been found only twenty yards from where he had been parked in the unmarked vehicle from the Fox River Police Department. The one thing Peanuts was sure of was that he had not had an adequate night's rest.

"I gotta get some sleep."

"Aren't you on duty today?"

"I can rest up in the newsroom."

"Keep your ears open, Peanuts."

"While I'm sleeping?"

Tuttle wasn't sure that one's ears closed while one slept. If they did, Peanuts never would have been roused and got out of the stake-out. After a suitable interval, Tuttle drove out to the scene of the crime with one thought succeeding another in his mind. A picture of the young woman on television made clear who she was—the girl Tuttle had met in the clubhouse when he had showed up with Jack Gallagher's neighbor Isabel. She was also the girl Tuttle had seen go into Jack's apartment, and had not emerged by one o'clock when Peanuts came to relieve him.

"There's a woman in there with him, Peanuts," Tuttle had said.

"Who?"

"It doesn't matter. What matters is when she comes out."

But the significance of this had been lost on Peanuts, who probably had fallen asleep as soon as Tuttle drove off. Now Tuttle wished he had given Peanuts daytime duty and reserved the nights for himself.

Where the body had been found was staked off and there was a uniformed officer on duty. Tuttle got out of his car and sauntered over to the cop.

"Tuttle," he said, tipping his tweed hat.

"Who?"

"I am Jack Gallagher's lawyer."

This failed to impress the officer. Peanuts might be on the bottom rung of the force but there were others not much higher.

"Quite a mess," Tuttle said, looking at all those footprints in the snowy interior of the marked-off area.

"I don't know anything about it."

Tuttle left him. The scene of the crime had been trampled all to hell. Not much would be learned from it. As he headed for the door of Isabel Ritchie, snow began to fall again. Great. At least it wasn't a thaw. Tuttle rapped on Isabel's door.

"Just a few questions, ma'am."

"Oh, it's you. I have only just now learned what has been going on beyond my pulled drapes." She let Tuttle in. There was the aroma of coffee in the apartment.

"That smells good."

"Would you like a cup?"

"Absolutely. What have you heard?"

"They keep mentioning Jack but that's ridiculous. Apparently this woman wasn't his niece."

"Is that so?"

"So what does she have to do with Jack?"

"Good question. I gather you didn't hear anything."

"No." She seemed indignant that Jack Gallagher's name would be associated with anything unsavory. Well, what is there to hear when a woman is being strangled? Tuttle opened his coat and loosened his scarf.

"Would you like milk and sugar?"

"I would." The coffee was that bad. "Jack had a lot of visitors this morning?"

"The police have been pestering him, of course."

"It was the girl we met at the clubhouse, sitting with Jack."

"But the girl they found wasn't his niece."

"I thought you saw her picture on television."

"That was some lawyer from Chicago."

It was too bad for Jack that there weren't more Isabels in the world. But others who had seen the girl at the clubhouse would know that the story of her being Jack's niece was bunk. Tuttle was in a difficult spot ethically, you might say. He had been keeping a watch on his client so as not to be surprised by anything Amos Cadbury might come up with as to Jack's character. What Tuttle had seen was damaging to his client, not to say demolishing. Big Bertha would have Jack's scalp if she learned that the plaintiff was leading a life of dissolution and vice.

Tuttle himself was scandalized by Jack's behavior. It was one thing for an old man to get a kick out of having a few laughs with a young woman, a drink or two, but it was pretty clear Jack had been shacking up with her. Now he was the bull's-eye of the investigation into the death of Agatha Rossner. The woman had spent the night, or a good part of it, with Jack. Her body was found almost outside his door. And then Tuttle remembered the little sports car. She had arrived in that last night but she sure hadn't left in it. She had left in the meat wagon on the way to the morgue. In his pocket Tuttle had a notebook in which he had scribbled the license-plate number of the little car. Finding out about that seemed more important right now than paying a call on Jack. What could Jack tell him but a bunch of lies? Tuttle had no desire to tell his client that he knew all about it. But that little car bothered him.

After he drank half a cup of what Isabel had the nerve to call coffee, he got to his feet.

"No rest for the wicked."

"Are you going to call on Jack?"

"Not right away."

After he got outside, he sidled toward his car, half fearing that he would be noticed and Jack Gallagher would call his name. But he was ignored, or at least unsummoned. He drove downtown and found Peanuts, out like a light in the pressroom.

"A favor."

"Go away."

"After you do me this favor."

"What is it?"

Tuttle gave Peanuts the license-plate number. "Do a check on this plate for me."

Grumbling, Peanuts toddled off. Mendel took notice of Tuttle.

"You going to drop that suit now, Tuttle?"

"What's the latest on the body found out at Western Sun?"

"She's dead."

"I wondered about that."

"Jack Gallagher won't wiggle out of this one."

"How much does the *Trib* carry in libel insurance?"

"I can wait for the indictment."

"How's the novel going?"

Mendel glared at him. It was clear that he regretted the day he had confided his literary ambitions to Tuttle. "The chapter in which you appear has bogged down."

"Ha. You got any portions I can read?"

"If you can't read, what do you care?"

"I think of you as catapulted out of here into sudden fame, the toast of the town, all that. 'Local Scribe Hits Best-seller List.' "

That Mendel was driven by such dreams was clear from the anger he showed. "Go to hell, Tuttle."

"Will your novel be on sale there?"

Peanuts came back and handed Tuttle a printout. The little lawyer folded it twice and put it in his pocket.

"What's that?" Mendel asked.

"A letter from my editor about my novel."

"Get out of here."

The car was registered to Agatha at an address on the near North Side. Well, why not? There were times when following whim and caprice was the reasonable thing to do.

One look at the street lined solidly with parked cars told Tuttle that any resident who counted on finding an open space when he needed it was an idiot. Agatha had been a lawyer, therefore she wasn't an idiot. He drove around until he saw Kopcinski's parking garage. He pulled in and flashed a badge Peanuts had purloined for him. He then held up the printout on which he had circled the plate number. The badge had come and gone but the printout bore the heading of the Fox River Police Department.

"You guys always check out one another?" the attendant asked.

"How long ago was my colleague here?"

"I don't know. Earlier."

"Big guy, linebacker type, face like a blank page?"

"That's him." That would be Cy Horvath.

"Have they taken the vehicle away yet?"

The kid had never learned how to tie a necktie. It hung like a noose down the front of his wrinkled shirt, which was visible because his leather jacket was unzipped.

"You ought to zip up. You'll catch cold."

The kid bent over to look at his fly.

Tuttle drove in and found the little car. It looked like it had been through a car wash. The doors were locked and there was nothing particularly interesting visible inside the vehicle.

On his way out Tuttle called to the necktie, "We'll be back for it."

Where to now? For some reason, he still did not want to see his client. These recent events might have shaken Jack Gallagher's eagerness to take Austin Rooney to court. Back to headquarters again, where he would try to pick Cy Horvath's brain, if he could get at it through his thick Hungarian skull.

3

Amos Cadbury was obviously disturbed when he came into the sacristy after Father Dowling's noon Mass, his second visit of the day. He stood just inside the door while Father Dowling took off the vestments and the old gent who had served as altar boy puttered about. Obviously Amos wanted to speak in private and Roger had little doubt what it was about. There seemed to be only one topic now, St. Hilary's pulled into it by Jack Gallagher's suit against Austin Rooney. But things had gone far beyond a tiff at a dance. Jack Gallagher was the prime suspect in the death of Agatha Rossner.

"I'm surprised he hasn't been arrested," Amos confided as they walked to the rectory for lunch. Then silence, as if the attorney remembered that even birds have ears.

Of course Amos had demurred when Roger invited him to lunch and of course Roger had insisted; but it was the suggestion that Marie Murkin would be abject if she knew he had come to the sacristy to talk with the pastor and then had not accompanied him to lunch that tipped the scales. Marie's cooking skills were largely wasted on Roger Dowling, who ate whatever she served, and preferred little rather than much and simple rather than complicated. Nonetheless, Marie always outdid herself at noon in the hope that he would bring someone back for lunch, preferably a trencherman like Phil Keegan, who was a man worth cooking for, though Marie would never have told him so. The spare and spartan Amos Cadbury had the look of a third-order Carthusian but Marie had found his weakness when he stopped for tea. Her buttered scones had melted whatever resistance he had. Her pineapple upside-down cake had elicited an almost tearful remembrance of his mother, as he devoured two slices. How Marie's heart must have leapt when she saw Father Dowling bringing Amos Cadbury along the path from the church. Not for nothing had she labored over her consommé, and the risotto with peas and mushrooms met even Marie's own exacting standards.

When they came into the kitchen Amos stopped, closed his eyes, and breathed deeply. Marie beamed but then shooed them into the dining room. "You'll want to hurry with the soup because the risotto is almost ready."

"Risotto," Amos sighed, passing into the dining room.

There is a time to speak and a time to eat, and for Amos the time to eat took precedence over what he had come to say. Father Dowling finished his soup and had a few dabs of the risotto, almost regretting that when Amos finished off the rest with sighs and exclamations. Marie had poured him a glass of Chianti.

"Father Dowling, I think I have a vocation. Do you have an extra room here?"

"There are seminaries for delayed vocations, Amos."

" 'Delayed'? In my case, it would be 'surpassed.' Not that I ever aspired . . ."

"I understand."

"Marie," the gallant lawyer said, and then gestured speechlessly his appreciation of the marvelous meal.

"Would you care for another glass of wine?"

"No, thank you. One is enough to speak the truth."

Marie withdrew and Amos lifted his brows in a question. Here or in the study? Father Dowling decided on the study. Marie, flattered to death, would be sure to eavesdrop on their conversation, if only to see if praise for her cooking continued in her absence.

When they were in the pastor's study, Father Dowling told Amos the latest he had heard from his friends in the Detective Division. It was of course Amos's expectation that Jack would drop his suit against Austin Rooney now that greater difficulties were upon him.

"Let me tell you what I know, Amos."

Phil had told Father Dowling of Cy Horvath's dogged pursuit. While the snowy conditions of the crime area did not offer much help, there was the undeniable fact that the young woman's body had been found there, but how had she got there? The guard in the shack had told Cy that on at least one other occasion when he was on duty the young woman had arrived in a very attractive-looking car, small, sporty, expensive. He would have noticed the car even if it had not been driven by such a gorgeous woman.

"She said she was here to see Jack Gallagher. They don't have to tell me why they come. Not a visitor like that. I am there to keep the riffraff out."

Cy woke up Rawley, the night guard, and asked about the make of the vehicle, trying to get more specific, but already it was specific enough to know that no such automobile had been around that morning. Rawley thought he had seen the car go out the gate. He knew he had seen it enter earlier.

Rawley's facial hair seemed to have been cleared away just enough for his eyes to see and a little bulb of a nose to show through the thatch. The mouth was never in evidence, but there was an undulating movement of whiskers and a voice came from somewhere.

"I'm positive. She got here about seven, seven-thirty."

"In her car."

"The Alfa Romeo." A laugh struggled through the hair. "What a brand! That should be Jack Gallagher's, not the lady's; for her, Alfa Juliet maybe."

Cy became interested in this walking argument for razor blades.

What did Rawley do before he guarded gates? He had been an accountant on the local campus of the state university, beginning on day one the campus opened. If he was retired, why was he still working? "You ever hear of a rolling stone gathering no moss?"

Cy was tempted to allude to the growth on what must have been Rawley's face. He did ask him if he had worn it that way when he worked at the university.

"I was clean as a baby's buns, so to speak. The day I walked out of there I quit shaving."

"You ever know a Professor Rooney?"

"Austin? My last task, I helped him figure out his retirement. They offer the faculty so many variations that they could grow old deciding among them."

"You heard he popped Jack Gallagher?"

"I envy him. Know what Gallagher calls me? Snuffy. You remember Snuffy Smith?"

Resentment in the guard house.

"You sure you saw her car leave?"

Rawley's eyes bulged. "My God, that's right. She was in no condition to drive."

"You didn't notice who was driving it?"

"It was already through the entrance when I noticed it."

Cy and Phil had already located the dead woman's car in Kopcinski's Parking on the North Side.

"Apparently it had been taken through a car wash before being put into its place in the garage, Amos."

"They can check on that."

"Phil put Agnes Lamb on it, but he doubts she'll find anything. There are too many self-serve car washes."

"Self-serving" had once been the name of a vice; now it was a pillar of the economy.

Amos pondered this, then said: "Obviously whoever it was knew where her garage was and her parking space in it."

The car had not been seen entering, but the recent car wash made it clear it had not been there all night.

"So she drove to the Western Sun development."

Phil had held up a hand when Father Dowling had said this. "Or was driven. Remember, this is Cy Horvath, who jumps at no conclusions. She could have been taken there in her own car and dumped in the snow. There's something else."

"What?"

"Her car keys were in the purse found at the scene."

When Father Dowling relayed all this to Amos, it was clear that most of it was news to the lawyer. It was the fact that suspicion had fallen on Jack Gallagher that intrigued Amos.

"The missing car is a tribute to Cy's thoroughness, but I don't think that Jack Gallagher can count on the police investigation to remove him from suspicion."

Father Dowling tried to imagine Jack following the young woman out of his apartment and then strangling her in the street. As if reading his thoughts, Amos said, "He could have dragged the body there. Pulling it down his glazed walkway and leaving it in the snow would not have taxed his physical strength."

"Dear God."

"Father, I must confess that I was one of the dedicated devotees of Jack Gallagher's show." A little pink showed on Amos's cheeks as he continued. "I found his chatter annoying, the heavy breathing and insinuating tone, as if he were making love to his audience, but the music he played more than made up for that. If he had not implicated the parish, I don't think I could have taken the role of his adversary."

Amos had now reached a surprising decision. He wanted to put his firm at Jack Gallagher's disposal if and when an arrest was made.

"I have a young man who is excellent in that regard."

"That is very generous of you, Amos."

"Of course, it may not come to that. In the event of his arrest, I will demand that Tuttle withdraw the suit and attempt to placate Judge Farner."

While Amos was still with Father Dowling the call from Phil Keegan came.

"We brought Gallagher downtown for questioning, mostly because reporters were beginning to grumble that favoritism was being shown to a onetime celebrity. Just routine. Except for one thing."

Phil fell silent.

"What is the one thing?"

"Jack Gallagher has confessed to killing the woman."

1

Jane Gallagher, with Tim off to work and the kids put on the school bus, returned to her kitchen and the cup of coffee that was usually the best one of the day, but not this morning. She had hesitated about letting the children go to school, fearful of their grandfather's plight being known to the other kids, but Tim had dismissed this. He had flown in early that morning and come home to shower and change. Fresh clothes and a shower and he was ready for the day, no matter how little sleep he could have caught on the red eye from wherever. She had given up trying to keep track of his business trips.

"The teachers may know, but they aren't likely to say anything."

"Tim, what is going to happen?"

"God only knows."

"I can't believe that your father would get involved with a woman that age."

He held her and kissed her forehead and told her he would be in touch. Sipping her coffee, Jane considered the events of the past week which had completely altered her impression of the father-in-law she had thought she knew. Jack Gallagher, after he became a widower, had been an unusual grandfather, playing the role as if it were just that, a role. Imagine Jack Gallagher a grandfather. Jane's parents had been fans of Jack's and he had been something of a legend when she and

Tim married, his presence all but eclipsing the bridal party, somewhat to Tim's annoyance.

"Imagine what he would be like if he were famous for something important."

But the day had been far from spoiled, she had laughed and danced and wept, she and Colleen crying like schoolgirls before she went off to the airport with Tim and the flight to the Cayman Islands. Tim's success had lifted them out of their former surroundings and there were new friends and activities, but Jane had always remained close to Colleen, watching with apprehension as the years passed and Colleen remained unmarried. Of course she was a whiz at what she did, but did she want to be a paralegal all her life? And then she had met Mario Liberati.

Jane had liked Mario instantly and told Colleen how wise she had been to wait for Mr. Right. Had it been even a month since she and Tim had met Mario? Since then the world seemed to have fallen down around Jane's ears. The absurdity of Jack's getting into a fight over a woman with Uncle Austin at a dance for old people at St. Hilary's parish was the beginning. As far as Jane knew, the woman was as old as Jack and Austin. Something Tim had said then came back to her now.

"Old or young, it doesn't matter to him. He's like Don Giovanni. As long as they wear a skirt . . ." He actually sang a few bars of Leporello's aria. How like his father he was, despite the undertow of animosity between the two men. With Aggie, Jack had apparently turned once more to the young.

That the woman was younger than herself gave Jane a creepy feeling. Jack had always been affectionate with her. He liked to have his arm around a woman, he liked to punctuate his talk with little kisses on her hair; sometimes she thought he was trying to annoy Tim, as apparently he had annoyed Austin. But with a man that age, and a man who was her father-in-law, it would have been ridiculous to take offense.

"Don't encourage him," Tim said once, ambiguously. Had he meant being too ready to listen to his father's reminiscing, or his playful displays of affection? Jane had liked the thought of her husband as jealous, however innocent the cause.

That morning second thoughts came. The young woman had stayed overnight with Jack before; presumably that had been the case last night as well. Jane had always assumed that with age people got over that sort of thing.

"He must be on Viagra," Tim growled.

Mornings had always been cherished by Jane. As soon as the kids had begun school, her house became in a special way her own. All day long, she could enjoy it. She was forever redecorating, imagining how a room could be more attractive, rearranging. But mainly just enjoying it. But this morning she did not want to be alone. Not that she could have been comfortable with any of her friends. What she needed was family. Colleen.

Good God—Colleen. How awful for her, with the dead woman a lawyer employed at Mallard and Bill. All this on top of the dreadful news Tim had told her before changing to begin a new day.

"Mallard and Bill have canned Mario."

"What? I thought he was their star."

"So he was. But it seems his sister is married into the mob in Milwaukee."

"Can they let a man go for that?"

"Image, my dear. Image. Of course he will be said to have resigned, and he will be more than amply compensated for the inconvenience. Nonetheless he will be out on the street. Of course, if he had mentioned it in the interview or on his application he never would have been hired."

How casually he took all this. The world in which Tim lived was ruthless, people rose and fell, but the march went on, the stragglers shot like those on Napoleon's retreat from Moscow. One of Jane's secret daytime vices was to watch videos on the VCR. She had just finished for the second time Anthony Hopkins in *War and Peace*, a wonderful movie despite the fact that Natasha looked old enough to be Pierre's mother. Jane had been reminded of the description of the little woman over whom Austin and Jack had quarreled at the dance. Now she thought of Mario, propped against a tree and, as the column moved on, the crack of a rifle. Could such an imposing and intelligent man be put out on the street for such a reason?

Her hand had gone to the phone and now she dialed Colleen's number, half reluctantly. She had to speak to her and yet she dreaded it. The phone rang and rang and then the recorded message came on. But at the sound of the beep, Jane said nothing, putting the phone back in its cradle. She was in the den, trying to decide between *Pride and Prejudice* and *Emma*, passports into the eighteenth century and out of her present concerns, when the phone rang.

"Jane?" It was Colleen!

"Colleen, I just called you but I didn't leave a message. Where are you?"

"In hiding. Mario wanted me to be out of reach of reporters."

"Are you at his place?"

"No! I'm in a motel."

This seemed an unnecessary precaution. What possibility was there that reporters would seek out the daughter of a man perhaps implicated in an incident in Fox River?

"Colleen, you should come here. You can be sure I wouldn't let any reporters in."

"Well, I'm here now. Jane, isn't this awful?"

"Tim told me about Mario."

"Don't worry about Mario."

"Has he really been let go?"

"Yes. I think he is already getting used to the idea."

"Colleen, tell me about this woman."

Colleen's account was given in angry tones. "I know I should speak well of the dead, and may she rest in peace, but Jane, she was dreadful. One of those women who imagine men are making conquests right and left and figures she has to do the same. And then brags about it. She was notorious at the firm, holding court in the ladies' room where she recounted her latest victim."

"But a man your father's age!"

"Jane, I blame myself for that. I invited Dad down to see the offices—he had never been there—and he met her. She actually walked off with him on her arm, but fool that I am, I didn't suspect a thing. I suppose his age added spice to it."

"And his name."

"She hadn't known about his career."

"But he would have told her."

Colleen laughed but it was not a happy laugh. "When I think that if I had not asked him to the office and he had not met Aggie, none of this would have happened."

"You don't think your father killed her?"

"Jane, I don't know. I just don't know. Suddenly everyone seems to be a stranger, not at all what I thought they were."

"Oh, Colleen, I wish you were here," Jane said at the sound of Colleen crying into the phone. Had Mario's connections in Milwaukee come as a surprise to Colleen as well? The poor girl. Jane's heart went out to her. Mario could handle this, men can, but Colleen, for all her success in the workplace, had never lost her feminine softness.

"I talked to Tim about Mario."

"I know."

"I mean about another job."

"Tim said this morning that the two of them may be in the same boat with your father in the news this way."

There was a ringing on the other line and Jane asked Colleen to hold. It was Tim.

"My father has confessed."

"Confessed?"

"He said he killed that woman."

"Oh my God. Where are you?"

"On my way to police headquarters." Tim made an angry noise. "Why couldn't he keep his mouth shut? He should have had counsel."

After Tim hung up, Jane hesitated before going back to Colleen. It seemed awful that she should be the one to tell Colleen this. She inhaled deeply and pressed the button.

"That was Tim. Colleen, brace yourself."

"What is it?"

"Your father has confessed."

"Oh my God."

"Colleen, just stay on the line. We'll talk. You don't want to be all alone in a motel room now. Tell me where you are."

"Jane, it doesn't matter."

"Can you come here?"

"I better not stay on the line. Mario may call."

With great reluctance Jane hung up. The sense that the world was giving way beneath her feet increased.

2

There was a convergence of lawyers at police headquarters. Tuttle learned that Tim Gallagher was already there, as well as Mario Liberati, the hotshot courtroom performer from Chicago, when he asked to see his client.

"Get in line."

That was when he heard that Tim Gallagher and Mario Liberati were in conference with Jack. Tuttle debated the wisdom of joining the party. It had its attractions, just walking in there and taking Jack's hand in his. The faded celebrity should know that his dollar had bought him the loyal services of Tuttle no matter what developed. On the other hand, Tim Gallagher might take that amiss. He could guess what the son had said when he heard his father had put himself into Tuttle's hands in the Austin Rooney matter. Tuttle sat and pulled his tweed hat over his eyes, his thinking cap, his lucky Irish tweed. But he did not pull it so low that he did not see Amos Cadbury enter. He felt the patrician eyes on him and awaited some scathing remark. But when he tipped back his head slightly, he saw Amos being admitted to the conference room. Tuttle felt like a little boy with his face pressed against the candy store window. The fight at St. Hilary's had promised weeks of publicity, and now with Jack confessing to murder, Tuttle would fight any effort to keep him out of it. The thought of himself, Tim Gallagher, and Mario Liberati as the defense team had the promise of the O. J. Simpson trial; Tuttle did not care if he were cast in the role of the schlemiel who hit the prosecution witnesses with every dirty trick in the book.

"Tuttle?"

Tuttle pushed back his hat to see Skinner before him. "What's going on?"

"I am pondering the defense strategy."

"You're still his lawyer?"

Tuttle didn't like the implications of the question, but then Skinner had put him on to a good thing, a good thing that now seemed to be slipping from his grasp.

"I've been assigned the case," the assistant prosecutor said. There was triumph on Skinner's narrow face but his next remark did not seem to bolster it. "Everyone else begged off when they heard that Amos Cadbury will be involved."

"Let's go to your office."

And off they went, two men low on their respective career ladders, but Skinner with a better chance of rising.

"I think we've got the bastard this time," Skinner said without preamble as he scooted behind his desk and sat. Tuttle saw in the mien of the prosecutor all the professors and devisors of bar exams who had tried to keep him from fulfilling his father's dream of having a son as lawyer.

"My client?"

"Surely you jest, Tuttle. Step one is they will have you dropped as counsel. In any case, you were not hired to defend Jack Gallagher from a charge of murder."

"Murder?"

"Murder one, or my name isn't Flavius."

Tuttle had wondered what the *F* stood for. "You're confident of your case?"

Listening to Flavius Skinner lay it out, Tuttle had to agree that Jack Gallagher was in an unenviable position.

"Item: He has been engaged in hanky panky with the deceased. Item: He has a reputation for inciting violence and being involved in same."

"Rooney knocked him on his ass."

"With provocation. Believe me, I know the type. The first blow is often a matter of body language."

This was a phrase with which Tuttle had often had difficulties. Stomach rumblings, belches, other unmentionable gaseous emissions had an arguable claim to be called body language. But that is not what Skinner meant. Turns of the head, unreadable gestures, posture, and movements of the limbs had a lesser claim on the label "language." Whatever else, Tuttle thought such extrapolations had only dubious grounding in the law.

"Item: The woman is known to have spent that last night, or a significant portion thereof, with Jack Gallagher. Item: She is found strangled on his doorstep. And item the last: The son of a bitch has confessed."

"I wonder why?"

"What?"

"Why would any sane man confess to a murder while the investigation is still under way?"

"How about because he's guilty and knows that he is cornered?"

"That's a possibility."

"It's a reality." Skinner sought and found, then flourished, a sheaf of paper. "This is his confession."

"You sound confident."

Apparent agreement subdued Skinner. "My question is, why has all this high-caliber legal talent rallied to his defense?"

Tuttle knew the feeling. For a week he had been imagining himself in the pit of the court, matched against Amos Cadbury. But Skinner would face Amos and Mario Liberati, to say nothing of the son, Timothy Gallagher.

"Well, I wish you luck."

"I need your help."

"You have the whole Detective Division at your beck and call."

Skinner emitted a barking laugh. "They don't really believe what Jack Gallagher has told them."

"I wonder why."

"You know why, Tuttle. They are the establishment and they have decided that Jack Gallagher is one of their own."

Different juices began to flow in the slumped figure of Tuttle. Skinner was appealing to him as underdog, not a bad idea, given his status in the local bar. Cadbury's bar. More than once the paragon of legal rectitude had sought to disbar Tuttle, failing each time for reasons Tuttle ascribed to his father's interventions from the next world. Tuttle *père* had not scrimped and saved and sacrificed to see his son at last a lawyer only to be driven forth from the professional status he had won.

"So what do you want?"

"What do you have on Gallagher? I know you and Pianone have had him under surveillance."

"Peanuts is a member of the Detective Division."

"And your bosom buddy. I know all about it. One or both of you were there last night, weren't you? You saw what went on."

"Peanuts told you this?" Tuttle knew this to be impossible.

"I will call you as a witness."

"I'll save you the embarrassment. I was not on stakeout last night."

"So it was Peanuts?"

"You want to put Peanuts on the stand?"

Skinner paled at the prospect. "Whose side are you on, Tuttle?"

"That depends."

"Aha."

Tuttle saw Skinner as his darker self, a zealot who thought he was interested in justice but was really driven by the basest of motives.

"Let me ask you this, Flavius. Do you think Gallagher would have been arrested and indicted if he hadn't confessed?"

"You don't?"

"Not on what they have so far."

"Have you talked with Pianone?"

"Anything he might have told me would be confidential."

"What do you want, Tuttle?"

"I haven't heard an offer yet."

They hammered one out in the next twenty minutes. Tuttle would be hired as special counsel, and investigator, for the prosecutor's office. Peanuts was already ex officio on Skinner's side. The fee proposed would have to be approved by the prosecutor.

"I'll be waiting to hear."

"Tuttle, this is a done deal."

"Sure it is. When it's done."

The air outside Skinner's office seemed more breathable. Jack Gallagher might be guilty as sin but a prosecutor like Skinner could make any jury sympathetic to the accused.

"He should have been a hangman," Tuttle concluded. "But he probably would have made a slipknot for a noose."

3

Marie Murkin was astonished by Amos Cadbury's decision to switch allegiance and become, if not Jack Gallagher's attorney, a member of the team that would defend him when he was brought to trial, having confessed to the murder of Agatha Rossner.

"He told me he was a fan of Jack's, Marie," explained Father Dowling.

"Then why did he agree to defend Austin Rooney?"

"Because he thought the parish was implicated."

Marie pondered that. More puzzling than Amos Cadbury was Father Dowling. Did he really think a confessed murderer should get off scot-free because of legal shenanigans? Not that she thought Amos capable of them, but as far as she had heard, he would not actually question witnesses or address the court or jury. But his presence would have a tremendous value for that rake Jack Gallagher.

"I wonder what Austin Rooney will make of it?"

"He probably will take it as a sign that he no longer needs a lawyer."

Marie decided on a tour of the school, not one she would call an inspection tour, not out loud anyway, but there was no harm in keeping alive the realization that the dance Edna had agreed to had been a mistake. A case could be made that, if the dance had not taken place, well . . .

The activity in the gymnasium gave no indication that the men and women there were aware of the day's news, or concerned with it if they were. Self-absorption is the mark of age, of course, aches and pains riveting one's attention on oneself. Not that many aches or pains were in evidence here. A cry went up as a small slam was made at a bridge table, and several people converged on the triumphant pair, who were only too happy to review the bidding, the play, the outcome. Among them were Maud Gorman and Desmond O'Toole, Desmond very much in possession of the clinging Maud. Marie joined the happy throng.

"I don't believe a word of it," Desmond replied, when Marie motioned him away from the table and asked what he thought of his friend Jack Gallagher. Of course Maud floated along with him.

"You don't!"

"A man that age with a mere girl? Impossible."

On his arm, Maud dropped her eyes and simulated a blush. Desmond patted her arm and said, "It's compensation for what happened here."

"I don't understand."

"It will all come out." He looked knowingly at Marie, then protectively at Maud.

Desmond O'Toole was a fool, of course. He reminded Marie of those who claimed the moon landing was a trick of photography not an actual space journey. Would he have to catch Jack in flagrant delight, or whatever it was, before he believed him? The police certainly believed him. More importantly, Amos Cadbury did. He would not be offering Jack his legal services if he thought it was a mere misunderstanding.

Marie went slowly up the school staircase, trying not to double over to make the ascent easier. Then she thought of Edna, bouncing up and down these stairs dozens of times a day. Her chin lifted, she smiled grimly, and moved swiftly upward, ignoring her creaking joints. Sometimes, climbing the stairs to her apartment, she stopped halfway and rested. No need to rush when no one could see her.

Edna Hospers, at least, had been flabbergasted by the news of the day. "Marie, I am so glad to see you."

This was unusual warmth, and Marie basked in it, taking a chair and regaining her breath.

"I didn't want to talk to any of my wards about it. If Austin Rooney had come in today, I could have talked to him, but the rest . . ."

"Are playing bridge and spooning."

"Spooning?"

"I just talked to Desmond and Maud. Desmond thinks it is a publicity trick on Jack Gallagher's part."

"Some publicity."

"I suppose he means being irresistible to a woman young enough to be his granddaughter."

"I keep thinking of her lying there in the snow . . ."

It occurred to Marie that the events recalled dark moments in Edna's life, before she had come to work in the parish, when her husband had come under just such a suspicion.

"Austin actually met the dead woman once."

"He did?"

"I don't know what the occasion was. I think he met her through his nephew."

"He must have meant *niece*. Colleen Gallagher works in the same law firm as the dead woman."

"I thought he said nephew," Edna said testily.

Marie let it go. Why argue when you know you're right?

It had not been much of a tour of inspection. When she got back to the rectory she found Father Dowling getting ready to go out.

"I am going downtown to talk with Jack Gallagher."

"I'd like to give him a good talking-to myself."

"Marie, try to think of him as innocent. At least until he's proven guilty."

"He's already admitted it!"

"That's one reason I want to talk to him."

15

1

Harry Paquette was taken into custody in Kansas City and would be returned to Fox River in two days. It seemed that Harry Paquette, not Lloyd Danielson, was his real name, the latter having been invented in Minneapolis. Apparently he had no wish to fight extradition, if that right had been explained to him. Coming when it did, this seemed more of a nuisance than a breakthrough, at least to Phil Keegan, but Cy had grown tired of the ceremonial treatment of Jack Gallagher. It was hard to take such a man seriously, no doubt about it, but confessing to murder is a serious thing. Skinner was inspired.

"There can't be this prolonged and unlimited access, Captain," the assistant prosecutor complained. "I'll want him ready for court in the morning."

"No need to hurry."

"Was his confession coerced?"

"Far from it."

"Was it explained to him that he had a right to a lawyer's presence?"

"He said he didn't need a lawyer to tell him what he had done."

Of the lawyers Jack had seen since, his son Timothy was understandably more shaken by his father's confession. Cy had heard of the episode in Jack's office during his heyday, when his brother-in-law had given him a beating. All in all, the Gallaghers were a combative family, including in-laws. It was not every day that you get a retired professor hauled in because he had thrown a punch at someone, but Austin Rooney had laid Jack Gallagher low twice in the same night. Their family reunions must be interesting. But so far, Jack had been receiving rather than giving punches, so his claim to be a murderer was a quantum leap.

"Why would you kill her?" Cy had asked.

"She wouldn't let me alone."

"Come on."

Jack lifted one eyebrow. "That was not a macho remark. This was a very odd young woman. She literally picked me up the first time we met, dragging me off for a drink, and the next thing I knew she was spending the night with me. A little bit of that goes a long way, at my age, and I don't particularly like a woman who is the aggressor. It saps one's manhood. I told her as gently as I could that this had to stop. I expected tears, the usual thing, but her reaction came as a shock."

"What was it?"

"She threatened to accuse me of sexually abusing her!" But his indignation faded into a wry smile. "I told her that was *my* complaint against *her*."

"So you killed her."

"It's a little more complicated than that."

"We've got time."

"She got dressed, there was a very chilly exchange in the living room, then she strode out the door, leaving it open. That's when I noticed she had left her scarf. I ran after her, in robe and slippers, with the scarf in my hand. She turned and saw me and immediately began to scream. I was trying to shut her up."

"With the scarf."

"It showed why I had followed her, I wrapped it around her neck, so she would understand. But she twisted away and began screaming again. Well, you know the rest."

"And you just left her there?"

"I panicked. I ran back to the house and stood in my doorway. Suddenly I became aware that the neighborhood was quiet as the grave. No one had noticed the scene in the street. I shut the door, made a drink and waited for morning. That is when you and Captain Keegan came."

A confession is not enough in itself. The case still has to be proved, even if it is like doing a math problem when you know the answer you're supposed to get.

"What do you think, Cy?"

"Quite a story."

"He sort of comes out as the victim, doesn't he?"

Cy could imagine the defense, the put-upon elderly man, the ravenous sex-mad young professional woman, him succumbing once or twice, then trying to escape her clutches. Her screaming reaction to Jack's chivalrous return of her scarf might rouse all the residents in Western Sun. The strangling came through as almost inadvertent, more the girl's fault than his.

"Women," Phil said, shaking his head.

Cy stared after Phil Keegan as he went down the hall to his office.

"Horvath!" Skinner approached with his head thrust forward, as if he were on a scent. "Guess what? Big Bertha has been assigned to this case."

"Gallagher isn't even indicted yet."

"This deal had to be worked out. The judge had been looking forward to chastising Austin Rooney. If that suit is dropped, she drops out of the spotlight." Skinner rolled his eyes at the folly of man, or of woman, in this instance.

"You think that will help you."

"On this issue she could be a hanging judge."

"She bulges here and there too."

Skinner was shocked. His own cynicism was part of the job description, but he retained a simple faith that police were neutral, partisans only of justice.

"I mean, if she was ready to lay it to Rooney and judge in favor of Gallagher, her sympathies may already be engaged."

"In a murder trial?"

"Manslaughter at best, Skinner. You should listen to Gallagher's confession. If the girl had survived, she would be on trial for leading him up the garden path."

Skinner dismissed this as facetious but he was flustered. He had envisioned months, years, of work ahead of him. The trial, conviction, appeals, the death sentence, at which point he would put to the test the governor's moratorium on the death penalty. How can you put a moratorium on the law?

Skinner scooted away in quest of the transcript of Gallagher's statement. He would have to wait in line to see the suspect. Jack was still in conference with his legal team.

"The scheme team," Tuttle muttered, when Cy found him in the press room. The intrepid representatives of a free press had taken notice of the lieutenant's entrance.

"The man suspected of shoving Linda Hopkins into traffic has been apprehended in Kansas City and is on his way here."

Blank looks.

"The woman who was killed on Dirksen a couple weeks ago."

Annoyed expressions.

"What do you have on Gallagher, Horvath?"

Mendel and his colleagues had begun a drumbeat of criticism about Linda Hopkins's death, demanding that the fiend who had done it be found. But the tide of history had passed on, and their discontent now had a different object.

Tuttle followed Cy out of the press room. "You caught the guy, eh?"

"The Kansas City police did."

"You were the only one who really gave a damn about it."

It was that kind of day. Faint praise from Tuttle was gratifying. Keegan hadn't been much more excited than the reporters. One piece of luck: Skinner would be occupied if they could make a case against Harry Paquette.

"When you tell him he has a right to a lawyer, give him my name," Tuttle said.

"Has Gallagher let you go?"

Tuttle pushed back his hat and scratched his forehead. "He will."

2

Thank God she had brought her computer. Otherwise Colleen would have gone stir-crazy in the Hacienda Motel. She had talked to Jane and that had helped, and of course Mario had called.

"Your father's confession is not as bad as it could be. Maybe he did better not to have legal advice when he talked to the police."

She listened as he told her how self-servingly her father had incriminated himself. Why did she think that Mario sounded as if he were throwing himself on his sword only as a dramatic gesture meant to draw attention to the incomparable Jack Gallagher?

"How are you doing, Colleen?"

"I was just going to check my e-mail."

"Have you talked to anyone?"

"Jane."

A pause. "Did you tell her where you are?"

"Just a motel."

"I'll call again in an hour or so."

When he hung up, the room seemed to close in on her. Room? It was a suite, almost as large as her father's condo. She looked at the great gray eye of the television. There was another set overlooking the bed. She had no desire to let in the outside world that would be babbling about what her father had done. At the desk she turned on her computer and, while it booted up, thought of all the work she would have been engaged in at Mallard and Bill. But how could she have thrown herself into it when Mario would not be there? Albert Fremont had been told to take over what Mario was working on. It could have been worse; it could have been Aggie. She logged on and called up her e-mail. Halfway down the list was a message titled "Cheers." She called it up.

Have a date with Dad. Cheers.

Unsigned, but of course the address of the sender was at the top of the screen: AGATHA ROSSNER, ESQ. And then she saw that it had been copied to Tim as well, at his office.

Colleen stared at the little line of vindictive words. For the moment she forgot that Aggie was dead. She thought only of the office sex symbol, the body with brains, taunting a daughter and son that she was going to see their father that night. The message had been sent the previous day in midafternoon. What would she have done if she had read Aggie's message yesterday?

But yesterday seemed ages ago. The author of the message was dead. Colleen's father had confessed that he had strangled her. How could such a confession not be bad?

She switched to the home page of Mallard and Bill. After the name of the firm, in Gothic script, the next item was a page of thumbnail photographs of the members of the firm. Clicking on any one of them would enlarge it to screen size. She clicked on Mario's photograph and her screen was filled with his face. It was all she could do not to kiss it—a virtual kiss.

There was a tap on the door and Colleen froze. She went back to the page of thumbnails and listened. Another tap and then a key in the door.

"Who is it?"

The door opened and a black woman in chambermaid uniform looked in.

"Housekeeping, ma'am. Everything all right here? Towels . . ."

"Oh, just fine. Thank you. I only now checked in."

The woman stepped inside, keeping one crepe-soled shoe in the door. "It's a slow day today. Not much going on at all."

"That's fine with me."

"Me too." The name tag on her ample bosom said RUBY, HEAD HOUSEKEEPER. She noticed Colleen noticing.

"You're in charge of rooms?"

"Keeper of heads, as my husband says. He was in the Navy. Where 'head' means bathroom?"

"The law firm I work for has held conferences in this motel."

"We get lots of professional people. Doctors, lawyers, beauticians, accountants . . ." Her voice slowed as she ticked off the litany. "A local firm?"

"Chicago. Mallard and Bill."

Just talking to someone was a relief, and she hadn't been here two hours. Mentioning the name of the firm to the head housekeeper didn't matter.

"I think I remember that name."

They looked at one another, then Ruby smiled. "Well, honey, I better get on with my appointed rounds."

The door closed shut. Crossing the room, Colleen's image was played back from half a dozen mirrors. *What am I doing here? Why am I in hiding?* Mario's plan had seemed to make sense earlier; she had willingly surrendered herself to his notion that she had to be put out of the reach of reporters. Now she felt in exile.

3

Descriptions and pictures of the wanted always made them seem larger than life, objects of universal pursuit, but in person they were just the usual losers who showed up on the wrong side of the law. Harry Paquette wore jeans and new cowboy boots he wasn't accustomed to yet, and his jacket hung open as if he defied the weather to cool his T-shirted chest. He hardly glanced at Cy when he took custody of him from the officers who had been sent to Kansas City to fetch him.

"Had anything to eat?"

"I'm hungry."

"Come on." He took him to the commissary after he had stowed the cuffs and leg irons in which Harry had been transported. The prisoner's step became more jaunty as they went down the hallway, as jaunty as was possible with the new boots.

"You get those in Kansas City?"

"I always wanted a pair."

"Never wore them."

"They take getting used to."

"The high heels go with your ponytail."

Harry gave him a look. His thin hair was skinned back over his narrow head and gathered in the back in what could be called a ponytail.

"You know when men began wearing short hair?"

"At birth?"

"Men, not babies."

This seemed to matter to the prisoner. For most of world history, men had worn their hair unshorn. Haircuts were a sign of the coming End. Harry had read it somewhere.

"Take Samson."

They were at the commissary and Cy led the way in. This was calculated in a way; he wanted to gain the confidence of the man he had been pursuing since the day Linda Hopkins got pushed into traffic on Dirksen. Cy could imagine him doing that. But then he could imagine lots of people doing it.

Harry filled up his tray as if this were going to be his last meal.

Cy said nothing. He settled for coffee and lemon meringue pie. "I've had lunch."

"Don't ever get arrested in Kansas City," Harry advised.

"I'll remember that."

"The food?" He made a gagging sound.

After they sat at a table, Harry went to work on the food he had taken. The guy didn't have a pound on him yet he ate like a horse. Pippen came in, looked around, and then her face lit up when she saw Cy. He motioned her over.

"This is Harry."

"Hi, Harry." She put out her hand.

"Mine's all greasy."

Cy said, "Have you done the autopsy on the girl?"

Harry stopped eating, and looked furtively at Cy and Dr. Pippen. Cy looked at Dr. Pippen. It was difficult not to. He would have asked her anything just to have her stay and talk.

"Let me get some coffee first."

"I'll get it for you."

"Oh, would you? I've been on my feet for hours."

She was deep in conversation with Harry when Cy got back. Harry was looking at her hair as he told her how recently it had been that men had cut their hair. She gave Cy a guarded look when he sat across from her again.

"She was strangled," Dr. Pippen began without preamble. "But then we already knew that. Her stomach was almost empty but she had been drinking. She looked to have been in remarkable health."

"Who was strangled?" Harry asked, licking his fingers. Would he want to shake Pippen's hand now?

"It's another case." Cy said.

"Another?"

Cy decided not to spoil his rapport with Harry by telling Pippen who he was and what he was accused of. Pippen yawned.

"I didn't get a wink last night."

"Don't ever get arrested in Kansas City," Harry told her.

She looked at him, startled.

"Noisiest jail I was ever in."

She decided to leave that alone, now that she understood Harry's status. She yawned again deeply, as if giving an advertisement for perfect teeth, front to back.

"I am going home and get some sleep." She stood and gave Cy the smile that tested his marital fidelity. But she was an all-American girl, a cheerleader type, clean as a whistle. Cy wondered if she realized how beautiful she was. She turned to Harry. "I'll remember that about Kansas City."

"She a doctor?" Harry asked, watching her leave.

"Assistant coroner."

Harry shook his head. Once men start cutting their hair, anything can happen.

When they were sitting in the interrogation room, with a stenographer present, Harry said, "It was the bank account, wasn't it?"

"Bank account?"

"The one I opened at the First Fox River."

"You left town without your money?"

"I beat it in only what I was wearing. You think I was going to stick around after what happened? Of course I left town."

"Well, I don't blame you."

"This is why."

" 'This.' "

"As soon as you found I had a record I'd be sitting in a room like this. I couldn't face that, not then." He shook his head. "One look at her and I knew she was gone."

"Harry, you have a right to a lawyer."

"What do I want a lawyer for?"

"You know why you were arrested in Kansas City and brought back here."

"Yeah, but I didn't do it. Not that I expect you to believe me."

"There is a lawyer in the building who would be willing to represent you."

"I told you, I'm innocent."

"Everybody is innocent until proven guilty." And those proved guilty went on claiming to be innocent. Probably some of them were. But most of them?

"Let me see if that lawyer is still around."

Tuttle was in the press room sipping coffee from a Styrofoam cup as if he were testing it for poison.

"I've got a client for you," Cy said.

Tuttle was on his feet. "Who?"

"The guy who pushed the girl into traffic."

Tuttle made a face.

"Don't worry. He just told me he's innocent."

They went back to the interrogation room and Cy asked the stenographer to read back what had been said so far. Tuttle sat straighter at the mention of the lawyer. "Tuttle is the name." They shook hands, after which Tuttle looked at his, then took out his handkerchief to clean it.

"I'll just go ahead, okay?" Cy said.

Tuttle bobbed his head.

Cy read to Harry highlights of the record of the investigation that had been conducted. Harry lowered his head as the description of the girl's body was read. Cy gave the original statements of witnesses—no point in mentioning that most of them had waffled later. Once they got a look at Harry their memories would be refreshed. Harry kept shaking his head.

"That's bull. Nobody saw me do that, because I didn't do it. I was coming toward her, we had agreed to meet there, and she turned and saw me coming. The expression on her face . . ." He stopped and then a great sob escaped him. "Oh God, God, God."

"Just tell it in your own words," Tuttle said.

"Why would you meet there?" Cy asked.

"That's the corner the bank is on. The First Fox River."

"You weren't going to rob it?" Tuttle cried.

"I had an account there. I was going to turn it into a joint account, that's why I told her to meet me on that corner."

"You were approaching the girl," Cy said.

"And then some guy came out of the crowd and pushed her. She was still looking at me when she fell." Again he stopped. This time his shoulders and chest heaved, but there was no sobbing.

"Did you recognize the man?"

"He was just some guy."

"Would you recognize him if you saw him again?"

"I don't know. It happened so fast."

"How was he dressed?"

Harry's eyes were swimming with tears. "I don't know. Like you, I guess."

"Wearing a suit?"

"He had a coat on too. And he wore a hat. A cap."

"He was a workingman?"

"No, it wasn't that kind of a cap."

Cy turned to Tuttle. "I can't get the witnesses down here until tomorrow. Right now I'd like to take Harry out to the Hacienda Motel."

"That's where she worked," Harry said to Tuttle.

"You've no objections to going out there, Harry?" Tuttle asked.

"Would it matter if I did?"

"I don't think it will do you any harm."

Harry needed the men's room and Cy had an officer take him away. Tuttle looked at Cy. "He's going to be something when he takes the stand."

4

Amos Cadbury had never practiced criminal law, and after some hours with Jack Gallagher, young Gallagher, and Mario Liberati, he thanked God for it. He preferred a world in which there were written contracts and the quarrel was over the meaning and application of carefully chosen words. Jack Gallagher was a flowing fountain of words—but such words. They could mean anything and everything. In the time since making his confession to the police, he had amended it time and again orally, discussing the events with his son and Mario Liberati, who was, Amos learned, also to be a son-in-law of the mellifluous patriarch. That voice brought back to Amos his love-hate feelings for Jack Gallagher's radio program. It had been the music he loved, but to hear it he had to listen to the breathy inanities of the host. Here there was no music as compensation for the voice.

"What do you think, Mr. Cadbury?" Liberati asked him when they had taken a break from the discussion.

"Did I understand aright that you are going to marry Jack Gallagher's daughter?"

"Yes."

Amos consulted the ceiling. "That makes his defense team seem a trifle incestuous. There is a young man in my firm . . ."

Liberati shook his head. "There is no law against having a relative defend you. It is true that it is not smiled upon in the profession because of the seeming lack of the objectivity a good defense requires. Jack Gallagher is my fiancée's father, but he is, for all that, a stranger to me. The courtroom is my forte, Mr. Cadbury."

"With Mallard and Bill?"

"I'm leaving there."

"That surprises me," Amos said diplomatically. "I should have thought it was a coup to be taken on there."

"It has its negative side as well. The young woman who was killed worked there too."

Amos had heard ad nauseam how Agatha Rossner had pursued Jack Gallagher with all the tenacity of the figures on Keats's Grecian urn, with the roles reversed, of course. *Forever she pursues and he pursued.* Her behavior, if accurately portrayed, gave a somewhat different image of Mallard and Bill than the one Amos had always had.

"Whatever the wisdom of representing him, Jack is fortunate in his son and soon-to-be son-in-law."

He decided against rejoining the discussion. He'd had all of Jack Gallagher that he could take for now. Returning to his office was equally unattractive. The workday had been ruined by this turn of events and he would get precious little of consequence done if he returned to his office. On the steps of the courthouse, Amos set his black homburg firmly on his head, buttoned his overcoat with its astrakhan collar, and looked out at Fox River. He had been practicing law here for nearly fifty years, since his graduation from the Notre Dame law school. He had seen the city grow and prosper and in recent years had watched a seeming reversal of that. It is not easy for a small city to retain its identity with the megalopolis of Chicago reaching out to digest it and turn it into a mere suburb. This would have affected his status if it had happened earlier, when he was younger.

His decision to begin a practice in Fox River had been deliberate. He had never really liked Chicago. A very large city attracts the worst as well as the best, and the good are affected by both, perhaps more by the former. Fox River had been a Norman Rockwell setting half a century ago, before the Pianones had made their iniquitous presence felt. His parish, St. Hilary's, had been made up of hundreds and hundreds of families, young people starting out in life, those of middle age who were well-established. Neither a workingman's nor a professional's parish, but both, melded into a community of believers. Kneeling together at Mass of a Sunday, their differences in education and income evaporated. But like the city, the parish had changed. For all that, in some perverse way he preferred it now, doubtless because of the pastor Roger Dowling.

He had walked to the courthouse from his office, the exercise evoking an earlier time when he had been perforce a pedestrian. Now he was driven wherever he went. But what was the radical difference between Amos Cadbury young and Amos Cadbury old? He had tasted too deeply of success to have any illusions about it. When Mrs. Cadbury died he had gone through a period that friends had described as depression but which he himself had thought of as a time of great lucidity. The death of his wife had brought back the kind of thoughts he had not indulged since he was an undergraduate. What does it all mean? Where are we hurrying with such single-mindedness? Now that Catherine's life span was closed, with a beginning, middle, and end, he had wondered at what point he was on the allotted span. The thought of returning to his practice and concentrating once more on the moment as if it bore some significant relation to the future was repellent. *"What does it profit a man if he gain the whole world and suffer the loss of his own soul?"* Amos felt that he had delivered himself over to a routine whose main advantage was that it diverted his mind from more serious matters. It was at that time Roger Dowling had been made pastor of St. Hilary's, replacing a line of friars who, whatever their avoirdupois, had a lean and hungry look when they greeted the affluent Amos Cadbury. How could he have spoken to such men of the condition of his soul? They would have recommended an increase in his financial support of the parish, perhaps of their order as well. Father Dowling had understood.

"We are brought low for a purpose, Mr. Cadbury." They were then on a quite formal level, of course, despite the matter that Amos had come to speak with Father Dowling about.

In the course of their meetings Father Dowling had told Amos his own story. The stellar career in the seminary, being sent away to study canon law, returning to play a major part on the archdiocesan rota, the presumption by everyone, including himself, that one day he would be named auxiliary bishop and eventually go on to his own diocese. But the work he did had pressed heavily upon him. In those days—better days, as Amos now thought—it had been almost impossible to have a marriage annulled, yet day after day Roger Dowling had reviewed applications for declarations that a marriage was null and void, that in effect it had never taken place. The anguish of dealing with people who had come to the point of wanting to discard their past without being able to assure them that this was possible became too much for the young canon lawyer. An evening drink with colleagues, to relieve the tension of the day, became supplemented by another in his rooms. And another. Soon he was in the grips of drink and it became necessary for him to receive medical attention. His clerical career was over.

"I thank God daily for that, Mr. Cadbury. To be sent here has meant that at last I can do what I was ordained a priest to do. I have stopped thinking of life as going anywhere."

"I don't understand."

"Don't you imagine some future time as the culmination of all your efforts?"

"I suppose I do."

"The culmination of our efforts is today. It is *how* we do what we do, and *why*, not what."

There was more, much of it obscure to Amos, but he had found a kindred soul. Reflecting on his conversations with Father Dowling, he had remembered things he had known from childhood—known but not known. The grace of the present moment. The sudden realization of the sense of the Gospel passage, "Thou fool, this night thy soul will be required of thee." Soon Amos was back in his office, his practice continued to flourish, and now he had become the dean of the Fox River bar. He was conscious of the honor shown him, but within himself he knew that in and of itself it did not mean a thing.

These memories prompted Amos to hail a cab and give the address of the St. Hilary rectory, hoping he was not abusing Father Dowling's hospitality. He had always allowed a decent interlude between visits, but today . . . He might have walked a few blocks to his office and made use of his driver, but taking a cab had some obscure significance that he welcomed. Would Father Dowling be at home? Would he be free? Amos left all this in the hands of God. And God was good.

"Amos, what a delightful surprise." But the pastor did not seem really surprised to see him yet again.

"I have spent much of the day with Jack Gallagher."

"Say no more. I will have Marie prepare tea for you."

And Mrs. Murkin's delicious tea was brought, with buttered scones, toast, and strawberry jam, and Amos was thankful that he had obeyed the impulse of the moment.

"Jack Gallagher has confessed?" Father Dowling asked.

"In a manner of speaking."

"How so?"

"There are ways of taking blame which have the effect, perhaps the intent, of exonerating the one confessing."

"You must have eavesdropped in the confessional."

Amos threw up his hands in shock. "Good heavens, no. Sometimes I have left a confessional because the person on the other side was audible."

"I only meant that there are penitents like that."

"I doubt that anyone would describe Jack Gallagher as a penitent. I rather think he is enjoying this."

"It's a somewhat dangerous enjoyment, isn't it? Saying he killed that young woman."

"Oh, there are legal ways of negating that folly."

"The deed or the admission?"

"Young Timothy Gallagher is a most impressive lawyer. And a man named Mario Liberati, lately of Mallard and Bill, is also advising him."

"He will marry Jack's daughter Colleen."

"So you know that."

"Amos, do you think it possible that this confession is meant to shield someone else?"

Amos smiled. "Very perceptive, Father. I must say that criminal law is not something with which I am experienced. But I have observed human nature over many years. The very insouciance with which Jack speaks of his guilt suggests he doesn't feel any at all. So, of two possibilities, one: either he did it and is so morally blind that he feels no guilt, or two: he did not do it, and saying he did cannot make him guilty of it."

"Phil Keegan is impatient with such a suggestion. He is understandably content to have the crime and its solution be all but simultaneous."

"A confession does not absolve him of the need to provide the prosecutor with independent evidence. No judge would allow anyone to plead guilty to such a charge. It will have to be proven pretty much as it would if he had not confessed. Let us hope that all plausible avenues of explanation will be explored."

The tea things were taken away. Amos very much wanted a cigar but would not light one now, as the pleasurable enjoyment of a cigar takes more time than he would inflict on Father Dowling.

"Could I use your phone to call a cab, Father?"

"A cab?"

"That is how I came. There is a taxi stand just in front of the courthouse."

The cab was called, Amos bade adieu to his old friend and, in the backseat of the jolting cab, felt that he was doing penance for indulging himself in his unscheduled visit to St. Hilary's.

5

Phil insisted that Cy bring an officer with him if he was taking the prisoner to the Hacienda Motel, given Harry's status.

"How about Peanuts?"

"You're kidding. Take someone else too."

"Tuttle is coming along. Harry has become his client."

Phil Keegan moved things around on his desk as if he were losing at checkers. He almost agreed that Cy didn't need any backup. Still, even Phil would have reacted if he had seen Tuttle and Peanuts go off in one car, and Cy in another with Harry in the passenger seat beside him and Agnes Lamb riding shotgun in the backseat.

"Why would anyone push that girl into oncoming traffic, Harry?"

"I told you I didn't do it."

"I meant anybody else," Cy said.

"The guy who did it, you mean. Who knows? There are a lot of weirdos in the world."

Cy said, "A cop doesn't like to admit that things just happen, no reason. Our work is based on cause-and-effect. Something bad happens and we have to find out who did it. Lots of times we don't find out, but we still think someone did it, that the effect had a cause. Even weirdos have to have reasons."

"Weirdo reasons."

"Maybe." Silence. "Tell me about the bank account."

Harry looked as if he now regretted having told Cy of his big surprise for Linda. He had been putting away a little now, a little then, and the balance had reached a point where he could show it to her and say, "Now we can get married."

"I checked it out," Cy said.

"You think I'd lie about a thing like that?"

Harry had opened a bank account, the day after Linda told him that the only way they could live together was if they were married. There was a balance of $1,289. "I was going to tell her when it went over a thousand. When it got there, I was going for fifteen hundred but then I couldn't wait. I wanted her to know that I was serious. If I hadn't decided to tell her . . ."

Causes and effects. Cy was beginning to believe Harry—against his better judgment. Harry had been in and out of reform schools, jails, and one prison, and would have learned the art of ingratiating himself with his captors, only Cy didn't think Harry was trying to convince him of anything.

"One thing's for sure, if they put me away for that, which I didn't do, I'd almost welcome it. I was like a lost soul in Kansas City. Stupid temporary jobs. When I knew you were after me, I was glad. You think I'm not sorry I didn't just stay here, no matter what. Running off like that . . ."

* * *

Mr. Lawrence Wagner was the assistant manager of Hacienda Motel. His eyes swept over the party: Peanuts, Tuttle, Agnes Lamb, Harry, and Cy Horvath.

"This way, please."

Down a corridor, through double doors marked STAFF ONLY, another corridor, and then a festive scene, lunchtime for the housekeepers. Wagner left them, his unsavory duty done. Cy motioned to Ruby.

"What is this, an arrest?" That got a big laugh but then Ruby saw Harry.

"You!"

"Hi, Ruby."

"I hope they put you away forever, I hope they hang you or sizzle you or whatever they do." Suddenly she rushed at Harry and began to pound on his bony chest.

Cy took her arms. "Take it easy. We're still trying to find out if he did anything."

A sullen Peanuts was looking around at the housekeepers with discomfort. It was as if he faced a roomful of Agnes Lambs.

" 'Did anything'! Do you know what she looked like afterward, Harry? You didn't stick around to find out, but I'll tell you what she looked like after several cars ran over her body." She tried to get free of Cy and her voice rose to an hysterical pitch. The others in the room looked on with stoic calm.

Cy told Tuttle to keep an eye on his client and led Ruby to a chair in the corner of the room, where she calmed down. "Seeing him again," she said, shaking her head. "Just go on with what you're doing," she called to her crew. "The fun's over."

"Ruby, he says he didn't do it." He held up his hand to stop her reaction. "Pretend, okay? Harry doesn't exist. Linda is pushed into traffic to her death. It could be a freak or it could be intentional. Who could have intended it if not Harry?"

"I don't know. There's nobody else."

"It was a man."

"It was Harry."

"You mentioned men who stayed at the hotel who were interested in her."

"They were just jollying her."

Ruby had told him this before, but now she refused to entertain the idea that anyone other than Harry could have killed Linda.

The other housekeepers left. Tuttle brought Harry back, Peanuts shuffling behind. Harry's eyes were red. Ruby found this disgusting. Agnes Lamb just took it all in. "Come down here where she worked and bawl like a baby. You're trying to bawl your way right out of this, but you can't fool me."

Harry just looked at her.

Cy had parked near the east wing of the motel because that is where the help ate and showered and had their lockers. Peanuts, Tuttle, and Harry went outside. Ruby was now talking of the Jack Gallagher confession.

"I should be working on that," Cy said.

Ruby leaned toward him. "His daughter's here. To keep out of the way of the press."

"The daughter?"

"Colleen Gallagher. She checked in this morning."

"Thanks, Ruby, I wanted you to see that we found him."

"Hang him high."

Outside, he said to Peanuts, "You're all going back in this one car. Agnes and I are sticking around. Tuttle, I remand Harry to your custody—meaning I'll kill you if anything goes wrong. Peanuts, if he tries to run, shoot him. Harry, if you run away I'll come after you personally. Everybody understand?"

Three heads nodded. Peanuts put the car in gear and rolled across the parking lot for the exit. Cy went back inside and found Ruby sitting at the empty table, staring into her cup of coffee. Agnes was sitting beside her.

"What unit is Colleen Gallagher in?"

Ruby refused to go with him, since then the girl would know who had told Cy she was there.

"Stay with her, Agnes."

There was no answer to the first knock on the door, nor to the second, though he stepped back to give Colleen Gallagher a look at him through the hole in the door. Then he went into the lobby and phoned her room from a house phone.

"Lieutenant Cy Horvath of the Fox River Police Department. There are no reporters in view."

"Who told you I was here?"

"I was in the motel on another matter. Can I talk with you?"

After a long silence she said reluctantly, "All right."

She had activated every security device the hotel provided, lock, bolt, and chain, and undid them as if she were the ghost of Christmas Past.

"I'm Horvath."

"What 'other business'?"

It seemed as good as any other way to break the ice. "Remember that girl who was pushed into traffic on Dirksen drive and died a horrible death?"

Colleen Gallagher shivered. "What has that got to do with the motel?"

"She worked here. In housekeeping."

"Good Lord."

"Her boyfriend has been sent back from Kansas City. I just presented him to the staff and got him away before there was a lynching."

"Did he do it?"

"He says he didn't. I am beginning to believe him. Which creates a problem."

"Would you like coffee? I can make it right here."

"If you want some. You brought your computer?"

"Thank God." She had begun the process of making coffee, filling the pot, putting in the little packet of coffee. Throwing the switch. "A motel room is a pretty boring place."

"Nothing on television?"

"Ugh. What problem were you referring to?"

"If he didn't do it, someone else did."

"How do you go about discovering a thing like that?"

"I come to where she worked and ask who else she knew, who else might have had any reason to do such a thing."

"And?"

"Nothing much. The best I can come up with are the people who stayed here, or came for conferences, and showed an interest in her."

"That sounds pretty far-fetched."

"It is." The coffee was already burbling into the little pot. "That's some screen-saver you have on your computer."

"It's a standard one."

Geometrical figures formed and morphed and fused on the screen, in a continuous pageant of pointless motion. She tapped a button and the screen changed.

"Who are those people?"

"That's the Web site of the firm I worked for, Mallard and Bill. In the Loop."

"Where Agatha Rossner worked."

"Whatever my father says, I am sure he didn't kill Aggie."

"He says he did."

"My father says lots of things, sometimes just for effect."

"Well, it's the same principle."

She looked at him questioningly.

"If he didn't do it we have to find someone who did."

"She didn't have many friends."

"You mean women friends."

"Any friends. Men didn't *like* her, they were mesmerized."

Cy got up and looked at the computer screen. As he did so, the pictures disappeared and the screen-saver began to swirl again.

"Press any key."

This brought back the pictures. She told him these were the lawyers at Mallard and Bill.

"I don't see you."

"I'm a paralegal. A lower form of life."

"Who's this?"

"My fiancé. Click on it and it enlarges."

Cy did this. "What's his name?"

"Mario Liberati."

"He's been with your father most of the day."

"I know. It was his idea that I hole up here."

"Well, it worked."

Again she looked at him.

"No reporters."

"Just cops."

But she said it with a smile. Cy was used to the fact that people felt at ease with him. Give him a minute or two and people thought he was a cousin or a big brother.

"Who do you think killed Aggie?"

"I could have."

"Did you?"

"Of course not. All I meant is, I had motive."

"She was flirting with your fiancé?"

"She tried to, before we were engaged. Mario can't stand her."

There was a tap on the door. Cy lifted a hand and went to the door and looked through the viewer. Then he opened the door. It was Ruby and Agnes.

"Is this man bothering you?" Ruby asked with a big smile.

"I'm glad for the company."

"Watch him, he's sly." But Ruby was looking at the monitor screen. "I know him."

"That's my fiancé. Mario Liberati."

"You are a lucky woman. He's been here in the motel, at conferences. Know what he said to me? When his mother came to this country she did the kind of work I do. Now she's gone back to the old country."

"Maybe you can end up the same way," Cy said.

"The old country? Not me, no sir. No way, José." She glanced at Agnes. "Never. I like it right here in the good old racist U.S.A."

"Do you get chummy with all the guests, Ruby?"

"He got chummy with me. Big-shot lawyer and plain as can be."

Colleen beamed at this testimonial to her fiancé.

Cy, at the computer, backed it up to the page where all the firm's lawyers were shown. "Take a look at these, Ruby."

"That's the girl, isn't it?" Ruby turned away. "The one who was strangled."

"Take a look at the others. They've all been at conferences here."

But Ruby had backed away to the door. When she was gone, Agnes going with her, Colleen said, "I checked my e-mail at the office." When he said nothing, she went on. She sat at the computer and tapped a few keys, then said, "Read this."

Cy bent over the machine and read the line that had appeared. *Have a date with Dad. Cheers.* He looked at Colleen.

"It's from Aggie, as you can see from the top of the message."

Cy saw that. He also saw that the message had been copied to Timothy Gallagher.

1

Rawley had shampooed his beard and it looked even fuller than usual. His eyes were bright with the terrible happenings at Western Sun as he talked with George Hessian.

"The guy who killed her must have driven right past the shack, not a foot or two from me, when he escaped, and all I saw was the back end of the car as it turned into the street."

"How can you know a thing like that?"

"It was her car."

George Hessian groaned. No need to ask who "her" was. Rawley had degenerated into a Kierkegaardian aesthete, carrying on an imaginary affair with the young woman who came to see Jack Gallagher. There was something unsavory about Rawley's description of the lissom way in which the young woman walked from her little car to the door of Gallagher's apartment, of the sight of the two of them, December and May, going arm in arm through the snow toward the distant glow of the clubhouse lights. There is a second adolescence as well as a second childhood.

"But Jack Gallagher has confessed to killing her."

Rawley's eyes crinkled and several teeth appeared in a separation of whiskers. He was smiling. "An attempt to grab center stage."

"That's crazy."

But there was something wistful in Rawley's tone, as if Gallagher had beaten him to the punch. But Rawley's facial hair was back in its accustomed arrangement and his eyes no longer glittered. Indeed, they became moist.

"Till my dying day I will think of her, lying out there in the snow, perhaps still alive, while I sat in my snug little guard shack, reading."

Of course it would be only imaginatively that Rawley would write himself into the unfolding drama. Still, it was an eerie thought, the one who might have strangled the girl using her car for his getaway, driving within inches of Rawley.

"Did you wave?"

"I did. After the car had gone by. He couldn't have seen it."

If George Hessian had world enough, and time, he might have listened to Rawley reenact what had and had not happened. There was the unstated implication that somehow his *amour fou* for the girl had placed her in danger, jeopardized her life, somehow led to her death by strangulation.

" 'In vain does the watchman watch . . . ' " George murmured, but he could not remember the words of the psalm.

"Indeed, indeed. I had come to regard this job as a joke. Gate guard! The only thing that menaces the inhabitants of Western Sun is death. I waved cars in and out, I paid no attention to anything but my book. You and I chipped in with the others and we put in a Mr. Coffee. FM radio, coffee, a book, and a very comfortable chair. This is work? No wonder I was derelict on the one occasion vigilance was needed."

On and on. George's shift was over and he excused himself and went on to Assisted Living to visit his mother. Pathetic old people inched along in wheelchairs, looking up in confused expectation as he passed on the way to his mother's room. George was a firm believer in the sacredness of life in all its stages, but there was irony in seeing these ancient people adding hours and days and months, sometimes years, to lives that were essentially over, while Agatha Rossner had

242   Ralph McInerny

been violently killed a short distance away. He thought, too, of the other young woman, who had been pushed into traffic, a horrible death. A suspect had been returned from St. Louis in that case, but who would answer for the more recent death? Jack Gallagher? Why not? Away from the mesmerizing voice of Rawley, George could imagine that his friend had only imagined the girl's sports car being driven past the shack; Rawley felt an overwhelming need to connect himself with the dreadful event.

"I want to go home," his mother said. She gripped the arms of her wheelchair and glared at the television screen. He leaned over and kissed her on the head.

"Of course you do."

"There is absolutely nothing to do here."

"You've earned the rest."

"Rest? I'm tired of rest."

"For now, it is better for you to be here."

"Better for whom?

And so the old quarrel went on, George feeling as much sympathy for her side of it as his own. Why shouldn't she resent the fact that she now spent her day with incontinent oldsters mewling and drooling their way through the day? Blame him if she wished; he felt guilty enough that she was here. But he would have felt worse if she were not. It was a problem without a solution. There must be crimes like that. What if it never would be known who had strangled the girl and left her lying in the snow twenty-five yards from the shack in which Rawley had read on, warm as toast, sipping coffee?

2

Austin Rooney had spent the day in his apartment, trying not to listen to the radio or television, both of which he had on. Even if he had wanted to, he couldn't get Jack Gallagher out of his mind, though he would have much preferred to think of Maud. It seemed the gentlemanly thing not to show up at the Center and embarrass her after last night.

When the news of Jack's confession came, Austin fixed his first drink, a very mild gin and tonic, a drink he did not particularly like in season and which therefore seemed safe as a daytime drink. Two days ago Austin had been sure that the suit Jack had brought against him would reduce his income to only his Social Security check; a court might award Jack the amount of his retirement fund, but they couldn't touch Social Security. He had faced the prospect of retrenching as the Woodhouse family had in Jane Austin's *Emma*, only it wouldn't be idle luxury at the equivalent of Bath. More like a room at the Y. Not quite that maybe, but one of the minuscule apartments available on campus for emeriti. He could eat in the student dining hall and avail himself of the entertainment and lectures on campus. Not all that bad a prospect, if he chose it freely, but that it might be imposed upon him by Jack Gallagher enraged him.

They had married one another's sisters and both sisters were dead, dissolving, as Austin thought, the relationship between them; like marriage, it lasted only until death. The news that Jack had confessed had given Austin only temporary relief; then the doubts set in. It made no sense that Jack would offer himself up as a sacrifice, so he had to have some ulterior purpose in mind, but what could it be? The relief Austin felt when it occurred to him that Jack was no longer in a position to press his suit, brought home to Austin how the prospect of falling afoul of the law had oppressed him. How could Jack feel otherwise when a far greater charge was laid against him? But he had rushed to accept it. It made no sense. Austin found that he was far more uneasy than he had been as the target of Jack's ridiculous suit.

His image of the dead woman was inseparable from the memory of Tim turning in that crowded bar and seeing his uncle there. Tim's expression had been eloquent of guilt but the girl had been unaware of Austin's presence. Even so, her image had been etched indelibly in his memory. That had been enough, he was sure, and he had left the bar without confronting his nephew. Only it had not been enough. The liaison with Tim had not been immediately discontinued and then she had turned her attentions to Jack.

The whole thing was mixed up in Austin's mind with his own infatuation with Maud Gorman, in escrow now, and his jealousy when Jack had sought to invoke droit du seigneur in her regard. The blow Austin had struck seemed to have been in reserve for years, through encounter after encounter with Jack when Austin's resentment, while concealed, was building to a flashpoint. When they were both left widowers, there should have been an opportunity to begin again, on a note of common bereavement, but the very sight of Jack had repelled Austin. Of course, sights of him were rare, and when Austin discovered the Senior Center at St. Hilary, it had seemed just the sort of thing he had been looking for. Getting together with former colleagues had its attractions, but how often could one relive the past and lament the present fallen condition of the academic world? At the Center he had found people he had known when he was a child, and others with whom he had nothing in common save the day-to-day diversions of the Center. And of course there was bubbly little Maud, making him feel like a man again. It was that innocent idyll that Jack Gallagher had sought to destroy. Austin regretted many things but he could not regret having felled Jack with what might have been a lucky punch, if he had not repeated the feat in the parking lot.

The young woman lawyer seemed Jack's retaliation. Austin could have Maud Gorman, Miss Haversham and her eternal youth; Jack would counter by getting involved with a truly young woman. After Austin's effort, in response to Colleen's request that he speak to Tim about Aggie, it was a bitter turn of events that he had released her for Jack.

The thought of Colleen prompted Austin to pick up the phone. He pushed away his third gin and tonic, thrice as potent as the first. But Colleen did not answer her phone. When the recorded request that he leave a message came on, he hung up. She must be at work. He looked up Mallard and Bill, rang the number, and asked for Colleen Gallagher.

"One moment, please."

A full minute later an apologetic male voice came on. "I am taking Colleen's messages today. Can I help you?"

"This is her uncle, Austin Rooney."

"Colleen didn't come in today. She called and left the message that she would not be in."

"With whom am I speaking?"

"Albert Fremont. Colleen and I work together."

"She doesn't seem to be at her apartment, either."

"The fact that she does not answer her phone . . ." Fremont's voice trailed away.

"Of course. Thank you."

After he hung up, he thought of Colleen, alone in her apartment, not answering the phone, overwhelmed by the events that had become the news of the day. He decided he would go there and, since he'd had three gin and tonics, he decided to go by public transportation.

He came to curse the decision not to drive, although the traffic at this time of day was probably as jammed as the CTA car he boarded. There were travelers coming from O'Hare, with their baggage taking up room, causing snarling comments from the other passengers. Austin stood gripping a pole, trying to keep his mind on his wallet. The train stopped endlessly at each station and then went on in a hesitant way, as if acceleration were merely prelude to another stop. When Austin escaped from the car, he went immediately into a bar and ordered a martini on the rocks. He would stay with gin, but he needed a restorative after his journey from Fox River.

Walking to Colleen's building, he was filled with the conviction that this trip was in vain. Colleen could be anywhere. If she had not gone to work, it was not to brood alone in her apartment. After all, she was engaged. Her fiancé, Mario Liberati, would not just leave her to her own devices at a time like this.

When he turned in to the apartment, a man came toward him. They passed and then the man said from behind him, "Are you Austin Rooney?"

Austin was flooded with confusion. Why would a stranger know him by name? He turned as if to face a raging lion, but there was only an ineffectual-looking fellow.

"Fremont. We talked when you called the office."

"Of course."

"We seem to have had the same idea. She doesn't answer her bell. I rang the manager and he offered to go up and see if she is in. Apparently she isn't."

"I was just telling myself I had made this trip in vain."

"Well, now you know where she isn't."

Austin felt an impulse to ask the fellow to come have a drink with him. But the moment passed, Fremont disappeared up the street, and Austin returned to the bar where he'd had the martini. He only drank in moments of stress.

3

The apparent indifference of the seniors to the plight of Jack Gallagher was only that—apparent. It was as if someone had to break the ice before they all acknowledged that their thoughts were full of the news of the day. The television set in the center always drew a crowd when the news came on, but today a cable station brought regular bulletins whenever there was a break for local news. When the news that Jack Gallagher had confessed to killing the young woman whose body had been found near his condo was announced, a great cry of protest went up.

"They know how to get confessions out of people."

"God knows what torture Jack has been subjected to."

Desmond O'Toole looked at Edna and lifted his brows. Not for him to tell these innocents that Jack had volunteered the confession. Edna had passed on to him what Father Dowling had been told at the rectory. The police had been surprised by the confessions and there was much skepticism about it.

Edna went back to her office, not wanting to get involved in the dozens of excited conversations. Desmond had shaken off his reluctance and was now holding court on the matter. Maud ignored the voice of authority, turning whenever the door opened, as if she were expecting someone. . . . Austin Rooney?

Having closed the door of her office, Edna sank into a chair and stared across the office. The only disadvantage of her job at the Senior Center, for which she thanked God every day, was Father Dowling's friendship with Phil Keegan and the frequent presence of the captain of detectives and his lieutenant Cy Horvath at the parish. Of course Edna resented the role of the police in her husband Earl's arrest and trial. The events that had led to his conviction and sentence were in one way irrefutable but there was a real sense in which Earl was innocent, technically innocent, of the charges brought against him. That he had not actually done what he set out to do was not a moral defense, and the fact that the deed had in any case been done, made his conviction inevitable. It had fallen to Edna to keep the family together, their two daughters and son, and to prevent them from becoming estranged from their father. That Earl did not want them to see him in prison, Edna understood, but that meant he had become a mythical person, someone she described to them and they reconstructed from their own memories.

The day when he would be freed drew nearer but meanwhile the children grew so swiftly that Edna did not see how he would recognize them when he got out. He pored over the photographs she brought him, but it was the pictures of them as they had been when he was arrested that meant most to him. And in their different ways the children resented not having a father in the home, resented the need of their mother to work, were constantly evading questions about their father. No wonder Edna felt seething anger that Jack Gallagher should confess to murder almost casually.

Did he count on his prominence cushioning the effect of that confession?

There was a tap on her door, and for a moment Edna considered not answering. She had the sense that she was hiding from events, that even the undemanding routine of the Center was oppressive. But the thought of someone reporting to Marie Murkin that Mrs. Hospers could not be found decided her. But the door opened before she got to it and Desmond O'Toole peeked in.

"Busy?"

"Come in, Desmond."

But he was already in. He wore a tortured, theatrical expression. "I have to talk with someone."

"Of course."

He went to the chair across from her desk and Edna seated herself in her desk chair.

"I can't talk to Maud about this, she is too good-natured to credit."

"Good heavens, what is it?"

But Desmond was not to be hurried. "I suppose I should go to the police about it, but I wanted to talk with someone first."

"Why would you want to go to the police?"

Desmond settled his bony frame in the chair, looked over her head, and seemed to be humming.

"It's Austin."

Edna managed not to groan. Was Desmond bothered about competition for Maud's attention again? But the police? "Has Austin come?"

"That's just it. He's not here today. Mrs. Hospers, you know what happened last night, to that young woman, outside Jack Gallagher's condo."

"Of course I know."

"Have you given any thought to who might have done that?"

"Jack Gallagher has confessed."

Desmond made an impatient motion with his hand. "That's just a play for attention. If we grant the story that he and the young woman, were, well, you know, why would he strangle her?"

"You always hurt the one you love."

"The Ink Spots." For a moment Edna feared that Desmond would burst into song. "Theirs is the only worthwhile version of that song." He brought his mind back to his reason for coming here. "Austin knew that young woman. He went downtown to talk to her. He told Maud about it."

"I didn't know that."

"Now that you do, what does it suggest?"

"I haven't any idea."

Desmond grew patient. "Think back over the past weeks. Remember the brawl the night of the dance. The brawls. Austin was in a rage because of Jack Gallagher."

"Go on."

"The fact that he hasn't come in today got my mind going. Austin's blood was up. I never saw a man with such murder in his eye."

"Are you suggesting that Austin Rooney strangled that young woman?"

"It makes sense when you stop to think about it, doesn't it?"

"No, it doesn't. I never heard of anything so far-fetched in my life. But I'm glad you came to me with your suspicions."

"There's more. As you say, it sounds far-fetched. But I checked with the manager of the building in which Austin lives. He didn't get home until dawn."

Desmond's speculation had seemed absurd; now it seemed dangerous. Edna had watched the way Desmond had pitted the two brothers-in-law against one another, holding Jack's coat, so to speak, so the two men could have it out. The prize would be Maud, and the prize would go to Desmond.

"What do you think I should do?"

"Nothing."

"Mrs. Hospers, this is very important information. What we know is not known to everyone, but his being out all night . . ."

"I meant you should do nothing. It's good you brought this to me. Let me take it from this point."

"You will let the police know?"

Edna nodded, as if this were less than a real agreement. "You've done what you think is right, and now let me handle it."

Desmond actually sighed. "What a relief."

"It was wise not to tell Maud. Let's just keep this between us until we see what the police think."

Desmond rose slowly from the chair, the picture of a man who had just laid down his burden.

"I can't thank you enough. I wouldn't want to be the one who pointed the finger at Austin Rooney. You understand."

"I understand perfectly. That is why we won't tell Maud about it."

He actually made a little circle with thumb and forefinger. Edna got up and went with him to the door. Before she could open it, he swooped at her and pecked her cheek. Then he was gone.

It felt like a Judas kiss. With the door shut, Edna vented her anger at Desmond. What a silly old busybody he was. But now she had a problem. If she didn't pass on Desmond's story he would keep after her until she did.

4

When Father Dowling arrived at the courthouse, Jack Gallagher's legal team had left. It had been a marathon session and had left quite an impression. Phil, when Father Dowling stopped by Keegan's office telling him he wanted to see the prisoner, waved him to a chair. The room was redolent of new and old cigar smoke, not an olfactory treat. Father Dowling did not accept the offer that he light his pipe.

"Skinner is nervous as a cat, Roger. He's been in and out of here all day, wanting to know if we have anything new on Gallagher."

"Do you?"

"Cy wanted to attend to another matter first. The guy who pushed the girl into traffic on Dirksen has been returned from Kansas City."

"Your plate is full."

"At least he denies he did it."

The comparison was with Jack. "Why are you so skeptical of his confession?"

"Wait until you talk to him."

"Is anybody with him now?"

"They've finally left. His lawyers know a lot more of what happened now than we do. Their main concern is to nullify the confession."

"Can that be done?"

"Jack won't hear of it."

Father Dowling was more anxious than ever to talk with Jack so Phil took him to the cell blocks and smoothed the way for him. He was shown into a conference room and waited there for the prisoner to be brought to him. It was a blank, featureless room, affording no distraction to the guilty eye. A smallish table, two chairs at either end of it. Another chair near the door. The door opened and Jack Gallagher swept in.

"Father Dowling," he cried, all smiles, hand out, advancing on the priest. "How good of you to come."

"I had to stand in line."

"Have you been waiting?"

"Just a figure of speech. I'm told you have been kept busy by your lawyers."

"Lawyers," Jack said, arranging himself in the chair across from the priest. "Even when they are friends and relatives, they live in a different world."

"They want you to take back your confession?"

"They explain it in legal terms, but that is something I cannot do. There is nothing I told the police that I am not willing to tell anyone."

"That doesn't sound too contrite, Jack."

Jack assumed a tragic look. "I still find it hard to believe that I did it."

"But you did?"

"Oh, yes. I must have gone out of my mind, temporarily. I became aware of the fact that I was twisting the scarf about her neck and then I just kept twisting." Jack shuddered and looked at Father Dowling for his reaction.

"Then there is another confession you must make."

"I suppose I should."

"There is no time like the present."

Jack shook his head. "Not now, Father. Not yet. I want it to sink in. As you say, I have yet to feel contrition."

"Such a confession should not be put off for a minute, Jack. You must not presume on God's mercy."

"I understand what you're saying."

But he continued to put off going to confession. He needed time to acquire a penitent outlook.

"For example, I am plagued by the thought that Austin Rooney must be enjoying all this to no end."

"I doubt that, Jack."

"It is my thoughts I refer to."

Jails are filled with guard-house lawyers, but Jack Gallagher invoked the bits and pieces of moral lore he had picked up over a lifetime as a Catholic. He had to be truly sorry and have a firm purpose of amendment.

"Surely you don't think you'll make a habit of strangling young women."

"That is another thing, Father. She stayed at my place. A serious sin. But it still doesn't seem serious to me. I am actually proud of it, like an old rooster. I have a long way to go before I will be ready to confess."

Father Dowling thought of the conversation on his drive back to his rectory. For a man who had been eager to confess to the police, Jack had dozens of reasons why he could not avail himself of the sacrament of penance. Perhaps he remembered what a grievous sin it was to lie in the confessional. The nuns would have made that clear to him.

"Edna wondered if you could come by her office," Marie said, her tone a commentary on the request.

"She's in her office now?"

"Until five."

"I'll go over."

"I could ask her to come here." Part of Marie's annoyance was that she would not be in the building where the conversation took place.

"No, it's no bother."

"Hurry back. I want to hear all about Jack Gallagher." She paused. "Only what you can tell me, of course."

"Father," Edna said, "Desmond O'Toole has concocted a story he wants me to tell to the police."

Edna told him about her conversation with Desmond, clearly trying to make it sound ridiculous. But the alleged fact that Austin had not been home last night made the speculation serious.

"Austin met with the young woman who was strangled?"

"The daughter asked him to talk with her."

"About her father."

"I am passing the hot potato to you, Father, as you can probably guess."

"I wish I could say thanks."

"I wish I hadn't answered the door when he came up here. Not that it would have mattered. He walked right in."

"A man with a mission."

"He's being vindictive, Father. That's the bottom line."

Edna was clearly relieved to have put the burden on the pastor, and Father Dowling managed to let her think that he was glad she had. But walking back to the rectory he knew there were two things the police should know: The young woman was not a stranger to Austin, who had apparently been deputized by Colleen to shame Agatha into leaving her father alone; and Austin had not been home until dawn. These were facts that would doubtless show up in Cy Horvath's investigation, when he got going on it. Only if he failed to discover them would Father Dowling feel the need to tell him. He hoped that time would not arrive.

5

Mario came for Colleen at four o'clock and was no longer worried that she would be harassed by the press.

"They've got something else to distract them now. The girl who worked here."

"Ruby told me all about her."

"Ruby?"

"The head housekeeper. She says you talked to her about your mother."

"Oh, sure. I remember. Anyway, the man who did it has been arrested."

"The police did find me here, Mario. A detective named Horvath. He was very polite and considerate."

"Did he wonder why you were here?"

"Oh, I told him. He seems to have contempt for the press. How is my father?"

Mario looked at her for a long time before answering. "I've never seen anyone quite like your father. Tim and I, and Amos Cadbury, explained to him that the confession he made will be thrown out because he did not have an attorney with him at the time. He says they asked him if he wanted one and he told them no. Even so, we can have it thrown out. But he refuses."

"Why?"

"I hoped you could give me a reasonable explanation. None occurs to me. Even if he did do it . . ."

"Mario, that's it. Whether he did or just says he did, it comes to the same thing."

"I think he is enjoying this."

"He wouldn't be my father if he didn't. That doesn't mean he isn't a serious man. He is. I remember how he pontificated at my mother's funeral, impresario one moment, disconsolate husband the next, always at the center of things. It is the life he has led."

At the desk, no surprise was exhibited at the fact that Colleen was checking out without having stayed overnight. Mr. Lawrence Wagner looked out of his office and lifted an eyebrow, absolving himself of all responsibility. Motels had ceased being the custodians of the nation's morals.

They ate at a little restaurant near her apartment and were accorded all the privacy and anonymity they could wish. Mario poured their wine and lifted his glass to hers.

256   Ralph McInerny

"Here's to the future."

How could they express such a wish without it seeming ironic? During the day, Colleen had resolved that she would indeed leave Mallard and Bill; telling Mario that earlier had been a show of solidarity. But she could not go back to those offices which had rejected Mario and which would now be haunted by the ghost of Aggie.

"Did Tim say anything to you?"

"Today? Believe me, his mind is completely absorbed in the problem of the moment. He and your father are very close, aren't they?"

"I guess so."

"More like brothers than father and son."

Colleen let it go. Who knew what a family looked like from the outside? To her it seemed that Tim had spent most of his adult life increasing the distance between himself and his father. For years he had turned a cold stare on anyone who mentioned having listened religiously to Jack Gallagher on radio. Colleen thought all that went back to the episode when Tim had had a summer job at the station, and Tim had accused their father of philandering. He had told Colleen reluctantly, feeling it was something she ought to know. Besides, he wanted her to have his story of what had happened before Dad developed the deluxe version. Her mother had not been told, but how much had she known without being told? What a crucifixion that must have been for her, knowing her husband's success brought him constantly in the path of the temptation he could not resist. At the moment, Colleen felt like losing her life in Mario's and letting her own family look after itself.

Mario said, "He doesn't seem to give two thoughts to what this is doing to other people. Tim's children, for example, to say nothing of you."

"They have Tim."

"Tim is one great guy, Colleen. You should be proud of him."

Oh, the things she could not say. Mario seemed unaffected by her telling him that she had enlisted first Uncle Austin and then her father to talk sense into Tim, who, surprisingly, seemed to be putty in Aggie's hands. She looked at Mario.

"No one is a total hero, sweetheart."

He smiled. "No brother is to a sister, that's for sure." His smile disappeared. "I called my sister and told her what effect Jimmy Kane's effort to get me to defend him has had on my career."

"She must have felt awful."

"Awful? She practically cheered. Now there is no obstacle to my coming up there and keeping that crook of a husband of hers out of prison. I'll have to call her again."

"Did you agree?"

"No, I hung up on her."

"You mustn't do it, Mario. You don't owe anyone that."

"Then why does my conscience keep nagging me? It's not him, it's my sister. But the truth is, she would be better off if he were put away for life. They have always lived in the shadow of this possibility. Now it's here, and suddenly it's my responsibility to make it go away. What I can't imagine is doing for him what a defense lawyer has to do—to at least pretend to believe in his client, assume he is innocent, use every device allowed to prevent justice being done. He would be convicted in any case, and it would be like Jimmy Kane to blame it on me. I myself would feel that I hadn't done my best."

"Mario, that is the best reason of all for saying no."

"What's the best reason of all for saying yes?"

She leaned toward him and his lips were briefly on hers. "Next week, marriage preparation. I think I'm ready right now."

"I'm glad you checked out of that motel."

"You're right. It was too impersonal."

Lovers' patter, nothing more. This was the man who had resisted Aggie's effort to add him to her list of conquests. His indifference had intensified Aggie's campaign. But the harder she tried, the more disgusted he became. Thank God.

"As soon as we finish Father Dowling's boot camp, let's get married."

"That could be only a month from now."

" 'Only.' "

So they sat on, planning their wedding on a day when their worlds had seemed to disintegrate. But what better time to think of a new world?

❧ Part Four ❧

1

Tuttle let Cy Horvath set the pace without protest because it was the quickest way to get briefed on his client. Harry and Cy were now the best of friends, with the lean man in the ponytail babbling away to the detective as if they were on the same side.

"Harry," Tuttle said at one point, "remember Horvath is a cop. He intends to put you in prison and throw away the key."

"He can't."

"That's good to hear."

"Because I'm innocent."

"That's good too." Good for nothing. But the trip out to the motel and meeting all the cleaning ladies had given Tuttle a sense of how anyone who knew Harry hated his guts. They were sure he had killed the girl and they looked like a jury to Tuttle.

Harry told him about the bank account and the reason for meeting Linda where the accident had occurred. Not that he accepted the term "accident" for what had happened.

"The guy did it on purpose, shoved her right into the path of oncoming traffic."

Harry's expression as he said this might work with the jury. Of course Tuttle assumed his client was guilty. Why else would he be his client? But having Harry to deal with took the sting out of being given the boot by Jack Gallagher.

"Of course my father will drop the suit against my uncle," Mr. Timothy Gallagher, all grand in his five-hundred-dollar suit, had said to Tuttle. "You can send me your bill."

"There's no need to withdraw it. You never know."

"It will be withdrawn. Thank you for your services, Mr. Tuttle. My father faces a far more serious problem now."

"If you need any investigative work done . . ."

No deal. He was being dumped and that was that. No surprise, of course; as soon as he had seen the two prosperous young lawyers and learned that Amos Cadbury too was in on the defense, he knew it was *Sayonara, Tuttle.* Jack Gallagher was making it look as if the surest way to rally everyone to your support was to confess to murder. If Harry confessed, the result would be something different.

"At least he's innocent," Tuttle said to Horvath, when the lieutenant got back to headquarters.

"Until you get him convicted."

"Hey, I'm his defense attorney. You're thinking of Skinner."

"As little as possible."

Skinner confided, at the top of his lungs, that the Detective Division was not taking the strangling of Agatha Rossner seriously. "If you're going to get killed, Tuttle, don't be from out of town and have the killer a local boy."

"I see what you mean."

"Now they're trying to nullify the confession."

"The Detective Division?"

"No, the platoon of prima donnas who have risen to Gallagher's defense. I don't suppose they have offered you any help with the crook you're defending."

"He's innocent, Skinner."

"Of what?"

If Timothy Gallagher had reacted differently, Tuttle might have told Gallagher what he knew about his old man and Agatha Rossner.

Mentioning that he had someone on stakeout all night when it happened would have melted some of that starch. He was not yet inclined to pass it on to Skinner. All he had to do was mention that it was Peanuts out there in the car that night and Skinner would scoff.

On a lark, Tuttle again went downtown to the garage in which Agatha had kept her car. The adenoidal attendant with the tie as wide as his face remembered him. "Anyone else checked on that car?"

"Another one of your guys."

"But it's still here?"

If Horvath knew the car had been given an A-1 wash that morning, he would put two and two together. The trouble with Jack Gallagher's confession was that it did not account for the return of Agatha's car to the garage on the near North Side.

"I been trying to reach you all day," Hazel said when he got to his office, sounding like a schoolteacher.

"You should have paged me at the courthouse."

"They should have booked you at the courthouse. What's going to happen with the case we've been working on?"

We. There it was again. If she kept this up, he would have a contract taken out on Hazel. Just kidding. Nothing less than a stake in the heart would do anyway.

"Gallagher decided to drop the suit against Rooney."

Hazel wailed. "I was afraid of that."

"Make out a bill and send it to the son. Timothy Gallagher. A very comprehensive and detailed bill."

"Say no more." Hazel settled at her computer. "By the way, I cleaned up your office."

Tuttle closed the door behind him and looked around. His office looked like a magazine ad. Desktop clear, wastebasket empty, a vase of artificial flowers on the windowsill. And his bookcase was unrecognizable. All the books lined up, none on their sides or jammed in any which way. Damn that woman. How would he ever find anything? In a spirit of rebellion he got on the phone and called Peanuts.

"Stop at the Great Wall and get me some hot-and-sour soup, shrimp fried rice, and tea. Order whatever you want and get over here."

"Is she gone?"

"If you mean Hazel, she is in her own office where she belongs. My office is my castle."

"I don't want to," Peanuts said.

"You'd rather have Italian?"

"She reminds me of Agnes."

"Hazel is white as your whatchamacallit. You going to let some woman decide whether you going to eat Chinese with an old friend?"

"I'll meet you at the Great Wall."

He hung up. Well, maybe Peanuts was right. It was food they wanted, not to make a territorial point.

"I'm going out."

"Bring me something to eat."

"What do you like?"

"Chinese. Anything. And tea."

Tuttle just stared at her. Was this his destiny, to eat Chinese food in his office with Hazel, Peanuts no longer his friend? He was going to slam the door when he went, but what the heck, why be childish?

2

When Nusbaum, the prosecutor, learned what the police had on Harry, he switched Skinner to that, saying he himself would take the high-profile case. All eyes would be on the trial of Jack Gallagher and one misstep could spell disaster. City hall would be watching, the press would be all over it; this was no case for the second team. Nusbaum said all this with no consideration of Skinner's feelings. Skinner seethed but kept his peace. The prosecutor was called "Noose" Nusbaum in the press, in ironic recognition of the number of convictions he failed to get. But then Mendel had been addressing Skinner as "Mule" so maybe he was better off out of that spotlight. He would bet a ticket to a Cubs game that with Nusbaum on the job, Jack Gallagher would end up a free man. Probably sue the city for wrongful arrest.

In the press room Skinner was told that Peanuts had gone to meet Tuttle at the Great Wall. The thought of Chinese food made Skinner salivate and he decided to have his conference with Tuttle there among the fortune cookies.

Tuttle, wearing his hat, but with a paper napkin tucked into his collar, was facing away from the door when Skinner came in. But Peanuts saw him and scowled.

"Move over," Skinner said, giving Tuttle a bump. Peanuts had stopped chewing and stared at Skinner. "I thought we could talk about the case while we eat."

"We're already eating," Peanuts said.

"I'll catch up." He waved for the waitress, ordered rapidly, adding, "Bring chopsticks."

Both Peanuts and Tuttle attacked their food with the usual utensils, but Skinner had mastered the art of chopsticks and was conscious his dexterity won the attention if not the admiration of his companions.

"Nusbaum wants me to prosecute your client."

"Which one?"

"Ha. I heard you got dumped by Gallagher."

"You saying we're on different sides?"

"Only on Harry Paquette. You indicated that you had stuff on Gallagher that would be very helpful in prosecuting the case."

"I don't remember that."

"Oh, come on, Tuttle."

"I thought Nusbaum was prosecuting Gallagher."

"If he is ever prosecuted. Look, Tuttle, I work for Nusbaum."

"I'm not doing your boss any favors."

"That's my point, Tuttle. He's my boss. I want him to fall on his face. Anything you got that could help me do that, I'd appreciate."

"You're prosecuting Harry."

"I figure a two-day trial."

"Yeah? I'm pleading him innocent."

"Of course you are. What else?"

"He denies killing that girl."

"Does he really? Well, that ought to be enough. We'll just drop the charges."

"You may get a surprise in court, Skinner."

"It hasn't happened yet."

It was difficult to eat and talk while Pianone sat immobile on the opposite seat of the booth, looking at Skinner the way primates look at visitors to the zoo. He seemed to be waiting for him to finish and go.

"Well, it was good food, anyway," Skinner said, getting up.

"This your treat?"

Skinner thought about it. Why not? "We'll call it a pretrial conference."

At the cash register he looked back to see Peanuts wading into his food at last. Strange fellow. But then all the Pianones were strange.

Back at his office, he was shown a message: *Talk to Edna Hospers at St. Hilary's if you want to know who killed Agatha Rossner.*

"What the hell is this?"

"That's the message."

"Who is Edna Hospers?"

"I'll check on it."

When he learned that she ran the Senior Center where Jack Gallagher had been clobbered by Austin Rooney, Skinner thought it worth a trip. If Tuttle had been around, Skinner would have asked the little lawyer what he thought of the message. As it was, he would just see what he would see.

Skinner had been born and raised in Poughkeepsie, attended law school at Northwestern, and stayed on in the Midwest because he found it an exotic place. He did not have the native's understanding of things, and of course one would have to be both native and Catholic to figure out how a parish school had evolved into a hangout for the retired members of the parish. It seemed like a good idea, but when he crossed the parking lot and pulled open the door which was a school door no matter where you were raised, and looked into a very large room that still had basketball hoops mounted on either end and was filled with old folks, Skinner decided that it couldn't be a barrel of laughs running this operation.

"May I help you, sir?" a lanky man with the compensatory stoop of the very tall asked him.

"Mrs. Hospers?"

"Right up those stairs and the first door on your right."

His hand sought the railing as he mounted the steps; schools are schools and age does not dull the habits they ingrain in us. There was no legend on the first door on the right. Skinner knocked. An attractive-looking woman opened it, her brows coming together but not affecting the smile.

"Edna Hospers?"

"Yes."

"I am Flavius Skinner from the prosecutor's office. Could I have a minute of your time?"

She was wary, backing around behind her desk and indicating that Skinner should take the chair that faced her.

"I have been told that you have information about the Agatha Rossner murder that would be helpful to us."

Her face brightened. "Father Dowling talked to you?"

Father Dowling? Skinner decided not to lie. He got out the slip of paper that contained the telephone message and handed it to her.

"Desmond O'Toole did this!" she cried.

"What is it all about?"

She was on her feet. "Wait right here. Desmond is here and I'll bring him up."

Skinner would have liked to have a cigarette but schools had been the first smoke-free zones and he thought better of it, no matter that the building was now put to a different purpose. A full five minutes went by. Skinner was beginning to wonder if Edna Hospers had skipped on him, when the door opened and the lanky fellow who had directed him to the office was brought into the room by Edna Hospers, who had a firm grip on his elbow.

"Desmond, this is the man who got your anonymous message. Perhaps you would like to tell him what it is all about. I will leave the two of you alone."

"Geez," Desmond said, when the door closed emphatically after Mrs. Hospers.

"You sent this message?"

He handed Desmond O'Toole the slip and he read it several times. "I told Mrs. Hospers about it. The idea was that she should tell the police. Even when I told her, I knew she wouldn't do it. So I called your office."

"Where did you get my name?"

"From the newspaper. You were going to prosecute Jack Gallagher. Well, he was guilty of hitting Austin Rooney, but he didn't kill that girl."

"But he's confessed."

But O'Toole was on another tack. He wanted to tell Skinner about the dance they'd had here, a tremendous night, great music and singing. Jack Gallagher was the star of the show, but it was all spoiled when Austin tried to break in on Jack and Jack just ignored him.

"You had to see the fire in Austin's eye. Murderous hatred."

"I know about that fight."

"The one in the parking lot was worse. If Maud Gorman hadn't been there, Austin would have killed Jack."

Skinner wondered why he had been chosen to be the beneficiary of this stick figure's power of total recall. No wonder Edna Hospers had left.

"The suit against Austin only added to the fuel. So what happens next? Jack starts fooling around with that young woman and Austin went downtown to meet her. He will say he was on a family mission, to save Jack from himself. Anyway, that's number one: Austin knew that girl. Second . . ." Desmond paused and opened and shut his mouth several times, making a smacking sound. "Second: Austin was out all last night. He did not get home until dawn."

That was the QED. Desmond leaned toward Skinner, waiting for him to get it.

"He was setting Jack up."

"You mean Austin killed the girl?"

"Think about it."

"So why did Jack confess?"

Desmond smiled slyly. "It's like a game of checkers."

Skinner felt like crowning him. He thanked the man and got up. They reached the door at the same time. Desmond seemed to be waiting for Skinner to open the door. Skinner outwaited him. But when Desmond opened the door he went out first and Skinner had to catch the door before it hit him in the face. Maybe he should have shown more interest in Desmond O'Toole's theory.

"Well?" Edna Hospers said, when she met him on the stairway.

"Nutty as a fruitcake."

Her look of relief was reward enough. She called good-bye after him. He hurried past the gym and out to his car. But he sat behind the wheel for a moment. There was no way in the world he could find out if Austin Rooney was hanging around Jack Gallagher's apartment last night, waiting to spring on the girl when she came out, but he could find out if Austin had been sent on a family mission to talk Agatha Rossner out of seducing Jack Gallagher.

3

Edna Hospers breezed into the rectory, by the kitchen door, and told Marie she had to see Father Dowling right away.

"For heaven's sake, Edna."

But something about Edna's manner told Marie this was no time to stand on her dignity as housekeeper. In any case Father Dowling had heard Edna burst in, and came into the kitchen. "I have to see you, Father."

"Of course, of course."

And down the hall and into the study they went. The door closed with the finality of the door to the confessional. The analogy brought a pious expression to Marie's face and she busied herself in her kitchen, making more noise than usual. Ten minutes later a considerably less agitated Edna came through the kitchen.

"Thank you, Father," she called to the pastor. Marie waited to be acknowledged but Edna pushed through the back door and outside.

"Well?" Marie said, turning to the pastor.

"What would you say if I invited Phil Keegan to dinner?"

"Tonight?" It was nearly dark outside.

"If he's free."

"Oh, if he's free, of course, ask him."

"He could come after dinner."

"No, no, it's all right."

"You're sure there'll be enough." Although Father Dowling ate as if Lent ran all year round, Marie refused to cook to his diminished appetite. This entailed a hefty intake on her part, but it was the principle of the thing.

"There'll be enough."

Still no word about Edna's mysterious visit. Marie was beginning to believe the woman *had* come in order to go to confession. A real emergency. But she wiped her mind clean: Judge not. Father Dowling went upstairs where Marie suspected he caught a ten-minute nap as he often did this time of day, if he could.

The dinner was more like it. Marie was as good as one of the party, and the conversation turned on Edna's visit to the rectory. Marie listened with both ears. What a sneak that Desmond O'Toole was.

"It all has to do with Maud," Marie said.

The two men looked at her. In the ensuing silence her chin lifted a notch at a time.

"What are you talking about?" Phil Keegan asked.

"It is very simple." But it sounded complicated as she laid it out. Desmond O'Toole had been accepted by Maud Gorman as her chief escort and companion at the Center. With the advent of the cultivated Austin Rooney, Desmond had been replaced. Then Jack Gallagher showed up and Desmond formed a plan. Of course he couldn't imagine any sane man not wanting to have Maud Gorman hanging on his arm. Given the choices, when Jack decided to dance, it was clear what partner he would want. So the two men fought.

"You think this old guy thinks the civil suit Jack brought, and now this confession of murder, is just a continuation of their three-way contest over Maud Gorman."

No, Marie didn't think that, and why didn't he just shut up and listen? It was foolish to give Phil Keegan an opportunity to act superior.

"However it is with that," Father Dowling said, "there are two elements in what Desmond told Edna to tell me."

"Timmons to Evers to Chance," said Phil, who was a student of the game.

"Austin was delegated, supposedly, to talk to this young woman about her affair with Jack. And he did not come home until dawn this morning."

"Maybe I ought to talk to O'Toole."

"Just more hearsay, Phil."

"And this guy gave this story to Skinner?"

"That's why Edna was so upset."

"Skinner." Phil rubbed his forehead with the heel of his hand. "Now he'll be telling us how to do our job."

"Is he prosecuting Jack Gallagher?"

"No, he got bumped. Nusbaum smells publicity."

"Rivalry?"

"Cats and dogs."

"Maybe he won't tell Nusbaum."

Phil's grin began small and grew large. He nodded his head, eyebrows lifted. "Let me use your phone, Roger. Cy has to know about this."

Much of Marie's disgust and anger with Desmond O'Toole was due to the fact that he had gone to Edna with his story, not to her. But later, in her room, yawning over her novel, the import of Desmond O'Toole's gossip dawned on her. He really thought Austin Rooney had killed that girl! If nothing else, diverting attention to Austin would be helpful to Jack Gallagher. Marie's problem was that she could not imagine either one of those two old men strangling a girl in the small hours of the morning and leaving her body lying in the snow. But then she could not for the life of her imagine what Jack Gallagher had been doing with a woman that age—with any woman, for that matter, but especially with someone young enough to be his daughter. There were times when Marie seriously doubted her knowledge of human beings: what they might do, what they might not do.

4

The following morning at eight-thirty, Cy called Colleen Gallagher and told her he would appreciate a few minutes of her time.

"Where should we meet?"

"Actually, I am parked right outside your place. This is a cell phone."

"Well, why don't you come up?"

"You sure?"

"There's still coffee from breakfast."

It was one of those apartments that looked like a college dorm room with desperate efforts to give it individuality. Cy remembered the lofts guys would build in dorm rooms, spending a fortune in lumber to create the impression of a two-floor flat. That got all the bedding up in the loft and freed the rest of the room for parties. Colleen had resorted to flair. One alcove was papered in garish red with big gold splotches on it.

"Rice paper," she explained, when he stared at it.

The furniture was kind of Oriental too, not comfortable for a man, certainly not a man Cy's size. So he took the sofa, sitting in the middle. She handed him a cup of coffee and he sipped it. Weak.

"Did Austin Rooney ever meet the woman Jack Gallagher says he killed?"

The question surprised her, as he had thought it would. She stared at him. He was counting on the way they had gotten along the day before. Her shoulders began to slump.

"Who told you—Tim?"

"I want to hear it from you."

"You have to understand what kind of a woman Aggie was. I never met anyone at all like her. She didn't want love, she wanted adventure. She wanted to be a serial man-killer, and then boast about it to other women. She met my brother Tim at some legal seminar and the next thing I knew she was claiming she had added his scalp to her belt. It was her way of getting back at me."

"For what?"

"Mario. My fiancé. She set her sights on him and he just dismissed her. When Mario and I got engaged and she met Tim, well . . ."

"And you believed her?"

"I asked Uncle Austin to check it out. According to Aggie, via the grapevine, of course—she never said these things directly to me—they met for drinks at the Willard Bar. Austin went there and there they were."

"What did he do?"

"He thought just being seen with the girl was all Tim needed. Tim looked so guilty that Austin let it go at that."

"Did it work?"

"Not according to Aggie. That's when I asked Dad to intervene."

"With your brother?"

"With Aggie. He came down to the office and I introduced him around and he was a star again. He didn't even have to ask Aggie. She led him away."

"All the way, apparently."

"Can you blame me for thinking this is all my fault? If I had just ignored Aggie, if I had let other people work out their own problems, Aggie would still be alive, Tim and Dad would have gotten over her . . ."

"You're not responsible. There's no crime in trying to help people out of the jams they get in."

Cy did not, of course, show it by any change in expression, but he had learned more things in five minutes than he could have learned in a week of investigation, a lucky week. The mention of Tim Gallagher was the big surprise. If he reviewed what Colleen revealed to him for her confirmation it would have run as follows:

Timothy Gallagher meets Agatha Rossner at a legal seminar, and Agatha learns he is the brother to Colleen, whom she hates. In a spirit of revenge and in her character as the firm's femme fatale, Aggie makes a successful play for Timothy and brags about it at the office in a way that is conveyed to Colleen. Timothy is a married man with a family. Colleen asks her uncle Austin Rooney to talk sense to the young man. Rooney shows up at the bar that is the rendezvous of the illicit couple, catches his nephew's eye, and the shamed reaction seems to accomplish his mission. But Tim is allegedly not deterred. Colleen now calls into play her father and the father gets into the act, replacing his son.

Taken as prelude to the discovery of the dead body of Agatha in the snow outside Jack Gallagher's condo, this account was full of possible explanations for what had happened. After Cy left Colleen, he drove to where Austin Rooney lived, a fourplex whose owner lived on the first floor east. His name was Fred and tufts of white hair sprouted randomly from his head as if someone had sprinkled it with hair restorer.

"Yeah?"

"You Fred Crosley?"

He poked his head out and looked at the nameplate next to his door. "Looks like it."

Cy showed him his badge and Fred let him in. "Is this about Rooney?"

"What about Rooney?"

"That he didn't come home until dawn that night."

"How do you know that?"

Fred pulled at his lower lip and his brows rose and fell as if in response. "Listen."

Cy leaned forward expectantly. There was the sound of creaking overhead.

"There. Rooney lives upstairs and I know when he's in because of that damned creaking. Nothing can be done about it."

"You lie awake nights listening to the creaking?"

"Funny. No, Rooney makes a trip to the bathroom along about five A.M. So do I. Like clockwork. He's the same. You reach a certain age and your bladder just can't wait."

"So you get up at five A.M."

"Every morning. The other morning, I was up a little earlier and when I got back to bed I thought I'd wait until Rooney made his trip before going back to sleep, otherwise he'd wake me up and I might never get back to sleep again. So I lay there and lay there, waiting for the creaking that would tell me Rooney was up and going. It didn't happen. By then I was wide-awake and mad as a hornet. And then I saw his car pull up outside. He shut the door very quietly, didn't slam it, and then almost tiptoed to the door. When I finally did hear him creaking around up there I started wondering where the hell Austin would be until that hour of the morning."

"What did you conclude?"

"The fellow that called me yesterday, O'Toole, said he had a pretty good idea which he would tell me someday."

"Do you know O'Toole?"

"He cut my hair for years."

Cy decided not to comment on the present state of Fred Crosley's hair. "Pretty good barber?"

"We called him 'News of the Day.' Go to his shop and you got caught up on everything. And he sang."

"In the barbershop?"

"People begged him to. He wouldn't sing while he was cutting hair, but afterwards, if the demand was insistent, he sang. Wonderful voice."

Cy thanked Fred and asked who was his barber now.

"I'll tell you a secret. I cut my own hair now."

18

1

Cy decided to check up on the men in Agatha Rossner's life chrono-logically in the light of what he now knew. That meant Timothy first. He could have asked him point-blank, and maybe he would later, but he took the indirect route first. If the thing had gone beyond drinks after work, where had the couple gone for the main act? Aggie's modus operandi was never to take a man home, but go to his place so that when she left, it was over. Imagine trying to get a man out of the house in the morning. Aggie had been full of such folk wisdom, a courtesan's guide to the etiquette of random coupling. That is why she had stayed over at Jack's.

Tim Gallagher could scarcely have taken her home. So, where? They had first met at the Hacienda Motel, where the legal seminar had been held. It was a place favored by many legal groups and firms. That might tell against it, from the point of view of discretion, but either there was some legal event on or there wasn't. If there wasn't, it was just another motel. There was a photograph of Tim in the morning paper, striding from the courthouse. Cy figured it would serve as well as anything for identification purposes.

While he was crossing the enormous lobby, Mr. Lawrence Wagner popped out of his office like a cuckoo, all but throwing up his arms at the sight of Horvath. Then he was scooting across the floor to intercept Cy before he got to the corridor leading to Ruby's office.

"Lieutenant Horvath. I asked specifically that you come around the back."

"You were expecting me?"

Lawrence frowned. "I called 911 ten minutes ago."

"What about?"

"Don't you know?"

"Not until you tell me."

Lawrence checked the lobby, then led Horvath into the corridor. "I don't want the guests alarmed. It's Ruby."

Cy started for her office, on the run, with Lawrence coming afterward, urging calm and consideration for the guests.

Ruby had been sitting at her desk in the little office that was more like a linen closet. The murder weapon had been a cord pulled from a laundry bag and twisted around her neck until she was dead. Her head was flung back and she stared unseeing at the neon light above her. The cord must have been dropped over her head from behind. A ballpoint pen had been used in the twisting, tourniquet style. Cy picked up the phone and called Dr. Pippen, but she was already on her way. While he waited, he kept gawkers out of the room and warned the 911 crew about messing up the scene.

"The coroner's on her way."

"Nothing we can do for her."

"Wait until Dr. Pippen gets here."

Why? Did he want company? Mainly he didn't want the housekeepers who took turns peeking in at Ruby, their eyes wide and horrified, to think that this was getting anything but the complete attention of the Fox River police. He wished Agnes Lamb was here to reassure them further.

Meanwhile he considered what Ruby's death meant for Harry Paquette. Harry was under lock and key downtown, so there was no way he was going to be accused of doing away with a woman who would have tied him tightly to Linda Hopkins and knew all the ups and downs of their relationship and thought he should be hanged. But Cy had come with the idea that Ruby might be able to identify Timothy Gallagher as the lawyer who had tried to be so friendly with Linda. It was not the sort of speculation he would have voiced, certainly not to Phil Keegan, but if Ruby had made the identification of Tim Gallagher, the two murders he was investigating would no longer be unrelated. But related in what way? Not even in the privacy of his own mind did Cy attempt an answer to that question.

2

If Cy Horvath had a primary virtue, it was his Hungarian doggedness. On the other hand, that was his main vice too. Phil Keegan had let Cy wrap up the investigation of the woman pushed into traffic but he was supposed to be devoting himself primarily to the Agatha Rossner strangling. So what the hell was he doing out at the Hacienda Motel and calling in to report the murder of Ruby Otter?

"Nine-one-one got that, Cy."

"Phil, this is the woman who knew the girl who was pushed into traffic."

"I thought you were looking into the woman Jack Gallagher claims he strangled."

"That's the funny thing. I am."

"You got anyone with you?"

"No."

"Why don't I come by there and hear what you've got."

Before a death could be turned over to the prosecutor as a case of murder of whatever degree, Phil Keegan's division had to establish a number of things. Identify a suspect, or suspects, of course, and then show there was motive and opportunity and, most important of all, gather physical evidence that the suspect had done the deed. What someone might have going on in his own mind, God only knew, and that went for the jury as well as the one indicted for a crime. Leave too much margin for thought on the part of the men and women of the jury, and all hell could break loose. The thing had to be tied down in such a way that, like it or not, whatever the defendant might claim he meant to do, no one could reasonably deny that he did kill the other person. A confession of guilt? These were so rare as to be nonexistent—even years afterward.

Justice is imperfect in this world, of course, and many of those who walked free after a trial, or who by bargaining and the like spent a short time in prison because their action had been redescribed out of all comparison with what the evidence showed, were guilty as sin and everyone including their attorneys knew it. There were protests against such decisions only if there were factors involved that could ignite a segment of the population. If a cop is set free by a jury when he is up for shooting a citizen, you can count on protests. Demonstrations on the other side are far more sure, particularly if it is a question of capital punishment. It didn't matter to anti–death penalty zealots if the prisoner himself accepted the justice of his sentence. It was barbaric to exact a life in the name of justice, however guilty that life was. Life imprisonment was the fallback position: Better to lock the murderer up forever and throw away the key. But now life imprisonment too, was coming under attack, now it is thought barbaric to confine a man in a penitentiary for life. The whole damned society has gone nuts, Phil was sure of it. It was punishment itself that horrified people.

"They don't think anyone is really responsible for anything, Roger," he had said to Father Dowling when he had philosophized about this subject at the rectory.

"A comforting doctrine. But I don't think it has many adherents, Phil."

"Come on." Phil had been ticking off examples of what he meant.

"Think of the ref at a ball game. Fans are ready to hang him in a minute for a bad call."

"It might bring back real baseball," Phil growled.

It was the anger he felt about Jack Gallagher that had brought all these thoughts up like heartburn. With Jack they had had a confession before he got his chair warm downtown.

"I did it. It's that simple. I strangled that poor girl and I am here to pay the price."

What good is a confession? They still had to do their job. Jack would not be permitted to plead guilty. Like everyone else he would be the beneficiary of the legal system, rival attorneys, the prosecutor trying to convince the jury he had done it, the defense rebutting and mocking the prosecutor's case. Jack Gallagher's confession was not going to figure in that procedure.

The medical examiner's team had been all over Jack's condo, fingerprints, photographs, the works. And the area outside where the body had been found was still marked off, but the word was that it was useless. The area had been stomped to death by the 911 ambulance crew and then Dr. Pippen and her bunch. What could they do? They had to walk on the ground. Now a slight thaw had made it even more worthless. The autopsy report, the lab's examinations of the site— meaning largely Jack's condo—would give them facts. But until someone like Cy got working on it, it would not take a shape that any prosecutor would accept. So why in the hell was Cy out here at the Hacienda Motel checking out a call that had been made to 911?

"I didn't come because of the call, Phil."

They were in Ruby's little office and Phil was bent over, studying the throat, still tightly caught in the laundry-bag cord. "Either she fought pretty good or the strangler didn't know his business. See how the marks jump all over before the final twisting?" Dispassionate. Of course Phil hadn't known Ruby.

"I came to talk with her."

"What about?"

Pippen blew in then, her leather coat open and flying around her, red hair swept efficiently back to set off her Grace Kelly cheeks. She nodded at the detectives and then she too was bent over Ruby.

"How about a drink, Phil?"

"Sure. Why not?"

The medical examiner's van was pulling in as they crossed the lobby to the lounge. Lawrence Wagner came athwart them, wringing his hands. "Must they use all those damnable sirens?"

"Those are the low ones," Cy said. "You should hear them full blast."

"Who's he?" Phil said as they entered the ill-lit, chilly lounge.

"The manager."

Phil made a sound.

They sat at the bar, and ordered glasses of stout. "The reason I was coming to see Ruby was to show her this."

Phil took the newspaper and looked at the picture of Timothy Gallagher. "She know him?"

"We'll never know." Cy drank off his glass in one steady swallow and shook his head when the bartender came over. Phil was a sipper, but this was no place to hear what Cy wanted to say. Phil put away half his stout and said, "Come on."

They sat in Keegan's car and, listening, Phil remembered his annoyance that Cy wasn't concentrating on the death of Agatha Rossner. Cy spoke matter-of-factly, of course, but not even his phlegmatic disposition could lessen the bizarre menagerie that had formed prior to the murder. The facts, as Cy would write them up when he got back to his desk, were these:

- Colleen Gallagher heard that her brother Tim was involved with Agatha Rossner, whom he had met at a legal seminar at the Hacienda Motel.
- Colleen thought this affair was revenge on Agatha's part because Mario Liberati, now Colleen's fiancé, had spurned her advances.

- Fearful that Agatha could, intentionally or not, ruin Tim's family life, Colleen spoke to her uncle Austin Rooney about it and he agreed to talk to his nephew. He saw the couple together at the Willard Bar downtown and thought being observed was all the lesson Tim needed.
- When the affair continued, Colleen asked her father to talk sense into her brother. She contrived a tour of Mallard and Bill so her father could see what Agatha was like, and the two went off together afterward, Jack indicating that he would work on the girl first.
- As a result of this, Agatha dropped the son in favor of the father. At least one previous time she had stayed most of the night with Jack. On the night she was killed, she left earlier and was killed not far from the entrance of Jack's condo.
- Jack confessed to the murder, but that was bunk. He was calm as could be when the police came to his door the following morning.
- If Jack is just a distraction, who are the possible suspects?

> *Timothy Gallagher.*
> *Austin Rooney.*
> *Mario Liberati.*
> *Colleen Gallagher.*
> *Unknown.*

"In that order?" Phil asked. He had lit a cigar and nodded his head among the clouds.

"I think so," Cy replied.

"What would Ruby have been able to prove if she had lived to see that picture of Timothy?"

"That he and Aggie went there after their drinks. We can't just take a woman's saying so for the fact that they had an affair. That may be good enough, or bad enough, for the man's sister, but we have to know."

"Who do you want working with you?"

"Maybe Agnes, in a little bit. There is one more item, Phil. How did Agatha get to Jack's place and how did she expect to get home when she left?"

"It would be hard to get a cab at that hour, except by phoning first."

"The hood of the car was still warm when we checked her garage, Phil."

Phil Keegan munched on his cigar and scowled.

"Maybe somebody drove her there and dumped her in the snow."

"But if she drove there . . ."

"The car may be the key to the whole thing."

3

Fred came up, knocked on his door, and told Austin Rooney that the police had been here asking about him.

"That's hard to believe."

"They seem to be interested in why you was out all last night."

Austin looked at the loathsome Fred Crosley. The man rented out units of his building but did not thereby lose interest in the space he himself did not occupy. Except when repairs were needed, of course. He was the most intrusive busybody Austin had ever known.

"So what did you tell them?"

"Me? How would I know where you spend your nights?"

"How would you know that I wasn't home in bed?"

"Were you?" Fred asked, a sly expression on his face.

"Maybe I'll hold that answer until the police ask me."

"Where were you?" Fred asked, unable to face the prospect of not knowing.

"A gentleman never tells."

Sometime later, Colleen called to tell him that the police had been to see Timothy. "At his office, thank God. I suppose we will all be grilled now."

"They've already been here."

"What did they ask you?"

"They came in my absence. The ineffable Crosley apparently told them I didn't come home that night so I will have to come up with a story to account for it."

Colleen laughed. Austin was impressed by the way the Gallaghers were handling what for any other family would be an unmitigated tragedy. The head of the clan's confession, of strangling a young woman, was all over the news. Of course the worst was yet to be, as Colleen herself must know. Jack's ridiculous confession would not dissuade the police from doing their job, and sooner or later they would find out that Tim as well as his father had had liaisons with the Messalina of Mallard and Bill. And they would learn that Colleen had asked Austin to do something about Tim and the young woman.

"Oh, Austin, what a terrible fool I was."

"That means they will learn about Tim and Agatha."

"Austin, I told them all about it."

"You can see now the reason for Jack's confession."

"What do you mean?"

"He must think Timothy killed her. This is the grand patriarchal gesture. ' "Shoot if you must this old gray head, but spare my only son," he said.' "

Grudgingly Austin admired Jack for what he had done, assuming that he had confessed in order to divert suspicion from Tim. It was credible that Jack would march off to prison with head held high if he were convicted, his consolation that he had saved Tim and Jane and their children. But what he could not very likely prevent was Jane's learning of her husband's infidelity.

Thinking of all that the various Gallaghers had yet to undergo, Austin nonetheless dreaded his own exposure more. He had mocked the news of Jack's liaison to Maud who had said, "Of course he wouldn't be capable of anything. Not at his age."

"Why do you say that?"

"Would he?" Her head was lowered and her innocent blue eyes looked at him, the palm of her hand warm in his.

Lusting after a woman Maud's age might be ridiculous, but it made more sense than wanting a woman half his age. Maud was a flirt, of course, but there was more than the mere memory of desire in her manner. He drew her close against him. They were in his car. Austin had gone to a doctor who did not know him and received a prescription for Viagra. Now he was stirred by its effects. He took Maud masterfully in his arms and kissed her. She clung to him, all shyness gone. Eventually, as he had hoped, they went inside and there in her chintzy bedroom, all blues and pinks, they fell upon the bed and outdid themselves.

He would die before subjecting Maud to exposure. That was why he had slipped away in the early-morning hours, though Maud thought it was an unnecessary precaution. There was that in her reluctance to see him go that suggested that she had not yet had her fill of carnal memories. He knelt beside the bed and put his face next to hers.

"I'll make an honest woman of you, Maud."

"I thought you'd never ask."

4

"Of course he didn't do it," Tim said to Jane.

"Then why does he say he did?"

"Why does anyone take the blame for something he hasn't done?" He shrugged and took her in his arms. "I've had a day making up for yesterday."

Jane's heart went out to him. Everything had seemed to be going so smoothly and suddenly things were falling apart. And Tim had to bear the brunt of it.

"Go into the den and relax. I'll bring you a drink."

"Where are the kids?"

"Austin has them."

"Austin!"

It had been a surprise, Austin's offer to take the kids to a hockey game. "You two need a little respite, Jane," he'd said.

"Hockey? That ought to thrill Becky."

"He gave them a choice. Hockey or a double feature. Go sit down, I'll be right with you."

Usually Tim made his own drink, a martini, and Jane was not that practiced in the art. All she remembered was heavy on the gin. She made a gin and tonic for herself, light on the gin.

Tim had collapsed into his leather chair, shoeless feet on the footstool, coat tossed over a chair, tie loosened, his head leaning back, eyes closed.

"Portrait of a successful young lawyer," Jane said.

He opened one eye. "I feel as old as the sea."

She put down the drinks, found room on his chair, pushing him over, and laid her head on his chest. Soon she could hear the steady metronome of his heart, rhythmically beating, something like the sea indeed. Her heart too went on like that. So had the young lawyer's, Agatha's, but now it was stopped forever.

"Why do people take the blame for things they haven't done?"

After a pause, he said, "To protect someone else.

"Is that what your father is doing?"

"He thinks so."

"Did he tell you that?"

"He didn't have to." The rhythm of his heart seemed to alter. "He thinks I did it."

"What!" Jane sat up with a start, nearly losing her place on the cushion. He grabbed her before she fell to the floor and then he held her tightly against him.

"Jane, I have to tell you something I would almost rather die than tell you."

Oh, God. Something awful was going to be said. Had she had some premonition of this? She waited, holding her breath. Perhaps her heart had stopped beating as well.

"Let me just say it all first. About Agatha Rossner. I met her at a legal seminar . . ."

Jane listened, understanding but not believing she was hearing this or that Tim was saying it. Whatever she had dreaded, it was not this. That Tim had been unfaithful to her, that he had succumbed to the lures of that Jezebel, was beyond belief.

"I had drinks with her a couple times. Only once was there anything . . ."

She pressed her fingers against his mouth. Dear God, she did not want to hear any more. She felt like someone on the TV news from some disaster area, their home underwater or burned or blown away.

For a time, they were silent in one another's arms. She should feel anger and rage, but she felt only emptiness. And she could sense his relief at having told her. What a weight it must have been.

"Your father knew?"

"The woman worked at Mallard and Bill with Colleen."

"She told your father?"

"First she told Austin."

Had everyone known what Tim had told her? She tried to think how they had acted recently, Colleen, Austin, but she could detect nothing even in retrospect.

"Why?"

"She did it for us, I think. For me and then for you and the kids. She was right."

"And now you think your father has confessed because he thinks you strangled that woman?"

"It's the only explanation."

"Well, tell him you didn't. Tell him you couldn't have." She sat up, surprised to see that his face was wet with tears. "You were out of town." And then she moved her face to his, mingling their tears.

Men are weak, of course, she had always known that, but sex alone cannot hold them. "If sex were all then any hand could make us squeak like dolls the wished for words"—Wallace Stevens, for whom she'd had a great enthusiasm in college. Disbelief, sorrow, anger, and finally something like peace. She would forgive him. He was suffering enough inside, knowing what he had done, how he had endangered their home, and telling her had to be worse than telling a priest in the confessional. It was the womanly thing, to forgive, the Christian thing.

The big meal she had planned when Uncle Austin took the kids went into escrow. They had scrambled eggs and ham and raisin toast, Tim's favorite, and coffee. The drinks she had made were in the study, ignored, diluted by the melting cubes. They turned on the television but muted the sound so it was just a flickering presence in peripheral vision as they sat side by side on the sofa, not saying much, two shipwrecks washed ashore but feeling no more need to talk about their ordeal.

"Don't put off confessing, darling," she said into the silence.

"What?"

"If you haven't been to confession yet, get it over with."

19

1

Father Dowling reflected on the irony of recent events.

Harry Paquette, the man accused of pushing his girlfriend to her death in traffic, had had his moment in the sun and then faded from attention. The death of Ruby, the head housekeeper at the Hacienda Motel, confused the issue. Harry had been in jail when the murder occurred, yet Ruby would have testified against Harry and given reasons why he would have killed Linda Hopkins. Perhaps his trial would elicit interest. For the sake of the parents in Appleseed, Wisconsin, he hoped not. Meanwhile, having asked about Harry while speaking to Phil, Father Dowling decided to go downtown and talk to him. He had been prepared for Harry by Phil's description: ponytail, cocky, and defiant.

"I ain't Catholic," Harry said, coming to a stop just inside the door.

"That's true of most people in the world. What are you?"

Harry seemed surprised by the question. "I don't know. Not Catholic."

"But Christian?" Father Dowling indicated the crucifix tattooed on Harry's forearm.

"I was drunk at the time." He pulled a chair some feet from the table and sat. "You the chaplain here?"

"Lieutenant Horvath told me you deny killing that girl."

"He doesn't believe me." Harry shrugged. "What do I care? I didn't do it. I wish it had been me was pushed into traffic."

"You were going to marry?"

"It's the only way she'd have it. I would have done anything for her."

"Including starting a savings account."

Harry made a face. "Horvath told you everything, didn't he?"

"He's your best bet, Harry."

"Horvath?"

"Horvath. I think he does believe you."

Father Dowling came away sharing the view that Harry Paquette was innocent.

Cy had said, "If he were still on the run and Ruby got killed, I would figure it was Harry, trying to cover his tracks."

Cy had given him an account of events at the Hacienda Motel. There had been no robbery, nothing other than the murder. The man was hidden in a linen closet behind Ruby's desk, waiting for her. When she settled at her desk, he stepped out and looped the laundry-bag cord around her neck.

"Man?"

"Size-ten shoes. That's about all he left, his footprints."

Cy had all this in reports from the medical examiner's crew. But his attention now was on the strangling of Agatha. The media had suddenly noticed that three days had gone by and the man who had confessed to the crime had not yet been indicted.

"Would you do me a favor, Father? There's one man I can cross off my list if I could learn one thing."

"Austin Rooney?"

"That's right, you know about that. I don't want to embarrass him and I sure don't want to give any satisfaction to Fred Crosley, his landlord, but I have to know where he was night before last."

"That's a pretty delicate matter, Cy."

"Maybe he was putting in his time before the Blessed Sacrament. Isn't it round-the-clock at the basilica?"

"Or an all-night card game."

"Anything, just so I can account for it. Skinner has hold of it and he's like a rat terrier."

With some reluctance Father Dowling took himself over to the Senior Center to talk with Austin Rooney. A call to Edna had assured him Austin was there.

"He was playing cribbage with Maud when I last looked."

First he would have to separate Austin from Maud, then he would have to rely on inspiration for a way to ask Austin the question. If inspiration did not come, he would forget it. A priest cannot go around like a moral policeman.

When he pushed through the door of the school, a figure burst from the gym, holding a bloody handkerchief to his face, and collapsed on the stairs, moaning.

"Desmond, what happened?"

Desmond O'Toole looked up at the priest. He took the handkerchief from his nose and gasped at the amount of blood.

"I need first aid," he cried, and began to move up the stairs, half crawling, then stopped, but on his feet, one hand on the railing, the other pressing the bloody handkerchief to his nose.

Austin Rooney and Maud emerged from the gym.

"I did it," Austin said, and there was pride in his voice.

"Father, he deserved it," Maud said.

"He insulted Maud."

"He insulted both of us."

"How so?"

"He asked a very personal question about where I spend my nights," Austin said.

Maud dropped her eyes, but crept closer to her hero.

This broke the ice. Father Dowling asked Maud if she would excuse them for a moment and she released Austin reluctantly. The

priest took Austin into a onetime classroom, not yet remodeled, recalling the original purpose of the building.

"I think I was in this room, in third grade." Austin looked around
as if in a time capsule, then moved down the row of desks nearest the
window and stopped. "Here. I sat here."

"Austin, you should know that Desmond has been making trouble for
you. He called your landlord and was told you were not at home the night
that girl was strangled and he has got it into his mind that you killed her."

Austin's laughter, more cheerful than derisive, was welcome. "But
I have an alibi."

Nothing more. Father Dowling, who had a logical mind, did not
choose to frame the question that suggested itself.

"You must stop hitting people, Austin."

"They have a common thread, Father: Maud."

"I'll let you get back to her. And think what you'll say if the police
ask you where you were that night."

"Maud is my alibi."

No need to comment on that. The trouble with this answer, Father
Dowling reflected on the way back to the rectory, was that no one was
likely to believe it. Maud would say anything Austin asked of her. Plus
the skepticism that two people of that age should be spending an illicit
night together. But then he thought of Jack Gallagher's enduring
machismo. When *does* the folly of the flesh subside?

2

"How will you make any money from a client like that?" Hazel wanted
to know.

"I'll be court-appointed. The county pays the bills."

"Welfare!" Hazel snorted. "You have to start advertising."

Tuttle shook his head. "It doesn't work."

"Of course it works."

"I've tried it."

"It's how you state the message. We'll call you 'Fox River's most experienced lawyer.' "

"That's Amos Cadbury."

"It's only an ad. And you have to appeal to women."

What had he done to deserve Hazel? Had he even hired her? She paid herself out of the dwindling office account, of which she had taken charge. Her efficiency was formidable.

"Officer Pianone called."

"What did you tell him?"

"That you were busy and would try to get back to him."

"He is my contact downtown. He keeps me informed."

"You could learn more from the janitor."

Tuttle closed the door of his office, picked up the phone, and dialed the Detective Division. Something about the line suggested that Hazel was listening in. She had ordered a new phone system, so that all incoming calls went through her.

"Detective Division."

"That you, Agnes?"

"Who's this?"

"Tuttle. Is Peanuts around?"

"I don't see him."

"Tell him I called. Oh, Agnes, you working with Cy on the Agatha Rossner murder?"

"Sort of. I am checking up on Ruby to get some lead on who might have killed her."

"Don't forget to tell Peanuts."

She hung up but Tuttle still held the phone when Hazel's voice emerged from it.

"Who's Agnes?"

He slammed down the phone.

* * *

He found Peanuts at the Great Wall, sitting morose and alone in a booth, the shells of a fortune cookie before him. He held the little ribbon of paper on which the message was printed. When he saw Tuttle, a great smile spread over his face. Tuttle slipped in across from him.

"These things are never wrong."

The message read, *You will find an old friend.* Tuttle was touched.

"Did you fire her yet?"

"It's not that easy." It was why he didn't like to handle divorces. There was always one party who resisted.

"I'm not going there until she's gone."

"Have you eaten?"

For answer, Peanuts opened the menu and began to read it greedily. Tuttle would not risk mentioning Agatha until they had eaten. He did not think of what he was doing as withholding information, since Horvath ought to know as much about the young lawyer's car as he did. He had got to the garage first and he must have seen that the car had just been washed that morning. Tuttle knew what Horvath could only guess—that the woman had parked that car outside Jack Gallagher's condo on the fatal night. Tuttle himself had watched her pull over, cut the power and lights, and then pick her way delicately through the snow to the shoveled walk and then go like a model on a runway to the door. The car was still there when Peanuts relieved him. Peanuts had brought a bag of tacos and enchiladas, still reasonably hot.

"She's been inside since seven-thirty."

Peanuts had continued to chew on an enchilada. You never knew whether Peanuts understood or cared what he was doing on such occasions. He would be asleep ten minutes after Tuttle left him but the hope was that anything like a car starting would wake him up. That night it hadn't. Nor had the arrival of the 911 paramedics. Only their flickering lights had disturbed his slumber and when the police arrived, Peanuts had had the sense to get out of there.

The woman's car was gone and she was found lying dead in the snow. So who had driven her car away and taken the trouble to run it through a car wash before putting it in her garage stall? Someone who knew where she parked the car. Or would there have been something in the car that told him where to put it? But why not just leave it? And how had the man who took the car gotten there in the first place? One thing was clear: Find the man who took Agatha's car back to her garage and you would have the man who strangled her and left her lying in the snow.

And that man was surely not Jack Gallagher. When would they let the guy go and get him off center stage so the media wouldn't keep waiting for him to be brought before a judge? Even Judge Farner had said something that was interpreted as surprise that Jack Gallagher had not yet appeared before her.

"How's Cy doing on the big murder case?"

Peanuts shrugged.

"I mean the woman lawyer who was strangled."

Peanuts moved his head from side to side.

"Agnes working with Horvath?"

Tuttle was ready for Peanuts's usual reaction when reminded of the young black woman who had been hired on the basis of affirmative action but had turned into a first-rate detective, quickly advancing beyond Peanuts, no great feat, but gaining the confidence and even praise of Captain Keegan. And Cy Horvath seemed to want her on any investigation he conducted.

"He dumped her."

"No kidding."

"She's on that motel thing."

"Motel thing."

He meant the girl who had been killed in traffic on Dirksen. She had been a housekeeper at the motel.

"Doing what?"

Peanuts grinned. "Keeping out of his way."

* * *

3

Rawley looked over his book, slyly, the way he was telling George Hessian he had looked when Lieutenant Horvath asked about the Alfa Romeo.

It had occurred to George's hirsute friend that when you thought of his testimony, you had a very interesting mystery on your hands. Rawley would swear on a stack of Bibles that the young lawyer's Alfa Romeo had been parked in the development when he came on duty and that the car had gone past the guard shack sometime in the early morning. That was why the car was not there when police cars and an ambulance came roaring up to the gate and found the body of the woman lying in the snow.

"But her car was gone."

"So she left during your watch?"

"I already told you that."

"Did you call the police?"

The whiskered face was still and Rawley's eyes drifted away. The two men were crammed into the guard shack, with the Mr. Coffee burbling and the windows steaming up. Rawley's answer was scarcely audible.

"No. God forgive me, no. But I had no idea . . ." He looked at George like a fugitive peering through foliage, his massive beard twitching from side to side as if he were working his mouth.

"You didn't call them."

"You could get the answer by asking the police."

"If they know."

Rawley was in the mood to invest his job with mystery and danger. In retrospect, at least, he enjoyed the thought that waves of violence and mayhem lapped at the guard shack, and that his presence there was the one sure thing that prevented the encroachment of the jungle on this more or less peaceful little island. But sometimes the gate was breached, and the world crept in, with fatal results.

"What gets me, George, is someone drove her car right past this shack. If I had been looking out that window I would have seen him."

"Don't blame yourself."

"What are you talking about? I'm not blaming myself."

"Who knows how many people drive in and out of here without your noticing."

Rawley didn't like that at all, but George was a little sick of the way his friend sought to dramatize his marginal connection with the death of the young lawyer. He had stopped here on his way to visit his mother with the hope that he could talk about his writing. He got to his feet and then nearly doubled over. There was a cramp in his leg from sitting so long in a less-than-comfortable position.

"Where you going?"

"Over to see my mother."

"Stop by when you leave."

George did not speculate that he could drive out without Rawley noticing. On the way to his car, he walked off the cramp. Stopping to visit with Rawley had been a way of postponing the visit to his mother. Now he looked forward to it. She would listen to him talk about his writing, even if she didn't follow what was said to her.

4

Agnes Lamb had not known Ruby Otter but did know Ruby's assistant, Gloria Daley, who had returned from vacation to find herself the new head housekeeper at the Hacienda Motel. Gloria had dropped out of the school Agnes graduated from and was from the neighborhood.

"I'm almost afraid to sit in that chair, Agnes. That's where he killed her."

"Who'd want to kill you?"

"Listen, if Ruby had any enemies, I don't know them. That

woman was so good." Tears glistened in Gloria's eyes. She had bal-
looned since the last time Agnes had seen her and the trouble with
the chair in the office of the head housekeeper was if Gloria could fit
in it.

"You were on vacation."

"Ruby called it sick leave."

"Where were you sick?"

"In Joliet mainly." She meant the casino boats anchored along the
banks of the Joliet River. "He won so we decided to go big-time and
flew out to Vegas."

And lost it all. Gloria had had to wire for money to get home. Her
man had sold the return portion of their tickets and stayed on to win
back what he had lost. Gloria got on a bus and saw parts of the country you wouldn't believe on the way home.

"So you heard nothing about Linda's death."

"Uh-uh. She was a sweet thing."

"Did you know the guy? Harry?"

Gloria whistled. "He acted like a cab driver."

"He was a cab driver."

"That's what I mean. Long hair, earrings, tattoos. What she saw in
that freak show, I don't understand."

"Ruby said she was trying to get rid of him."

Gloria thought about that, then shook her head. "More like she
wanted marriage if he had any big plans."

"He says he didn't do it."

"Uh-huh."

Cy's assumption was that once they had Harry in custody, the witnesses who had gone from being sure to being vague would become
sure again. But that wasn't happening. Agnes had been assigned by Cy
to talk to the three that might have been any help in court, and they
studied the photographs of Harry without having their memories
refreshed.

"I may have seen him there, but I didn't see him push her."

"Earlier you seemed pretty sure you could identify the man who pushed her."

"I still think so. But this isn't the one." That was Baxter, James, mail carrier.

Pettigrew, Phyllis, Mrs., shook her head as soon as she saw Harry's pictures. "I saw him in the paper and knew right away you had the wrong person. Mabel said I was wrong; that's the man," she said. "It's so sad."

"What's sad?"

"The way she died."

"Mabel Wilson is dead?"

"They found her yesterday, at her kitchen table, oven door open, place full of gas."

In the interview she had given at the time, Mabel had said she would never forget that man's face if she lived to be a hundred. She was fifty-nine when she died. With her went the case against Harry Paquette.

"He must have someone doing it for him," Agnes said to Cy at that juncture. "Ruby, now Mabel Wilson." Mabel's remark that she would never forget the murderer's face had appeared in the news stories after Harry was brought from Kansas City.

"All the housekeepers knew about Harry. Why kill Ruby?"

So Agnes had come to the motel with another photograph in a manila envelope to test out a hunch of Cy's.

"Gloria, Ruby mentioned what a hit Linda was with groups that held conferences at the motel, lawyers and such."

"She told you that?"

"Isn't it true?"

"Well, it wasn't her fault he liked her so much. Lots of guests were friendly but this one was serious. I think they had a date, when she was on the outs with Harry."

"You ever see this man?"

"Honey, we all made a point of seeing him. Ruby warned her about it. That man was interested in only one thing and Linda wasn't that kind of girl. Ruby might have said something to him too."

Agnes slipped the black-and-white photograph out of the envelope and handed it to Gloria.

"Is that him?"

"He looks familiar."

"Is he the man who showed such interest in Linda?"

"Oh, no. That's not him. But he does look familiar. Who is he?"

"You might have seen his picture in the paper."

"He got a name?"

"Gallagher. Timothy Gallagher."

"He's not the one," she told Cy.

"Definite?"

"Definite."

There was no use expecting any explanation from Cy Horvath, but Agnes could see that his hopes that there was a connection between the two murders the Division was investigating had just gone up in smoke.

5

Cy went personally to Timothy Gallagher to tell him his father would be released from detention, though he must hold himself available for any further questioning. The son nodded. "Thanks, Lieutenant. He'll want to make a great exit."

"I'm still trying to figure out why he would have claimed to have done such a thing."

"Two reasons at least. First, he saw an opportunity that morning to play a role he had never played: Jack Gallagher, murderer. Besides, it drew attention to the fact that the young lady had been infatuated with him."

"Is that the second reason?"

"No, the second reason is he thought I did it."

"Did he say that?"

"Not in words. It was the main point of the exercise."

"Why would he think a thing like that?"

"Lieutenant, I know some of the things you've learned in the past few days. What you may have heard about Aggie and myself is true. My father became involved with her when he went to speak to her about me. My wife now knows of this, but of course I would appreciate as little publicity on the matter as possible. Unlike my father, I do not thrive on public self-laceration."

"When was the last time you saw her?"

"Aggie?" He had to think. "A week? At least a week, maybe more."

"How could your father imagine you'd killed the woman?"

"You'll have to ask him that."

"And you're assuming that he confessed in order to divert attention from you."

"Technically, yes. I am assuming it. But I am certain that is the reason."

Timothy Gallagher followed Cy downtown and in the courthouse there was an emotional, and media-recorded, reunion of father and son—who had spent the better part of the previous days in consultation. Jack beamed at the cameras without seeming to notice them; he looked around as if he was surprised to find anyone at all awaiting his appearance.

"I feel like Saint Paul being led out of prison by an angel."

"That's better than being led in by one," someone cracked, but

Jack ignored it. This was not a time for levity. He could not, in the understandable elation he felt on regaining his freedom, forget the wonderful young person who had lost her life three nights before.

"Why did you say you killed her?"

Jack acknowledged this question. "I confessed the guilt I felt. I considered myself to have been the occasion, if not the cause, of her death. Who could have exonerated himself if he were in my position? Mine may not be a guilt in reach of the law, but it weighs on me all the same."

Father and son went arm in arm from the courthouse. Phil had come down to the rotunda to watch this performance.

"We should charge him rent," he growled.

What Phil did not mention was that they were running out of suspects. Jack had never been seriously in the running, Austin had cleared himself, and now Timothy Gallagher seemed to have defused what they knew of him by a candid admission. Cy imagined the man telling his wife about the affair. What could he fear after that? And then he had heard from Agnes Lamb that his wild hunch had not paid off. Timothy Gallagher was not the lawyer who had shown more than a passing interest in Linda.

"So there's no connection," Agnes said. "Between the two murders."

"Apparently not."

He should have known she would guess the implications of the test he had asked her to make. If Timothy had turned out to be a womanizer, Aggie only one episode . . . if he had been the lawyer who took Linda Hopkins out at least once . . . well, then the two murdered women would have been connected through him. Because if Agnes had gotten a positive response, Cy would not have ruled Timothy out as a suspect. Even so, he was not convinced that Timothy was completely in the clear.

"Want to get something to eat, Cy?" Phil asked.

Cy was due home but this was the time of day when Phil Keegan's loneliness closed in on him. He was not eager to go home to his apartment looking out at an artificial lake and other apartments overlooking the same lake. His wife was dead, his daughters settled elsewhere with their families; Phil's only interest was in his work. And shooting the bull with Father Dowling.

"I'll have a drink with you, anyway."

They went across the street to Stub's where Phil ordered a Guinness, in the bottle, and Cy had a Coke. They huddled at the end of the bar.

"I suppose tomorrow we'll be escorting Harry Paquette out to the waiting media."

"Skinner is the only one who thinks we have a case."

"Skinner." Phil drank deep. "Say, was there anything worthwhile in that stuff of Harry's you picked up from where he lived?"

Cy looked at him. "I haven't had a report on it."

"You forgot it, didn't you?"

"I haven't looked into it yet."

But Phil would not drop it. Most of the time he praised Cy to the skies so he probably had a right to make a lot of his flaws. The truth was that, what with one thing and another, Cy had forgotten the stuff of Harry's he had turned over to the lab.

"It will be worthless," Phil said, letting up. "You can bet on it."

Phil said he would eat at Stub's, then maybe give Father Dowling a call. Cy said good night. Outside, he crossed the street to the courthouse and went up the stairs to the top floor. Putting off until tomorrow the discovery that what Harry had left behind when he fled to Kansas City was worthless did not appeal after Phil's razzing. Coming toward him in the corridor was Dr. Pippen, the assistant coroner, and Cy's ticket to heaven or hell.

"Still here?" she asked brightly.

"I want to check something at the lab."

"Me too. They've had more than enough time to go over the contents of Agatha's purse."

Finley was on night duty and he looked dumbly if beatifically at them because of the plugs in his ears. He removed them. "Mozart," he sighed. "What can I do you for?"

Cy let Pippen go first, politeness, of course, having the bonus of letting him just stand there and look at her. She was given the purse and a sheet listing its contents. Each item checked.

"She had the purse of a call girl," Pippen said, turning her wide innocent eyes on him. Doctors, especially pathologists, knew dark secrets, but if they were like Pippen they did not take root in the soul. "Two sets of keys."

"Two? Let me see." They were both house keys. Was one to Jack Gallagher's condo? He dropped both sets in his pocket.

"You better sign for those."

"Anything else interesting?"

"I thought you had another reason for coming here."

"Finley, give me the Harry Paquette stuff."

It still looked like a stack of dirty laundry, but the itemized list indicated the tests that had been run, without result.

"This one really shrunk," Pippen said, holding up a T-shirt.

Cy did not say what he thought—that the item belonged to Linda; that like the savings account, it was another proof of Harry's helpless love of the girl. But that was not all. There was a framed photograph of Linda Hopkins, and a bank statement. Dr. Pippen studied the photograph. "Pretty. Has his trial been set?"

"There may not be one."

She tucked in her chin. "Really?"

"He denies it, the witnesses can't identify him—those that are still alive—and he intended to marry the girl."

"But did he do it?"

"No."

"But then who did? She was pushed, wasn't she?"

"She was pushed."

Finley had his earplugs in and did not acknowledge their departure. In the hallway, Pippen stopped, and looked around, lost.

"Care to have a drink at Stub's?" Cy asked.

"Do you have time?"

"Just."

Phil had left, probably having wangled an invitation to dinner with Father Dowling, but Cy did not let out a silent cheer. He had told himself it was all right if he took the beautiful Dr. Pippen for a drink if Phil could join them.

"You haven't had much of a week, have you? Jack Gallagher walks and Harry can't be tried."

"That's the way it should be, if they're innocent."

"I keep remembering the condition of that girl's body when we got it."

"You chose an odd speciality."

"I figured I couldn't harm anyone. *'Primum non nocere.'* That's part of the oath we don't take anymore."

"Hippocratic."

"I suppose it became the Hypocritic. But I'm keeping you. You should go home."

"When are you going to get married?"

She brightened. "You noticed!" She splayed the fingers of her left hand to show the diamond. Cy looked at her.

"Who is he?"

"A pediatrician."

"Foot doctor."

She kicked him. "You must come to the wedding."

"I wouldn't miss it."

Driving home he felt both relieved and saddened. He had imagined an unchanging Dr. Pippen—tall and beautiful and competent, unmarried—as a fixture of his life, someone with whom he could just sit and talk and . . . Oh, the hell with it.

"So who's left?" Gladys asked. She was watching television while Cy told her of his day. She did not really like to hear about his work. Who could blame her?

Mario Liberati was left. Cy had gotten the impression from Colleen that she and Mario thought Agatha had had something to do with his being let go by Mallard and Bill. Maybe revenge was a more promising motive than ruptured romance. But sitting on the couch, not watching the program his wife had on, he thought of Agnes's report on the witnesses to Linda's death. They seemed to have been disappearing one by one.

1

Being in jail had taken Jack out of his shell. There was never a dull moment, he had been in the eye of the hurricane, the cynosure of every reporter, lawyer, detective, prosecutor, as well as assorted female clerks who came by just to take a look at him. Of course the other prisoners had resented all this, until he sang for them.

"Give us Frankie's 'My Way.' "

He gave them Frankie's "My Way." Silly lyrics, but most lyrics are. The song had become the favorite hymn of the losers of this world.

" 'Dat's Amore'!"

He gave them Dino Martino. He felt like a jukebox. But he was loved.

After that, returning to his condo was deflating. He closed the door of his condo behind him and felt more in a cell than he had in the cell. He had been expected to be taken home to dinner with Jane and the kids, but Tim brought him directly to the condo, came in, and shut the door.

"I'm back in jail," Jack sighed.

"Dad, what you learned about me and Aggie? I've told Jane."

"You shouldn't have done that." The voice of experience.

"She would have found out some other way. I wanted to tell her."

"That must have taken great courage."

Tim sat, still wearing his coat, arms on the arms of the chair, chin down. Napoleon in thought. "I don't know the difference between courage and cowardice anymore. I was afraid she would find out before I told her."

"She's a wonderful woman."

"I didn't strangle Aggie."

Jack feigned surprise. "Good Lord, who ever thought so?"

"Just about everyone after you confessed. You were sacrificing yourself for your son."

"Why would I think you did it?"

"We both had similar motives."

"I am going to have a drink. Do you realize that I have not had a drink in days?"

"I'll wait until I get home."

"Wise, wise."

"So who did do it?"

"Who's left?"

"Mario?"

Jack paused in the process of pouring scotch over the cubes in his glass and looked at his son. "Are you serious?"

"You know he was let go by Mallard and Bill."

"Whatever for?"

"His sister is married to an underworld figure in Milwaukee who has just been indicted."

"They fired him for that?"

"He thinks Aggie made sure the founding partners learned of it. It had the effect she must have foreseen."

"I thought that young man was their courtroom star."

"He was. 'If you are to be one of us, you must be like Caesar's wife.' Mario had been there long enough to believe that. So he resigned when he was asked to."

"But still blamed Aggie."

"So Colleen told me. Mario is too proud to go on about it. He pretends he has been liberated, that this is a great opportunity for him."

"Maybe it is."

"He asked about coming in with us. Not a chance. For the same reason."

"And Colleen has resigned."

"If they're smart, they will postpone the wedding."

"People aren't smart about such things."

Silence, as son and father applied that to each other. It was hard to enjoy his drink with his son sitting there morosely. Finally Tim got up to go.

"I can't thank you enough, son."

Tim hesitated, then took his father in his arms. Jack was as embarrassed as his son. Gallagher men were seldom demonstrative. Tim avoided his eyes as he pulled open the door and left.

Jack sat, drank, looked at the dead eye of the television, sighed. Was it for this that we fought the war? When Julia had died, Jack had mourned like Hamlet for Ophelia but he would not have been human if he did not sense a little leap of joy that he was free at last, thank God Almighty, free at last. He had loved Julia, he had lived a double life in order to spare her sensibilities, and yet freedom had a salty taste. But the salt had lost its savor. His life seemed to be ending in farce, not tragedy, high-school antics at the senior dance and actually getting knocked on his ass by Austin Rooney, twice. He had deserted that arena, and then took up with the insatiable Agatha. That had led to his last great scene, the confessed murderer, but he sensed that he was more pitied than admired. What next? How long, O Lord, how long?

There was a tap at the door. Jack sat still. Eventually another tap and a voice, faintly audible, a female voice. He got to his feet, slowly, and shuffled to the door. But when he opened it he was upright and imperious.

"Isabel?"

"I am a delegation, Jack. People want you to come over to the club for a little welcome-home party. Of course if you don't want to, they'll understand. It can be tomorrow night. It can be any night you wish."

"Come in, Isabel."

"What you have been through!"

Jack sighed. "However heartrending, it is over—over for her, over for me."

Isabel had been advancing into the room with little baby steps as if Jack were the captain issuing orders.

"I was sure they had the whole thing wrong from the beginning."

"Isabel, I do not wish to put the blame on others."

"But this woman wasn't your niece."

Jack looked at her with real fondness. "Dear Isabel. The male animal is a beast forever."

" 'The male'! The way she came after you?"

"I hope you weren't spying on us."

"Why would I spy on you and your niece?"

Jack looked at her. "Why indeed?"

"What I don't understand is why that little lawyer didn't come forward. He must have seen everything."

"What little lawyer would that be, Isabel?"

"Your lawyer. The one with the tweed hat."

"Ah, Tuttle."

"As you know, he was parked out there night and day, him or his partner."

"A very reliable fellow, Tuttle."

"When he came to my door I thought at first he was investigating you."

"No reason for him to do that."

Jack was trying to sift the wheat from the chaff in Isabel's remarks. The little lawyer in the tweed hat could only be Tuttle. Tuttle had become his lawyer some days before the strangling of Aggie, filing Jack's suit against Austin Rooney. Jack longed to see Tuttle—he had been kept from the conference room by Amos Cadbury, Tim, and young Liberati. Of course, being on the wrong end of a murder investigation and on the right end of a suit for damages are very different things. But Tuttle was still his lawyer, now that the trio of giants had saved him from himself.

"Isabel, tell my friends at the clubhouse I would rather postpone our little party. I find I am more fatigued than I realized."

"It is absolutely up to you."

"Perhaps tomorrow night."

"If that is your wish."

"Let's say tomorrow night."

Jack took her to the door and as he reached for the knob, pecked her on the cheek. She went giggling into the night. Jack retrieved his now watery drink, tossed it off, and got on the phone to Tuttle.

2

Cy Horvath's list of suspects in the death of Agatha Rossner was shorter now, both Gallaghers having been eliminated. Tim Gallagher's alibi, that he had been out of town on business on the night Agatha died, took the son as well as the father off the hook as far as Phil Keegan was concerned.

"So who is left, Cy?"

"I suppose I ought to verify that he was out of town."

The information had come from Jack Gallagher who, in what had to be a first in the experience of the Detective Division, had dropped by to thank Phil and his department for the unfailing courtesy and fairness that had been shown him during the days he had been locked up.

"I wouldn't go so far as to recommend it, Captain, but it did afford me a welcome opportunity to regain my perspective on things."

"Is that why you confessed, to get a little quiet time?"

Jack could appreciate wit when he heard it and he accorded Phil's remark a generous laugh. "My son thought I was trying to protect him." There was a chuckle in Jack's voice as he relayed Timothy Gallagher's interpretation of his father's confession.

"And all along he had an alibi." Jack paused. "Not that I for a moment thought he was involved."

"You mean in her death?" Cy said.

Jack looked at him. "In her death. Like his father, he was susceptible to her charms."

"What is his alibi?"

"He was out of town on business."

And that, Phil told Jack, took both Gallaghers out of the target area.

"Who do you think did it, Jack?"

"Gentlemen, there I must defer to your professional skills. I haven't the faintest idea." He brought his hands together. "Now can anyone tell me where I can find Tuttle? I called his office and got the biggest runaround of my career."

"From Tuttle?"

"No, from what I took to be a woman. His secretary, I suppose."

Cy and Phil exchanged a look.

"Try the press room."

When he was gone, it took minutes for the atmosphere to return to normal. Phil was scowling in the usual way when he suggested that they turn their professional skills to the task of finding who had strangled Agatha Rossner.

"Who was next on your list, Cy?"

"Mario Liberati."

"Maybe he's got an alibi too."

But Cy found himself still wondering about Tim Gallagher's. They couldn't accept on hearsay that he had been out of town the night of the murder. Maybe he had and maybe he hadn't. What was for sure is that he, like his father, had succumbed to the charms of Agatha Rossner. Jack had laughed at the interpretation of his confession as an effort to protect his son, but what other explanation for it was there? And if he had thought that, then it could not be assumed that just because Aggie had transferred her affections to Jack, that Tim had gracefully bowed out.

The law firm with which Tim Gallagher was associated occupied the fourteenth and fifteenth floors of a building near the Outer Drive. Barth, Brach, Frailey, and Kelly. Cy felt like an astronaut as he took the elevator to the observation floor. Swoosh. His ears popped before they got to thirty-five. The view of the lake and the Loop was impressive, though somewhat unreal. Everything had been done to prevent anyone using the observation floor as a springboard into eternity. Double-paned windows were guarded by a railing that kept observers a foot away. But the sway of the building could be felt. Cy was glad to get into an elevator and descend to fourteen where he asked to see Timothy Gallagher.

"He's in conference right now. Would you care to wait?"

"I wonder if I could see his secretary."

The receptionist had a repertoire of answers for standard questions, but nothing for this. "His secretary?"

Cy had hoped to avoid making this official. He showed his badge and said in a lowered voice, "This won't take a minute."

"Is it about his father?" She was whispering too.

Cy nodded. "I would rather not bother him."

She nodded as she rose. They were on the same wavelength. "Come this way."

She led him down a corridor, telling him how terrible they had felt for Mr. Gallagher and wasn't it wonderful how everything worked out? She ducked into a doorway.

"Phyllis, this is Lieutenant Horvath."

"I didn't want to disturb Mr. Gallagher."

"He's in conference."

The receptionist withdrew, wearing a Girl Scout smile.

"You keep a calendar of Mr. Gallagher's activities, appointments, trips, that sort of thing."

"Of course."

"We're just tying up loose ends about his father."

"Thank God that's over with."

"I just need to see the appointments for the week of November 30."

He leaned over the book she turned toward him and he was aware of the musky scent of her perfume.

"Could I have a photocopy of this?"

"Is it important?"

"It clears up one point, that's all."

She scooped up the book and dashed down the hall. Two minutes later, Cy was on his way, the photocopy in his pocket. He took it out in the parking garage when he had located his car and read it in the eerie light. Agatha Rossner had died on December 3. Timothy's day was accounted for until after five, and the following morning his appointments began at nine. There was no record of travel or of his having been out of town.

3

Father Dowling had been intrigued by Cy Horvath's attempt to link the death of Agatha Rossner and that of Linda Hopkins via the Hacienda Motel. The law firm for which the young woman worked had held meetings at that motel and the housecleaning crew had worried about the attention one young lawyer had paid Linda, suspecting that he was up to no good and she was too naive to see that. The death of the head housekeeper Ruby Otter had the effect of exonerating Harry Paquette, but thus far Agnes Lamb had been unable to find any lead or motive for Ruby's death. That she had been garroted suggested the way Agatha had died, but of course strangling with a scarf and garroting with a cord were not completely identical methods. Cy decided to talk it over with the pastor of St. Hilary's.

"Your thought was that she had been silenced because she knew something," Father Dowling said.

"Something bearing on Harry Paquette."

"But you had already taken him there to be identified by her, hadn't you? What more could she do to him?"

"It's a moot point anyway. Harry was in a cell at the time."

"Who else would have wanted to silence Ruby?"

"Harry had no friends."

"I wasn't thinking of him, Cy."

"There is also Mabel Wilson."

This was the witness to what had happened on Dirksen Boulevard that snowy November evening, the woman who had said she would not forget the face of the man who pushed Linda into traffic if she lived to be a hundred. She had not lived until her next birthday, having died an ostensible suicide in her kitchen with the oven door open and the gas going full blast.

"So Ruby Otter and Mabel Wilson could be the victims of the man who killed Linda Hopkins," Father Dowling mused.

"I did manage to eliminate the possibility that someone from Mallard and Bill was responsible for Ruby's death."

If Harry Paquette could not have killed Ruby, Cy had turned his attention to the lawyer who had pursued the beautiful and naive young woman from Wisconsin.

"When Colleen Gallagher stayed at the motel the day her father was arrested, to keep away from the press, she brought her laptop with her. I was talking with Ruby and she told me that Colleen was in the motel, so I stopped by. Her computer was on and she showed me the Web page for the firm. There were photographs of all the partners and lawyers and paralegals. Ruby popped in while Colleen was showing me this, and recognized Mario Liberati's picture. Colleen had enlarged it to fill the screen."

"Mario Liberati."

Cy shook his head. "That's what I thought too. But Ruby said he was not the man who had been pursuing Linda. She knew him because he had been kind to her, telling her his mother had worked in a motel too. After Ruby was killed, I asked Agnes Lamb to show Gloria another picture. With the same result."

"Whose picture was it?"

"Timothy Gallagher."

Father Dowling raised his eyebrows. Of course Cy would have thought that if the young man had been unfaithful with Agatha he might be unfaithful with someone else.

"And that eliminated him. I am told that his alibi for the night of Agatha's murder puts him in the clear there as well."

Cy said, "We were told that he had been out of town on business."

"And was he?"

Cy handed Father Dowling the photocopy of Tim Gallagher's schedule for the week in which the murder had occurred. Every minute of the lawyer's day was accounted for, doubtless in order to facilitate billing clients. There was no mention of travel that would have taken him out of town on the night Agatha was murdered. Father Dowling looked at Cy.

"The first thing to be said is that Tim Gallagher himself did not tell us he was out of town that night. It came to us secondhand."

"Ah."

"From his wife. Through Colleen and from his father. I guess that makes it third-hand."

"His wife said he was out of town?"

"That's why I've come to you, Father."

This was what Roger Dowling had been dreading. It was frequent enough that Phil Keegan kept him au courant on an investigation, talking about it over lunch or in the evening while they were watching a game, but Cy was far more reticent. That he should have stopped by the rectory in midmorning to brief the pastor of St. Hilary's on the present status of his investigation had come as something of a surprise. And now the reason for it was revealed.

"I could go to the house and ask her point-blank if her husband had been away that night."

"But you'd rather not."

"She would immediately suspect I had a reason for asking. I mean, even if he wasn't home, that doesn't mean he had anything to do with the death of Agatha Rossner. But maybe Colleen misunderstood her. Maybe he was home. His appointment book indicates he should have been. The whole thing could be a misunderstanding."

Father Dowling was not surprised at such considerateness from the stolid Cyril Horvath. Phil Keegan stood in awe of Cy's way with women, who seemed instinctively to trust him and want to confide in him. This was all the more remarkable because the only explanation seemed to be Cy's unchanging facial expression which conveyed the thought that nothing could come as real news to him. Perhaps he would have the same effect on Jane Gallagher, but still, a detective lieutenant checking on her husband's whereabouts on the night Agatha Rossner was killed would doubtless alarm her.

"I'll talk to her, Cy."

How he was going to redeem this promise was not immediately clear. He did not know Jane Gallagher, he had never met her, and she lived in Barrington which, while it wasn't a million miles from Fox River, could sometimes seem that way during peak traffic hours. The pastor of the parish in Barrington was an acquaintance if not a close friend, but resident in the parish, in semiretirement, was Jimmy Weigel, a classmate of Roger Dowling's. Jimmy had developed an almost crippling arthritis that had necessitated giving up his parish. The opportunity to be resident at St. Anne's in Barrington had come as a reprieve.

"I wish you'd talked to me about coming to St. Hilary's, Jimmy."

"Maybe I will if they get tired of me here."

That seemed unlikely. Jimmy said an afternoon Mass on weekdays and several on Sunday. The parish had grown exponentially with the addition of development after development so that the presence of three priests there, an almost unheard-of luxury nowadays, was a practical necessity in order to minister to the rapidly expanding flock. Father Dowling's promise to Cy Horvath seemed closer to fulfillment when Jimmy said he knew the young Gallagher family well. So it was that Father Dowling drove to Barrington for a reunion with his classmate.

"What do you think?" Jimmy extended his hands. "They broke all the bones and reset them."

"They look good as new."

"An illusion. But they are easier to manage."

Some of the crosses people carry are more obvious than others and Jimmy's arthritis was difficult to conceal. Any priest learns the weight that can press on even the most fortunate of souls. And of course the cross is proportionate to the bearer. What for one might be a small thing, can bow down another. For all that, Roger Dowling was filled with admiration for Jimmy and his determination to continue with pastoral work despite his constant pain. After twenty minutes of reminiscing, Roger Dowling turned to the Gallaghers.

"The father put them through a wringer, Roger. What a thing to do, confess to a murder!"

"Apparently he was trying to protect someone else."

"He was willing to be thought a murderer to save a murderer?"

"He thought Tim was involved."

"My God."

"The young woman had shown interest in both father and son."

"Well, she wouldn't get anyplace with Tim, I'll tell you that."

"We've heard that he was away on a business trip the night it happened."

"There you are."

"The police have learned this just as hearsay."

"Why don't they ask him?"

"The fact is that his office calendar does not record any travel on that day."

Jimmy thought there must be an easy explanation of this. "Does every trip a man make have to be recorded?"

"You may be right. For that matter, it's not clear that it matters whether he was on a trip or not. The detective who told me all this wants to avoid causing any pain to the Gallaghers. He thought that if there was some way Mrs. Gallagher could be asked without seeming to be questioned . . ."

"Let's go see her, Roger."

"I had hoped you would suggest something like that."

The Gallagher home was suburban imperial style—massive, many roof lines, a three-car garage, a multitude of chimneys, and, of course, the mandatory basketball hoop. The driveway was not level with the road, actually rising steeply from it, not the best design for this kind of weather. But it had been cleared of snow and presented no problem this afternoon.

"Two priests!" Jane Gallagher cried when she opened the door. "I feel like I've won the lottery."

She was an exuberant and charming hostess. They sat in a sunny room at the back of the house and heard about her children, her background, her years at Georgetown where she and Tim had eventually become engaged.

"I had known him in Fox River; his sister Colleen was my best friend. I guess he needed to see me in a foreign setting."

"Washington, D.C., is foreign?"

"When you're from Fox River it is."

"Colleen will be married in St. Hilary's, as I suppose you know. She and her fiancé will begin marriage preparation soon. Recent events have put that on hold, of course."

"What a time it has been. Imagine my father-in-law confessing to a murder."

"Why would he do that?"

"Tim has a theory." She smiled and then made an effort to look serious. "He thinks his father thought he did it and this was a grand gesture to save Tim."

"For heaven's sakes," Jimmy blurted out.

"If he had asked Jack would have known how silly that was. Tim wasn't even in town."

Jimmy said, "Where was he?"

"On business somewhere. I really don't know. But he flew back that morning and came here to get ready to go to the office."

"How long have you lived in Barrington?" Roger asked. He had learned what he had come for. Jane Gallagher knew that her husband had not been home the night Agatha Rossner was killed. Whether or not this meant anything, Roger Dowling would leave to Cy Horvath. Cy had thought Tim might have been the lawyer who had pursued Linda Hopkins. Tim had become involved with Agatha. Perhaps there was yet another woman who could explain his absence from home on that fateful night. But it seemed an odd thing to hope for.

4

Tuttle was more than happy to consult with his client Jack Gallagher at his condo in Western Sun Community. For one thing, it got him out of the office, though Hazel made an alarming suggestion.

"I better come along to make a transcript."

"No. Jack wouldn't like that."

"Let's find out."

Tuttle fled to his inner office and closed the door. Now he felt trapped; the only way out was through Hazel's office, and she sounded as if her mind was made up. She intended to go with him to Jack Gallagher's. His eye fell to the new phone that sat on his desk. Hazel had gone all-out. Not only could calls be switched back and forth, there were several lines now, one of which seemed to function as Hazel's private line. Tuttle had resolved to speak to her about that. Now he was glad he had put off the evil day. He picked up the phone, dialed her number, put down the phone and then crept to the closed door. When her phone began to ring, he opened the door and raced through the outer office to freedom. Hazel was calling after him as the elevator doors closed.

Jack Gallagher was a picture of relaxed rectitude when he opened his door to Tuttle. Mahogany loafers, pale green slacks with a pleated waist, black shirt. His smile was benevolent, his silver hair undulant, his eyes atwinkle.

"Counselor. It has been too long."

"I came as quickly as I could." Tuttle had the wild thought that if he told Jack Gallagher about Hazel he would understand. So he did.

"I won't suggest that you strangle her."

It helped to laugh about it. "As your lawyer I would counsel against such advice."

"It's time we got back to my suit against Austin Rooney, wouldn't you say?"

"Of course I kept in the background while the other matter was going on."

"My confession of murder."

"That was very risky."

"Oh, I don't know. Given your vigilance, I should have been able to produce the best excuse of all. You and your man must have seen what happened. Who killed her, Tuttle?"

This was asked with such jovial good humor that Tuttle did not bother to deny the stakeout he and Peanuts had kept.

"Were we that obvious?"

"Night and day? We're not all plagued with deafness and poor eyesight, Tuttle. But come on, let's have a drink and get comfortable."

Tuttle accepted a beer and watched Jack splash a glass half full of scotch. Tuttle put his tweed hat on the coffee table and lay his coat on the floor beside his chair. Jack sat, arranged the creases on his trousers, and lifted his glass.

"Cheers. May Austin Rooney eat crow."

"We can't lose."

"Why would you keep your own client under surveillance, Tuttle?"

"When I go up against someone like Amos Cadbury, I want no surprises. I want to know everything he could learn that might help his case. I interviewed people at the station. Hove and Judy."

"Hove!"

"Exactly. If Cadbury talked with Hove and I didn't, well, I would have been caught off-guard. Judy, of course, was very positive. Is it true that Rooney assaulted you in your office at the station?"

"The man is a menace."

"So there is a pattern."

"Exactly. Another beer?"

His instinct was to say no. With Peanuts he would polish off a six-pack without giving it a thought, but Jack Gallagher was the most promising client he had ever had and a clear head seemed indicated. But then he thought of Hazel and half wished she could see him yakking it up with Gallagher, lawyer and client having a drink, going over the case.

"Maybe I will."

"Good man."

Jack Gallagher had not forgotten the vigil that had been kept outside his apartment and he wanted a complete report on what had been seen the night of the murder.

"Of course we saw the girl arrive."

Jack nodded. "What time was that?"

"Seven-thirty. I'd have to check . . ."

"No, you're right. Did she come by cab?"

"No. The usual way. The Alfa Romeo. That car is the real mystery."

"How so?"

"What happened to it? The young woman arrived in it, but she sure didn't drive it away. It ended up in her garage near Old Town."

"You must have seen who drove it away."

"This is embarrassing," Tuttle said.

He told Jack about Peanuts, and yes, he belonged to the famous or infamous Pianone clan, but he was a good friend of Tuttle's. Peanuts had been keeping watch on Jack's place, with Tuttle taking turns.

"Who was on that night?"

"Peanuts came on duty at two, driving an unmarked police car. When he got there he had brought tacos so I sat with him while we ate those. The way he was yawning I worried he wouldn't be awake for long. I told him the girl was in your apartment. When I went back to my car, I thought I should stick around awhile, keep an eye on Peanuts as well as the house. How I wish I had."

"So you yourself weren't here when she left."

"No." It sounded like dereliction of duty.

Jack leaned forward, looking anxious. "Was my son . . ."

"Peanuts fell asleep, just as I had feared. It was the lights on the paramedic ambulance that woke him up. He got the hell out of there."

Jack Gallagher sat looking at Tuttle. All the previous camaraderie seemed gone. "In the military he'd be shot."

"He's lucky to be a cop."

"So you know nothing about what happened."

"The car. I may not have seen it, but someone drove her car away, ran it through an automatic wash and parked it in its regular place. Whoever did that had to know where to take the car."

"That must have been the one who killed her."

Tuttle nodded. "If the police knew what they were doing they would concentrate on that Alfa Romeo."

5

When Father Dowling told him that Jane Gallagher herself had brought up her husband's alibi, that he was out of town on business the night Agatha Rossner was killed, Cy once more drove to the Loop and ascended the elevator to Barth, Brach, Frailey, and Kelly. He had to assume that Timothy was there in midafternoon; calling in advance was too risky. Young Gallagher would want to know what Cy needed to see him for, and it was not wise to lie in the course of the search for the truth. His gamble did not pay off.

"Oh, he's gone for the day." Phyllis's manner was chillier than it had been earlier.

"You wouldn't try to fool me, would you?"

"I wish I had used more sense when you were here this morning."

"Something go wrong?"

"Mr. Gallagher came in and wanted me to enter something in the appointment book and wondered why it was opened where it was. I forgot to put it away after I made the photocopy."

"You tell him about the photocopy?"

"He found out in the copying room. I'm lucky I still have my job."

What could Cy say that would reassure her? He had shamelessly relied on the fact that women trusted him implicitly when he'd asked for the photocopy of Timothy Gallagher's appointment calendar.

"If you have any trouble I'll take the blame."

"That ought to help."

Well, it was the best he could give. "Any idea where he went?"

"He didn't even say good-bye."

"Guess."

"He called his sister."

That Tim would go to Colleen now that he knew his supposed alibi was exploded made some sort of sense. He had to go somewhere and probably going home early did not appeal. Sooner or later he would have to tell his wife that he had not been out of town on business that night. So where had he been? Jane Gallagher would not want to know the answer to that question any more than Cy Horvath did. Calling her was out, even more than calling Timothy's office had been. Now Tim would know that Cy Horvath had seen his appointment calendar and knew the story he had told his wife about a business trip was phony. If he was at Colleen's and she got a call from Cy, he wouldn't stick around to talk about where he had been on the night Agatha was killed.

As he drove, Cy thought of Agatha's Alfa Romeo, which had finally cleared the red-tape hurdles and was being given a thorough examination, courtesy of the Chicago police lab. Agatha must have driven that car to the Western Sun condominiums on the last night of her life. Someone else had driven the car away and left it in the garage where she rented space. Why? Whoever it was had taken it through a car wash and probably had cleaned up the interior as well, making chances of the police lab turning up incriminating evidence minimal. But it was the thought of someone waiting around outside Jack's condo, someone who seemed not to have come by car, that intrigued. He would have had to have known where Agatha's car was. He would have had to have reason to think that she wouldn't spend the entire night in Jack's apartment, but would emerge in the wee hours. Had he been waiting for her when she came out? Had he killed her and then, for whatever reason, driven off in her car, washed it, parked it in its stall in the garage? This faceless person took on the face of Timothy Gallagher; he would have known of his father's liaison with Agatha. Had he been driven by jealousy of his own father? Or—a darker thought— had he done what he did in order to implicate Jack Gallagher?

Cy found a parking space within walking distance of Colleen's apartment. When he turned in at the building, Tim Gallagher was coming toward him.

"She isn't here."

"It's you I want to see."

"Yes, yes, I know. But I called Colleen on my way over and when I got here she was gone."

"Did you get in the apartment?"

"The door wasn't shut tightly enough to engage the lock."

"Did you leave it that way?"

"No, I shut it. It's locked now."

"Well, let's find the building manager."

Checking out Colleen's apartment might loosen up Timothy. He knew why Cy was here, that he had come to see him rather than his sister. He had as much as acknowledged that, but his concern for his sister was real.

Lazenby, the superintendent, wrinkled his nose. "You're her brother?"

"Yes."

"And you are a policeman."

"That's why I carry this badge."

"Well, I don't see why I should let either one of you into her apartment."

"Can I use your phone?"

Lazenby seemed ready to veto this as well. Cy picked up the phone and dialed. "Inspector of Buildings? Look, this is Lieutenant Horvath. Could you get an inspector out here immediately? I think we've got—"

"Stop!" Lazenby cried.

"Just a moment," Cy said to the busy signal.

"I'll let you in but I must go in with you."

They went upstairs and the superintendent managed to get the door of Colleen's apartment open.

There is an emptiness that feels like absence. With Lazenby dogging his footsteps Cy went through the apartment. A glance around sufficed to show she wasn't there, but he looked in the closets and even under the bed. "What time was it when you spoke to her?"

Timothy looked at his watch. "Not an hour ago."

"She left without her purse."

"That's a computer case."

Cy took the strap and lifted it, trying its heft, then put the strap over his shoulder. It was still on his shoulder when Lazenby let them out, and watched them go down the stairs.

"You're welcome," he called after them sarcastically.

"What time would you like the building inspector to come?"

Lazenby clattered down the stairs after them. "But I showed you her apartment."

"I won't report that." At the curb he turned to Timothy. "Where are you parked?"

"That's me there."

"I'm two blocks away. Let's sit in your car."

Cy got into the passenger seat and waited for Timothy to settle behind the wheel.

"You weren't out of town on business the night Agatha was killed."

"No."

"Where were you?"

"I spent the night at a motel."

"Why?"

"I wanted to sort out my thoughts, review what I had been doing. I had made a damned fool of myself with that girl and I was determined to get over it. I didn't realize then that I would have to tell my wife about it."

Cy thought about that. He didn't envy Timothy that ordeal. "What motel?"

"The Hacienda."

"Why the Hacienda?"

"Why not? It's the only local motel I ever stayed at."

That was something easy to check. Maybe Timothy had an alibi after all.

"Why did you take Colleen's computer out of the apartment?" Tim asked.

"I thought you could check her e-mail. See where she might have gone."

Timothy got the laptop out of its case, turned it on, connected it to his cell phone, and hummed while he waited. "She should get a new one. This is slow."

Her code name was recorded on AOL so he logged into the server and then brought up new mail. Most of the messages were from Mallard and Bill.

"Fremont," Cy said. There were half a dozen messages from Fremont.

"She's been working with him as well as Mario."

"Is there a message there from Mario?"

"No."

"Do you know his number?"

He didn't but he called information and then waited. The corners of his mouth turning down. "No answer."

"Give me a lift to my car."

When he had directed Timothy to where he had parked his car, he opened the door and stepped out.

"You can check at the Hacienda Motel, Lieutenant."

"I will."

21

1

Phil Keegan was annoyed with the way things were going. Mario Liberati was nowhere to be found either, suggesting that he and Colleen had gone off together. At least that was the hypothesis Phil Keegan invoked to explain why his department was not involving itself in the matter.

"People go off without telling anybody all the time, Cy. It's not a police matter. And when a man and a woman go off together, well . . ."

"But when the two people are mixed up in an ongoing investigation?"

Cy's pursuit of the possibility that Timothy Gallagher was once more a suspect, given the fact that he had not been, as his wife had believed, out of town on business the night Agatha Rossner was killed, had come aground at the Hacienda Motel. Tim had indeed spent the night there.

"To gather his thoughts," Phil said, his attitude toward Timothy's reason for going into seclusion a product of his disappointment that the young lawyer was no longer a suspect.

Cy was not sure that registration in the Hacienda settled the matter. He had become quite the confidant of the housekeepers there and the new head housekeeper looked into it and found Timothy had had dinner in his room and seemed to have stayed there until morning. That still did not absolutely close off the possibility that Timothy had used the motel as a base of operations from which to go to Western Sun and strangle Agatha.

Of course Mario Liberati had a motive too, if he was right to suspect that Agatha had informed Mallard and Bill that their star courtroom performer had underworld ties in Milwaukee. For the moment, Phil Keegan was sick of it. He got into his car and stopped at the St. Hilary rectory.

"The Bulls on?" he asked when Roger Dowling answered the door. "Come on in."

But in the study Phil found himself reviewing the annoying details of the investigation, ending with the suspicious disappearance of Mario Liberati. "Maybe that's why he took a powder, Roger."

"With Colleen?"

Phil shrugged. His eyes drifted to the screen where the Bulls, in the post-Jordan era, were disgracing themselves as Larry Bird's Pacers went up by twenty points. Phil groaned.

An hour later, alone, Phil having gone home, Father Dowling sat on in his study, puffing pensively on his pipe. The events of the past several weeks occupied him as he tried to make sense of what had happened. He longed for the time when it had been the rumpus at the parish dance that had held center stage. Two elderly men, brothers-in-law still, although the sisters they had married were dead, had vied for the favors of an equally elderly lady, and the suit brought by Jack Gallagher against Austin Rooney had threatened to bring unwelcome publicity to the center so capably run by Edna Hospers. The death of Agatha had made that dispute seem more trivial than it already was, and Jack Gallagher's dramatic confession to the murder of Agatha had drawn the attention of the media away from the parish but in a way Father Dowling could scarcely find comforting.

Jack's confession had been a diversion, as Father Dowling had been convinced it was when Jack had shied away from confession in the sacramental sense. If he had sought Divine forgiveness for the deed to which he had confessed to the police, it would have been impossible to dismiss it, but Jack had avoided making the confession that he knew would count. The assumption had been that he confessed to the police in order to divert attention from the one he assumed to be the murderer, and his son was the obvious candidate for that role. The alibi, if it could be called that—after all, Timothy's business trip had been the excuse he had given his wife, not a public claim—had now dissolved and it seemed improbable that he had registered at the Hacienda Motel and then somehow gotten to Western Sun and done away with the woman who had led him up the garden path before she had succeeded in capturing the fancy of his father.

But his motive remained a strong factor. Agatha had exposed the weaknesses of son and father, and had led Tim into a dalliance that had threatened his home and career. But the fact that he had bared his soul to his wife told strongly against his being guilty of the death of Agatha. So where did that lead?

Roger Dowling had been intrigued by Cy Horvath's hypothesis that there was some connection between the death of Agatha Rossner and the horrible incident on Dirksen Boulevard when Linda Hopkins had been pushed into oncoming traffic and died a terrible death. The arrest of Harry Paquette in Kansas City, given his past record, negated his claim of innocence. But the decisive fact that Harry had been in custody when Ruby Otter was killed in her office at the Hacienda Motel was in his favor. That Ruby had been witness to his love for Linda scarcely made her a menace. But another of the witnesses, Mabel Wilson, had died in a suspicious manner, though that too had happened when Harry was out of the picture. Unless Harry had friends who were responsible for getting rid of the one whose testimony would have been decisive against Harry, and killed Ruby in the bargain, these deaths seemed unrelated to that of Linda Hopkins. But how could all this be linked to the death of Agatha Rossner?

Cy had thought that Timothy Gallagher would provide the link, but when Agnes Lamb had showed his picture, taken from the Web site of Mallard and Bill, to Gloria—Ruby's successor as head house-keeper at the Hacienda Motel—the result had been negative. But someone who had attended a conference at the motel had shown interest in Linda. Perhaps looking into all the conferences held at the Hacienda during that time frame was the most promising avenue now. Father Dowling had a hunch this would have occurred to Cy Horvath.

2

Cy was keeping vigil outside the apartment of Mario Liberati. He had learned that Liberati's car was not in the parking bay he rented but was unable to learn anything helpful as to when the lawyer had last been seen at his place of residence. It was possible, maybe even prob-able, that Mario and Colleen had decided to go off together, to get away from the scene of recent events, perhaps to marry, but every-thing Cy knew of the couple told against it. They were due to begin marriage-preparation classes with Father Dowling; both of them seemed to regard marriage in such a way that an elopement would be an unlikely course.

The biggest decision Cy had taken was not to go to Milwaukee. Mario's departure from Mallard and Bill had been precipitated by his brother-in-law Jimmy Kane's demand that Mario defend him against the charges he faced. Pressure had been put on Mario by his sister, and her plea had been difficult to ignore. Lining up these thoughts did not produce anything like an argument. Nonetheless, Cy was parked outside Liberati's apartment on the unformulated assumption that the missing lawyer would return.

And so he did. At two in the morning, when the street had dissolved into shadows and the rows of parked cars lining each curb seemed to be taking their rest along with their owners, a pair of headlights came slowly down the street, a driver looking for an opening. Cy sat forward and turned the key in the ignition and waited. The car crept by him, only one person visible, the driver. The car continued down the street and accelerated. Cy pulled away from the curb, made a U-turn, and followed without turning on his lights. He followed the car to the garage into which it turned. Cy parked and got out of the car and was waiting when Mario Liberati walked slowly up the ramp to the street.

"Liberati?" He stopped and Cy stepped into the light. "Lieutenant Horvath."

"Have you found her?"

"Where have you been?"

But Liberati advanced on Cy as if he would force an answer from him. "Where is she? Where is Colleen?"

"I don't know. Where can we talk?"

"Talk? For God's sake, you have to find Colleen!"

"That's what we're going to talk about."

After some hesitation, they started up the street to Mario's apartment.

"How did you know she was missing?" Mario asked, when he had let them into his apartment.

"Her brother Timothy became worried when he couldn't reach her."

"I talked to her last night. But today . . ."

"Where have you been?"

"Milwaukee."

The story came easily when Liberati realized that Cy knew of his brother-in-law Jimmy Kane and Kane's effort to enlist Mario as his defense attorney.

"He tried to work on me through my sister. Then, when I couldn't find Colleen, I had the thought that he was trying to work on me through her."

"And?"

Mario shook his head slowly. "I'm going to make a drink. What would you like?"

"What have you got?"

Cy settled for a beer.

3

Edna needed a day off when she realized she couldn't stand the sight of Desmond O'Toole and that the girlish laughter of Maud Gorman was driving her nuts. She needed some peace and quiet. But the hope of having the house all to herself was dashed when the kids reminded her the night before that tomorrow was December 8, the Immaculate Conception, a holiday of obligation.

"And there's no school!"

"Oh, good," she managed to say.

But after Mass she made waffles and it was better than the weekend. Janet helped her with the dishes and Carl went off to his computer. By noon the house was as quiet as Edna could have wished and she couldn't stand it. Before she could suggest a visit to the mall, Janet got a call and arranged to go out with her girlfriends. When Edna looked in on Carl, he was engrossed in an astronomy program on his computer and was way out in space in several senses.

"I think I'll go over to the Center, Carl."

"Hmmm."

"I'll be back in a few hours."

He nodded. She doubted he had heard a word she said. She headed back to the St. Hilary Senior Center almost with relief.

"Father Dowling was looking for you," Desmond O'Toole said.

"Thank you." Edna looked into the converted gym. There seemed as many here on a holy day as any other day. Of course, they would have attended Mass at St. Hilary's before coming to the Center. On a corner table near the coffee urn were doughnut boxes, suggesting an improvised breakfast.

"He asked me if you were in your office," Desmond said over her shoulder. "I said I suppose so and he went upstairs."

"Thank you, Desmond."

"He said you weren't there."

"I wondered where I wasn't."

Edna skipped up the stairs as if fearful Desmond might follow. She closed her office door behind her and felt a fleeting impulse to lock it. She slumped into a chair and wondered if this is what people meant by "burnout." Her planned day at home had proved a disappointment and it didn't help to have Desmond O'Toole almost scolding her when she showed up at the Center.

Her hand went out to the phone, then stopped. Maybe she should go over to the rectory to find out what Father Dowling had wanted. But the thought of Marie Murkin dissuaded her. She dialed the rectory.

"Marie? Is Father there?"

"Edna, where are you?"

"In my office."

"Oh, thank God. When Father came back and said you weren't there I called your house and talked to your son. He didn't know where you were."

"Well, here I am. Let me speak to Father."

But Marie had not exhausted the subject of Edna's mysterious disappearance. "I tried to remember if I had noticed you at Mass this morning . . ."

"Marie, I've been to Mass, I spent the morning with my kids, I am now in my office, and please put Father Dowling on."

A silence. "One moment, please."

After Edna's phone call Father Dowling walked over to her office in the school.

"It was nothing at all, really, Edna. I wanted to ask you a computer question."

"Have you bought a computer, Father?"

"I never rose to the level of an electric typewriter."

One becomes an expert on the computer when asked questions by someone who knows less about them. Father Dowling professed to know nothing at all. Could Edna get onto the World Wide Web? She could. Is it true that any Web site in the world can be brought up on the screen? "How do you summon them?"

"They have addresses."

He looked disappointed. "So if I had heard of such a site but didn't know the address, you couldn't show it to me?"

"What Web site is it?"

"Mallard and Bill are a firm of lawyers in the Loop. I am told they have a Web site."

"I'll do a search."

Edna typed *Mallard and Bill* in the little box, and clicked on SEARCH. Moments later the results appeared on the screen. "Is that it?"

Father Dowling leaned toward the monitor, which of course was difficult to read at an angle. "Is that all there is?"

Edna highlighted the entry and pressed ENTER and the Web site for Mallard and Bill formed on the screen.

"Ah," Father Dowling said. He pulled a chair up next to Edna's.

Edna showed Father Dowling the various subdivisions of the site that could now be reached.

"Let's look at partners and associates."

"All right."

"They're very small, aren't they?" he said a moment later, looking at the array of photographs on the screen.

"Oh, they can be enlarged." She clicked on one to show him. It was Mario Liberati. At least he hadn't been removed from the roster.

"And you can print it out."

"Of course."

Edna printed out Liberati's picture. It was not photograph-quality, of course, but amazing nonetheless.

"I would like printouts of all of them."

"You would?"

Father Dowling lifted his hands. "Just a wild idea. Too wild to bother Cy Horvath with."

He had fifteen printed photos when he thanked her, ready to go.

"What is the wild idea?"

"I'll tell you later. Do you have an envelope for these?"

Edna found a large manila envelope and put the photographs in it for him, enjoying the thought that he did not want Marie Murkin to see what he had come to the Center for.

4

"Cy Horvath called," Marie said, meeting Father Dowling at the door. "I didn't want to call you at the school. Colleen Gallagher is missing!"

"Missing?"

"They don't know where she is. She isn't at her apartment, she didn't go to work, Mario Liberati has no idea where she might be, and he is frantic."

If Father Dowling had had any doubts about what he would do with the pictures Edna had printed out for him, they were gone now. He told Marie he would be away from the rectory for an hour or two and would try to reach Cy or Phil Keegan by phone somewhere.

"You should have a mobile phone, Father."

He showed her the palm of his hand. Technology was all very well. He was glad that Edna was so adept at the computer, and he had heard much unsolicited testimony on the practicality of cell phones, doubtless all of it true. He was no Luddite, but he had no desire to encumber his life with such gadgetry. Besides, there were pay phones scattered throughout the city, at intersections, in parking lots and malls and other stores.

The Hacienda Motel was a familiar building though he had never been in it before. It was simply one of the objects that slipped past in peripheral vision as he drove by. The parking lot was surprisingly full, but he found a place, tucked the manila envelope under his arm, and headed for the entrance. Inside, he had to get oriented. The registration desk was not as prominent as he would have expected, having to compete with dining areas, a bar, sofas and chairs in various formations and configurations. Finally he saw it.

"Good afternoon."

The girl looked up and then straightened at the sight of his Roman collar. "Yes, Father."

"Where would I find Gloria, the head housekeeper?"

"You want the housekeeper."

"That's right."

"See those doors at the far end of the lobby? If you go through those, there is a long corridor. You just keep going down that and you will find her office. The door will say 'Housekeeper.' "

He thanked her and started across the lobby when a man fell into step with him. "Lawrence Wagner. I'm the assistant manager. Can I help you?"

"Thank you, I've been helped. I've come to see Gloria."

"Gloria!"

"The housekeeper."

"I know she's the housekeeper." His voice rose. "I'm sorry. I'll take you to her."

"That's not necessary."

"At the Hacienda, we do not confine ourselves to what is necessary. You're a priest?"

"Yes."

He gripped Father Dowling's arm, his eyes wide. "Is something wrong with Gloria?"

"No. This is just a visit."

Lawrence Wagner peeled off as they neared the double doors. "You're sure you can find your way?"

"Oh, yes."

He pushed through the double doors and as they closed behind him he looked back to make sure Lawrence Wagner was no longer with him. Of course he was only doing his job. But he had something of Desmond O'Toole in him.

A sound of humming came from the open door of Gloria's office. Father Dowling tapped on the door frame.

"Door's open, come right in."

"Gloria Daley?"

She turned slowly in her chair and her eyes traveled from Father Dowling's face to his collar. She pushed back and tried to rise from her chair.

"Please. Don't." He brought another chair next to the desk and sat. "My name is Father Dowling. You don't know me."

"I know I don't."

"I want you to do me a favor." He undid the clasp of the envelope and slid the photographs from it. Gloria followed this warily.

He told her of his friendship with Cyril Horvath. He said he knew Agnes Lamb.

"We were in school together."

"Here in Fox River?"

"Yes, sir."

Father Dowling nodded. "I've come about Linda Hopkins."

"Uh-huh."

"The police talked to you about a man staying in the hotel, here for a lawyers' conference, who pursued Linda."

She frowned. "He was a bad man, but she was such a good girl she didn't realize it. Not that anything came of it. We looked out for her."

"Gloria, I want you to look at these pictures."

He handed them to her, and she turned them over, one by one. But then she turned one back the other way. "That's him."

"The man who was bothering Linda?"

"Oh, yes. That's the man."

"Thank you, Gloria."

She stared at him as he got up.

"Is that all?"

"You may have to do this again for the police."

When the priest passed through the lobby, Lawrence Wagner, behind the reception desk, looked as if he might leap over it and help Father Dowling find the door. But he restrained himself and soon Father Dowling was outside breathing the brisk winter air. He was halfway to his car when it occurred to him that he could have called Cy or Phil from one of the phones in the lobby of the Hacienda. But the thought of Lawrence Wagner deterred him. There were phones everywhere.

But he drove several blocks until he found one, on a street corner, looking the worse for wear. He was almost surprised to hear a dial tone when he picked it up. He called his rectory.

"Has either Cy or Phil called?"

"Cy called before you left."

"If they call again, tell them I am going to Colleen's apartment."

"Do you know where it is?"

"I want you to look at the notes I took when she and Mario came to talk about their wedding. Her address should be there somewhere."

"I answered the phone in your study. Where should I look?"

He told her where to look, and after a great deal of sighs, shuffling of paper, and other sound effects meant to convey that Marie Murkin could shoulder any burden, no matter how inane, she sighed a final time into the phone.

"You found it?"

"Why do you want to go there? Cy has already been there—he and Mario went through the apartment. She's not there. That's why they think she's missing."

"What's the address?"

Marie read it out reluctantly. Father Dowling repeated it. "Thank you, Marie."

5

Tuttle sat in a booth at Stub's, exiled from his office by the predatory presence of Hazel Barnes, sipping a Dr. Pepper and pondering the significance of the mysterious removal of Agatha Rossner's Alfa Romeo from the scene of her murder. The young lawyer had arrived in that car, but when police had descended on Western Sun, alerted by the call to 911, the car was no longer there. Peanuts had proved to be of no help in the matter, and Rawley the gate guard was little better. Rawley had seen the car after it passed the guard shack, exiting the development, but he was far more intrigued by the relation of this fact to himself.

"Of course I thought it was the goddess who had driven by."

" 'The goddess.' "

"Her name was unknown to me. I preferred it that way. She was gorgeous, and a mythical designation seemed appropriate. I will never think of her as Agatha. It's a good Greek name, of course."

"Is Rossner a Greek name?"

Rawley ignored the question. "Agatha means 'good.' "

Tuttle gave up. As he sat in the booth at Stub's, tweed cap pulled down over his wrinkled brow, he realized that his former admiration of Cy Horvath and Phil Keegan was shaken. They knew of the mysterious removal of the car. They had traced it to its accustomed stall in Kopcinski's garage. They had to have noticed that it had been recently washed. Couldn't they see that the car was the solution to Agatha's murder? Who but the man who had strangled her would have driven it away?

He pressed his back against the seat on which he sat. For all he knew, Cy Horvath *was* concentrating on the car. The Chicago police had gone over it without results. No wonder, since it had been run through a car wash. Anyone who would do that would be unlikely to leave traces of his presence in the car.

Tuttle left his soda unfinished and went out to his own car. He could not bear the thought of going to his office. How could he ever get rid of Hazel? When he pulled away from the curb, he headed for Kopcinski's. Inspiration or just a cowardly avoidance of Hazel? Tuttle sent up a prayer to his sainted father. Despite his pep talk to Jack Gallagher, Tuttle felt foreboding when he thought of presenting the case in Judge Farner's court. If he were denied that triumph, where was he?

The kid with the dangling necktie squinted at Tuttle as if he felt he should recognize him. Tuttle accepted the ticket, but before driving on into the garage, lifted his hat to the kid, hoping for an unequivocal recognition.

"Did they bring the car back?"

"What car?"

"The Alfa Romeo."

"Look, it's not for sale." He stroked his sallow face. "What vultures. A woman is murdered and people want to buy her car."

" 'People.' "

"Well, you're not the first."

"Did I say I wanted to buy the car?"

A horn sounded behind Tuttle. He was blocking the entrance of the garage. He drove on in.

When he got to the Alfa Romeo, he saw the man; he was stooped over and peering into the car. Tuttle drove by slowly, rounded the ramp, and ducked into an empty stall. He got out of his car, eased the door shut, and hurried to a point where he could look down at the car. The man was no longer there. Tuttle walked down the ramp but before he reached the car he saw that the man was sitting in it. The engine started. Tuttle turned and ran back to his own car and got behind the wheel. He would have to go down the up ramp or risk losing sight of the Alfa Romeo. When he rounded the curve, he slammed on his brakes. So did the car coming up. There was an angry blasting of horns. Tuttle leaned out the window.

"Back up. Back up."

"You're going the wrong way!"

"Just let me get by you."

Tuttle started toward the other car and was almost bumper-to-bumper with it when it began to move backward. Tuttle swung into the place vacated by the Alfa Romeo, then backed out and headed for the down ramp. When he reached the exit of the garage, the Alfa Romeo was pulled up at the guard shack. The kid with the loose necktie was reading something, lips moving. Tuttle pulled up behind the sports car, trying to get a look at the driver. The paper was handed back, the bar lifted, and the Alfa Romeo shot forward. Tuttle went out right after him, ignoring the protesting squeal of the attendant.

The Alfa Romeo proceeded slowly up the street, its speed mocking the potential of the car. Whoever was in it had unlocked the door and had an ignition key. Whoever had driven it away from Western Sun had to have the keys to it. But Agatha's keys had been in her purse. It dawned on Tuttle that he was tailing the man who had strangled Agatha Rossner.

The sports car went south three blocks and then, stopped by a light, its turn light winked on and off. He was turning toward the lake. The light changed, the turn was made, and Tuttle followed. Why would the murderer risk being identified with Agatha's car when he must realize the significance of its removal from Western Sun could not escape the police? They were on a narrow street made more narrow by the parked cars lining both sides of it. The Alfa Romeo crept along until it found an opening, then ducked into it and parked. Tuttle stopped in the middle of the street. There was no other parking place in sight. A horn sounded behind him. In the rearview mirror Tuttle could see at least three cars he was holding up. But he did not move until the door of the Alfa Romeo opened and the man got out. He looked toward Tuttle's car and the forming traffic jam. Tuttle took his foot off the brake and started forward.

The man was not Tim Gallagher.

Tuttle did not know if he was relieved or disappointed. At the corner, he turned and double-parked and hopped out of his car, looking back up the street where the Alfa Romeo was parked. The man was disappearing up the walk, toward the far intersection.

Tuttle hopped back into his car, intending to make a circuit of the block, but the first street was one-way the wrong way and he raced on to the next. He had lost all hope of seeing the man again. But when he finally made the second turn and was heading north, he saw the man get into a cab.

Good God, what luck. He wished Hazel could see him in action. Hazel! He gripped the wheel and shook the thought away, and followed the cab.

Not more than a mile away, in another narrow street, the man got out of the cab and hurried to the door of an apartment house. This time Tuttle found a parking space. He got out of his car, slammed the door, and looked up to see Father Dowling going along the walk.

6

"Father Dowling!"

Recognizing Tuttle was a matter of recognizing his tweed hat which concealed the facial features that might otherwise have identified him. Father Dowling had turned when he heard his named called, and there was the tweed-topped lawyer coming toward him.

"Father Dowling," Tuttle said excitedly. "I've seen him. I've seen the murderer."

"Where?"

"He just went into that building."

"Just as I feared."

"But how would you know . . ."

Father Dowling unfolded the photograph that Gloria had identified at the Hacienda Motel. "Are we talking of the same man?"

"That's him!"

"And he entered this building?"

"Just minutes ago. Who is he?"

"A lawyer at Mallard and Bill in the Loop."

Father Dowling had started toward the entrance of the building with Tuttle in tow. The door was locked but there was a bell marked MANAGER. Father Dowling pressed it and turned to look up and down the street. He had the sense he was on the threshold of danger, and Tuttle was not an imposing companion. Would Cy be able to retrace his steps to the Hacienda Motel and, having talked with Gloria, come here?

"This is where Colleen Gallagher lives," he said to Tuttle.

There was a clicking sound, and Father Dowling tried the door. It opened. The manager awaited them inside and was suitably affected by the sight of a Roman collar.

"Could you take me up to Miss Colleen Gallagher's apartment?"

"All you have to do is ring that bell."

"I'd prefer it if you'd take me up." He turned to Tuttle. "Will you find a phone and call the rectory and tell Mrs. Murkin where I am?"

"You think he's up there?"

"Did he let himself in the door?"

"Yes."

"Please make the call."

The manager was both fascinated and annoyed. From the open door of his room came the roar of a television. Tuttle hesitated. "Will you wait for me?"

"What floor does she live on?" Father Dowling asked the manager.

"Eight. Eight-oh-nine."

Father Dowling said to Tuttle. "When you return, just come up to eight-oh-nine."

"How'll I get in?"

"Use my phone," the manager said as he pushed the elevator button.

Father Dowling decided that the phone call would be insurance enough.

The elevator door slid open and he stepped into the car. "Come up after you've called," he said to Tuttle.

As the door closed, the manager was taking Tuttle toward the open door of his apartment.

The car lurched upward when the door closed, and seemed to grope up the shaft as if finding its way. Cloudy mirrors on the sides of the car made it seem full. A sign announced that the elevator had a capacity of five.

At the eighth floor the door slid open and Father Dowling stepped into a narrow hallway running east and west with a window at either end. Sunrise, sunset. Ceiling lamps gave a grudging light. He found eight-oh-nine and rapped firmly on the door. A minute went by and then another. He knocked again, more loudly. Finally there was the sound of a lock turning and the door opened several degrees. Looking at him over the chain was Albert Fremont.

❧ Part Five ❧

1

Sometimes, in her heart of hearts, Marie Murkin wished that Father Dowling would get out of the rectory more often, leaving the house as her unequivocal domain, but she fretted more in his absence than when he was ensconced in his study reading, praying, whatever he did there when no one came to see him. Actually it was more trying when he had someone with him behind closed doors and she was not privy to what was going on. But today his absence was particularly trying, since he had left the rectory on an enigmatic note. She really had no idea why he would go off to the Hacienda Motel.

Of course, it was the place where so many strange things had happened of late, as she had managed to learn as much by indirection as by any confiding from the pastor. After he had left, she tried to convince herself that she was glad he was not in. Of course, when he went over to the Center she was always uneasy. The thought of him chatting away with Edna about who knew what was unnerving. She had never been able to convince him that Edna was more or less her assistant. This was a suggestion that Edna resisted, of course, but Father Dowling should understand Marie's need to be kept informed of everything that was going on in the parish plant itself. Of course there were things that were confidential, she had no real problem with that, but surely there was nothing about the Center that she did not have a right to know.

Sitting at the kitchen table, having tea, thinking of recent events, she felt an impulse to review them. What the pastor did not seem to see as absurd amazed Marie. For example, that Maud Gorman should be such a queen bee at the Center, with men hovering around her as if she were half a century younger than she was, should have provided a rich source of those mordant exchanges Marie had come to cherish in her relations with Father Dowling. That a man with the background of Austin Rooney should be smitten by Maud was beyond belief, but Father Dowling had not encouraged Marie's critical remarks on that subject. When things had flared up with the advent of Jack Gallagher, she had surely had a right to expect that he would appreciate her negative attitude toward Maud, and he had certainly been concerned that the parish might come under a cloud after the fiasco of the senior dance. The brawl should have put the kibosh on that brilliant idea, but Father Dowling had encouraged Edna to think that the dance was the beginning of a Center tradition. The dance had been the first of a chain of happenings. The next thing they knew, Jack Gallagher was confessing to having murdered a young woman found dead in the development where he lived, and rumors had spread through the Center, fomented by Desmond O'Toole, that Austin Rooney might have done it. Marie went to talk to Edna.

"Desmond says that Austin's landlord said Austin was out all night when the girl was killed," Edna said.

"That makes him a murderer?"

"He had been asked by Colleen to speak to the girl."

Edna's mouth closed as if she had just locked her lips and thrown away the key. Well, Marie wasn't having any of that. But Edna did not really open up and give Marie the kind of report she could sink her teeth into. It still sometimes surprised her that people had lives beyond their involvement in the parish. Suddenly everybody seemed to have been busy about so many things she hadn't known.

"Anyway, Austin had an alibi."

"What was it?"

"He had spent the night with his bride-to-be."

Edna's eyes widened and that was all. Marie was flabbergasted. Maud was a pain in the neck but it had never dawned on Marie that her coquetry was anything more than that. Some women cling to men, mooning around the sun, basking in borrowed glory. The marvel was that Maud had remained single so long since becoming a widow. But had her flirting been serious? Marie rapidly reviewed the arms to which Maud had clung in recent months. Had she granted them all the favors of her bed?

"He slept with her?" Marie whispered the words as if she had never before used any of them—and probably had not, in this combination.

"He spent the night at her house."

"Are you suggesting that he was there all night and . . ."

"Marie, I am suggesting nothing. I am sorry the subject came up."

Edna had never been a person with whom you could have a good talk. "The subject," as she called it, had enough gristle on it to be chewed on for hours. But it was clear that Edna did not want to dwell on this shocking revelation. Honestly, Marie thought on her way back to the rectory, people are a mystery and an enigma. Maud Gorman. Honestly. And of course Marie's attitude toward Austin Rooney had been irrevocably altered. It would be too much to say that Marie felt scorned, but she had thought that Austin Rooney had regarded her with, well, with something beyond the respect due the housekeeper of St. Hilary's rectory. He was welcome to Maud, that's all she had to say.

The phone was ringing when she came into the house. Without stopping to stamp the snow off her shoes, Marie tracked across her kitchen floor and picked up the phone. It was Tuttle.

"Marie, Father Dowling asked me to tell you that he is at Colleen Gallagher's and the murderer is up there."

"What!"

"I have to get up there myself. Father Dowling wants you to tell Keegan and Cy Horvath where he is."

"What murderer?"

"Tell them. I have to go."

He hung up and Marie stared at the phone. *Murderer?* The little lawyer's excitement, as well as what he had said, made Marie's heart flutter with fear. She hung up the phone, then snatched it up again and dialed Cy Horvath's number.

2

When Albert Fremont opened the apartment door, he seemed mesmerized as he looked over the chain at Father Dowling. But then he began to close the door. Lowering his shoulder, Father Dowling threw himself against the closing door, then he stepped back, his shoulder smarting, and again hurled himself at the still-open door. There was a splintering sound as the chain came loose. Father Dowling was carried by his momentum into the room and nearly tripped over Fremont, who had been knocked backward by the door. Colleen Gallagher, a gag over her mouth, hands behind her back, was tied to a dining-table chair that had been pulled into the room. Father Dowling started toward her but her eyes widened and she shook her head. Father Dowling turned to receive the full force of Fremont's fist. The priest staggered backward and received another blow, in the stomach, which doubled him up. He sank to the floor, gasping for breath.

When Dowling was able to breathe again, Fremont was walking Colleen from the living room. She was still tied to the chair and moved awkwardly, and Fremont pushed her savagely along, crying, "Move, move, move!" Finally he pushed her through another door and closed it on her. Then he turned to Father Dowling.

"Who are you?"

"Well, you're Albert Fremont. That's the important thing. You've come to the end, you know."

Fremont's mouth assumed a smile. "The end of what?"

"People at the Hacienda Motel can identify you as the man who importuned Linda Hopkins."

" 'Importuned'?" He laughed.

"She was your first victim, wasn't she? It must have seemed easy, just pushing her into oncoming traffic, one little shove from the midst of a crowd. You were recognized there too."

"How do you know these things?"

"The police know them too, Albert."

"Don't call me Albert."

There was a sound from the hallway. The door hung crooked on its sprung hinges. Tuttle looked in. "What happened?"

Father Dowling got to his feet and Tuttle came around the door, looking warily at Albert Fremont.

"Did you make the call?" Roger Dowling asked.

"Yes. You all right, Father?"

"Better off than Mr. Fremont's other victims."

"Where's the Gallagher girl?"

Fremont sprang at Tuttle, grabbed his wrist and twisted it behind his back. In the same motion he began to propel him to the door he had shut on Colleen Gallagher. He pulled it open and was about to push Tuttle inside when he yelped with pain. There was another yelp when Tuttle once more drove the heel of his shoe into Fremont's shin. Fremont let go of Tuttle's arm and danced backward on one foot. The little lawyer went in a swift fluid motion across the room to a position behind the couch.

"What's going on?"

"Colleen is in the other room. I have been confronting Albert Fremont with his sins," Father Dowling said.

"Sins!"

"They are that as well as crimes, you know."

"You don't know what you're talking about." He glanced at Tuttle. "Who are you?"

"A man who will bring charges of criminal assault against you. Father Dowling witnessed what you did."

But Fremont's mind was on other things. There were three witnesses in Colleen's apartment, if not to the murders he had committed, at least to the fact that he was beginning to unravel.

"Were you going to add Colleen to your list of victims?" Father Dowling asked.

Fremont looked at Father Dowling distractedly. Then, his mind made up, he started toward the priest, a grim look on his face. Father Dowling held his ground. Courage came more easily because he could see Tuttle scrambling over the couch. Fremont hooked his fingers into Father Dowling's Roman collar and ripped it free just as Tuttle brought the statue of Saint Anne down on his head. The first blow sounded like a *bong*. The second shattered the figure so that pieces of it fell to the floor with Albert Fremont.

Father Dowling knelt beside the fallen Fremont and quickly ascertained that he was merely unconscious. Nonetheless, he whispered the Prayer of Absolution. Fremont might not believe in God, but God believed in him.

"Call 911," he said to Tuttle. "No, I'll do that. Go untie Colleen."

3

Cy was in his car when Marie's message was transferred to him, and he immediately set off for Colleen Gallagher's apartment. The murderer must be Mario Liberati. But he had no urge to interpret the message. He wished he were in a car with a siren so that he could clear traffic from his path. He called in to ask if Phil Keegan had been given the same information.

"He's on his way there."

Marie Murkin had spread the word. Had she called Phil first? That possibility brought his foot down on the gas pedal and he leaned on the horn as he wove through traffic and got through an intersection on a red light just as the traffic from left and right began to accelerate. He half hoped a patrol car would flag him down so he could use it as an escort.

But it was the maze of one-way streets rather than traffic that was the final obstacle. Finally Cy turned and went the wrong way to a corner where he could reverse direction and go to Colleen's address. Coming toward him was a patrol car. Lights flashed at him; there was the warning purr of a siren. Cy got out of his car to explain just as Phil Keegan hopped out of the patrol car. The two men stared briefly at one another, then decided to act as if the meeting had been planned.

"Take care of his car," Phil shouted at the uniformed cop. To Cy he said, "I hope you left the keys in it."

"The motor's still running."

"What's the address?"

"There."

Cy got to the door before Phil and held it open for the puffing Captain of Detectives.

"I gotta exercise more."

Lazenby the manager emerged from his room, wild-eyed, when Cy and Phil pushed through the inner door.

"How did you get in?"

"By the door. Who are you?" Phil growled.

"Me? Who are you?"

"Has the building inspector been here yet?"

Lazenby turned to Cy and stared. "You!"

Cy flashed his identification, but Lazenby grabbed his hand and studied the badge. "Fox River? Where's that?"

Phil gripped his upper arm and felt mainly bone. The manager winced. "I want you to take us up to Colleen Gallagher's apartment."

"A priest is up there. God knows what they're doing."

"What floor is it on?"

"Eight."

Cy took Lazenby's other arm and they hustled the protesting manager onto the elevator. When they came to the eighth floor, they found Father Dowling standing in the hallway.

"Thank God you've come."

"What's happened?"

Cy pushed past the priest and into the apartment where he stopped. Colleen Gallagher sat on the couch, wide-eyed, in semi-shock. A man lay sprawled on the floor, facedown.

"I called 911," Father Dowling said. He knelt down beside the man. "He's been out for several minutes."

"What happened to him?"

"Tuttle stopped him when he was attacking me."

"Tuttle!"

The little lawyer took off his tweed hat and moved the brim nervously through his fingers.

"Tuttle. He acted heroically. God knows what would have happened to Colleen and me if he hadn't come."

Phil and Cy looked as if they would need time to digest this description of Tuttle. The prone man groaned and Cy knelt on his other side. He lifted a shoulder and gently turned the man onto his back.

"Who the hell is he?" Phil Keegan demanded.

"Fremont," Colleen whispered from the couch. "Albert Fremont."

"He's a lawyer with Mallard and Bill," Cy said.

Keegan went to the kitchen, brought back a glass of water and dashed it in Fremont's face. With sputtering indignation the lawyer came to. He sat up and looked around. Just in time to duck. Colleen had hurled one of the couch cushions at him. Now she stood, grabbed another cushion and began to beat him over the head with it. He yelped and covered his head with his hands.

It seemed only right to allow her to vent her anger at the colleague who had so disrupted her life. Cy gently took her arm after she had hit Fremont a dozen times with the cushion.

Sirens announced the arrival of paramedics and soon they swarmed into the room. Cy pointed at Fremont, still seated on the floor.

"Check his head."

"Inside or out?" Cy asked.

"He was out for some minutes," Father Dowling said.

"That's it?" said a paramedic whose huge belly seemed on display, his unbuttoned jacket suggesting curtains just drawn aside.

"He was hit with a statue."

Phil was talking to the other paramedic and apparently reached an agreement. While they strapped Fremont onto a stretcher, Phil said, "Go with them, Cy." He stepped close to his lieutenant and whispered. The slightest nod was the extent of Cy's Hungarian reaction. And then the crew, Fremont, and Cy went through the shattered door.

Lazenby looked in. "What's going on?"

"Get out of here," Phil growled, and the manager scooted away.

Father Dowling was sitting on the couch with Colleen, listening to her first account of her ordeal—kidnapped by Fremont, tied up and locked in her own apartment.

"Why would I have suspected him?" she asked.

Epilogue

Tuttle was granted his evanescent hour in the glare of public notice and acclaim. Mendel's story in the *Tribune* was free of irony and full of details that owed more to his imagination than accounts of witnesses; unless his source was Tuttle. Prominent in the accompanying pictures, informal shots in the hero's offices, was Ms. Hazel Barnes. She was the principal acknowledged source of Mendel's account. "The man is a weapon when aroused. He should be registered."

The benevolent smile the secretary cast at her employer, immortalized on film, suggested the city office in which she would love to register Tuttle.

Just when the publicity was fading, it flared up again. Tuttle had disappeared.

Mendel excitedly called for a national dragnet to rescue the little lawyer, certain that the forces of evil had been unleashed. But Peanuts Pianone had put in for leave and Father Dowling knew that the two old friends were in the wilds of Wisconsin, holed up in a cabin, far from the predatory designs of Hazel Barnes.

"Did he really bop Fremont?" Phil asked.

"He did. He acted with great courage."

"Well, he has gotten more than enough credit," Marie said. "What on earth made you suspect Albert Fremont?"

How often he had been asked that question since the arrest, arraignment, and indictment of Albert Fremont. The scorned lawyer would answer for the murders of Linda Hopkins, Agatha, and Ruby. The death of Mrs. Wilson, the woman who had seen Fremont push Linda into traffic, was not named in the indictment, though Skinner had pressed for it.

"We'll keep her in reserve," the coroner said. "Three's plenty."

That Fremont should have been attracted by both the naively innocent Linda and the unabashed Aggie Rossner was a puzzle Father Dowling would leave to those who imagine there is logic in human affairs. Fremont had indeed pursued Linda and had not taken her rebuff easily.

"When I saw the animal she wanted to marry . . ." Fremont's narrow lips assumed the disapproval of a disappointed eugenicist.

"No wonder she told him to buzz off," Harry said, when he got a look at Albert Fremont. "I'd like to have five minutes alone with that wimp." Harry had offered Tuttle two hundred dollars' reward for smashing the statue over Fremont's head.

"I just hope it doesn't bring bad luck," Tuttle replied when he magnanimously refused to tap the bank account Harry had amassed in hopes of marrying Linda. "She said it was a statue of Saint Anne."

"You superstitious?"

"Of course not."

"So don't worry."

Tuttle accepted Harry's comforting theology and went with a clear conscience into the wilds of Wisconsin. Harry decided to let the sum lie in the bank.

"In fifty years I'll be rich," he said without enthusiasm. "I read about it somewhere. Compound interest."

"If it weren't for that poor girl, it would all come back to Aggie," Colleen said. She and Mario had come to the rectory for their initial marriage-preparation session, but the first half-hour was spent on the harrowing events of recent days. "She teased him and led him on, and given her reputation he must have thought he was in luck. It was bad enough when she ignored him for Tim, but when she took after my father . . ."

"Aggie does bear a lot of responsibility," Mario said. In a bid for favorable publicity to balance the bad, Mallard and Bill had pled with Mario to return to the firm. He was inclined to accept but it seemed well to hold off telling the partners for several weeks.

"She didn't just tease Fremont," Cy said. "Maybe if they hadn't had their own little affair he would have dismissed her interest in Jack Gallagher."

Fremont had watched the liaison with Jack spring up just when Tim Gallagher was fading from the scene. To lose his love to a septuagenarian was more than he could take. He had rented a car, parked it outside the gate of Western Sun Community, and taken up his vigil. When Aggie had emerged he was half frozen from waiting, and seething with rage. He had strangled her with her own scarf and left her in the snow. And he had left her purse there as well, after extracting her car keys.

"Why did you take her car?"

"For the hell of it."

"That makes no sense."

"I thought the same thing before I'd driven half a mile," Fremont said. "I was going to abandon it but then I thought taking it to her garage would confuse the issue. How was I to know that Jack Gallagher would confess?"

"Why did you take the car from the garage?"

Fremont did not answer. Had he thought of abandoning it with Colleen's body in it? When this was mentioned, his reaction suggested that was the reason.

In June, Colleen and Mario were married at St. Hilary's and there was a general turnout of Gallaghers, colleagues, and old friends. Old people from the Center filled many pews. Jack Gallagher gave away his daughter with great panache; Jane was matron of honor. Maud Rooney, previously Gorman, improbably filled the role of maid of honor with Austin as best man. This arrangement symbolized the reconciliation of Jack and Austin. Marie gave the happy couple a statue of Saint Anne to replace the one Tuttle had used as a weapon.

"I think I can use it," George Hessian told Rawley.

"Go back to writing the parish history."

Hessian shook his head. "Not until I finish this biographical memoir."

"You're wasting your time."

The wedding reception was held in the parish Senior Center, where Desmond O'Toole was induced to sing with the band that had been hired. To general delight, he and Jack Gallagher sang a duet, Desmond doing Satchmo and Jack, Bing Crosby. Amos Cadbury smiled wistfully as he stood with Father Dowling near the back of the converted gym.

"You should dance, Amos."

"I don't think I will ever dance again, Father." He did not have to explain that his decision was due to the fact that Maud was now Mrs. Austin Rooney.

"What do you think of Albert Fremont's plea of insanity?"

"A sign of the times, Father. A sign of the times. The evil men do is now taken to be the result of illness. Is Original Sin an illness?"

"Not in that sense, Amos."

Marie Murkin joined them and the band began a waltz. "Marie," Amos said. "Would you care to dance?"

In confused delight the housekeeper accepted and was swept away in the arms of the stately lawyer. Father Dowling smiled benevolently over the gathering and then slipped away to the rectory, his study, his pipe. An hour with Dante and a renewed perspective on the human comedy seemed called for.

RALPH MCINERNY is the author of twenty Father Dowling mysteries, as well as a series set at the University of Notre Dame, where he is the director of the Jacques Maritain Center and has taught for more than forty years. He lives in South Bend, Indiana.